REBELLION IN THE MIST

MARLEY FERGUSON

Map by Marley Ferguson

Book Cover by Vivien Reis

Edited by Ana Hansen

ISBN-13: 979-8-218-68055-8

CONTENTS

For everyone who is the only person that can save the realm.
Especially when the realm is your household.

FOREWORD

The following story is interpreted into modern English from the original texts. All units of measure and time are shown as their closest modern approximation. All idioms, expressions, and colloquialisms are used to convey their original spirit.

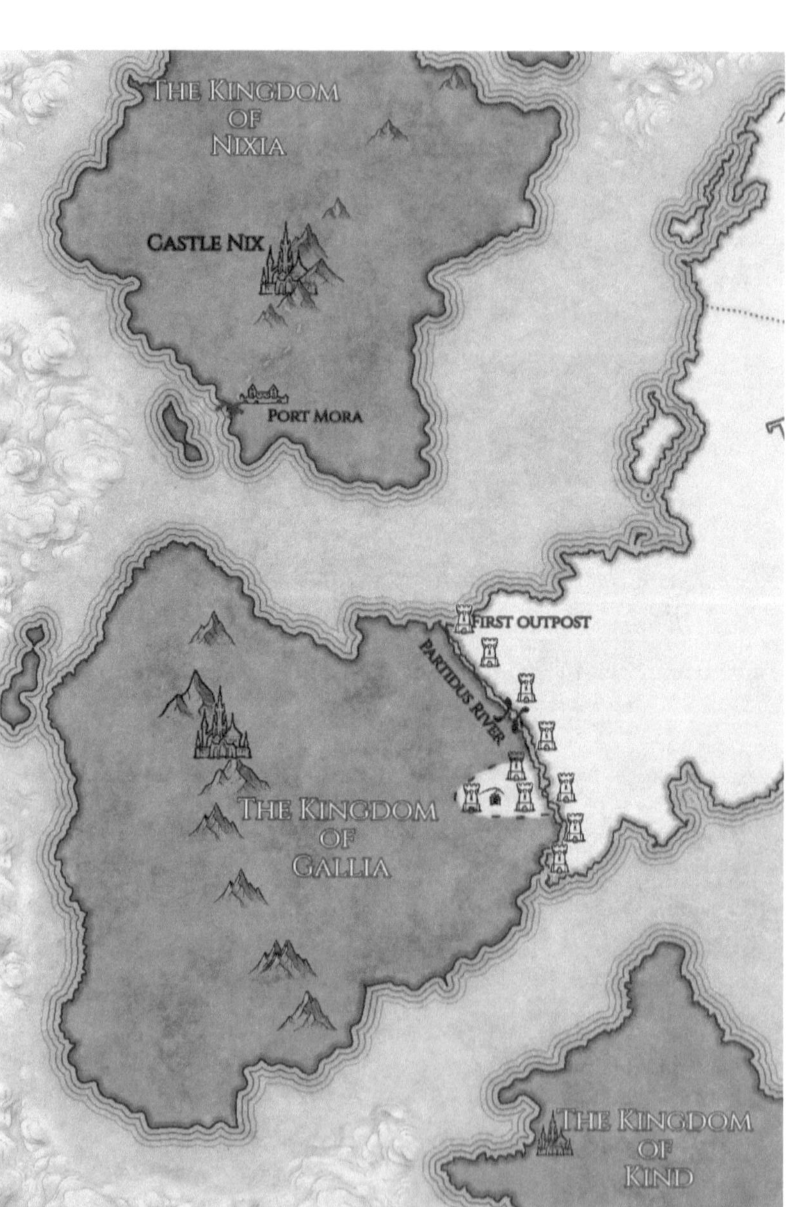

THE KINGDOM OF NIXIA
CASTLE NIX
PORT MORA
FIRST OUTPOST
PARTIDUS RIVER
THE KINGDOM OF GALLIA
THE KINGDOM OF KIND

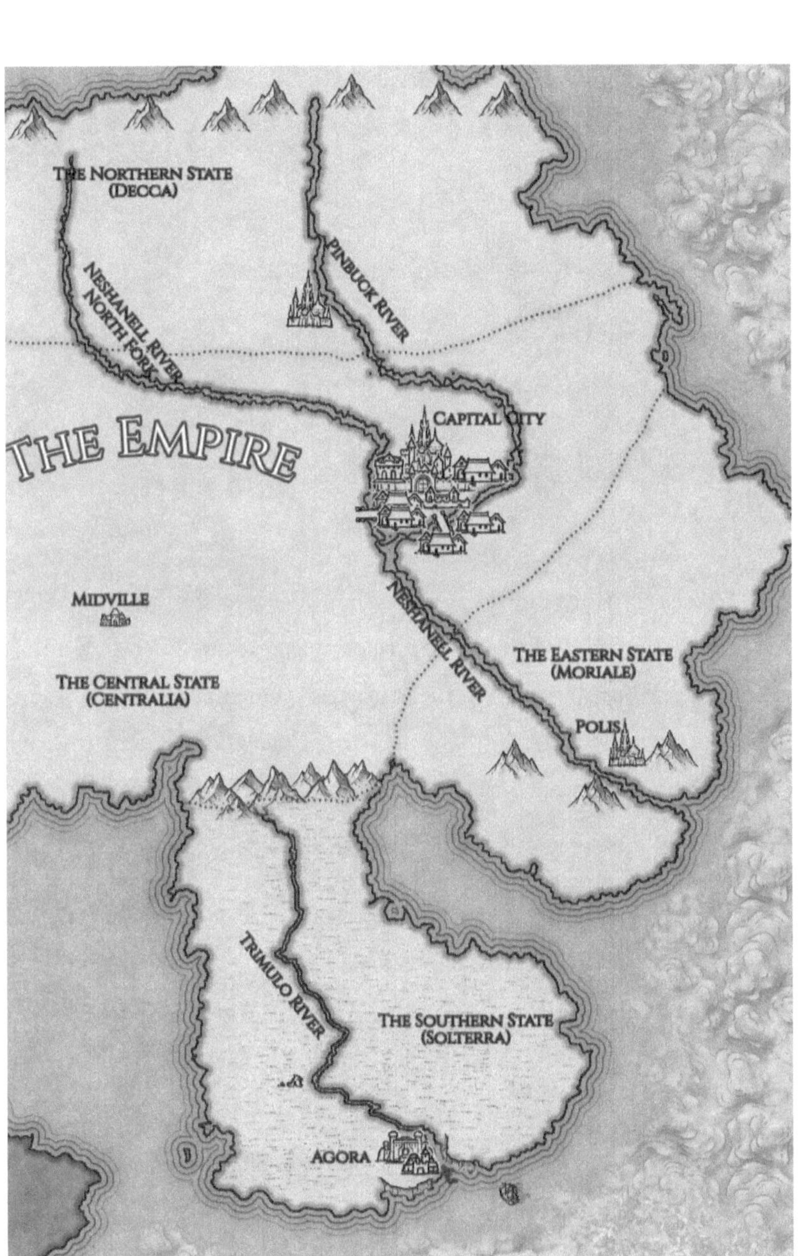
THE NORTHERN STATE
(DECCA)
NESHANELL RIVER
NORTH FORK
PINBUOK RIVER
THE EMPIRE
CAPITAL CITY
MIDVILLE
THE CENTRAL STATE
(CENTRALIA)
NESHANELL RIVER
THE EASTERN STATE
(MORIALE)
POLIS
TRIMULO RIVER
THE SOUTHERN STATE
(SOLTERRA)
AGORA

CONTENT WARNING

This story is intended for an adult audience and contains subject matter that is not suitable for younger readers. There is content that may be triggering to some including: explicit language, alcohol consumption, parental loss, gaslighting, sexually explicit content on-page (and mentions of non-consensual sex and dubious consent), mentions of suicide, and graphic violence including blood, gore, and death.

CHAPTER ONE

Golden rays of morning sun poured in from the open windows, illuminating motes of dust drifting lazily through the air. I watched them tumble along the breeze until they were lost to the shadows.

The serene moment was ruined for me by the presence of dozens of seventeen- and eighteen-year-olds chattering throughout the amphitheater-shaped room and acting like, well, teenagers.

From my vantage point facing the class, I could easily pick out the groups with budding friendships making tentative conversations, the circles that knew each other before last month telling raucous stories, and the most entertaining—individuals trying to flirt with other first years.

A gangly teen that fell into the last group picked up a piece of parchment that had blown on the floor, handing it back to a fellow fae, who smiled much more broadly than necessary as she tucked a strand of hair behind her ear.

It would be a sweet moment to witness, if I hadn't seen it so many times before. The same love stories wrote themselves year after year with a different cast of characters. After a decade of training newly unlocked magic wielders, the specks of dust were less predictable than the students.

I cleared my throat, and the students quieted to stare at me expectantly. "Today we'll begin wielding water," I announced.

Smiles bloomed in front of me, excitement lighting the faces of the Protectors. The first few times I had announced this to a class, I'd been just as excited as them, but the tenth time around, I just wanted to get it over with. Now the most exciting part of the water unit for me was discovering which days I would finish teaching with water in my boots and a wet uniform.

"But we still don't know how to do that wind shield thing you showed us on the first day," said one of the students sitting in the first row. His rusty hair was already clumped with sweat from the summer heat blanketing the room.

"There's still a lot to learn with air, Henson," I said, "but you have the basics. We're going to move on to the fundamentals of the other three elements, and then you will learn the more complicated magic wielding for each one, like the wind barrier."

"Does that mean we'll learn to heal soon?" asked a girl in the second row, her long black ponytail bouncing around as her eyes widened.

"Not just yet, Kayer," I said, tucking an escaping curl behind my ear. The braid I typically wore was the only defense I had against the tangle of frizz my hair would become. With the humidity coming from the nearby rivers, it seemed the plait was already losing the battle today.

"We'll spend a month on water, just like we did for air, then we'll do another four weeks on fire before moving to Earth magic." My eyes moved across the three rows of fae who'd had their powers unlocked on the solstice four weeks ago. "But learning to heal with Earth magic will take one to three months."

"Why is there a range, Trainer Riseworth?" asked a slender wielder in the back row, whose name I was pretty sure was Tarwin. I used to pride myself on memorizing everyone's name within the first two weeks. This year, I hadn't tried as hard. After all, I wasn't even going to finish out the year with them.

"Didn't Commander Ianth cover all this with you after you touched Cavilth and went to the unlocking orientation?" I asked rhetorically.

I had been there along with the other trainers when they'd pulled the wielders aside from the rest of the new Protectors. Each summer solstice, hundreds of residents of the Empire signed their contracts to serve in the Imperial Protectorate. Their signature on that contract gave them permission to touch Cavilth, a magical stone that would unlock the ability to wield the elements if they had enough fae lineage left in their blood.

If the stone glowed when they touched it, they were beholden to ten years in the Protectorate and officially a magic wielder, with their life span tripled and a year of learning to use those powers ahead of them. Those who found out they were mortal on the solstice only had to serve the Protectorate for three years and were given a month of combat training before being placed throughout the Empire.

"She did," said Tarwin, his interest seemingly to the floor rather than the unintentional scowl on my face. "But it was a lot to take in on our first day."

I leaned my arms on the lectern in front of me and tried to remind myself that I only had five more months of this. These students had just left the life they had known before this. Everything was new to them, their future unknown. No one made the best choices or remembers everything in times like those.

"After you have the basics of the four elements, your time spent training with each will be individualized based on your aptitude. If you take to healing, you'll do rotations for an extra two months with the Healer's Wing to see if you have what it takes to be assigned there."

"Aren't the Healers the best of the best?" Kayer asked, practically bouncing out of her seat with excitement.

"No, the most elite become Compound guards," a blonde wielder said from the middle row. Jeffers, maybe?

"You're both right in your own way," I said. "Only the best of the best with Earth magic are selected to be Healers. The most elite fighters become guards for the Compound. As I said, it will be individualized to your strengths."

Tarwin raised his hand. "If you aren't selected for either of those—"

I cut him off, knowing where his head was. "You will continue honing the elements and rotate through all the duty stations until command determines the best assignment for you."

"Can we request our station?" asked Henson.

Better to warn them now.

"You can put in requests for reassignments, but don't hold out hope. Command does *not* like having their decisions questioned. Reassignments are few and far between."

"What if we're not good at any of the stations?" Tarwin asked quietly.

"Then you get assigned to be a Trainer," said a voice from the doorway. "But don't worry, I only know of one wielder who was assigned to start training right after her first year. The rest of us served our duty station until a Trainer position opened up."

I turned my head to the door behind me. "Trainer Sheab," I said, trying to keep my tone even in front of the class, even as I stared daggers at him. "You're a little early for small group practice. We're still in instruction."

He pushed off the doorframe, running a hand through his coiffed hair as he swaggered into the room. I barely suppressed an eye roll. A few of the first years gazed at him dreamily.

"Commander Ianth told me to take over your lecture. She wants to see you in her office immediately."

He didn't completely hide his smirk as the room full of teens gasped and whispered. Even only a month in, they knew being suddenly pulled aside to speak with your commanding officer was not a good sign. Sheab could have pulled me into the hallway to tell me this. *Dick.*

"We were just starting water basics," I started to explain.

"Don't worry, Riseworth. I can handle it. You don't want to keep command waiting."

CHAPTER TWO

The dark slate floors of the Imperial Compound passed under my feet unnoticed while my mind skittered along the dozens of tiny infractions that could have landed me a disciplinary meeting.

Spending the night in another Protector's dormitory room wasn't strictly allowed, but no one was ever punished for it, and it had been a long time since I'd fallen asleep in one of my friends' rooms.

Using the secret passageways of the Compound was certainly forbidden, but it had been a while since I'd done that too. And I had never been *seen* using the tunnels.

As I entered Commander Ianth's small, windowless office, I was no closer to figuring out why I was being summoned. She sat behind her desk, straight-backed with her hands folded over a piece of paper. Her hawkish gaze followed me as I closed the door and sat in the simple wooden chair across from her. She smoothed her hand along her already impeccably tamed hair to the low bun at the nape of her neck.

The sparse room was furnished only with her desk and the two chairs we were seated in. I had been in her office many times before and always took her minimalism as tidy and professional, but today it made her seem austere.

"Trainer Riseworth," she said in greeting.

"Commander." I tucked my hands under my thighs, trying to prevent myself from fidgeting like a first year.

She took a deep breath and splayed her hands over the paper, covering it almost entirely. "You have been asked to cover a patrol shift this morning."

"Ma'am?" My brows drew together in confusion. I was missing something, clearly. In ten years, I had never been asked to cover a patrol shift.

She sighed, her eyes softening slightly. "You are our most experienced trainer, but your service to the Empire is over in five months. My understanding is that you do not plan to extend your contract." I shook my head. "It would be beneficial for the other trainers to have practice teaching without you, then."

I spiraled into doubt. Was I so bad at my job that they didn't want me to pollute the other Trainers' lessons? I wanted to voice my concerns, but I had just lectured the first year wielders on how command hated being questioned. Thankfully, she volunteered a small amount of reassurance. "This is not a permanent reassignment. You are only being asked to cover this one shift."

I could handle that. One, single shift walking around the streets of Capital City.

"Who am I paired with?"

"They are very short on patrol Protectors today. It seems you will be unaccompanied."

I frowned. "What route am I supposed to patrol?"

"That was not provided in this missive. You are to stop by the guards at the gate for further instruction."

She lifted her hands to point to the parchment, but stopped short, covering the parchment again and clearing her throat.

"Riseworth, this request came from the general's office." She tapped her index finger on it several times before continuing. "Just patrol how you should, and you'll be back in the classroom tomorrow."

A cloud of uncertainty hung around me as I left Commander Ianth's office. I didn't have much experience with patrols, unless you counted accompanying the first years on their trial rotations, but that was always overseen by experienced patrol Protectors. I was only there to answer wielding questions.

I hope I don't have to bring in any law-breakers during my shift.

I snorted a laugh to myself. The arresting of citizens was the main duty of the Protectorate—in fact, protection patrol was where the majority of Protectors were placed after their training, hence the title—but I had never done it outside of those training rounds.

I stopped by my room to strap on my rarely used leather armor before heading back down toward the front gate.

As I was passing near the wielding classroom, a ball of water as tall as me rounded the corner and rolled toward me. Henson from my class followed the orb as he guided it along the wide hallway, moving it from side to side, cleaning the dirt from the dark stone floor as he went. Behind him, the bouncy-ponytailed Kayer was blowing gusts of air along the floor to dry it in his wake. Trainer Sheab was following behind the two first years.

My brows raised at Sheab when he looked at me. Cleaning tasks were usually reserved for a few weeks from now, to ensure the new wielders had enough control before allowing them to potentially ruin a passing noble's day.

"Alright, Henson, let's bring the water to a controlled stop while holding its form," Sheab said, ignoring my look. "Gently roll your hands back to get it to slow down."

Henson tentatively started the motion, but the ball of water continued to tumble my way. I shuffled to the side of the hallway, making myself a smaller target as I waited to see if he would get it under control.

I really hoped I wasn't about to start my patrol duty doused in dirty water.

The ball crept closer to me, now only two feet away.

"Whoa, bring it back!" Sheab called.

Henson panicked and jerked his hands back as far as he could. That was enough to keep the water from drenching me, but it reversed directions and began barreling toward the others.

Kayer forced a gust of air at the water, trying to shield her group from getting soaked without knowing the proper technique. Her air slammed into the ball, and it exploded, drenching their end of the hallway in grimy water.

After the initial shock wore off the first years' faces, I stepped over the murky pools to their end of the hallway.

"You need to hook your fingers more when changing the direction of the water," I said to Henson. I demonstrated the motion as a dingy drop fell from the ceiling into his hair. "It helps control the pull and makes it more nimble to your will." I moved to Kayer and her now-drooping ponytail. "And Kayer, remember, if you are panicked while wielding, your magic will respond in kind. Especially when trying to do something new."

Sheab shot me a look as a drip fell from his soaked tunic with a *plop* to a puddle on the floor.

"Henson, Kayer, practice those motions while working together to collect the water again," Sheab said, taking me by my elbow to lead me into a shadowy alcove. "I was handling it," he hissed, low enough that the two new wielders wouldn't hear.

"Sorry, it looked like you could use some help," I said. "Coaching after mistakes is your biggest opportunity to make a memorable impression. I was just passing along the things that have worked best for me."

"Just because you've been training wielders since you got here doesn't mean you're better at this than everyone else, Riseworth." His dark eyes narrowed on my face. "Despite what you think."

"You made that clear to the entire classroom," I said, pulling my arm from his grip. "Apparently ten years of training just makes me inferior. I can't help where I was placed after my first year, or that all my requests for reassignment were denied. But don't worry, you can teach them however you see fit." I waved a hand at him, gross water and all.

He turned, shoes squelching, and strode back to Henson and Kayer, his earlier swagger washed away.

CHAPTER THREE

As I made my way out of the shade of the Compound buildings and crossed the hard-packed dirt path to the wall's main gate, I tried to shake off my annoyance at Sheab. His accusation that I thought I was a better trainer than everyone else was unfounded. I was only trying to help him and the first years.

When he became a trainer a year ago, we had started off amicably. He only became unpleasant after I turned down his invitation to join him for dinner outside of the Compound, which sounded too much like a date for my taste. It wasn't a reflection on Sheab. I just didn't date other Protectors anymore.

As I passed through the arched gateway I heard, "Riseworth?" echo after me.

Shit. I forgot I needed to check with the gate Protector for my route.

I spun around to correct my mistake, but the force of the turn made my braid whip around my shoulder and strike me in the face.

The Protector's blonde hair was glistening and slicked to his head. It was oppressively hot in the direct sun, despite it still being before noon. Sweat began to drip down my back beneath my long-sleeved black tunic and pool at the waistband of the leggings that I wore beneath the armor. I looked back longingly at the huge sandstone wall and the shade only available directly under the archway this time of day.

His round cheeks suppressed a laugh as I rubbed my cheek. "The commander said to pass orders to you. You're supposed to replace Bannu and go help the executioner in the Old Square today."

Morning duty with the executioner, when they took down the bodies from the last hanging, was one of the least desirable jobs a Protector could be assigned. At least I wasn't given evening duty with the executioner. Even though there was always a large group of Protectors assigned together on those shifts, watching the hangings was far worse.

The portly Protector saw my open distaste at the assignment. "I'd rather do that than catch what Bannu has," he said.

"What's wrong with Bannu?"

He snorted. "Some illness in his stomach. He can't stop shitting long enough to go to the healers."

Bannu and I had equally bad lots today, in my opinion.

He shaded his eyes with his hand, staring at me. "Hey, you're that wielder I heard about."

I sighed. I had never seen this Protector before today. He was probably a new recruit just starting his service after the summer solstice. When I met new people, it was always this. This year's new wielders had already gotten over the initial novelty, and I hadn't had to deal with this for a few weeks.

"I didn't think it could be true," he said, looking at my eyes with an uncomfortable intensity. "But they really are gold, not hazel or light brown or anything."

He was staring at my irises so hard, I felt like I was being examined by a Healer.

"Yeah, that," I said, not bothering to hide my fatigue with this topic as I gave a lazy wave toward my face. "Been like this my whole life. No one knows why. They don't do anything special. Probably some abnormality from birth or a vestigial fae trait."

I rattled off all answers to the typical questions before he could ask. The sun was burning into my patience along with the top of my head.

"You probably didn't have to worry before you touched Cavilth." He leaned in closer to my face. "If you have enough fae blood to have a fae trait, you knew you'd be able to wield."

I had never heard of a fae with golden eyes, but I didn't have a better explanation for my strange irises, so I nodded to try to kill any further discussion.

"Thanks for passing the assignment along." I turned, hoping the sound of grit under my foot would force finality on this interaction.

"I was just having a look," he grumbled behind me.

I needed to pass through most of the City to reach the Old Square. Closer to the Imperial Compound, the wealthy in Capital City were insulated by homes with tidy stone fronts and sturdy slate roofs. I wound my way past people chatting idly with their neighbors on the clean, broad avenues, shaded by awnings and trees. Vendors sold their goods in neat shops with their windows thrown open, and the delicious smells of sizzling spiced meats perfumed the air.

As I moved further away from the Emperor's residence and closer to the Old Square, the buildings became shabbier, the thatched roofs sagging with mold and holes. The streets were grubbier, the smell of sweat on hot bodies getting thicker with each step I took.

"Watch it," a man pushing a cart filled with cabbages huffed at a small boy darting across the narrow lane before the child scampered off into a dim alley.

The poorest neighborhoods in Capital City surrounded me, where the river was clouded with sewage and the more pungent trades kept shop. I considered deviating the few blocks it would take to walk past the run-down flat my mom raised me in, but no matter how much I wanted to delay this duty, I wanted to see the echo of my previous life even less.

I was sweating through my tunic, which bunched up and chafed me where the leather was snug. This armor was certainly not designed for Protectors with a full bust.

I pulled at the strap under my armpits more out of annoyance than to provide any actual relief from the rubbing. My duty had not truly started, and I already smelled about as good as the streets around me.

Five more months. I took a deep breath. *You can do this, Ness. You don't have much longer, just push through.*

Each cobblestone beneath my feet felt like it was one step closer toward my own execution. The families of those sentenced to death had few other outlets besides harassing the executioner. The trials of citizens were private matters. The rationale was that no one could face backlash for giving testimony to the Committee against any other citizen. This was supposed to be more fair, because wealthy nobles could be accused by poorer citizens without fear of repercussions. However, this meant that once a person was taken in by the Protectorate, their families rarely knew the details of the trial, much less what was said to lead them to the gallows.

The Empire might not be perfect, but it was more good than bad, in my experience. It provided me with an education and gave me a place to go in the Protectorate after schooling. As a Protector, I saw some of the grittier sides of the Empire, but I trusted the system worked.

The smell of death confronted me as I entered the plaza, telling me the bodies had been swaying from the gallows for a few days with the sun beating down on them. My armor was downright pleasant in comparison.

I crossed the dusty cobblestones, avoiding the divots where some pavers had long since been removed for one reason or another and sidestepped some of the lumps of dirt that looked like dried horse shit.

The only other person dressed entirely in black on this stifling summer day was an older man with sparse, gray hair combed in stringy clumps to one side to try to hide his glistening crown, which was visible without the cloak of the executioner's hood.

That was odd even from my limited knowledge of this duty. People would know who he was with his face exposed. It took a bold man to be proud of being an executioner. Or stupid one.

He was sitting atop a cart attached to a donkey under the shade of the only remaining tree in the square. The donkey looked just as pleased to be here as I was.

"You my help today?" he asked with the casualness of a man who wasn't about to handle the twelve rotting corpses behind us.

"Yes, Bannu is sick. I'm Riseworth."

"Where's your second?"

"Apparently, none were available."

"Hmm, well, name's Jenkins." His eyes lingered for a moment on mine, but he didn't comment on my irises. "Not much to this. I need to get these criminals down so I can string up another twelve at sunset.

Keep a wall of air up so none of those shit disturbers can interfere with the Emperor's justice. And I wouldn't be mad if you gave me a breeze so that I could get some fresh air while I'm at it."

That was simple. This wouldn't take too long, but I still wasn't happy to be here. The thick, humid air trapped the stench of the bodies, which clung to the inside of my nose. I wondered if I had unknowingly pissed off the General recently.

The Old Square had once been a thriving market near the center of town, filled with trees and fountains, but that was hundreds of years ago, before the Great War that united the Empire. Once four of the kingdoms in the mainland were unified, the Emperor moved his quarters to the Imperial Compound at the edge of the then-smaller city and transformed this square to carry out his justice against traitors that still supported the old crowns. All the former liveliness of the square was lost and now it was just a dusty, open area where we kept the gallows.

People started to gather in the square, seeing something was about to happen. I hated being face-to-face with the families of the executed. Today would be their last chance to say their final goodbyes before the Empire returned them to Father Earth.

I knew what it was like to lose a family member. To stand by, feeling hopeless, as an Imperial cart collected their body.

But not everyone stood by peacefully as their loved one was taken away. The family members could get disruptive, which was the reason I was here. It was also the reason I was a bit surprised Jenkins was unafraid to wait on his cart alone before I arrived. But it was probably the same reason why he wasn't masked yet, proud to do the Emperor's dirty work.

He pulled on the black hood to complete his official ensemble and signaled his readiness.

I drew the powers from the well of energy behind my sternum, making a wall of wind to protect him as he worked. The hum of my magic moved through my hands as I shifted the barrier of air along in unison with him, coaxing the donkey closer to the platform. He dismounted and began taking down the decomposing bodies. I remembered his request for a breeze and began to flow some air into his bubble to help with the smell.

As I focused on the different directions I needed to make the air move, the people in the square began to congregate tighter around me. "I guess the Emperor needs to make room to kill more of his people," a middle-aged man said as he stepped closer to me than I was comfortable with.

The people were bold today. I was getting crowded on all sides and they were nearly bumping against me. Jenkins began to cough behind his wall of air.

Shit. I had gotten distracted by the people talking around me and forgotten to keep up the circulation in there. I ignored the growing crowd and concentrated on the wind I was manipulating.

I was jostled from behind. Not hard enough to move my feet, but it was noticeable. "Better watch your back, Protector," said the greasy man who pushed me. "Those who serve the Emperor will get their just due. In this life or the next." He spat at my feet before disappearing into the crowd.

Well, fuck. I'd forgotten to place a wall of air around myself for protection too. If I tried to add that right now, I would probably drop the shield of air entirely around Jenkins for a second before I could get them both back up. Could I do it quick enough? It had been a while since I'd had to do practical wielding like this and not just examples in classrooms.

Normally, a Protector wouldn't have to shield both themselves and the executioner. There would usually be at least one other with them to watch their back. If anyone harassed a member of the Protectorate, they could immediately be arrested by the second.

It'll be fine. That man said his bit and walked away. I was going to get through this just fine. After my shift, I would be one day closer to the end of my service and never have to deal with this again.

More people pressed in near me. It seemed unusual for citizens to have this much dedication in the summertime, when the square offered no shade and the smell was so offensive. This batch of offenders must have been particularly well-known in their neighborhoods.

Jenkins was almost half done by now, shifting the fifth person into his cart.

I wondered how a man so old could still lift people like that. Maybe he was much younger than he appeared. Did being an executioner age you prematurely? Or maybe his love for the Emperor kept him strong—

I was shoved again, this time at my lower back.

I flicked my head back to where a very dirty, scraggly boy dressed in tattered clothes was scowling up at me. His brown, shoulder-length hair was matted with grime.

"Get out of my way, you Imperial bitch. He's taking down my dad!"

I looked back to see Jenkins removing the noose from a man with similar brown hair. I felt for the boy, even though I could do without his name-calling and pushing. Losing a parent was so hard, and his father was probably his family's breadwinner. I would try to give him a few coins from my pocket when I was done here. I didn't have much to spare, but I would have food later, and I wasn't sure this boy would be able to say the same.

I turned from the boy, ignoring him since he wasn't a real threat. I focused back on the wall of wind I was making to protect Jenkins. The mass of people was growing more restless. I willed Jenkins to hurry up. He only had four left to get down.

An abrupt pain shot through the back of my knee, collapsing my leg under me and pitching me forward. My hands were raised to control the wind around Jenkins and not prepared to break a fall. I smashed my nose directly into the cobblestones. Pain shot through my face as blood flowed freely from both nostrils.

Even without another Protector to back me up, this was too far for me to ignore. I rolled over to my back to see who my assailant was so I could seize them and turn them into the Committee.

The same boy stood over me and stomped a dirty, shoeless foot hard into my ribs, forcing the breath from my lungs.

I gasped as I lay there trying to breathe again. Air slowly crept back into me.

Air.

Fuck!

Jenkins!

I rolled back over and rose to my hands and knees to see the executioner being swallowed by the horde that had converged on him the moment my shield had fallen.

"Stop," I tried to yell, but the breath still had not fully returned to my lungs, and it came out as a wheezing gasp.

I felt a kick to my backside, and I lurched forward on all fours. I did the first thing that came to me. I thrust my leg back like an angry mule, catching the same boy in the thighs and sending him to the ground. I jumped to my feet and didn't have time to process the shrieks of, "The

Protectors are beating our children!" through the chaos around me as I tried to force a gale around Jenkins to get the mob away from him.

My mind was darting from the crowd to Jenkins to the boy to the throbbing pain in my nose, and the air was sluggish to respond to my will with my lack of focus. I continued to force the air around Jenkins, slowly pushing the crowd away from him.

Jenkins lay on the ground, covered in blood, his arms covering his head. He hadn't moved since the crowd retreated.

This is really fucking bad. Where the fuck are the patrols of Protectors? There should be about six patrols walking near the Old Square right now.

I took a step toward Jenkins to check on him, but my foot caught on one of the divots left by a missing cobblestone. My face slammed into the ground a second time. This time my cheek took the fall, making my eyes water and teeth rattle.

Another stomp from a bony foot to the small of my back made me reel. I glanced over my shoulder to see that fucking kid run off, disappearing with the crowd out of the square.

I got my palms to the ground under my shoulders to push myself up, and a hand closed around my bicep. I whipped my head to see who was attacking me now.

It was another Protector trying to help me up.

The nearby patrols had finally shown up, in time to see me get humiliated by a ten-year-old and get a black eye from the shit-covered stones.

As the Protector helped me to my feet, I surveyed the damage in the square. The donkey was gone, four bodies still swayed gently from the gallows, the cart was on its side.

Jenkins still hadn't moved.

CHAPTER FOUR

Getting back to the Imperial Compound was a haze of throbbing pain in my face laced with concern for Jenkins. The Protector who had helped me up stayed with me, steadying me by my arm as we navigated through the streets with my eyes nearly swollen shut.

I had to stop and catch my breath at one point on the journey, leaning back on the warm stucco wall of a temple that had been painted by the zealous Children of the Mother, as they liked to be called. The donkey carrying Jenkins continued on to the Imperial Compound ahead of us.

Pressing my back against the mural depicting the creation story, I looked through my slitted eyes to the first section showing an image of the Mother, Creator of all things, bestowing her gift of nature spirits to the Father, Earth itself, to honor their marriage. The painting—showing the trees, rivers, mountains, and oceans being inhabited by ethereal humanoid nature spirits—was flaking at waist height where people leaned.

I twisted slightly to see if the section I was resting against was chipping as well. Slivers of paint were missing from an image of the first fae, but I couldn't tell if that had been me or not. The panel was still clear even with that damage, showing the Father's delight for the Mother's beautiful gifts and his desire to honor her by creating the fae from his soil to protect the delicate nymphs. I slumped back against the wall.

"Are you alright?" the Protector asked me as he leaned against the third panel, crumbling away the pitiful expressions of the first humans the nature spirits created when they became bored.

"I just need a minute." My breathing was ragged, the air seeming to snag in my chest.

He scuffed his boot along the dirt as he shifted to look at the third panel. It was the one where the humans bred too fast and began destroying the beauty of nature that all of these beings had been placed here to protect. The Children of the Mother intended that section to be a warning about humans trying to act beyond the control of those that knew better than them, but I had always thought they made the throngs of people overindulging look like they were attending the party of a lifetime.

I quickly realized my shaky breath was not going to steady by standing here. I needed to find out how Jenkins fared.

"Ready." I moved to walk past the two final panels of the creation story.

The next one had always been my favorite, even though it was a dark and foreboding image of the witches the Mother and Father had created to subdue the humans. It showed the witches sucking the lands dry of all life to channel a fierce lightning from their hands. It had struck me as mysterious and exciting ever since I was a young child—a power beyond those that we knew. The potential in it felt endless.

The last image on the side of the temple showed the Emperor defeating the witches and standing over their bodies on a land filled with plants and animals once more.

The nature spirits were left out of the end of the story. Maybe that was supposed to entice any citizens who didn't already attend their services to visit their temples and find out what became of them.

"Hold on," he said. "You have some of your brethren on your back." He ran his hand between my shoulder blades. Shards of paint cascaded off my armor, littering the ground around my feet with flecks of the faces of the first fae.

The fae no longer existed as a separate race. They had long been intermingled with humans, and there were no full-blooded ones left. Now we just used the term *fae* to indicate a person like myself who could wield magic, no matter how distantly related to the first fae.

I nodded my thanks to him before we finished our walk back.

Once in the Compound, I was taken directly into the Healer's Wing. My nameless companion deposited me on a narrow cot covered with blankets before disappearing to talk with the other Protectors that had been at the Old Square.

I squinted around the large, open room that served as the triage area, trying to keep my mind from racing back to Jenkins and what a spectacular failure I was. He had been my responsibility. My thoughts tumbled to Commander Ianth's comment that I needed to do well in this shift, since the Ancient Bastard of a general had assigned me there himself.

I took a deep breath, trying to reduce the mountain of dread that was pressing into my shoulders and knotting my stomach.

I had never been injured badly enough to be treated here before. Typically, I was only in the Healer's Wing when I brought the first years here to start their Earth Magic section. As we made our way to the wing, I would explain that Earth magic gives us our longer-than-mortal lives and the ability to heal more quickly, since we are made from the soil of Father Earth.

A tall, lean figure jogged my way, her coily black hair bouncing around her shoulders. My chest eased at the sight of one of my best friends, and my hands relaxed around the scratchy blanket.

Normally, Lina's long limbs moved with a grace I could never achieve. She had warm eyes that always felt kind, set in a face of elegant beauty. But right now, she looked frantic, her brows furrowed in concern and a sheen of sweat dappling her rich brown skin.

"Ness! Are you okay?" She bent over me and began inspecting my injuries. "Shit, your face is bad."

Before she even finished her sentence, the hum of her magic began to seep into my face and ease the pain. The taut skin around my swollen eye lessened as her healing reduced the inflammation.

My own small amount of Earth magic would heal my wounds faster than a mortal, but I didn't have it in abundance like Lina. She was the strongest Healer in the wing, and had already been asked to stay on as a Lead Healer after her term of service to the Empire ended in two years.

Lina sat on the cot next to me as she grabbed my hands, making the scrapes and cuts begin to fade away.

"They said there was a riot. Why were you there? What happened?" She spoke quietly so none of the passing Healers could hear.

"I got pulled from training to cover a duty with the executioner in the Old Square." The words tumbled out of my mouth. "I was supposed to protect him, but the crowd got out of hand. And shit, Lina, I fucked up. I forgot to shield myself from them. They started attacking me and

I lost my focus. I couldn't keep the shield up for the executioner." My voice dropped to a quivering whisper. "Do you know if he's dead?"

Tears burned down my cheeks. Her eyes softened, and she wrapped me into a hug.

"I'll go see what I can find out," she said, giving my freshly healed hands a squeeze before leaving.

I wiped at my face. I had never heard of anything like this happening before. How did it get out of hand so quickly? Hands shaking, I poured myself a glass of water from a nearby pitcher, trying to steady myself with a drink.

Lina came back to my cot a short time later with a damp cloth and small mirror. She sat down next to me to wipe the dried blood and dirt from my face. When she was finished, she handed me the mirror. "Good as new."

Looking into the mirror, I found nothing out of the ordinary on my fair skin besides a little extra pink in my cheeks under the sprinkling of freckles there. My eyes were a bit red from the crying, but the swirling molten gold of my irises looked the same as ever. My chestnut curls looked a wild mess, but there was little I could do for that at the moment.

"Do you want the bad news or the really bad news first?"

I lowered the mirror, setting on the cot next to me. "Which one is that Jenkins is dead?"

She took my hand in hers. "That's the bad news."

"Shit. I didn't see him move since the crowd was pushed away. I was hoping he wouldn't be," I said, my hand trembling in hers. "So then, what's the really bad news?"

"You've been summoned to go before the Committee."

"Fuck. Did you hear what day I'm supposed to go?"

She squeezed my hand, looking grim. "Immediately."

"What do you think is going to happen? I mean, a man died because of me," I said desperately.

"It was the crowd that killed him, keep that in mind. And point it out to the Committee if they don't say it first."

"Yeah, the crowd I was supposed to be controlling."

"Jenkins was old." She shrugged. "Maybe they'll go easy on you."

"Jenkins loved the shit out of the Emperor, so probably not," I said.

We sat there in silence, watching the other Healers pass by as I attempted to gather my courage. My legs bounced restlessly as my thoughts churned over the memory of this morning. And what was to come.

"I did hear one other part from the Protectors that were there," she said, a smile starting to form on her lips.

"What?" I couldn't think of a single thing to smile about right now.

"That your injuries were caused by someone much smaller than you." Her smile widened. "Some might refer to him as a young child."

"Lina! Now is not the time," I said.

"So, is it true?" she asked, barely concealing her uncontrolled delight. "You had your ass handed to you by a child?"

"Yes." I sagged. "You can't tell George or I will never hear the end of it." I braced my elbows on my knees, slumping my forehead into my hands.

She laughed and drew stares from a few Protectors still milling around. They quickly followed the looks with whispers to each other. Great. My defeat at the hands of a ten-year-old would be known to everyone in the Compound before I was even in front of the Committee.

"You know we can't keep secrets from each other," she said. "It's wrong to not tell George."

"It's not that we *can't* keep secrets from each other. It's that we don't *normally* keep secrets from each other. This is an extraordinary circumstance, so I'm asking you to not treat it normally."

"He's going to hear about it. George knows everything that goes on around here. He might as well hear it from me, because I'm assuming *you* don't want to tell him."

"Ugh, fine!" I conceded. "I hate you."

"No, you don't," she said, squeezing my knee.

"No, I don't."

The muscles that had loosened during my talk with Lina tensed back up, making my spine rigid as I stood to go face my judgment from the Committee.

CHAPTER FIVE

By the time I reached the large oak doors that led into the Committee Hall, the tension in my chest felt like a dam about to burst once more. Everything sounded oddly far away.

Whatever was about to happen in there, I just needed to stay calm and stick to the facts. And downplay the fact a child took me down in the middle of the square. And hope no one actually liked Jenkins that much.

Fuck, that was a terrible thing to think about a dead man. I was a bad person. I probably deserved whatever horrible punishment I was about to receive.

The Empire has always given you a path forward. This will turn out fine.

I entered Committee Hall for the first time in my life. The room immediately made me feel small with its towering ceilings connected by intricately carved arches. The walls were covered with detailed frescos, showing the Great War when the Empire was united and the witches were killed off. The paintings didn't skimp on the depictions of gruesome deaths, which felt foreboding in this place of judgment.

Directly in front of me was a long, raised dais where ten people were seated. I had never done this before. I didn't know the process. They all stared at me expectantly until one said, "Nessamia Riseworth, please approach."

The walk across the flagstone floor seemed to take years. My expedition ended next to a plain wooden chair in front of the ten Committee members. As I stared at them, my mouth went exceptionally dry. I wondered if I'd ever been able to swallow, or if it was something I'd dreamed up.

"Sit."

They all were dressed in decadent clothes that had been expertly tailored. I had heard the Committee was made up of the Emperor's friends and those with the wealth to buy power. A woman in the middle with long red hair and a green dress covered in intricate embroidery that looked like it cost more than I was paid over my entire term of service cleared her throat. "We have reviewed the events of this afternoon as reported by the Protectors who witnessed the incident."

I wondered which Protectors they interviewed and what they said. No one else had been there to witness everything. Suddenly, I had a whole lot more sympathy for those families of the hanged. There were a lot of gaps I would sure love to be filled in before my judgment.

"We came to a determination that based on the particularly unruly crowd, you will not be charged with a capital offense for the death of the longtime executioner of the Empire, Putino Jenkins," Green Dress went on.

I breathed a sigh of relief. That still left a lot of room for other unpleasant punishments, but at least my death was off the table.

"We were instructed not to sentence you to any punishment yet."

I hadn't been asked to tell my side of the story, so that was probably what they were waiting on. My side of the story also included my negligence to shield myself. Yet they did say they were taking into account the rowdiness of the crowd, so maybe my honesty wouldn't damn me.

No one had prompted me to say anything, and I was debating whether or not they were waiting for me to start speaking on my own accord when the door groaned open behind me. The breeze rushed around me, stirring the smell of dust and wood polish.

I twisted to see the Emperor's general walk in. He stood well over a head taller than me and had broad shoulders. He was a formidable man with a shaved head and a large fair beard. His sharp blue eyes cut to me as he walked past.

The General appeared to only be a few years older than myself, but I knew he fought in the Great War over five hundred years ago. He was one of the few who survived the illness following the war. As the Emperor's right-hand man, he took care of all the Imperial dirty work.

His nickname wasn't Ancient Bastard because he was well-known for his kindness. If he was here, it would not be good for me.

"Thank you for waiting for me," General Drakemore said.

A servant hurried in from a side door, carrying a chair that looked far more comfortable than mine, and set it next to the Committee members facing me. I adjusted my legs against the press of the unforgiving wood beneath my thighs.

His clothes were all black, like all those in the Protectorate, except his were of much higher quality and tailored to him. He remained standing, his hand rested on the pommel of his sword hanging from his belt. His fathomless blue eyes caught me in a stare that weighed down my hopes.

"Nessamia Riseworth." I sat up straighter in my chair. "You were instructed to protect a long-dedicated civil servant to the Emperor today. You failed at that duty."

His expectant look pulled a conditioned response from me. "Yes, sir."

"The crowds at the Old Square have been growing increasingly disruptive with each new hanging, going so far as to throw stones at the two Protectors assigned to that service earlier this week. Between the two of them, they barely managed to subdue the offenders and bring them in. Therefore, it has been determined you are not totally at fault."

I dipped my head in acknowledgement. If he already knew the crowds were getting worse, why hadn't they pulled a second Protector for that duty today? I felt a bit like I had been set up to fail. I pressed the palms of my hands against my thighs to stop my trembling legs.

"Your punishment will be reassignment," he said.

I stared at him, my eyes wide with surprise. It was completely unheard of to reassign a Protector with less than a year of service left.

"You will be expected to leave for the First Outpost tomorrow morning. There is a small group of mortal Protectors traveling there that you will accompany. Have your bag packed and be at the main gate at first light."

The finality in his words reverberated through me as he strode out.

Reassignment wasn't truly the worst punishment. But in a matter of hours, I would be leaving Lina and George, and that thought cut deep.

I was dismissed by Green Dress, and I peeled my legs from the hard wooden chair to go back to the Healer's Wing and tell Lina the verdict.

I was making a mental list of what I would need to pack as I walked up a wide stone staircase, when George's voice reached me over my thoughts.

"Ness! Thank the Mother, you still have your head!" He grabbed my shoulders and shook me slightly as if he was checking to see if my head was, in fact, still fully attached to my neck.

"George." I sagged with relief at his presence. "I'm surprised you don't already know."

"I can only listen in to Committee Hearings with prior planning." His brows arched over his gray-blue eyes, giving me a pointed look. We couldn't speak about using the secret passages in the open.

"I'm being reassigned," I said.

"That doesn't sound bad at all. I know you like training the first years, but you've been getting tired of it. Spending the next five months on patrols in the City isn't so bad." His eyes widened. "Or is it sewer duty?"

"No, not reassigned duties in Capital City. I'm getting moved to an outpost."

His hands fell from my shoulders. "You're leaving us! Does Lina know yet?"

I shook my head. "I was headed to the Healer's Wing to tell her right now."

"Before me? That's almost as painful as this news."

We cornered Lina in a semi-private alcove and told her about my reassignment.

"I have an hour left in my shift," Lina said, sadness dampening her voice. "What's the plan after that?"

"I still need to clear out my room, but I want to get in a last night at our favorite spots," I said.

"Right, so meet in the entrance hall in an hour for dinner at the Pony, and we'll go from there," George said.

"Yeah, it's going to need to be in two hours," Lina said, gesturing to her clothes stained with various bodily fluids. "I need to bathe first."

"I don't really want to wait near the doors to that stupid Committee Hall. Can we meet somewhere else?" I asked. "Maybe the front gate."

"That works for me," Lina said.

"No, please not the front gate. Randall is on duty this evening. I really don't want to have to wait near his post," George said.

"George," Lina said, "we told you so many times not to sleep with him. So many times."

"It's easy to see that now," George said with a shrug. "He gets jealous every time I leave the Compound. I feel like I'm being interrogated."

"Maybe you need to set Randall up with someone else and he'll leave you alone," I suggested.

"Never. He should pine over me. Just in a way that is less annoying."

"Lina!" called a Healer from the other side of the room. "We need your help over here."

"Shit! See you guys in two hours at the gate." Lina dashed off.

"And what is the most elite of the Emperor's Protectors supposed to be doing right now?" I asked as George and I walked from the Healer's Wing to the Protectors' dormitories.

"Oh, protecting the most important people in the Imperial Compound buildings. So believe it or not, I *am* doing my job right now," he replied with a wide grin. "And as a matter of fact, I thought I saw some suspicious activity under your bed, so I should probably protect you while you pack."

CHAPTER SIX

With still-wet feet, I padded from the shared bathing chamber to my small dormitory down the hall for the last time to finish packing. George had left a while before, saying he needed plenty of time to get ready.

I changed into a simple, loose-fitting dress. It was one of the two outfits I still possessed that hadn't been issued by the Empire. The other was a pair of pants and a tunic that had seen much better days and would be staying in the Imperial Compound when I left.

Most of my days were spent training new recruits or with George and Lina, which I could do in standard issue uniforms. I learned quickly that spending any of my meager wages on new clothing was impractical.

You could ask for advances on your wages, with the trade-off that you would extend out your contract. Every advance was another month added to the end of your service.

So far, Lina and George had managed to scrape by without any advances. There were a few close calls, like the time George lost a game of cards in a tavern so badly that Lina had to offer her ring from her aunt to cover the debt. They didn't talk for weeks after that.

Given I could only take a saddlebag of my belongings, most of the trinkets I had collected over the last decade were still piled on the small desk in the corner of my room.

I had already packed uniforms for the road, a few books, and the personal effects I wanted to keep—a necklace from my mom I never could bring myself to sell after her death, and the random scraps of parchment Lina, George, and I used to record the places we wanted to visit after our service was over.

I looked over the bed, desk, dresser, and single small window that made up everything I had been able to call my own for ten years. The confined space. The shared bathing chamber down the hall. This wasn't what I would miss.

Lina and George were.

I saw them every day. I told them pretty much everything in my life. I wouldn't have that for the next few months. Their lives would go on together without me. A feeling I hadn't experienced in some time opened inside of me, a hollow pit of loneliness. They would have jokes and memories I wasn't part of. The thought made my eyes prickle, and I left my room before I could dwell on it any longer.

I found Lina walking down the hall toward me as I made my way down to the front gate.

"Tonight was worthy of changing out of a uniform, huh?" she teased.

"To be fair, our uniforms are more flattering than this dress." I plucked at the skirt of my shapeless garment. It was a pleasant slate blue color, though, which nicely complemented my chestnut hair.

"How are you doing?" she asked as we passed through the stone corridors, the heat of the day finally starting to abate.

"I just keep reminding myself I can handle whatever comes next," I said, trying to sound convinced, but knowing Lina would be able to see through it. "I can't change what's about to happen and it will only be for a few months."

Lina gave me a bittersweet smile. "I know you can handle it. If anyone can, it's you, Ness."

"It's a lot of change," I said, my voice rough. "Leaving you and George, the City I lived in my whole life."

"You've been through a lot today, even without the reassignment." She shook her head and said quietly, "Sometimes I wish I could heal more than people's bodies."

I smiled at her, tucking an errant curl behind my ear. "We just have to trust that this is going to be a good thing," I said with far more confidence than I felt. "Every time the Empire has guided my life, it's turned out for the best." When I was young, my mom supported us by working in the Imperial Compound. Imperial primary schools taught me everything I know. Then when my mom died and selling everything wasn't enough, the Protectorate gave me an opportunity to get back on my feet. Plus, it's how I met Lina and George. "I have to tell myself this will bring me the best windfall yet."

She took my hand in hers. "I hope it does."

George was waiting for us by the gate, where Randall was indeed on duty tonight and trying his best to ignore George's existence. George was looking pointedly anywhere except at Randall, but both kept sneaking secretive glances when they thought the other wasn't looking.

We leaned behind a bush and watched him as he suffered, stifling our laughter. We could feel the tension from behind the bush. The other

Protector on duty with Randall kept darting his eyes between the two men as though they were powder kegs with the fuses lit.

"Beautiful sunset this evening," George broke the silence.

Randall rolled his eyes and gave a sigh that could be heard all the way to our bush. "Look, we don't need to do this."

The other Protector shifted slightly further away from them, looking like he would have gladly jumped in front of an oncoming cart to get away from this.

"I'm not trying to do anything. Just commenting on the weather," George said, his voice squeaking at the end.

"Right, and I'm sure it wasn't your idea to stand by the gate during my shift," Randall said.

"It wasn't."

I looked at Lina next to me. "We should put him out of his misery."

We emerged from our hiding place and approached George.

"Thanks for meeting up at the gate, George. It really made our lives easier to meet here even though you asked to meet by the fountain," Lina called out. Randall glared at her from the corner of his eyes.

We exited the Compound quickly, stifling snorts, not trusting ourselves to contain our laughter. George glared at us, before breaking into a smile of his own.

The Blushing Pony was closer to the Old Square than it was the Compound. Being in a lower-class area of the city, the drinks were far cheaper and more suitable for a Protector's salary. But the walk was short in the company of my friends.

As we entered the tavern under the creaking wooden sign painted with a Pony's head with pink cheeks and sultry eyes, I was immediately wrapped into the familiarity of our favorite establishment. The smell of ale and savory foods layered with chatter over the musicians playing near the back wall.

We navigated through the crowd swathed in dim light and took our seats around a high table against the wall.

A tall, thin man with dark golden skin and closely cropped white hair approached our table. "Evening, Jarvis," George said.

"Ah, my favorite trio. What are you drinking?" Jarvis asked with a smile.

George dropped a handful of copper coins on the table. "Whatever we can get a lot of."

"This is about three rounds of house ale," Jarvis said, scooping the coins from the table and counting them.

"Could it be four rounds if we told you our dear Ness is getting reassigned at an outpost tomorrow morning?" George asked.

Jarvis gave an exaggerated sigh. "Alright. But only if you two promise to still come here without her. My wife will never forgive me if we lose your business."

"Of course we will! You can't possibly think Ness is the cause of all of our terrible decision-making? She's only responsible for about half of them."

Jarvis laughed as he left to go get the first of our ales.

"Did they tell you why you're being sent to the First?" Lina asked.

I shook my head.

"I've been trying to figure that out all afternoon," George said, tracing some old gouges in the wooden tabletop with his thumbnail. "The Third Outpost is by the only bridge that crosses the boundary line, and it's always heavily guarded. The Sixth is closest to the silver mine which has the occasional attack on it by Gallian rebels. But the First has nothing. It's an uncontested part of the border that, as far as I know, has never had an attack in all its time. The bulk of the Protectorate presence there is mortal."

"I bet it's because there's that group leaving for the First tomorrow morning," Lina said as our drinks arrived. "The General didn't want anyone to have time to question his decision and wanted to get you out of the City as soon as possible."

"Yeah, but why is he making a questionable decision in the first place?" I took a drink of the frothy deliciousness in front of me. The Pony's brew was my favorite in Capital City.

"He's probably trying to resolve this quickly to hide that command fucked up by not finding a second Protector to cover that duty with you," George said.

"What's the normal punishment for an offense like this?" Lina asked George. He patrolled the halls of the Compound almost every day, and he overheard plenty of things most Protectors wouldn't know.

"I'm not sure I know of another Committee ruling for something quite like this," he said as he held his chin, elbow resting on the table. "But last year, there was that mortal Protector who was out with some woman from the City. They were swimming in the river and she drowned. He wasn't on duty at the time, but the Committee said he made the Imperial Protectors look irresponsible. They dismissed him from the Protectorate and banished him from Capital City."

"Do you think I'm being banished?" I asked with a grimace.

"No, they never said you couldn't come back."

"They probably don't want to lose a wielder five months before her contract is up," Lina said as she waved down Jarvis. "Better to stick you in an actionless outpost and hope you rack up gambling debts so you'll extend your contract rather than dismiss you altogether. Three plates, please, Jarvis." She handed him enough coins for all of us before I could reach for my own coin purse.

"That does sound right for the Protectorate," George said, his thumbnail now following the grooves on the cup. "Especially because I haven't ever heard of any wielder being sent there whose parents don't own half a state."

George was right. The First seemed like the type of place a rich wielder would be placed, and I was far from that. Every person, rich or poor, had to commit to service before touching Cavilth. The Empire liked to advertise this was part of their dedication to a fair and just system.

However, it was impossible not to notice how children of nobles were never sent to any of the insecure outposts or to patrol the Old Square. They all seemed to be assigned to quiet hamlets or luxurious estates.

George liked to say that if the system actually was fair and just, the Empire wouldn't need to point out how fair and just it was all the time.

A plate of roast and vegetables appeared in front of me. "My husband says you're leaving us, Ness." I followed the pale hand setting down the plate to the plump face of the owner standing behind me. She flicked her gray-streaked, wavy blonde hair behind her back before setting down the other plates.

"Polly." I smiled. "Yes, Mother only knows what the future holds for me these next five months." I poked a piece of beef with my fork, about to raise it to my mouth.

"Only five months?" she asked.

I lowered my fork with my food still uneaten. "I'm just serving out my extensions now. I'll be done this winter solstice." I would have been released four weeks ago if I hadn't taken advances on my pay at the start of my service. At the time the money felt worth it, but now on the other end of my service—well, I wouldn't have been on duty in the Old Square today.

"Extensions? But you three are so frugal."

"They're from before I met Lina and George."

"I always forget you three didn't all enter in the same year," Polly said. "So George and Lina, you two get out at the next summer solstice?"

"Lina is our baby," George replied. "I get out next summer and Lina the one after that."

"You already turned down the offer for Head Healer?" Polly asked Lina.

"No," Lina said slowly, not meeting anyone's eyes. "Not yet. A lot can change in two years."

Polly wiped her hands on her apron. "What are you three going to do when you're all done?"

"We want to travel," George said. "Go around the Empire, the seven kingdoms—shit, even beyond the mist."

The curtain of fog that hung over the seas around our realm made travel to other continents difficult, and it was rarely crossed. On one of our less sober evenings, we had made extensive plans to attempt the notoriously dangerous journey.

Polly huffed a laugh and left us to drink.

I wasn't drinking enough ale to get drunk. My nerves about the following day, months, years were getting the better of me. Large swaths of silence blanketed our group more than once. My thoughts continually strayed to our future rather than remaining in the moment.

"Do you know what Millie told me?" a nasal woman asked loudly from behind me. "She said Junie Foster's husband went to petition the Committee about there not being enough Protectors on patrol near his shop at night. There were three break-ins on his block last month. He never came back from the Compound. I bet he'll be swinging tomorrow evening for questioning the General's judgment."

George, Lina and I exchanged frowns. People weren't executed because they petitioned the Committee, otherwise no one would request anything. Yet, talking about the Empire like this so openly wasn't a great idea. Her sentiments were only a hair away from what some patrol Protectors might consider treason, and that would give them just cause to bring her in.

Lina whispered to us, "Junie Foster's husband likely committed a crime, and Junie hadn't wanted to admit he was arrested."

I nodded while George twisted his mouth to the side, taking another drink from his mug.

"Doesn't seem right to me," said the gruff voice of the woman's companion. He leaned in conspiratorially to the woman and lowered his voice to what I was sure the drunk man thought was a whisper. "Makes you wish you could change the powers that be."

The tension that jolted over the three of us could have cut stone. We looked at each other with wide eyes. If any of us were on patrol duty, that sentiment would certainly have been enough to bring him into the Committee. We were already struggling to relive our usual revelry at the Pony, but that broke any delusions we held that we could achieve it.

It didn't matter if the couple behind us was right or wrong—we couldn't change that we were born in the Empire. It wasn't as though we could buy political power like the nobles. Personally, it didn't seem worth my time to worry too much about a system I would always have to live within.

"We should start heading back to the Compound to get there before curfew," George said.

We abandoned our half-finished cups and found Polly and Jarvis behind the bar on our way out.

"Leaving already? You only had two rounds," Polly said as she wrapped me a quick hug. "Behave yourself and we'll be seeing you before you know it. Come back to us in one piece."

CHAPTER SEVEN

The sun had begun to set and darkness was slowly draping over the City as we traced the cobblestones back to the Imperial Compound. George moved a bottle of brown liquor to his other hand.

"Where did you get that?" I asked.

"Jarvis slipped it to me while Polly was hugging you. He said we should have it, since we never got those last two rounds."

George and Lina talked while I listened, my attention meandering between their conversation and the people we passed closing up their businesses for the night.

"No, after all that, it didn't happen. I was put off by this weird mole he had on his—"

"Do you think I'll see a real bear?" I cut Lina off. "On my way to the First? Or maybe while I'm living there?"

George raised his eyebrows at me. "I was about to hear a very interesting tidbit about Tellis and you interrupted to ask about bears?"

Lina gave a mischievous smile. "Trust me, my story is very small compared to bears."

"Disappointing," George said. "And no, Ness, I don't think you'll see a bear. They mostly live in the mountains and try to avoid people."

"Oh, that's good. Did you ever see a bear when you lived in Chatsboro?"

"Yes, a few, but never close up," she said. "Just make a lot of noise if you have to walk through the mountains and they'll avoid you. If you do run into one, make yourself seem as big as possible by waving your arms or moving to higher ground, and back away slowly. That's it. It kept me alive for eighteen years in Chatsboro, so you'll probably be fine living in a coastal outpost for five months." She chuckled at me. "Why are you concerned about bears all of a sudden?"

"I've never been further than a two-hour walk from the City gates."

When I was younger, my mother would occasionally take me on picnics in the countryside near Capital City. We would sit in the sun, feel the grass beneath our feet and swim in the clear waters of the creeks nearby. It was a world away from the cramped and dirty confines of daily lives, even if it was only a few hours outside of the City walls. Those times had been few and far between, and they would hardly prepare me for the days of trekking across the countryside to the First Outpost.

"You're going to be with other Protectors the entire time. I don't think you'll have to worry about bears for a single second," George said.

"Only worry about them if you surprise one, or if it's a mother with cubs. Or it seems hungry," Lina said.

We were within sight of the towering Imperial Compound gates, already closed even though curfew wasn't for fifteen more minutes. Fortunately for us, Randall was already off duty. Unfortunately for Lina—

"Tellis, hello," George smirked to the Protectors in front of the gates as he elbowed Lina.

"Shit," Lina mumbled so only I could hear. Then at regular volume, she said, "Hi, Tellis. Could you have them open the gate for us?"

"Lina, Lina, Lina," Tellis tutted. "I haven't heard from you since that night after the solstice party. I think we should catch up. My shift is done at midnight." Tellis spoke with entirely too much bravado for a man who had an off-putting mole somewhere.

Lina smiled sweetly at him. "Maybe you should let us through the gate before we're late for curfew, otherwise I won't have privileges to catch up with anyone for a while. And I won't tell anyone you closed the gates early."

"Hmm," he mumbled as he stepped out from the wall and signaled to the Protectors above to open the gates.

"I mean, I do feel bad for him," Lina said once we were out of earshot. "But not bad enough to meet up with him after his shift."

"You two have got to stop it with the gate guards. It makes our lives so much harder," I said.

"Not all of us are strong enough to swear off other Protectors, Ness," George said. "Despite the uncomfortable endings, they're pretty much the only people we get to interact with."

Our feet carried us along the gravel path we knew well, around the buildings and into the Imperial garden. Colorful, flowering bushes and hedgerows manicured to perfection lined our path until we arrived at my favorite destination within these walls—a crystal-clear pool surrounded by granite boulders that were perfect to sit on while dipping your toes in the water. The air was fresh and clear here, unlike the smells of sweat, wood smoke, and waste that clouded much of the City and the Compound.

We took seats on the rocks around the pond as a few stars began to poke out, twinkling overhead, the sound of insects discernible over the distant noises of the City. We discarded our shoes and stuck our feet in the cool water, passing around the bottle Jarvis gave us. The fish in the pond darted around our swinging toes as we talked about Tellis and other Protectors. Eventually, we fell to retelling of our favorite misadventures over the last eight years. By the time the moon was truly up, we had moved on to the classics.

"Remember when George tried to cut his own hair," I snorted.

Lina tipped her head back, laughing loudly. "Who knew you could be so bad at cutting hair that your own Earth magic wouldn't be enough to fix it? I had to come help him grow it back out."

"Let us never forget the time Ness got too drunk at the Pony and couldn't walk back to the Compound." George raised the liquor bottle in salute to the memory.

"It's not my fault those streets are so windy. It's very confusing," I laughed, taking the bottle from him.

"Ness, you can't cut me off before the best part," George said with a smile as he took the bottle from me. "You realized you weren't going to make it back before curfew, despite our help, so you paid that man to let you ride his horse back to the gate."

"But you couldn't stay on it," Lina picked up the story through gales of laughter. "So we had to throw you over the side of the poor thing and tie you on. And when we got to the gate and let you down, you tried to haggle with the man that it should be less than you agreed because you had rope burn across your back and 'I don't pay for what I can get for free.' And when he refused, you tried to shame him by saying—"

"It's too late for this horse to be out on the streets! Take him to bed," we all said together.

"Well, that was really to distract him from the fact that I threw up down the side of his horse." I grimaced at the memory. "I was hoping he wouldn't notice."

"Trust us, we all noticed," Lina said. After our laughter died down, we all went silent again. "You know George and I had to pay him extra."

I frowned. "You guys never told me that before. I would have paid you back for it."

"We know. That's why we didn't tell you. We didn't want you to add to your service any more than you already had," George said as he handed the bottle back to Lina.

I looked into the dark pool to watch the shadowy outlines of fish skate back and forth. They darted between the reflections of the scant stars that were visible through the blanket of chimney smoke in the City.

I finally voiced the dread that had been building in me since this afternoon. "Even if I'm only gone a few months, what will happen when I get back? You two have a lot more service to go. What if we're different people in two years and don't want to stick together and travel anymore?"

"I don't think that will be the case," Lina said. "We're more than just friends, you're my family. You can see the resemblance in our bad taste in men. No matter what happens in the next two years, as long as we choose to find each other, we will."

She leaned over and hugged me. George joined the hug from my other side.

"I hate this," I said, discreetly brushing some wetness off my cheeks. "I feel like I'm back where I was ten years ago. Alone. No idea what the future holds."

"Tell you what," George said. "Why don't we do something we've never done before? Make a real plan for the future, not scraps of paper.

How about no matter what happens, we promise to meet up in two years at the Blushing Pony?"

"You're not planning for the worst," I said. "What if I'm not allowed back in Capital City after my reassignment is over? Maybe George finally overheard the wrong secret and is in hiding. Maybe the Pony has burned down. What if we're released from duty and the rivers all flood and we can't make it back here?"

"We get it, we get it," Lina said. "Winter solstice in two years, then. A full six months to get our affairs in order and travel. And we meet somewhere that will always exist."

"Agora," George said. "Even if it burned down, they would always rebuild. We would always be welcomed there."

Agora was the only major city in the Southern State. Technically still within the Empire, the Southern State was run by a rogue governor while Protectors only maintained order within the ports. This agreement was a strange vestige of the aftermath of the Great War and was never discussed in detail in Imperial schools. The governor was commonly referred to as a crime lord, since the normal laws of the Empire weren't enforced there, and any vice could be satisfied.

"If any place would survive the worst, it would be Agora," Lina agreed.

We let the muffled sounds of the Compound fill our silence until we finished the bottle.

"We should head up," I said. "I have a full day of riding tomorrow, and need to be ready to leave by sunrise."

As we stood and collected ourselves, I knew this was likely the very last time we would all be around this pond to enjoy each other's company. After I returned, I would no longer be in the Protectorate and wouldn't have access to the Compound anymore. I took a final deep breath of the fresh air in the garden before leaving behind this part of myself.

The fullness in my heart welled up inside of my chest and poured out through my eyes. Only at the sound of my sniffle did Lina look over at me. Her eyes immediately began to fill with tears.

"I told myself I wouldn't cry. Not until someone else did first," she said with a watery smile.

"Oh, thank the Mother. I've been holding it together all night," George said thickly as a single, fat tear rolled down his face.

We stood there sniffling and hugging for some time.

"Starting tomorrow, every place, person and experience will be totally new to me. Which is really fucking scary," I said.

"At least your body will be getting new experiences," George added, raising his eyebrows. "You're finally going to end your dry spell since what's-his-name, the sailor."

Lina laughed. "That's true."

I crossed my arms. "You two don't *know* that." Lina and George exchanged a look. "What?"

"Come on, Ness." George gave me an annoyingly knowing look. "You dated Joss because you were lonely, even though he's a dick, and you hung on to him like he was the Mother's greatest creation. Even when you had to take all those pay advances to try to keep up with him."

"And you know," Lina twisted her lips to the side, "that summer we were all fighting, you got so serious with that mortal in just a few weeks, you actually met his family. But outside of them, you just..."

"Face it, Ness," George said. "When you feel alone, you bury yourself in a relationship."

I chewed the inside of my cheek, and couldn't come up with any evidence to refute their points.

"Maybe some time apart will be good for all of us," Lina said. "Give us a chance to grow into our own people."

"I'm sorry, you don't enjoy our oddly close group bonded through the shared pain and the torment that is being a Protector?" George joked. "That's it, no Yule gift for you."

Later in bed, I started to feel a small spark of excitement about what the coming months would bring. I had a plan to meet up with Lina and George again. And I had always been intrigued by stories I'd heard and paintings I'd seen of untamed mountains, sprawling deserts, and frozen wastelands. Now I would have a chance to see them with my own eyes.

Perhaps I *was* ready to be my own person, away from what everyone thought of me. Average Ness, whose magical powers turned out to be nothing special. Sad Ness, who was a shell of a person after her mom died and needed George and Lina to help her back up. And apparently, Dependent Ness, who latched on to romance when she felt lost. It was better to tell myself that I wanted this change, and that I wanted to be alone.

I slipped into a dream of walking along an unfamiliar road in the countryside. The stones below my feet were trembling. When I tried to deviate from the path, high walls sprung up on either side of me and the sounds of a rioting crowd swelled behind me, threatening to trample me if I didn't move. I had no other way to go and began to run forward.

Suddenly the path opened onto the Old Square. Jenkins was there, being surrounded by a crowd while dozens of Protectors lined the walls, watching idly. I screamed for them to help, but no sound would come out, like when the boy forced the air from my lungs.

I tried to pull my magic and force the crowd away, but it didn't respond to me. I was shoved to the ground from behind and pain exploded through my face. I tried to push up to see who knocked me over, but my hands were covered in blood and too slick to get purchase on the stones.

When I looked up to the gallows. General Drakemore was standing next to them, pointing at me.

CHAPTER EIGHT

A puffy-eyed Protector trudged across the grass still wet with dew to escort me to a brown mare the following morning. I stood in the early morning light trickling over the Compound wall as I tried to attach my bag to the saddle. Five others were lined up to ride with me to the First. Of the four mortal Protectors, three were men and one a woman. She had short, dark hair and spied on me frequently as she prepared her horse. I hoped that meant she saw us as allies, being the only two women on the journey, and I made a note to talk to her when we took a break. I might be alright without friends for the next five months, but I wouldn't turn one down if she was staring at me repeatedly.

The fifth member of the party was a mortal commander who was transferring to the First with us. I hadn't spoken to him yet, but if he was going to be spending the next few months at the First with me, at least my reassignment would have a decent view.

The commander was well over a head taller than me with broad shoulders and a strong, clean-shaven jawline. He flashed a disarming smile of straight, white teeth as he talked to the other Protectors. His short, fair hair looked soft and touchable as it flowed over his brow, and he didn't look much older than me.

I balked, realizing how right George and Lina were. I typically stayed clear of men in the Protectorate, and I couldn't look at a commanding officer with anything other than appreciation. It didn't matter if I didn't report to him directly, I was still a Protector. Relationships with any commanding officers were strictly forbidden and would result in immediate dismissal of both parties from the Imperial Protectorate. I still had a few months left to serve for pay advances and if I was dismissed early, I would have to pay them back immediately with money I didn't have. And if I couldn't pay, I would be back in front of the Committee.

I shoved the quick breakfast I had snagged from the dining hall into my mouth, finishing the dry bread before we left. Focusing on buckling the well-worn leather strap of my saddle bag to my horse, I tried to swallow the lump of bread that seemed to be stuck in my throat.

When everything was fastened, I hooked my foot into the stirrup and got ready to mount the horse. I'd only done it a few times before. It was generally impolite to be the only wielder in a group and use your magic for tasks the mortals around you had to do manually, so I couldn't use wind to boost me up. With no mounting block, I really needed to focus to get on my horse on the first try without looking like a fool. I knew I could do this, I just needed to get every part of it right.

Hands on the saddle, I started to launch myself up to get my leg over.

"Need a hand?" a deep voice asked from behind me, plucking a twinge of recognition in me. Turning my head to see who it was threw my balance off enough to make me lose momentum and start to fall back down.

"Shit!"

The commander grabbed my waist and reversed my fall to help me get on the horse without any further embarrassment. Of course I recognized his voice, he had been speaking to someone five feet away from me moments ago.

When I was soundly seated, he asked, "Are you alright now?"

"Yeah, thanks."

"You're Nessamia Riseworth, the new addition to our company," he said with a smile. He was shading his eyes with his hand as he looked up at me on the horse, but it didn't hide his dazzling blue eyes as he did the usual observation of my golden ones.

"Ness," I said a little breathlessly. I blamed that on finally getting down the extremely dry bread. "I go by Ness."

"I'm Commander Densen." He smiled. "Nice to meet you."

He looked at me expectantly.

My need to prove George wrong and not immediately start flirting with the first man to speak to me warred with my inability to remember how to talk at that moment. I looked around at the other Protectors, mounted and starting to gather near the gate, hoping for inspiration for a casual response.

The silent search went on until he clapped his hands. "Alright then, let's get to it." He left me to go mount his own horse.

Once we passed beyond the drab walls of Capital City, the dusty cobbles and cramped spaces opened into a packed dirt road. The fresh air filled my lungs, lifting some of the weight from my shoulders.

The distant shape of the hill where Cavilth sat came into view.

The last time I was this close to it was the summer solstice just over ten years ago now. I remembered that warm day, climbing the path along the grassy hill, turning back to get a view of the tight streets of the City beyond the wall and the looming Imperial Compound beyond.

I had signed the parchment, agreeing to serve the Empire in any way commanded of me, as I waited just outside of the gate that kept Cavilth shuttered other days of the year. Once that paper was signed, I was at the whims of my commanding officers until my term was up, under penalty of death.

On that blustery day, I'd crested the hill to catch my first glimpse of the red granite rock that reached to hip-height of those waiting in line ahead of me. I watched as the people in line in front of me touched Cavilth one by one.

My hands were shaking as the woman two in front of me placed her hand down and the rock remained unchanged. The Protector keeping roll proclaimed her a mortal, to serve for three years, and she was sent down the other side of the hill.

The person ahead of me, a handsome teen with pristine clothing, turned to me and smiled before slapping his hand on Cavilth. The ruddy hue of the rock began to radiate a soft amber light. The teen whooped in victory during the reading of his name, but I clearly heard he was a wielder and would serve for ten years.

Then it was my turn. I was trembling as I reached out to touch the sun-warmed stone. Beneath my fingers, the rough points of granite were smoothed over from centuries of hopeful hands. The heat from the rock spread up my arm and into my body as the light from Cavilth grew brighter and brighter.

Everyone on the hill went silent as the typical dull glow turned blindingly white. When the light receded, the Protector recording the roll cleared his throat and said, "Nessamia Riseworth, *definitely* a wielder. You'll serve the Empire for ten years."

As I walked down the other side of the hill, the teen who went before me was waiting. "That was you? That light?"

"Yes," I replied nervously. "I guess it was."

"I've never heard of Cavilth glowing that bright before. I think you're going to be very powerful." He tossed his head to the side to get his dark brown hair out of his emerald green eyes. "I'll have to keep my eye on you."

"Hmm." I wasn't sure what to make of that, but a spark of hope bloomed inside me. Maybe everything would turn around now that I would have a job and place to call home for the next ten years. For the first time since my mom died, I wouldn't have to worry about where my next meal would come from.

"I'm Joss, by the way," he said, holding out his hand to me. "Joss Milton." A smile lit his charmingly handsome face.

"Milton, as in the family that owns most of Capital City?" My jaw dropped at the casual way I was meeting a child of one of the most influential families in the Empire.

"That's the one," he said. "And I think you and I are about to start spending a lot of time together." His eyes looked me up and down before a smirk spread across his lips. I had felt my cheeks heat as I smiled back, and seventeen-year-old Ness had really thought her luck was changing.

Cavilth had glowed brighter for me than it had for anyone else in memory, but it turned out my abilities were far from great. They were exceptionally average compared to the other wielders, sometimes below average.

That might have been the reason they assigned me to be a trainer all those years ago—maybe they hoped training the new wielders might help me find the deep well of power Calvilth had seemingly promised I had.

Only it didn't.

Instead, I'd begun a monotonous ten years of teaching and constantly being overshadowed by the powers of my students. Sometimes it took wielders a few years to get to their strongest. But mine stayed the same. Eventually, hope that my magic would suddenly flourish had faded, as did my relationship with Joss.

I shook the memories from my head and spent the rest of the morning basking in the wide-open spaces as our horses trotted further away from Capital City. Squirrels skittered away from us as we approached, and the noise of our party scattered birds into flight from the canopy of trees lining the road. Of course I had seen these animals before, but wildlife was rare in the City and still very much a novelty to me.

Once the sun began baking into my skin, the excitement wore off. I spent the late morning lamenting the lack of amenities outside of the City, like shaded alleyways and fountains of potable water.

And there were the bugs. After a trip into the brush to relieve myself, I was covered in dozens of itchy red welts in places that made riding a horse all day less than enjoyable. As our group stopped for lunch, I tenderly dismounted. I gently sat on a rock next to the only other female Protector.

This was my chance. If I wanted to stop lying to myself about being fine with spending the next five months alone, I needed to take this opportunity to get to know her. We could be new at the First together.

The commander walked away from our group to scout ahead. I looked her over from the corner of my eye, assessing how to best win her over. She was taller than me and athletic looking. Her straight, dark hair had a deep reddish tone to it and was cut into a bob.

She handed me a bit of bread, some dried salami, and an apple from a bag that was being passed around the group. Not too shabby. I was concerned meals on the road would be foraged berries and question-able mushrooms.

"Thanks," I said as I took the food from her, my smile forced. The enthusiasm I had for trying to make a new friend was already waning under how awkward I felt.

She nodded, her brown eyes watching me carefully. "Wynn Part-son," she said as she gestured to herself, her mouth already full of bread.

Introductions. I could do this without messing up. "Trainer Riseworth." *Shit.* "I mean Ness Riseworth."

I rarely introduced myself to any other Protectors besides the first years I was training. In the Compound, all the other Protectors always ignored me.

"I know," she said around the bread she was still chewing. "I've heard of you." Her eyes narrowed on my face. "And how you think you're better than everyone else."

Well, fuck. My smile dropped into a frown. "I'm not...I don't—" How could this be going so poorly so quickly?

She looked right back at me, eyebrows raised, waiting to see how I would respond.

She could wait a long time.

"I don't think I'm better than everyone else," I finally said. "I just don't usually talk to anyone else besides my friends."

"Only talking to those you deem worthy. Next you'll tell me you don't tell the other trainers how to do their jobs."

"What? Where did you hear that?" I tried to understand where this had all gone wrong.

"Trainer Sheab sat at my table last night at dinner. All anyone talked about in the dining hall was what happened in the Old Square, and

Sheab had quite a lot to say about your character." Her words dripped with scorn.

She raised her eyebrows as though waiting for me to deny these unknown allegations. I completely forgot I had even seen Sheab yesterday, much less interacted with him. So much had happened between his perceived slight with the water lesson and right now.

When I woke up yesterday, I had no reason to think it was going to be anything but normal, and today someone was dead because of me. I had just left the only city I ever knew and the only people I cared about in this world, my entire future was in question, and now I couldn't even make small talk over lunch.

My shoulders began to shake and I hid my face in my hands, my elbows propped on my knees. Laughter was huffing out of my nose uncontrolled. The more I tried to calm myself, the harder I wanted to laugh.

I peeked through my fingers. The three other Protectors were staring at me while eating, as though I was a busker on the streets of Capital City and they were enthralled by my performance. I couldn't blame them.

Wynn was looking at me, clearly as uneasy about my mental state as I was. "I think I'm beginning to see why you don't talk to other people. You seem unwell."

"A man died because of me yesterday," I said between laughs. "I'm not alright. I doubt I'll be well for the next couple of months, years, who knows."

I would only know these Protectors for five months. I couldn't make myself care that they were seeing me like this. I took a drink from my waterskin and tried to go back to eating, but food was no longer appealing.

CHAPTER NINE

We continued on until the evening with everyone riding in an uneasy silence. At our camp that night, I found out Wynn and I would be sharing a tent for the rest of the journey. *Great.*

I was asked to help another Protector set up the tents. Unlike my companion, I had never seen a tent set up before. He begrudgingly answered my countless questions and corrected my many mistakes. I probably made the whole process twice as long as if he had done it alone.

Wynn took a seat around the fire she had just finished building and stretched her legs out, crossing one boot over the other as she watched my progress with the ropes and canvas. "Well, at least you're enthusiastic."

My uneasiness with her was temporarily forgotten as I focused on untangling a rope that was wrapped around my boot. "No point in not trying to learn something new if I can. My service is over in a few months. I'm going to be off on my own soon enough, so the more skills I have, the better off I'll be."

"A surprisingly rational sentiment, considering how you were earlier today."

"I'm just in a bad place right now. I'm handling it as best I can," I said, finally freeing myself from the rope.

She frowned at the flames licking the logs. "I heard you and your friends thought you were better than the rest of us. I figured I would give you a hard time before you could be rude to me first. I don't know the hierarchy of the Protectors, with you being fae. I didn't want to end up being your next victim with the way Sheab painted you." When I got back to Capital City, I would be having words with Sheab. "And I didn't know you were so…" She gestured vaguely to all of me.

"Yeah, well, you aren't exactly catching me on my best day. But generally, I try not to be rude to anyone."

Wynn looked at me thoughtfully. "I think I owe you an apology."

"You didn't know I was a fragile mess when you handed me lunch. You don't owe me anything." Well, I wouldn't let an opportunity pass me up if presented. "But a second chance would be appreciated."

She nodded. "You're not the only person to leave everything and everyone you know behind." Poking the fire with a stick, she sent embers into the dusky sky settling around us. "I'm not exactly looking forward to my posting at the First."

"Really? You never left Capital City before either?"

"Not quite. I grew up in the Eastern State, but before I went to Capital City to join the Protectorate, I'd never left Polis before," she said.

So she was from Polis, what used to be the capital of the Eastern State when it was still an independent kingdom. I'd heard the culture and customs there were different from those in Capital City.

"Is it true you celebrate Yule on a different day each year instead of the twenty-first day of the last month?"

"We used to when we were still Moriale. The tradition was to celebrate with the last full moon of the year."

It probably *was* just as hard for her to leave for the First as me. If she was a mortal heading to her first posting, that meant she had been on her own for a month already.

"It's a hard world out here," she said. "It's easy to forget that there's no reason to be hard on each other too. We're going to be posted together, so we might as well be moderately nice to each other." She stared into the flames again, the flickering light moving shadows along her face and making it difficult to determine her expression. "It wasn't exactly the highest point of my life to sign my Protectorate contract at twenty-five."

I hadn't really considered that Wynn appeared closer to my own age than the usual seventeen- and eighteen-year-olds who touched Cavilth. There was no upper age limit to the ritual, but most people didn't usually choose to leave their established lives for the Protectorate, even with the chance of unlocking magic. Something must have been pretty bad in her life to force her to the Protectors at this age.

The other Protectors in our group all appeared to be closer to typical age, now that I paid attention to their gangly limbs and sparse facial hair. Maybe I would ask her about her circumstances later. Our acquaintanceship was too fledgling to start asking those kinds of questions now.

The Protector who was showing me how to set up the tent finally finished fixing my help and joined us by the fire. "I don't think anyone who is pretty certain they're mortal signs on with the Protectorate because their life is going great," he said.

I frowned a little. "The Protectorate may not be glamorous, but the Empire wouldn't function without us. We go to bed safe at night because people like us sign up for the Protectorate."

The other two Protectors nodded in agreement as they set down buckets of water and took seats by the fire. The commander appeared from around a copse of trees with two dead rabbits.

We quickly abandoned any further talk that could have been remotely seen as political and began making casual introductions. The Protector who helped me with the tent was Crist. The other two were Smith and Nok. It was unclear if those were their given names or their family names. Everyone already knew my name, that I was a wielder, and I was being reassigned. They had all heard about the crowd in the Old Square, despite it having only happened yesterday. That wasn't too surprising, given Wynn's comments about the dining hall the night before.

"I don't really want to talk about yesterday," I said after multiple requests for what really happened and questions about if various rumors were true. I glanced at the commander standing by the fire, now cooking the cleaned rabbits. "Besides, we're not supposed to discuss matters handled by the Committee." I sounded like I swallowed the book of rules. The commander dipped his chin in approval as he handed me a leg of cooked meat.

That killed the conversation around the fire. I wanted to be able to get along with these Protectors, but I was grateful I didn't have to recount the events that replayed in my mind every time I closed my eyes.

As we lay on our bedrolls that evening, I tried to focus on the sounds around me to prevent my mind from creeping back to Jenkins. Buzzing insects. Chirping frogs. The grass crunching beneath the thin bedroll as I shifted to stare at the beige canvas covering our heads.

"What is that!" I pointed at the blinking lights glowing through the fabric ceiling of our tent.

"Fireflies," Wynn said. "Have you really never seen fireflies before?"

I was about to. Wynn rolled over and gave me her back, but I rushed outside without her. The pulsating dots glowed over the nearby field as far as I could see. I couldn't make my eyes wide enough to take in all the thousands of little beacons winking in and out as the concert of tree frogs and crickets continued on.

I knew I could produce magic, but this was powerful in a different way. The sight made my heart hum under my breastbone.

I looked up to see how high these glowing insects went and was met with a different wonder. Capital City had stars, but not like this. Thousands more lights twinkled here than I had ever seen before. A cloudy stripe ran overhead, as though there were too many pinpricks of light in that space for my eyes to comprehend.

"I do love the sights when I get away from the City." I startled at the calm voice of the commander from behind me. I had been so engrossed in the sky, I hadn't heard his approach.

"I've never seen anything like it." I couldn't pull my eyes away from the stars.

"Have you ever left the City before?"

I shook my head.

He pointed across my field of vision to a group of bright stars. I could feel the warmth of his body next to me. "That constellation is my favorite. It's supposed to be Lacee and her lover, Gollen."

"I don't know that story." I looked at the cluster of six bright pinpoints above the horizon as a sweet breeze surrounded us.

"Lacee was a princess in ancient times and Gollen was the prince of a rival kingdom. They met while fetching water from the same river by their fathers' war camps. They had secret meetings every night and quickly fell in love, but of course, their families were mortal enemies and it was forbidden. Gollen's father found out about them and followed him to their rendezvous. He went to murder Lacee, but Gollen tried to defend her. In the end, Gollen's father killed them both, and was soon filled with regret. He begged the old gods to take his life in exchange for letting the two lovers be together once more." He smiled as he looked over at me. "And the old gods agreed. Only a life can't be given back once it's taken, so Lacee and Gollen were sent to the skies to be together forever among the stars."

"And why is that tragic story your favorite?" The tale filled me with heartache for everyone involved.

"Sometimes it's nice to think of a love so enduring, it hangs in the skies for all eternity."

"And what about the other times?" I crossed my arms around myself against the goose bumps that had appeared on my skin.

His eyes danced along my form. "Other times, it's a good reminder some romances are forbidden and the consequences for them are steep."

A blush crept into my cheeks as his words brushed across my prickled skin.

"We have to be up early tomorrow morning." He reached out and lightly brushed my arm as he smiled. "Goodnight, Ness."

I smiled in response. "Night."

I knew what George and Lina would say about it, but after that interaction, it seemed like I wasn't going to be the only one enjoying the sights at the First.

As I lay back down, distracted by my interaction with Commander Lev Densen and his touch still warm on my arm, I didn't think about Jenkins or the First Outpost before falling asleep.

Yet I woke in a cold sweat the following morning after my dreams slipped to scenes of cobblestones, blood, and gallows.

CHAPTER TEN

I crawled out of the tent in the morning bleary-eyed and joined Wynn by the extinguished fire.

"Still enamored by your new journey?" she asked.

My body was sore from laying on the ground, legs aching from being on a horse all day yesterday, and the bug bites on my lower half itching beyond what I thought was possible.

"I will admit, it will be nice to put my ass down for a meal without having to check if the surface is covered in bugs." I jumped back up and dusted off the now-damp seat of my pants. "Or wet. But I'm trying to look at this experience as a new chapter. I spent the first twenty-seven years of my life cooped up in a city. Last night was really spectacular. For right now, I'm telling myself the change is good."

"Your outlook is much better today than it was yesterday," Crist said. I flushed, even though he had said it with kindness.

"I'm just trying to strike balance. I think I'm in pretty good shape, considering what a shit hole this week has been."

The second day of travel was uneventful. Even when the party had to ford a river, it was less exciting than I imagined it would be. I had always pictured riding a horse through a river would be like riding into battle. We would charge forward with great splashes and it would be very theatrical. But the horses trotted out into the very shallow water, barely even registering that they were on different terrain. My horse stopped to take a drink midway.

I helped Crist set up our tents again that night, and this time I might have actually provided a minor amount of assistance. Dinner was much better for me than the night before. No one brought up the events of two days ago.

However, there were also no fireflies or cloudless skies to distract me from falling into nightmares about swelling crowds and unmoving executioners.

The third day dawned with everyone in good spirits, including Wynn, even though I knew I woke her several times last night with my fitful sleep.

"Why's everyone so..." I searched for the right word. "Talkative this morning?"

"We should make it to Midville tonight. We'll get to sleep in beds," Wynn said with a cheerfulness I had yet to hear from her. The prospect made me perk up too. It had only been two nights since we left the City and already, the idea of bathing off this smell of sweat and horse was sublime.

The whole party stayed cheery even when a drizzle started in the late afternoon, which progressed into a downpour by the time we rode into Midville. Undaunted, we approached the only inn in the small village with soaked clothes and morale still high.

Dinner in the dining room of the inn felt so different than having dinner at the Pony. I walked through the quaint and quiet room, only dodging a few tables. The dim lighting in the Pony evoked mystery and incited revelry, but the low lighting here just felt like it was concealing floors that needed to be swept. Either way, a warm meal out of the rain and giving our clothes time to partially dry was a welcome evening.

As we were finishing up meal, Commander Densen looked around at all of us. "We're leaving at first light tomorrow morning. If we press, we'll just have one more night in tents before we reach the First. No staying up late and drinking yourselves to the point you can't keep pace."

He didn't need to tell me. I didn't feel the need to spend what little coin I had to drink with relative strangers. I knew the other Protectors in the party were fresh from training, and they probably hadn't even had their first payday yet.

"We'll be doubled up in rooms tonight, since they only have a few," he added. I grabbed the key that he extended my way and headed upstairs.

It took me a few tries to find the correct door for the key. By the time I found the right room, Crist was opening the door next to me and Smith on the other side of him.

I heard the rest of our party coming up the stairs over a satisfying *click* of the lock. I pushed the door open to reveal one large bed in my room.

"We'll be cozy tonight," Densen said as he stopped behind me in the hallway. He leaned on the doorframe mere inches from me as he looked into the room, his body heat warming my side and making my heart race. Was he going to be doubling up with *me* tonight?

The key fell from my hand with the thought I could be sharing a bed with him. My cheeks heated as I recalled the many books I read involving one bed.

None of them ended innocently.

I squatted down to grab the key. Lev continued past me to go into the room with Crist and two beds.

"Alright there, Riseworth?" Wynn asked as she stepped over me through the doorway of the room that—once my senses came back to me—I realized would obviously be shared with her.

"Yeah," I said, standing up and following her in. "Just letting my mind wander." There was yet more credence to George and Lina's observations of my romantic habits. This was a very inconvenient time to become infatuated with him.

She smirked, looking toward the hallway Lev had just vacated. "Are you going to have better dreams tonight?"

I tried to put on my most innocent face and feigned ignorance. "What do you mean?"

"You're still blushing."

After I grumbled that she was mistaken and she laughed at me, we started to get settled for the night. "Sorry if I kept you up last night. I'll try not to do that again tonight."

"I'm not sure how you're going to control what you dream about, but if you say so."

"I'm just trying to say I know I bothered you last night, Partson. I didn't want to and I'm sorry it happened," I said a little more coarsely than I intended to. I was trying to be nice to her, and maybe prove to her that Shaeb was the dick, not me. Why was she making it so hard?

"And I'm just trying to say you went through some pretty fucked up shit a few days ago and shouldn't blame yourself for dwelling on it like a decent human being would," she said.

We didn't say anything else to each other for the rest of the night. Laying in the darkness next to Wynn, I thought maybe she would become my friend after all.

We arrived at the First as dusk was falling on the fifth day. The little stone fortress looked serene against the glowing orange sky. Overall, the outpost was much better than I imagined. The military structures sat against the banks of the Partidus River, which constituted the frontline to Gallia.

I was led to a stuffy third floor room that would have been better described as a closet with a bed shoved in it. Its features included a window that had been painted shut and an impressive amount of dust on the windowsill. It was certainly less comfortable than my dormitory room in the Imperial Compound, which was a feat. I really hoped this lodging was temporary due to the fact I was a last-minute addition, and not what I would be using for the next five months.

Either way, you can handle it.

The other Protectors, including Wynn, were housed on the same floor, but in much better accommodations. I stopped by her room on the way to dinner. Her shoulders slumped as she showed me what was going to be her home for the next three years. She had a single room which contained her bed, a desk, and a dresser in it, not unlike my dormitory in the Compound. Her bathing chamber would be shared with the woman next door to her and was located between their two rooms.

"I had to share a bathing chamber with a whole floor full of people in the Compound, not just one," I told her. "It's really not bad by Imperial Protectorate standards."

"That's what it was like in training," she said. "I was hoping that was just for the new recruits and it would get better once I was placed for service. My old quarters in Polis had private washrooms for everyone."

"I'll have to show you my closet later. They didn't even tell me which washroom I'm supposed to use." Her shoulders seemed to straighten a little at my words.

We went to dinner, and I was thankful I had her to sit next to. All the other Protectors sat in tight groups, talking amongst themselves, and didn't so much as look up as we walked by with our plates. I had a new appreciation for any person that had ever spoken to me in the last few years, considering they had to overcome this same cliquish feeling from George, Lina, and myself.

"Protectors," Wynn said with an eye roll at the unfriendly tables as we sat down at an unoccupied one in a dark corner. "I can't see how this still appeals to you after all these years."

"It's lost its luster. I'm looking forward to doing something new after the solstice." I shrugged. "But not like I had anywhere better to be. My friends are Protectors."

"You know there's this thing called family."

I snorted. "Maybe for you there is." She looked at me with a wide-eyed expression. Fuck, it had been a while since I'd talked about my past to someone who didn't already know it. "My father was never part of my life. He abandoned me before I was born. And my mom died in the winter of my final year of school," I clarified much more gently.

She grimaced guiltily. "Shit. And you don't have anyone else?"

I shook my head. "I'm an only child and the only other family I ever had was my grandma, who died when I was young." I felt the need to defend my choices to her. "The Protectorate has generally been pretty good to me. I was really out of other options by the time I signed up."

She looked like she had questions about that, but I was already enough of a mess without dredging up the hardest time of my life, so I changed the subject. "Now that we're here, I guess you don't have to put up with any more emotional conversations or nightmares from a tent mate. Tomorrow you could be sitting at any one of these tables without me." I wasn't sure I should be pointing this out, but felt it was only fair to release her from my chaos.

"True, you are slightly unbalanced. Fortunately for you, it keeps things interesting in what appears to be an otherwise dull outpost. I can keep sitting with you. At least until I make some other friends." She smirked as she stabbed a potato.

I poked around my plate, unable to stop the small smile from spreading on my face. From what I knew of Wynn, that felt like an open declaration of friendship.

I could do this for five months.

CHAPTER ELEVEN

The newly arrived Protectors were given a tour of the First and the surrounding town the following morning. We saw the posts where we would do sentry duty and the field that was nothing more than hard-packed dirt from the thousands of boots training there. We were also shown the docks at the north end of the outpost that exited to the sea beyond.

I took in the roaring waves of the sea for the first time in my life. Wynn had seen the ocean many times before, but she stood by my side as I stared out into the endless blue that rippled in a way that felt similar to my magic. The expanse in front of me seemed limitless and full of opportunity, if only I was brave enough to dive in after it.

The tour finished with a walk through the main building that contained our dormitories, the dining hall and the administration offices.

Moving through the hallways, this all felt normal, uncomplicated, not that different from the Imperial Compound at its core. It would be easy to find a routine in my new station, even if it wasn't training new wielders.

A spark of hope blossomed in me. This was a decent place to wait out the last few months until I could start my real life, or start figuring out what I wanted my real life to be.

Our guide told us to wait in the hallway in front of the plain wooden door to the outpost commander's office. As we stood there, I wondered why Commander Densen was assigned here if there was already an established commander. They couldn't possibly need two at such a quiet outpost, and by the way our tour guide talked, the current one wasn't going away anytime soon.

The door opened and Commander Densen himself stepped out of the office. "I'll wait, then," he said over his shoulder. He nodded at our assembled group, his eyes lingering on me.

I reflexively smiled, and I was so focused on if it looked stupid or not, I didn't notice when the rest of the Protectors began to file into the office and was almost left standing alone in the hallway with Densen.

Question answered, I definitely looked stupid.

I followed them into the office, contemplating the effect Densen had on me and if it would go away if I truly became friends with Wynn and the gap in my life left by Lina and George's absence was filled.

The Commander of the First sat at her cluttered desk in the small beige room across from two chairs. The morning light streamed in from the two windows behind her, seeming to emphasize those seats no one was willing to take.

"You two, sit," she ordered, pointing to Wynn and me, the last two to enter the room. Crist, Smith, and Nok were already standing in a row behind our seats.

The commander was as brief as the guide told us she would be. "Welcome to the First Imperial Outpost on the front with Gallia. I am Commander Bennington. We're the northernmost station of Protectors along the Partidus River. This outpost was established after the Great War to keep the Gallian forces at bay after they took issue with the treaty. Since we are so far north, we rarely see action, but we still maintain constant vigilance on the front."

She handed out parchments to the other four seated around me. "Here are your rotations for sentry duty, training, and other work we all take turns with to keep the outpost running." She turned her gaze to me, her eyes lingered for the typical golden eye review. "Riseworth, stay back for your assignment."

As the four Protectors rose to leave, Wynn shot me a look with eyebrows raised. I gave the smallest possible shrug in response.

When they were through the door, Densen entered and sat in the chair Wynn vacated. I swallowed at his nearness. His smell of leather and fresh soap filled my nose, and suddenly the room was much warmer.

"You're aware you are one of the few wielders assigned to the First," Commander Bennington said as she straightened a pile of quills on her desk. "Our mortal Protectors have never had any trouble defending this position with minimal fae assistance. Times have not changed in that regard, and your wielding abilities are not needed here."

I nodded slowly at her words, trying to think through what my role would be here if I didn't need to wield magic.

"You were assigned a room, as is standard for all Protectors, and to all accounts and records, you will be serving at this outpost through the end of your service."

That didn't sound normal. The assignment wasn't adding up. I waited for her to continue, but this was stretching into an eternity.

"But you'll be leaving," Densen said.

"Leaving?" I said blankly, staring between the two of them, unsure who would be providing answers.

"Yes, you're being assigned to an outside mission," Bennington said.

"Outside mission?" I asked. "But I'm a Trainer, not a Ranger."

"Do I need to remind you, refusing to participate in your assigned duty will get you right back in front of the Committee? I doubt they would be lenient with you a second time," Bennington snapped, her fingers pressing against a folded piece of parchment on her desk.

The quick change in her demeanor took me aback. "Sorry, ma'am. I wasn't refusing. This is just unexpected."

"Yes, it is, but we all follow the orders given to us." She shot an unreadable look at Densen.

"Bennington," Densen said with a certain degree of warning in his voice. To my shock, she gave a quick nod and exited the room, closing the door firmly behind her.

"We need to get you on a ship as soon as possible," Densen said. "It's why we had to assign you to the First, at the northern coast. We needed to make it seem like you were reporting to a regular posting, but now that you're officially recorded as stationed here, we can leave tomorrow."

"What? Why?"

"Riseworth, do you know what the Gathering of the Seven is?" Commander Densen asked.

"No, I've never heard of that." I shifted in my chair to face him fully now that it was just the two of us.

"Before the Great War, there was a conference where the leaders of the seven kingdoms came to discuss matters that concerned all of them and build stronger ties. It used to happen every twenty years. They rotated the location of the Gathering among the kingdoms.

"Each kingdom would use it as a chance to show off with great displays of their prosperity through feasts and events. It took place over two months, ending with a grand ball on the autumnal equinox." Densen's eyes shone, as though this was a bit of historical trivia he was eager to share with someone.

"They stopped having them after the Emperor united four of the kingdoms on the mainland. The remaining kingdoms were on strained terms with the Emperor, even after the peace treaty was signed. They decided to discontinue the Gatherings. That is, until we discovered another Gathering is going to be held in the Kingdom of Nixia for the first time in five hundred years. A Gathering of the Six."

"Six? But only three kingdoms remain, plus the Empire."

He nodded. "Six. The six old kingdoms, excluding the Kingdom of Centralia. Aside from the obvious leaders of Gallia, the King and Queen of Kind, and naturally the Queen of Nixia, they invited the current de facto leaders of the other three kingdoms that the Emperor united many years ago.

"The Southern State is sending Ransom Dimitris," he said. The crime lord governor running the Southern State from Agora was well-known enough across the Empire that even I had heard his name before.

"The Northern State is sending Mira Galfrey, matriarch of the Galfrey family that once ruled there when it was known as the Kingdom of Decca. And the East sent a woman called Aurora Fey.

"This whole event is of great concern to us. We need ears in that conference to know what is being talked about, what possible coup or attacks are coming to claim the innocent lives of those in the Empire. There is obviously a plan hatching there, otherwise they would have invited the Emperor and not those false figureheads," said Densen. I hardly noticed the venom in his last few words while trying not to look as lost as I felt. It didn't make any sense why I was the one being told this.

"Aurora is a new, untested leader in the East," he went on. "She recently took over for her uncle after he passed away a few months ago. The East was known to pass leadership on to those who are most capable within the family and not necessarily to direct descendants. She is young, about your age, and not well known. She must have shown great promise. She didn't reside at the family estate before being named heir and has never made a public appearance. These other leaders have never seen her.

"In order to attempt to keep their involvement in this meeting a secret, the East's delegation decided to sail a small cargo ship the entire way around the continent, rather than travel on foot across the Empire. One of our Imperial Protectors recognized that something was off with their ship when they stopped to trade in Agora. We sent a ship after them and were able to overtake them. When we boarded the Eastern Ship, Aurora and her small crew decided they would rather end their own lives than submit to questioning by the Empire."

This was a lot. There was going to be a secret meeting, probably to start a rebellion. The Empire had chased a ship and the people on board decided to die rather than be captured. Fuck.

I still didn't know where I fit into this.

"No one except the Protectors that boarded that ship and ourselves knows that Aurora no longer lives," Densen went on. "She is still expected at the Gathering, which will be starting in a few days. None of the rebels will know what she is supposed to look like. However, the Fey family mostly have brown curly hair, and it was known that Aurora had golden eyes. Quite a unique and noticeable feature, one a substitute Aurora would need to have."

Ah, there it was. I was a body that could fit the description they had.

That still didn't feel like enough, considering I was nothing special. I had no special training in espionage. I knew nothing of the current dynamics between the other kingdoms. I had no knowledge of any potential uprising in the other states of the Empire, and I had lived my entire life in the heart of the Empire, within the walls of Capital City.

I didn't normally push back on command, but this didn't seem like something I could do. "Isn't there anyone else who could go?" I shifted my weight, the leather of the chair seeming to echo my distress by groaning beneath me. "We can't be the only two people in the Empire with gold eyes."

"You are," Densen said. "As far as we know, there is no one else."

"But...I've spent the last ten years training other wielders. I don't know the first thing about the Eastern State, or being a leader." If Aurora was willing to die for her cause, I would wager getting discovered as imposters at this Gathering would have a similar penalty.

I wasn't even sure how I could begin to pretend to be this woman. She was a leader chosen for her capability. Up until last week, my biggest concern was how much ale I could purchase with my wages. Now, I was barely keeping myself together.

"That's where I will come in," he said. "I will pose as your personal advisor. I have a great deal of experience with this type of intelligence and can teach you all you need to know while you are undercover in Nixia. Also, we still have Aurora's ship and her chests. You will be able to arrive as she would and wear the clothes she was planning on using to increase your credibility. People will believe what they are told to believe. If you arrive as her and act like you should be there, they will think you are her. She never touched Cavilth, so your magical abilities will not be necessary."

I looked down at my hands fisted in my lap and exhaled slowly, relaxing my grip. "I'm not sure I'll be able to do this."

"You have the potential to save hundreds of thousands of lives preventing this rebellion, if we can get the information we need. And you won't be doing it alone." Densen leaned forward over the arm of his chair, the blue of his eyes shimmering in the sunlight pouring in from the windows. "We'll also bring with us three other Protectors. Five is a traditional number of delegates to the Gathering and it works well for us. Ameal Poltz and Jonas Beckworth will pose as your guards. Poltz was part of the crew that originally recovered the ship and sailed with it to the First. Beckworth was on dock duty when the ship arrived at the First. He scoured it, and his familiarity with the items found on board will be helpful. We do need to pull a female Protector from one of the rotations to use as a lady's maid."

"Wynn Partson," I said quickly. "She's the one who just arrived, so she's not expected on any rotations yet." I was just starting to feel like she was a friend, and I wasn't ready to give her up yet.

"I'll check with Bennington about Partson," he said.

"You have the evening to go prepare yourself. Be on the docks tomorrow morning first thing after breakfast," he concluded.

I still had so many questions that were churning too fast in my head to be voiced. I supposed I would have to rely on him to answer those tomorrow once my thoughts calmed down. I took my leave of the office and Densen followed me out.

"I hope you realize how special you get to be," he said as we started walking down the hallway. "We'll be the first ones in the Empire to hear information that may change the course of history. It's very exciting."

"Exciting is one way to put it, commander," I said.

He chuckled. "You need to be Aurora in every way. For the next two months, I am not your commander but your advisor, so call me Lev."

CHAPTER TWELVE

What the fuck.

> *What.*

The.

Fuck.

The longer I sat on my cot in my closet and replayed the conversation in Commander Bennington's office, the more *what the fuck* I felt.

Less than a week ago, a man had died because of me. Now *hundreds of thousands* of lives were my responsibility.

I had just arrived at the First and was already turning around to head back out the door. I had just started to think that I could handle the changes around me. That maybe after my five months here, I might find a small amount of healing and recover from the events in the Old Square.

But that didn't seem to be the hand that was being dealt to me. I was getting thrown right back into the fire.

Commander Densen—or Lev, I guess—had spoken of the mission as though it were easy, but the more I thought about it, the more I worried about what would happen to me if I was found out. If the other members of the Gathering knew I was from the Empire, would they kill me? Torture me for information I didn't have?

The possibility that I might never come back from Nixia slammed into me.

I might never see George and Lina again.

All I fucking cared about was getting to live my own life. I was so close to that end. I wanted to be able to explore the world outside of Capital City, but not like this.

Sifting through my bag, I removed all the items I didn't think Aurora would have. She certainly wouldn't take standard Imperial Protector uniforms with her. It left me with a very light load. Really, I only had the leggings I wore under my armor that would pass for a normal citizen's clothes.

I weighed the bundle of paper with the travel plans I made with Lina and George and my mother's necklace, which I had never worn. I hesitated over them for a long time. I didn't see a way the necklace could pin me to the Empire. In fact, my grandmother had once said it was a Moriale crystal.

After reading through all the travel plans, I burned the ones that could have been perceived as not made by friends living in the Eastern State. The small releases of my fire magic helped ease some of the tension in my body.

I held an old book, debating whether or not Aurora Fey would travel with a fictional account of a futuristic society where everyone had destroyed so many of the gifts of nature from Mother Creation that magic no longer flowed, and everyone made strange inventions to exist without it. I decided Aurora wouldn't, no matter how much Ness liked it, and threw it across the room as hard as I could to help with the remaining tension.

The book slapped into the opposing wall, bouncing halfway back to me and landing on the ground, scattering some pages onto the floor. Aurora Fey probably wouldn't have angry outbursts that involved abusing innocent books. I would have to work on that over the next few days.

"Between you forcing me to get on a ship tomorrow and destroying good books, I think I've officially decided to not be friends with you," Wynn said from my doorway.

I looked up at her from my crouch on the floor as I picked up the loose pages from under my cot. "I guess it's what you get for barging into people's rooms without knocking."

"It doesn't seem like a fair trade-off," Wynn said as she stepped in, closing the door behind her to sit on my bed. "Lady's maid? What about me has ever given you the impression I know about styling hair and dressing people?" She gestured to her short hair and Imperial uniform.

"Nothing. But I don't know anything about it either, so at least we'll fail together. And how hard can it be to put a dress on someone? Plus you're from the Eastern State. I had to ask for you." It was a fact I had forgotten when I requested she come with me, but now that I remembered it, I was extra glad she would be joining me on this disaster. And happy to use it as an excuse for a friendly face on this mission.

She considered it for a moment. "Have you done a mission like this before?"

"Not even close. I was in no way trained to be a spy. I don't know the first thing about how to covertly listen for information or ways to make people tell me things. Or what I should be listening for besides outright mentions of treason."

She sighed deeply and pinched the bridge of her nose. "Please don't get me killed."

"I'll certainly try my best." There was another thing to worry about with this stupid mission—everyone else's lives too. "I don't understand at all how the Empire thinks I'm going to pull this off. Densen said it was *exciting*." My voice quivered more than I cared to acknowledge.

We sat in silence for a long moment. "Well," she said, pushing herself up from my bed and going to the door. "At least you're going to make my next two months in the Protectorate fly by."

"I'm not sure if mortal danger makes time feel like it's going by faster or slower."

"Hopefully faster, but either way, it will be really entertaining to watch you fumble and blush after Commander Dreamy. Oh look, there you go, turning red again."

I was up most of the night worrying. When dreams found me, they were more scenes from the Old Square. The push of the crowd, getting knocked down, seeing Jenkins on the ground, but when I looked back to the gallows from the ground, five bodies were hanging—two faceless men, Wynn, Lev, and myself.

The next morning, my stomach was too nervous to add food to the mix, so I skipped breakfast and headed straight to the meeting point. I greeted the dawn on the small dock with puffy eyes. I watched the beautiful sunrise, the yellows and oranges streaking the skyline like autumn leaves caught in the wind.

I had been observing the tide roll out for some time, slowly revealing more barnacles on the rocks nearby, when I was joined by two men I didn't know. I assumed they must be my "guards." No one else knew about this trip, in theory.

"Hi," I said and stood to shake their hands. "I'm Ness Riseworth."

"Hi, Ness. Or should I call you Aurora?" joked the first. He was a few inches taller than me with a lean build. He had short brown hair with cowlicks on the back of his head. His face was plain, but his large eyes were crinkled at the corners like a laugh was always just beneath the surface. "I'm Jonas Beckworth. So it seems like we're both *worth* something."

I gave him a smile that was strained more due to my nerves rather than the quality of his humor.

"Sorry," he said. "Terrible joke. Please call me Jo, though."

He would be easy to get along with. I was glad I wasn't going to be stuck with stuffy, hard-line Imperialists for the next two months.

"Ameal Poltz," the other said. Everything about Ameal was proper and by the rules. He was a full head taller than me, his broad shoulders and muscled arms on display with the form-fitting black tunic. His face was handsome, even with his closed expression. He stood stiffly, feet shoulder-width apart, and extended his umber hand to shake mine. His grip was firm and his palm covered in calluses from swordwork, such a contrast to my soft, pale hands. As soon as the greeting was over, he straightened and returned his hands behind his back.

He definitely gave off the *stuffy Imperialist* air.

Before anything else could be said, Wynn appeared on the dock. "Hello," she nodded to the men. "Wynn Partson."

Lev joined us on the dock shortly after. With all the pleasantries and introductions exchanged, we began loading our items.

A surprising number of crates of food and supplies were loaded onto the small boat. "How long will we be at sea?" I asked.

"Hopefully, we'll be there in the middle hours of the night," Lev said, "but we're bringing supplies for twice that, in case the weather doesn't cooperate. If someone could wield the wind or waves to assist us, we could be there as early as midnight." He gave me a wink.

"I'll see what I can do." I had never tried to move a boat before. I had known a sailor well in Capital City, and my understanding from him was that it involved both pulling on air and pushing water magic at the same time.

If I was able to competently wield two kinds of magic at once, I never would have dropped the shield on Jenkins. I wouldn't have been reassigned. I wouldn't even be getting on this boat.

I tried not to focus on that. I'd just have to do my best. Before last week, I wouldn't have doubted my wielding. I certainly wanted the journey on the boat to go as quickly as it could. Being on open water frightened me. I wasn't a strong swimmer, this boat was so small, and the sea was so vast.

The lapping waves reminded me of the paintings on the temple I had leaned against just a week ago and old tales of Nereids, the nymphs in the sea who protected the waters and the animals that lived there.

I cast the thought from my mind as we unfurled the sail and began our journey to the Isle of Nix's main city, Port Mora. Once we were truly underway, Lev called us all together. We formed a semicircle around him as the cresting water against the hull made the deck boards creak beneath our feet.

"Now, I know this type of mission will be new to you all, so I want to cover some basics with you before we get to the island." Lev looked at each of us in turn to make sure we were listening. "The most important thing to remember is to trust no one. We will be there for two months. That is plenty of time to develop friendships or relationships more romantic in nature. You must not do that. It is crucial to our mission, to the Empire, and to our lives to remember that everyone is there for their own interests and will use any means necessary to get what they want. No matter how deep those connections feel, reveal your true mission to no one.

"That being said, we may have to imitate some of those relationships in order to be trusted by the rebel delegations and get the information we want. I will help you as much as I can to play your parts and carefully walk those lines."

The boat jostled us as it got further into open water. "The next thing to remember," Lev went on once his feet were firmly under him again, "is that we will be in another kingdom's castle. We are not familiar with it. We don't know who has access to our rooms. The enemy could be listening at any time, even when you think you're in private. Nowhere is safe. Always refer to Nessamia Riseworth as Aurora Fey from this moment forward. Maintain the act at all times, even in your most private moments."

He pointed at me. "I cannot stress enough that this woman's only name is Aurora Fey."

Everyone's scrutiny pressed in on me as we all nodded and murmured our understanding that I was now transformed.

"The Imperial Protectorate has been very clear to me that we are not to intervene with any plans for a rebellion. We are there to observe, report, and maintain the illusion that Aurora Fey is alive. Any actions or words that could prevent alliances or undermine their activities are strictly prohibited. They would not be in line with Aurora's views and could lead to our exposure. I shouldn't need to tell you, we are going into the lion's den. These are people willing to start a war for what they think they are owed. They would happily kill us to further their delusion that they could govern better than the Emperor. Our discovery would result in us never returning from Nixia."

My acting abilities would be the difference between life and death for everyone standing here. I usually enjoyed being right, but confirmation of what I'd feared last night didn't feel good.

"Additionally," he continued, "we need to be consistent with our details regarding our delegation and this journey. Jo, Ameal, Wynn, and myself will all go by our real names to help keep things as easy as possible. It is normal to use casual address with guards of private households.

"Now, about why we're a few days late. Once the Empire had the ship, we were able to sail it up the Partidus River to the First. We made up a few days of time with this. Aurora would have had to sail around Gallia to avoid detection from the Empire, but we are still several days behind her original schedule. It's best if we stay as close to the truth as we can, that way we can try to avoid detection. Keep in mind, no one at the Gathering has seen Aurora before or knows who was traveling with her."

Another swell in the waves caused the boat to pitch up sharply and everyone to lurch forward. I caught my balance before I toppled over with a clumsy windmilling of my arms. Mother, I hoped Aurora was not a graceful woman. This information was important, but I wished we had been briefed somewhere we could be sitting down.

Lev continued as though nothing had happened. "We know that Aurora's ship stopped off in Agora to resupply and trade. Merchants may have reported this to Ransom Dimitris already. After that, no one spoke to the delegation from the Eastern State, so we can control the narrative. We will say we ran into bad weather after the Southern State and stopped off at a port near the Twelfth to make repairs."

"Seems pretty straightforward," Jo said.

"That's the idea," Lev replied. "Any questions?"

We all shook our heads. "Good. Remember, keep things as close to the truth as you can, to avoid discrepancies. People will believe what you tell them." He dismissed us back to our jobs aboard the ship.

"Aurora," he said. "A moment." It took me a beat to remember that he was speaking to me.

"Yes, Lev?" A thrill went through me at using his given name.

"I wanted to apologize. We've had to act very quickly and in complete secrecy to get this mission underway. Your preparation for this has been minimal, but I'll be here for you the whole time. The most important thing to remember when we arrive is that you are a leader. When we arrive in Nixia, carry yourself as though you're the most powerful person in the room and no one will question you. They will believe what you tell them to believe if you say it with confidence."

"What can we cover right now to get me ready?" I asked with as much confidence as I could muster, standing up a bit straighter.

"The basics," he said, leading me to a wooden bench on the side of the boat. A smile played at the corner of his lips when he noticed my improved posture. "You are in your mid-twenties."

"Obviously." I gestured at myself.

He smiled fully, locking eyes with me. "You are succeeding your uncle, Caurus, who was the leader of the rebels in the East for thirty years before you. He died over three months ago, but the Eastern State has a tradition of mourning for a month before announcing their new leader. I have heard it also took some time to locate you, so you only took over as leader four weeks ago. Like many of those seen as leaders in their states, the Fey family purchased their old keep back from the Empire after the Great War, when the Emperor was in desperate need of funds."

"Alright," I said with a pleased frown. "I live in a castle."

He chuckled and opened his mouth to say something else, but was stopped by Jo's request for an extra set of hands with the sail. Lev jumped up to assist Jo, leaving me to my thoughts.

The rocking of the ship over the waves didn't help my still-nervous stomach feel any better. I decided the practical action was to not continue sitting there with my eyes closed, waiting for it to be over, but to try to wield enough magic to help hurry us along.

I pulled from the well of magic that hummed in my chest and hoped that I wouldn't upset the fabled Nereids, which proved to me that I was losing my mind. There was no reason to worry about mythical creatures when there were so many other realistic concerns at hand.

I refocused on myself—my existence, sitting on the hard boards of the bench beneath me. The same way I reminded new wielders to ground themselves when they were unsure about their magic. The breeze off the sea blew across my face and tousled loose pieces of my hair that escaped the braid hanging down my back. I could taste the brine in the air, and I envisioned the wind carrying us faster—gently, but faster. The clear sky allowed the sun to warm my skin, the warmth soaking into me, feeling as though it was filling my well of magic as fast as I was using it.

The waves gently rocked us as they carried us along. The fact that these swirling waters had seen many boats before us and carried them safely home calmed me. I envisioned the creatures living, swimming, and playing in the waters below. I even imagined the Nereids swimming gracefully in the depths, part of a world I would never be privy to. Their beautiful faces surrounded by hair drifting in the current. Their skin tones in shades of blue and green. They had powerful tails instead of legs, beginning near their hips where the skin seamlessly transitioned into iridescent scales. I imagined them welcoming our journey. We were not here to take or destroy, but only passing through, enjoying the beauty they protected. Nereids, like all nymphs, wanted others to see the beauty in their lives' work.

I opened my eyes, and we were moving swiftly, much more so than when I closed them. I could feel it. The gentle buzz of my magic as it coursed through me. It started in my chest and hummed throughout my body, before it connected to the wind and water. The more I looked around at the beauty of the bright blue sky, puffy white clouds, and the clear blue water, the more the magic poured from me.

I allowed myself to sit and enjoy the sea. Watching the way the wind brushed the tops of the waves. The salty spray that sprinkled my body. I lost track of time in my trance of being present with the wind and water, and how they connected to my magic. An extension of me.

At one point Jo offered me lunch, but I wasn't hungry.

I imagined the nymphs of the wind, the Aurae, guiding us along with the Nereids. They were tall and lean, all with pure white hair and unnaturally bright blue eyes, despite their skin tones being as varied as the humans of our world. They guided the clouds along the azure sky and reveled at birds that flew between them.

I wasn't sure where my mind was conjuring this image from. I had never seen any depictions of them like this, not even in the temples throughout Capital City. Certainly not in any of the art the Children of Mother painted.

My imagination told me that the nymphs, too, enjoyed us travelling, being aided by their domain. They liked the presence of my magic playing with their wind. I imagined telling them that I didn't want to cause them any distress, and I would only use what they would willingly give.

Their appreciation for my respect was evident in the exquisite sunset that painted the sky as we neared the shore, and I prepared myself to step out of the Empire for the very first time.

CHAPTER THIRTEEN

Only once the sun was fully beneath the horizon did I feel my magic wane. By then, we were nearly bumping the dock in Port Mora, with plenty of time to get dinner at a local inn. We planned to spend the night in town before the half-day ride from Port Mora to Castle Nix.

"That was some great time we made on the voyage, wasn't it, Aurora?" Lev said to me with a wink.

"I was just doing my assigned duty." I kept my tone modest, but I was very pleased with myself.

A longshoreman helped us moor our boat, and Lev paid him to stay and help us unload. He had a distinct accent, pulling vowels out longer than I was used to, but we had the same native tongue. It occurred to me then how little I knew about the other kingdoms in our realm.

The longshoreman suggested an inn to us that was a short distance from the docks, the Traveling Cat. It was bland, brown, and everything was made of wood, but the dining room looked clean.

Our group sat down at a large, round table far away from the door. Despite the pleasant summer weather in Nixia, I was relieved to get indoors. My cheeks were raw from being in the wind all day and red from the sun.

The constant use of my magic caught up to me. Now that I was sitting down again, it was a challenge to keep my eyes open until the food arrived at our table. I knew I was supposed to be transformed into Aurora Fey at this point, but when the stew and bread arrived at the table, I ate like no lady should.

I had never used my magic for that long before, and I assumed that this insatiable hunger was a result of our quickened travel, along with skipping breakfast and lunch.

"Hey, you're splashing me over here," Wynn said as she inspected the sleeve of her tunic.

"Sorry."

She glowered as she wiped at the bits of stew off her sleeve. I sat up straighter and took more measured, less enthusiastic spoonfuls after that.

Once the food was consumed, I excused myself for bed. We couldn't openly discuss much in the inn, and I was still exhausted from my magic use. Wynn headed upstairs with me to the room we would share. I didn't notice anything about the room through my haze of fatigue, except two small beds. I had no idea what the sleeping arrangements were for the men, and I couldn't find it in myself to care.

I visited the shared toilet down the hall, and was pleased to see that Nixia had running water. As I washed my raw face and arms in the sink, the soap stung my sunburned cheeks. I must have been as red as an apple, but it was hard to tell how bad it was without a mirror.

After brushing my teeth, I returned to our room to find Wynn pulling on sleeping clothes. Without a word, I kicked off my boots and lay down in my bed with my clothes still on.

"Aren't you going to change?" Wynn asked. "I brought up some of your things in my bag from the ship, like a good lady's maid should." She pointed to a rough, brown sack on the bed next to her. I mumbled an unintelligible "no" before sleep overcame me, the depleted well of my power finally forcing me to recover.

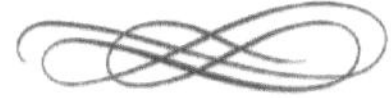

It seemed as if only one minute passed before Wynn was shaking me awake as sunlight streamed through the gritty window next to the bed, pulling me from the panic of the Old Square that haunted me nightly.

"Time to get going, Lady Aurora."

"I'm pretty sure I'm not a lady," I replied groggily, wiping the sleep from my eyes.

"Then why do you have a lady's maid, *Aurora*?"

"Because it sounds nicer than the poor soul who helps me put on shoes when my corset is too tight." I swung my legs out of bed and stretched my arms above me.

My whole body was stiff, as though I had spent all day yesterday in the training ring doing conditioning exercises with the Imperial Protectorate and not sitting on a boat. I suppose this was another aftereffect of me using my magic for so long yesterday.

I changed into the clothing Wynn brought up for me, black riding leggings and forest green tunic. I added a well-worn brown leather belt with a knife sheath, complete with a knife. It made me feel less helpless to be armed, now that I would no longer be able to use my magic. I frowned as I threaded the long end of the leather through the two loops of metal that tensioned the belt.

"What?" Wynn asked, noticing my expression.

"Well, it appears that the Aurora before this journey was a bit smaller than the Aurora that arrived in Nixia," I replied. I pointed to the obvious wear in the leather where the buckle usually sat, a few inches from where I needed it to rest on me.

"Hmm," Wynn said as she walked over to me. "I'm guessing Aurora was not as full in the hips when she started this trip—or chest. Look at the way the stitching lays there."

I looked down at the taut shirt. "I hoped that was just the fit."

"Not in the East. Let's hope no one here notices. Here." She folded over the extra length of leather, and tucked it through the loop she made, covering the wear. It formed a fashionable knot, the way someone would intentionally wear this belt.

"Thank you. How did you know to do that?"

"It's the fashion in the Eastern State. Wearing belts this way is common enough that even I do it when not in uniform. I guess I'll start doing it again now."

She pulled a belt akin to mine from her bag and put it on the same way. It was odd to see her in anything outside of the Protector uniform, but the ruby color of her shirt suited her.

"You're turning out to be a good lady's maid," I joked. "Your knowledge of fashion in the Eastern State is unparalleled in our party."

She chuckled at me.

"Did you know her?" I whispered. She looked at me with a degree of panic in her eyes, and I immediately wished I hadn't asked. We were in enemy territory now, not to mention that we were on an Imperial mission. Her response was a trap I had accidentally set for her, no matter how she answered.

Wynn shook her head and said quietly, "No, I was just another resident in Polis. I was too far away to know anyone from Stronghold." Then at my confused look, she added, "Stronghold is the name of the palace that was used when the Eastern State was still the Kingdom of Moriale. It's where the Fey family lives."

I nodded my thanks for her explanation. "I didn't think you were...involved with anyone...there." I was trying to walk a delicate line. "I just thought if you did...if you could tell me anything that would help me be the best Aurora Fey of Stronghold. It would help us all survive."

She looked at me in a way I couldn't interpret. "I'm just a woman from the East trying to survive. Trying to complete her duty without anything bad happening, so I can go back to my life there."

I knew that feeling all too well.

After breakfast, we ventured down the main road of Port Mora to the stable the innkeeper had directed us to. There, we would be given horses as guests of the castle. I took in the town around me as we walked the packed dirt. It was my first time in a different kingdom. Yet, everything was so similar. The people walking past in their work clothes looked the same as the people who would be out at this early hour in Capital City. Vendors behind their carts selling breakfasts that smelled like home. The shops opening up for the morning had the same routines.

We arrived at the stable and were greeted by a man who provided us with five horses and a small cart already loaded with our belongings.

The longshoreman seemed to have been the correct person to help us last night, as he had sent our belongings from the boat to the stable.

"Ah, Miss Fey, we've been expecting you for some days now," said the stable owner with a slight bend from his waist. "Hopefully it is seamless from here on out. Our queen takes pride in the hospitality of Nixia."

"Yes, our journey took some unexpected turns, bad storms," I said, hoping he wasn't going to ask for more details. I hadn't gotten comfortable yet with the lies we needed to tell. I reminded myself to practice in the mirror when we got to my room in the castle.

"Aye, the weather will do that," he said. I breathed a small sigh of relief that I wouldn't be required to think on my feet this early in the morning. "Well, these will be your beasts for the duration of your stay at the Gathering. The castle's arranged it all. Just return 'em to me when you leave."

Jo said he would drive the cart, since he had done it many times before at his family's farm. I was relieved that it wouldn't be my responsibility. While I was taught the basics of how to ride while in the Imperial Compound, I didn't think my skills extended that far. Then I remembered I was Aurora Fey, the leader of the Eastern State, and I probably would not be driving the luggage cart either way.

I approached a bay mare who looked sweet enough. The stable owner told me her name was Sugardrop, which made me smile. "My lady, you don't want that horse. You can select another."

"Oh, I definitely want a horse named Sugardrop," I said gleefully. "Unless it's a misnomer?"

"No, it's accurate. If you try to feed her sugar cubes, she'll pester you until you drop 'em all. Apples too. Really, she'll harass you out of any snack. She's a bit of a menace to those she doesn't care for."

"I refuse to believe such scandalous lies about you, Sugardrop," I laughed as I patted her nose.

"You'll believe 'em soon enough, Lady Fey." He handed me three cubes from his pocket. I fed her one, then she nosed my hand aggressively until I released the other two, fulfilling her namesake. I squeaked in delight that anything could be so adorable. Wynn rolled her eyes.

As we started our journey along the path, we could see Castle Nix from where we rode. The stone structure perched about halfway up this mountain was a steely gray megalith of spires and parapets that jutted out from the surrounding evergreen forest and with a crown of endless blue sky above it. Getting to live in a beautiful castle not hemmed in by a city and a horse to call my own made me feel like I was in an enchanted story.

Once out of town, I rode up next to Lev. "So am I able to be briefed further yet?"

He looked around sharply. "No," he hissed, "not out in the open. Once we're all settled, I'll stop by your room and give you the basics."

Not able to use my time to get prepared for what we were riding into, I considered riding with Wynn, but she was still standoffish with me after my question about knowing Aurora this morning. Ameal gave off the impression that I would have better luck getting a response from Sugardrop than him, so I rode as close to Jo as I could.

"What is your family like, Jo?" I asked.

"Not much to tell. We farmed vegetables," he said, careful to keep his answers neutral, in case there were listening ears around the trail.

"Did you like it? Do you have any siblings?" I asked.

"I did. But it can be boring, and if we have a bad year of weather, it can be really stressful," he said. "And yes, I have two sisters and a brother. My brother is older and will inherit the farm from my pops. Both sisters are younger. One is already married to a nice smithy in a nearby town with a family of her own. My other sister is much younger and still in school. I miss them, miss my parents too. And the farm. But as a second son, the farm is going to my brother. Picking up work as a...guard for the Fey family is an easy enough way to make a living."

He looked at me thoughtfully over his shoulder. "I've been missing it more and more recently. I was thinking after my current term of service is up, it might be time to head back to my family for a while."

We chatted for a bit more about benign topics and as much of our pasts as we could reveal, which was not a lot on my part. It felt good to have someone talk to me about normal life. It distracted me from the lump of nerves and anxiety hardening inside me. I wanted to share with him like he had with me, but I didn't have much to say. Since I was Aurora Fey, I had no powers and lived my entire life tucked away in the Eastern State.

I already hated this. I hoped it would get easier in time.

The conversation eventually lulled, and I began to look around at the large pine and cedar trees that surrounded us. I was right to be excited about living close to this. The air felt so crisp in my lungs. I could smell the scent of the evergreen boughs waving lazily around us. Birds chirped freely among the trees, a sound I almost never heard unless I was in the gardens at the Imperial Compound.

As we rode higher up the side of the mountain, the landscape provided more dramatic features. A crystal-clear stream tumbled over rocks, creating a rushing fall. I had never seen a waterfall before. I watched the water spill down into a froth, the swoosh of the current drowning out everything else.

Watching the water tumbling down, I couldn't help but think that it reminded me of the spill my life had taken recently, striking stone after stone, the course of the flow being forced in a different direction each time. Sprays of water left behind on the rocks at each juncture. The falls disappeared beyond a bend in the trail, and my chest ached for all I was leaving behind.

CHAPTER FOURTEEN

As we approached the castle shortly after lunch, my time for introspection ended. I no longer noticed the beauty of the landscape around us. Instead, I noticed that lunch was sitting heavily in my stomach, threatening to make a reappearance.

This was the moment of truth, the moment I would be assessed as Aurora by the people who truly mattered. The people who could kill me if we were discovered. We were about to find out just how bad these next two months would be. I tried to take deep breaths to steady myself, but it sounded like I had just finished running up the trail from Port Mora on foot.

Riding toward the open stone archway in the wall surrounding the castle, I sat up straight in my saddle, shoulders back and chest proud, trying my best to channel Aurora, leader of the East. So far, my best interpretation of her mostly consisted of not outwardly showing signs of distress.

A castle guard greeted us at the thick wooden doors that would bar the opening against unwanted company. I tried to push away the thoughts that we would definitely be unwanted company if found out. He pointed us to the main door and told us someone would take our horses and help us from there. It was going smoothly enough. So far, Lev had been right—people would believe what we told them as long as we gave them no reason to think otherwise.

At the main door, servants helped us down from our horses and informed us they would bring our luggage up to our rooms. They also pointed the way to the stables. I was glad to know where Sugardrop would be if I wanted her. I hadn't really spent much time on horses before this past week, but I liked Sugardrop and didn't want to spend the next two months without her company.

Another servant guided us through the entryway into a stately side room and offered us refreshments. It was filled with comfortable chairs and a crackling fireplace. Despite it being a midsummer day, the heat from the fire was pleasant in the large stone room.

Soon, the servant came back. "Her Majesty of the Kingdom of Nixia, Ruler of Castle Nix, Queen Elara."

I turned to see a beautiful, elegant woman walk in with her face schooled into a cordial expression. She looked to be about my age, with long blonde hair that swept in silken waves to her lower back. She had large blue eyes and a wide, full mouth arranged in a pleasant smile that made me feel at ease until she widened her grin, exposing her sharp canines that were longer than I was used to seeing. Interesting. Longer canines, along with pointed ears, rarely showed up in people anymore. They were some of the old fae traits that people assumed my eye color was as well.

"Ah, the golden-eyed woman we've been waiting for. Welcome, Aurora Fey, it's so good to finally meet you. My condolences for your uncle." She spoke with the same smooth grace as her movements.

I stared at her for a moment, frozen. I had never met royalty before. I may have lived in the Imperial Compound for the last ten years, but I never met the Emperor, only saw him in passing a few times. After a long pause, I remembered that she was talking to me, and I was expected to answer her.

Giving a quick curtsy, I said, "Ah, sorry, I'm just tired from the journey. Thank you. It's so nice to meet you. You have a lovely home. Thank you for welcoming us to it." The words tumbled out, less eloquent than I would have wished for a first impression.

She gave me a look of understanding. "I was very nervous on my first official duty as queen too, and at the time, I still had my husband by my side to help. These types of state matters can feel a bit overwhelming at first." She smiled. When I simply nodded, she added, "Now that all the guests have arrived, we will have our welcome dinner tonight at seven. You look like you've had quite a hard journey. I will have Mansby show you to your room so you can wash and rest until then." She gestured to the servant next to her.

"Thank you," I said, curtsying again.

We were taken up countless flights of stairs and down long hallways as Mansby explained directions to various features of the castle grounds. He made mentions of altitude and hot springs, but I retained little of what he said. My thoughts remained in a chaotic flurry over what I had done wrong with Queen Elara, and what the future would hold.

We arrived at a door that looked identical to dozens we'd passed. "Miss Fey, this will be your quarters. Miss Partson will have a room next to you with an adjoining door between the two," Mansby informed us, unlocking the room and handing me the key.

He held the door open as I stepped inside, closely followed by the others. We entered into a small sitting area centered around a fireplace with the most comfortable-looking sofa. Next to it was a full bookshelf, stacked with more titles than I had read in my lifetime.

On the opposite wall from the door was a large, arched window that looked out to a wild, grassy area with a small pond, in front of a gorgeous vista of a line of trees before the mountains beyond the castle. The view was outstanding. A finely carved table with four ornate chairs around it sat in front of the window. This was easily the most comfortable place I had ever lived, even without seeing the sleeping chamber.

Wynn gave a low whistle. "I hope my room is a mirror of this." The side-eyed glance from Mansby told me it was not.

"As your personal guards, we should do a quick once-over before you settle in, Miss Fey," said Ameal. He and Jo circled the room and headed through the open doorway to the left, into what I assumed was my sleeping chamber.

"You are certainly welcome to check, but I assure you our hospitality is purely altruistic. We believe that our realm can only thrive through unity and balance. We would not jeopardize that in any way," Mansby said, straightening his posture.

"We think so too, but we can never be too sure. One of the other guests may not be as altruistic as you. Just our presence here, after all, would be punishable by death in the Empire," Lev said.

I was glad to stay out of it, and focused my attention on the bedchamber. Ameal was lying on his stomach, head craned to check under the bed. He may not have been someone I could picture having drinks with, but at least he took his job seriously.

"Your trunks have already been brought up and placed in your dressing chamber," Mansby went on. "Should you need any help unpacking, or anything at all, pull this rope next to the door and someone will come to assist you. You also have a rope over here." He gestured to the closed door on my right framed by a velvet cord. "To ring a bell in your lady maid's room, should you need to summon her."

Jo and Ameal, finishing their inspection of my rooms and perusal of my drawers, returned to our group by the door.

"I'll show you to your room next, Miss Partson," Mansby continued as he led the others from my room. I was relieved to see the door close behind the group and to be by myself again. I had hardly had a moment alone since last week. I could feel my body start to relax.

Despite Mansby's assurances that I was perfectly safe, I felt better locking my door before exploring the rest of my space. When I entered the bedroom, two more doorways branched off from it. One led to a dressing chamber that was larger than my dormitory room in the Compound. The other led to a glorious bathing chamber finished in marble and beautiful mosaic tiling.

I caught a reflection of myself in a mirror placed over the sink. I now understood why the queen was so pointed when she said I looked like I had a hard journey. Two days of not caring for my curly hair had created a mess riddled with flyaway strands forming a frizzy halo around my head. A day of being sprayed by salt water, then sleeping, followed by a day of riding, was not my best look. My face was crimson and raw from the sun and the wind the last two days. I could hardly see the freckles sprinkled across my cheeks and nose under the tender redness. The small rinse I was able to do in the inn was no match against the smell of horse and sea that lingered on me.

There were curiously two taps on this bathtub, so I turned them both on. The first flowed with cool water. But the other, it poured out steamy, hot water.

I couldn't believe what I was seeing. In the Imperial cities, we had running water in almost all the buildings. Intelligent engineers and wielders had long ago crafted a system of aqueducts that utilized natural forces and magic to provide us with functional indoor plumbing. But all our water in the taps came out the temperature it was outside. We had small stoves next to our tubs to heat the water with a fire. Once my powers had been unlocked, I was able to heat the bathwater with my own magic. It was one of the things I was most excited to do after I touched Cavilth. It gave me a small sense of self-importance to know it was an ability not everyone had.

My stomach sank a little at the loss of some of that prized sense of superiority. This would be easier on me, I reasoned. Especially if I was already exhausted, I wouldn't have to exert myself to heat up a bath or stoke a fire. This was better.

Why did I dislike it a little?

Shit, maybe Trainer Sheab was right about me being stuck up.

I pushed past my feelings on it and slipped into the water. I scrubbed my skin, watching the dirt and sea spray melt away. As I washed, the final layers of Ness the wielding trainer were scoured off to fully become Ness, the spy.

I moved on to tame my wild nest of curls. Thankfully, a few bottles sat next to the tub filled with serums for hair. Their sweet, floral scents made me feel more ladylike. The silky balms smoothed the gritty mess of knots as I slowly, painfully raked my fingers through the tangles.

The knots were stubborn, and it took a long time to get all of them out. I grimaced at the pile of hair that came away during my work. I would have to be more careful with caring for it from here on. I really needed to start sleeping with my curls wrapped in a length of silk, like Lina constantly encouraged me to do.

After my bath, I wanted to look through the trunks of Aurora's possessions and get a feel for who she was, but walking past my bed was too tempting. I told myself I would lay down for a few minutes.

I still had hours before dinner. There would be plenty of time for the trunks, and to seek out Lev to discuss anything I should know before walking into the mouth of the bear.

I lay on the soft, comfortable bed covered in cozy blankets that were so smooth against my bare legs. It was so pleasant and warm. My eyes drifted shut.

CHAPTER FIFTEEN

I woke to the sound of bells chiming six times outside of my window.

Fuck. Get it together! Napping too long on your first day here.

I didn't have any time to get to know Aurora through her belongings or even spend much time getting ready. I needed to throw a dress on and find Lev. There was no way I would be able to survive a dinner as the leader of the East if I didn't talk to him first.

I dashed into the dressing chamber and threw open the lid of the first trunk I came across. I was lucky, it was full of dresses. I remembered the belt and tunic and panicked that none of these would fit me. In the trunk, folded clothes were arranged in three neat stacks. I rifled through the organized stacks until I came across a dress that looked promising. It appeared to be a flowy fashion that was supposed to be a rather loose style worn with a belt to define my waist. I hoped this would work for me. At least it was in the same slate color that complemented my complexion.

I pulled on the dress, admiring the delicate flowers embroidered along the hem and cuffs. It was a good choice to leave all my personal clothes behind in Capital City. I didn't own anything that came close to this quality.

This may have been a loose fit on Aurora, but it only just covered me. It fell down to my feet, but was tight across my bust and hips. I glanced back into the trunk, but didn't see another belt. I dashed back to my bathing room and rummaged through my clothes still on the floor to find the belt I was wearing earlier. It would have to do. I begrudgingly removed the knife sheath and left it among the rest of my clothes scattered across the tile. I didn't want to walk into this Gathering as a threat, but it also made me feel naked to be unarmed. I looped the extra leather of the belt around in the way Wynn showed me that morning.

I threw open the lid to the next trunk, hoping there would be appropriate shoes. I found slippers that were only slightly too big for my feet. These would work.

Now, Lev. I dashed out of my room, but once in the hallway, I realized I didn't know where his room was. I looked around as though there would be a sign to point me in the right direction. Shit. I had to think about this sensibly. I knew that Wynn was next to me, but that was it. I knocked on her door, and didn't get an answer. I considered knocking on one of the two doors next to Wynn's in hope it was one of my group.

I tried the next one, figuring that if it was another leader's suite, they might take pity on me and help. I hoped.

The door opened to Jo's face.

"I need to find Lev. Is he in here with you?" I asked.

"Hello to you too," he smiled. I appreciated his upbeat nature, but now was not the time.

"Sorry, hi, I don't have much time before dinner. I'm in a rush."

"This suite is me and Ameal," he said. "Lev is in his own next door."

"Thank you!"

I dashed away and practically slid to a stop in front of the next door. I knocked on Lev's door and waited. Finally his door opened.

"There you are," he said with the touch of a grin. I wasn't sure if it was his tone or smile or combination, but my cheeks heated. Hopefully he wouldn't notice it under my sunburn. I stepped in his room and Lev snapped the door closed at my back. "I went to your room earlier, but you didn't answer. I tried a second time a little while later, and when you didn't answer again, I tried to let myself in, but your door was locked."

His room was smaller than mine, with a second sleeping chamber where mine would have led to Wynn's room. It also appeared the washroom was set off the sitting room, rather than his bedroom. I wondered if I would ever get the chance to see his bedchamber. *Stay focused, Ness!*

I cleared my throat, pushing those thoughts away. "Sorry, I fell asleep. I suppose my body really needed it if I slept through all that. What do I need to know to get through this dinner?"

"Too much," he said honestly. "And definitely too much for me to cover in the twenty minutes we have before we need to head to the great hall."

I hadn't realized how much time I had wasted trying to find a dress.

Wynn walked into the room, followed by Ameal and then Jo, who locked the door behind himself.

"What do we know about Aur—me?" I caught myself. "Have you heard if people expect someone outgoing or reserved? Is she known for anything? Does she have any reported quirks or habits?"

"Very little is known about you outside of the palace in the East," Lev replied. "You were a bit of a surprise after the unexpected death of your uncle. There hasn't been time for any rumors or expectations to spread."

"That's good. I have a blank slate."

"The best tactic you can employ tonight is to stay quiet and observe as much as you can. Leaders tend to enjoy talking about themselves, so if you need to deflect, ask them a question about that," Lev said.

"There's one thing I do know. That her lady's maid probably wouldn't let her attend her first official function in this role looking like she has a rat's nest on her head," Wynn said.

"What? I just washed it," I said quietly, feeling the wild strands on the back of my head. "I fell asleep before it dried."

"I can tell."

Wynn moved behind me and gathered my hair on top of my head. Jo handed her a square of fabric from his pocket. She tied my hair back with it in a loose bun. I slipped into the bathing chamber and took a look. My hair was loosely back, allowing the texture of the curls to still show, while a few framed my face. The overall effect worked well, even if it wasn't exactly high fashion in Nixia. Wynn was meant to be a lady's maid after all.

We entered the massive dining hall in a tight group to find a single long table set for about forty. Most of the opulently cushioned seats were already occupied with guests dressed in beautifully made clothing, making me even more aware of my ill-fitting dress and frizzy hair. A servant next to the door showed us to our assigned seats as the conversation at the table filled the air around us. A small jolt of panic ran through me when

I found out I was seated near the head of the table where the queen was, next to the other leaders of the kingdoms, while the remainder of my group was seated among other groups along the table.

Queen Elara sat at the head of the table, radiating the same elegance and power she had this afternoon. To her right sat a couple wearing crowns, both with similar dark hair and flawless features, who must have been the Queen and King of Kind. Next to the king sat a woman who I was able to quickly identify as Mira Galfrey, rebel leader in the Northern State.

To the queen's left was a woman who looked about my age, with shiny auburn hair. She had bright hazel eyes with a smattering of freckles across her nose and cheeks, and when she turned her head, her pointed ears poked out from her hair. She must be the Queen of Gallia, our neighbors to the west. It was rumored that they were able to maintain the fae traits of pointed ears and sharp canines in their nobility by ensuring none of those with magical blood bred with mortals of their land, whom they kept enslaved.

Next to the Queen of Gallia sat Ransom Dimitris, the crime lord of the Southern State. He was a tall, muscular man who seemed to take up the entire room. He had a very closely kept dark beard and dark silken hair that fell just past his chin. His muscular bronze arms were littered with tattoos, starting on the backs of his hands and extending beyond the sleeves of his tunic. The single arm I could see well looked like it belonged to some of the rougher residents of Capital City.

I sat on Ransom's other side. The banners hanging from the ceiling dampened the sounds from the other end of the table, and I was peppered by the scrape of silverware against plates and chatter around me. I focused on the conversations already in progress, to pick up as much as I could about these leaders.

Polite nods and murmurs of agreement got me through the first two courses. As dinner progressed, I began to feel at ease. This really wasn't so bad. I was assessing, getting a feel for these people. Maybe I could make it the whole dinner without talking to anyone. My eyes fell to the black ink that sprawled across Ransom's corded arms next to me as I listened to the ongoing conversation from his other side. My eyes traced the swirling patterns his pushed-up sleeves revealed.

"My port has everything we need to keep my people happy and commerce flowing," Ransom was saying to the queens around him as I noticed the flowers just below his left elbow.

The images appeared random. I wondered if they extended to his chest and back as well, creating more of a full story. What would he have inked there? The top of one peeked out from his collar on the right side of his neck. He paused whatever he was saying and faced me. "Don't you agree?"

I felt his eyes on me and froze like a small animal caught unaware by a stalking wolf. His voice was as rough as the image I had painted of him in my mind, an almost-growl that stirred a tingle below my ribs when it was directed at me.

I had been doing my best to pretend I wasn't there, hoping the air of authority and power everyone else gave off at this end of the table would shroud me from them. My eyes moved slowly up from the study of his tattoos, along his broad chest, and to my first full view of his face, prolonging the silence.

I was surprised at how handsome he was. And young. He only looked to be a handful of years older than me. I would have thought that tales of his good looks would have come with the rumors of his illicit activities, but the gossip in Capital City was lacking. Or maybe those who got this close to him didn't live to tell about it.

He had a slightly rugged appeal to him that I would expect from a crime lord, but his features—the cut of his jaw, how his beard was actually more like evening stubble, and especially how the amber in his brown eyes danced in the light—made words harder to find.

"I'm sorry, I missed that last part," I squeaked, trying to pass as the capable leader of the East.

"I was saying that the shops of Agora are filled with everything a person could want. Didn't you stop at one of my merchants to resupply before you hit bad weather? Did Agora give you everything you desired?" Ransom asked, drawing out the last word as his eyes unabashedly swept my face and upper body. I ran a hand along my hair to make sure the mess was still contained in a bun. My dress felt tighter than it had a moment ago and my face more sunburnt. I certainly wasn't giving off the appearance of dominance and strength like everyone else around me. I was a kitten trying to conceal herself among wolves.

"Oh, yes, I did," I said, my hand moving to my raw cheek.

The entire end of the table was now paying attention to our exchange. I straightened my posture and dropped my hands to my lap. They were getting their first impressions of the leader of the East and how I would engage with the personalities at this Gathering. I needed these people to think I was competent.

Why had Ransom pulled me into this conversation? Was it possible Ransom had seen Aurora in Agora and he was already aware I was an imposter?

I needed to know how bad this situation was on my very first night. "I don't recall seeing you on the docks."

Ransom laughed. I started at the loud, booming sound that revealed a gold tooth near the back of his smile. "I don't suppose you would. I was preparing Solterra for my absence when you docked. My associates reported your resupply to me. Those golden eyes of yours were worth noting." His gaze narrowed on my face and his tone dropped. "They failed to mention how lovely they are up close."

The gentle description from his low voice made a tingle run up my spine and my cheeks redden further. Hopefully my sunburn was concealing it for me.

I could feel the close scrutiny on me from all the leaders at the table. The more they looked at me, the more exposed I felt. Like their assessing gazes were burrowing into my soul, and they would soon uncover that I wasn't who I presented myself to be.

Shit, say something, anything.

"The same could be said for you," I said, slightly breathily, my nerves getting the better of me. "My reports failed to mention that you're not nearly as brutish in your looks as you are in your reputation." That certainly sounded more flirty than I really wanted to be. Especially to a man who was rumored to torture people for fun, but the first thing that occurred to me was to mirror him with an equally suggestive statement.

My response earned another booming laugh from Ransom, followed by gentle chuckles of the other leaders whose attention slid off me as they resumed their conversations.

I reminded myself not to allow my relief to show. I fixed my gaze on my water glass and focused on calming my mind. I tightened my posture, drawing my spine up, pushing my shoulders back, tilting my chin high, and pushing out my chest. The dress pulled taut across my bust, and I couldn't stop my nose from wrinkling briefly at the stretch of the fabric.

"My reports of the new ruler of Moriale were very limited, it seems."

I jumped at the words in my right ear and looked sharply over at Ransom to catch his eyes traveling over me again. He leaned in closer still and whispered, "But then again, it might have been indecent to report on how deliciously curvy you are." He gave me a mischievous smirk. "Good thing I've never been afraid to be indecent." He turned back to the other leaders.

The crime lord's words should feel lewd. My body was probably just confused because of how anxious I was tonight, and the heat he made course through my core was nothing to concern myself with.

I would have to pay closer attention to him to see if he used this strategy on everyone here or if the flirtatious draw was a special kind of torture just for me. Maybe he found that if he charmed people with suggestive comments, they would give him what he wanted more easily.

It was also possible he was doing it to throw me off balance, in an attempt to get a truer read of Aurora. It was a damn good strategy, considering how my mind was reeling from this very short interaction with him. I would probably be thinking about this for days.

Those stupid comments from Lina and George cropped up in my mind again. I was probably extra susceptible to his tricks because of how out of sorts I was right now. After all, Lev was making me fumble more than I usually did for men. But Ransom. Fuck. With only a few sentences, he had made my body react in such a visceral way. It was unsettling.

Queen Elara stood up from her place at the head of the table and began speaking in a loud, clear voice. "Welcome, guests, to the Kingdom of Nixia. We are so honored to host you here at Castle Nix. Joining all our kingdoms together in one room has not been done since before the Great War, and these five hundred years have been a long wait.

"We waited and gave the dust time to settle after the war. We let the new borders be drawn in the mainland and the peace treaty be signed.

"We waited until the overreaching Kingdom of Centralia felt secure. We waited until leaders reemerged in our former allies' territories. We waited until the powers aligned again, and those born with the strength to change history were ready to take lead. The perfect pieces in the right places at the right time."

I shifted uneasily in my seat at her almost prophetic proclamation. One of those "perfect pieces" was already dead and replaced by an imposter.

"We feel the time is right to meet again," Queen Elara continued, "but now we meet as something new. A new Gathering of the Six to usher in a new era for the realm. The six true kingdoms, ready to put Centralia back within its borders." Her words were met with cheers from the entire length of the table. I clapped along like a good rebel leader should.

"The Emperor has not shown any signs he is aware that we have gathered, but we cannot assume that to be the case. He didn't conquer his neighboring kingdoms without being cunning. While we should all remain aware of our surroundings, rest assured, I have no qualms with eliminating unwanted visitors."

My fist clenched around the fabric of my napkin, and I tried to remember to breathe at normal intervals. The full weight of what was happening here settled on me like a boulder falling on my chest.

"I cannot organize anything against the Emperor, as the terms of our peace treaty from the Great War dictate. The Emperor will not try to invade the remaining kingdoms as long as we do nothing to aid any resistance against him.

"However, these types of magically bound treaties can offer loopholes if you know where to look. So, this is simply me hosting a gathering of my friends." She spread her hands wide with a conspiratorial smile. "I cannot and will not hold any planning sessions or offer suggestions for the future of the mainland. I cannot say what Mira Galfrey of the region formerly known as Decca will discuss with Ransom Dimitris of the territory formerly known as the Solterra. I will have no knowledge of what the Chancellor Parisa Harrow of Gallia will plot with Aurora Fey of the region formerly called Moriale."

Chancellor, not queen. I wasn't sure why I thought Gallia was a monarchy.

"I can't help what the royals of Kind will overhear at our weekly events, and the trade decisions their kingdom will make after this Gathering will be in no relation to that talk. I will not be able to stop my ears from hearing the plans that may be discussed at our weekly dinners. Any movement of my forces after this will be entirely unrelated." Queen Elara grabbed her goblet and raised it. "Here is to all my friends visiting me for the next two months and talking amongst themselves. Cheers."

She drank deeply. The echoing cheers that erupted were probably heard down in Port Mora. The queen sat back down and began talking to the king and queen of Kind once more, a smile wide across her face.

Servants entered and began to clear the plates. I watched them as they moved up and down the table. I should try to befriend one of them. They got to hear every conversation at this table, and that would be useful information to have.

The servants reappeared with fresh plates and trays of desserts. As they moved along the table the second time, I reconsidered. I might need to ask someone else in my group to befriend them. They were all much more closed off by my end of the table, and more at ease further down near where Wynn was seated. I kept forgetting I was now one of *them*. No longer a commoner in the background, but a main player.

After dessert was enjoyed and the dishes cleared, the Queen of Nixia stood once again. The room immediately fell silent. "I hope you enjoyed your meal. I know leading people, even unofficially, is laborious, and correspondence with your homelands will take up most of your time, but don't forget to experience the beauty and leisure we have to offer in Nixia. You are free to eat here in the great hall at any meal you wish, even if historically in Gatherings, most delegations have dinner in their suites. My staff can bring food to your rooms at any time.

"There are two exceptions to this each week. On the third day of the week, we will dine together as we have tonight. Also on the sixth day of each week, there will be an event that you must attend. The events will vary week to week, and will be a great opportunity to socialize, as locals will attend them as well to further the impression that this is a trade conference. You will be notified in advance with the specifics of each event. In our final week together, the event will be moved to the seventh day so that our ball falls on the evening of the autumnal equinox.

"That is all for tonight. Please go enjoy your rest."

I waited until a majority of people were rising before I excused myself. I was still the first of the leaders to leave the table, but I didn't care. I wanted to get away from them as soon as I could.

My group reassembled outside of the hall before making our way back to our rooms. Once in the Moriale wing, we started to discuss the best way to use the days we had before the first event.

"I will meet with you tomorrow after breakfast, Aurora," Lev said. It startled me once again to be referred to as Aurora. "That way, we can start to talk about the state of the East and what specifics we want to accomplish."

"I should probably join too, to speak to anything discovered on the boat," Jo said.

"That would be fine," Lev agreed slowly.

"Alright, with eating breakfast and getting ready, I think I'll be ready around ten—" I paused as we came to my door, noticing that it was slightly ajar. Everyone stared at the fraction of an inch of light shining through my doorway.

Ameal stepped in front of me without hesitation and walked into my room, followed by Jo. They searched my room much more thoroughly than they had the first time.

"It seems as though the drawers and trunks have been rifled through, but we couldn't find anything else," Ameal reported back.

"I was the one who checked the trunks before the journey. I didn't notice anything missing," Jo said as he reappeared from my room. "They did spread some clothes around your dressing chamber and bathing room, and there were letters on the floor, but nothing seems to be gone." I didn't mention that the clothing mess was probably my doing.

The security in this castle had been drastically overstated by Mansby. I wasn't allowed to use magic as Aurora, but if my life depended on it, I wouldn't hesitate to defend myself in that way. We all stood in the hall for a moment in silence, unsure what to do next.

Ameal gave me a firm look. "It's clear we need to keep your defensive training in top shape, especially considering your resources to defend yourself here are fewer. Be ready in the Southern Courtyard at six tomorrow. Then you can have your breakfast and talk strategy."

CHAPTER SIXTEEN

My eyes were reluctant to open to the watery morning light streaming in through my window as I dragged my feet out of bed. I tied my hair up in a quick bun on the top of my head and dressed in the first loose-fitting pants and tunic I could find. I also found a leather jacket in the trunks that must have been huge on Aurora, because it fit me surprisingly well. Since I couldn't bring any standard issue Protectorate gear, Lev had picked up a pair of generic boots for me in the town near the First. I was grateful to have shoes to train in that actually fit my feet.

I was as ready as I could be for whatever Ameal was going to throw my way. I found the courtyard with time to spare, since he seemed like one of the types of trainers that would make me pay for my tardiness.

I took in the pleasant freshness of the mountain air that I hoped I would never get used to as I leaned against the low gray stone walls that surrounded two sides of the Southern Courtyard. The morning was cool this high up, despite it still being midsummer, and I pulled the jacket tighter around me as I waited.

Ameal stalked across the grassy yard from the castle, looking formidable. He was an imposing figure normally, but with his all-black attire, carrying a large bag, I knew this training session was going to be more serious than I was used to.

He set down the bag next to me. "We'll start with a few stretches, a jog to warm up, some conditioning, then we'll get to training."

"*Then* we'll get to training?" I repeated. He had described three days' worth of exercise for me back at the Compound.

"Yes." He eyed me as though he was unsure how intelligent I was.

He was as good as his word. After what I would consider an entire week of training, but he called "just a warm up," we did lunges, squats, and holds on my forearms. He made me lift heavy rocks in various ways. When my body finally felt too tired to go on and all my limbs were as limp as cooked noodles, we began with hand-to-hand combat.

It went as poorly as I expected it would.

"You're not blocking when I come from the left," Ameal critiqued, just as I felt I was finally progressing a little. "I know you're new to this, but you need to protect your left as well."

"I'm not a total novice, they taught the wiel—me defense too," I corrected myself. I tried to protect my left while gasping for air. "We trained for an hour, three times a week!"

"You trained hand-to-hand for three hours each week and your left side is still open?" he asked, swatting away my strike as though I was nothing more than a gnat buzzing by.

"Well, it was three hours for everything. Hand-to-hand, archery, swords, conditioning, strength training."

He sighed. "I think I understand why your left is always exposed." He jabbed my ribs with a quick tap that I could tell only held a fraction of his true strength. "Plan on being here every morning that we are here."

"*Every* morning?" I thought longingly of all the sleep I was going to miss out on.

He breathed in and out deeply through his nose. "You can have off the mornings after the Gathering events. Seventh days are yours."

It was a much bigger concession than I ever thought I would get from him. After that, he began to show me the basics of how to use the knife that I had reattached to Aurora's belt. By the end of our session, most of my hair had fallen down from the bun and was plastered to my face and neck with sweat. My shirt was stuck to my back and the leather jacket had been long since abandoned in the grass.

I hurried off to bathe before my meeting with Lev. When I entered my room, Wynn was sitting at my table eating breakfast. I would have to remember to lock the door between our rooms too.

"Good morning. Your lady's maid requested you some breakfast." She waved her hand at the food on the table. Maybe the shared door *could* stay unlocked. "It would be stupid to let it get cold, though, so I started without you."

My path deviated from the bathing chamber over to the table. "It's still hot?" I asked, as I looked over the spread. She nodded, and that made my decision to eat now, bathe later.

Wynn watched me as I began piling my plate with bacon, eggs, toast, and fruit. "Worked up an appetite, huh?"

"You have no idea," I replied between bites. If she was going to ignore the awkwardness between us since my questions about her life in Polis, then so would I. Selfishly, I would have much rather had her as a fledgling friend than get insider information on Aurora. I told her what Ameal planned for me with the amount of time we would be training and everything we would be covering.

"I can't believe they didn't train you as much...before. You can't rely on your...*political powers* for everything."

"Well, I see that now. How am I supposed to know I was so unprepared? I could always use my *political powers* before coming here."

"Such a mentality of a person with power. That you're so superior to us mere mortals that you don't need to be in shape when you go out into the world." She might have been carefully choosing benign words, but their tone and true meaning echoed through me unpleasantly.

"Yeah, I see that now," I said quietly to my toast.

I didn't have much more time to dwell on Wynn's words, although I did want to revisit them when I could. After eating, I was out of time to fully bathe and settled for a fast wash with a cloth. I went to find another flowy dress that fit me. Nothing was suitable in my quick flip through the trunks. I would have to go to Lev's room in my sweaty training clothes.

I made a mental note to inventory the dresses that I could wear and set them aside later today for quick access to less smelly clothes.

I knocked on Lev's door right as bells outside chimed ten times. He was dressed casually, his light hair mussed from sleep or running his hands through. The look was very becoming on him. I was overly aware of my still-sweaty clothes and barely washed body.

"Right on time," he greeted me.

I joined him at the table covered in maps and books that awaited our lesson. A moment later, Jo joined us. We discussed the geopolitical history of the Empire before the Great War for most of the morning. I was glad most of what we covered was information taught in primary schools. The review was welcome, since I was so tired from training, the journey, and the stress of the dinner last night. I nodded along to Lev's history lessons and Jo's perspectives.

I lifted my cheek from the cradle of my hand as we began to cover how the Southern State, then still Solterra, became a stronghold for witches after the war broke out due to its inaccessibility to the rest of the mainland; they'd thought they stood the best chance there, being surrounded by mountains and water. I lifted my pen to take notes on the first topic all day that piqued my interest.

"This was before Agora was the only true city remaining in the Southern State. The witches congregated in a town whose name is lost to time," Lev said as he pulled a map of the Southern State to the top of the stack for me to inspect.

"How could there have been any other town in the Southern State? It's all desert. And how is the name lost to history?" I was always hungry to know more about witches. The subject was taboo and not discussed in schools or polite company.

"There's much we don't know, due to the witches' interference. Once they realized their cause was lost, they used their remaining strength to protect their secrets. They summoned a huge surge of power to wipe the minds and history books of their misdeeds, hiding the ability to do their magic from all who knew it. Apparently, it was stronger than they intended. They only meant to punish the mainland in this way, but their effects rippled across all seven kingdoms, stopping only at the mist. After that, the witches began dying off. Within two years, there were none left," Lev explained.

"But the Emperor and General Drakemore were alive during that time. Wouldn't they remember those names and places?" I asked.

"The witches' sorcery became locked away. It was very different than the fae powers we know today," Lev said. "Their history simply vanished along with all their abilities, even to those alive during their time. There's no known way to bring back the powers the witches once conjured."

I tried to parse through what he just said. It was strange to think there used to be an entirely different way magic worked that no one understood anymore. Or could we just not access it without witches? I always felt like my magic came from somewhere near my heart in a pool that was finite and needed recharging. What would witches' magic possibly feel like?

"Oh, it's already well after midday," Lev said. "We can stop for the day. I'm sure you're looking forward to some rest."

"Rest is high on my list, but I have a few other things on my schedule first." I stood, and my eye caught a map under some books. I pulled it out. Leaning over the table, I studied the paper.

"Me too," Jo said. "I need to grab food from the great hall and meet with Ameal to discuss our plans this afternoon." He packed up his books and hurried to the door. Lev walked with him and pulled the rope by his door summoning a servant, I assumed to request his lunch.

"Unfortunately, after lunch I need to go through the trunks and find suitable outfits," I said, still looking over the map I uncovered of the seven kingdoms before the Great War. The Southern State did look different than how they were depicted today. I wondered if that lost city was once on this paper.

"What do you mean?" he asked, his attention drawn over to me. I stood up straight, but kept my eyes on the paper.

"Apparently, when I left the East, I was a bit narrower in the hips. And smaller in the bust. And rear. It seems it was a long journey."

I wasn't able to meet his eyes. I had never compared myself to other women much before this mission, but faced with mountains of too-small clothing in my room, it was impossible not to feel inadequate against a woman neither of us would ever meet.

My self-consciousness sat heavily between us and made it evident that my interest in the map was not what kept me from looking up.

"Go through the clothing and set aside the items that need to be adjusted. We will send them down to Port Mora and have them altered. Let Wynn know which ones need to go. She'll need a task until the next event."

His gentle tone eased my embarrassment and allowed me to finally look up to him. I found his eyes roving over my silhouette. He lingered on all the parts of my body I'd mentioned, and a slight smile curled on the corner of his mouth.

Just then, a servant appeared at the door from Lev's summons.

"Yes, could you please bring up lunch for two?" he asked.

I tried to hide my surprise as he cleared the table and sat back down, indicating that I should do the same. We chatted about our personal impressions of Port Mora and Castle Nix so far, never straying into what I would have considered mission talk. His easy nature around me made the wait for the food breeze by. He spoke to me with a calm familiarity while we had our lunch, as though he'd been around me my whole life.

"Do you have anyone waiting for you back home?" he asked. We'd both finished eating long ago, but I wasn't ready to peel myself away from his room and go on to my next task quite yet.

"Just a few friends," I said as I twisted a loose string on my shirt around my finger.

"Really?" he asked. "No boyfriend?"

"No." I paused my fidgeting. What a personal question from a commanding officer. He must have wanted to know for some mission purpose. "Not much interest there."

"I find that hard to believe," he said with a smile.

I swallowed hard at the way that response sounded completely unrelated to the mission. "I–I mean more casual arrangements are my preference." I internally grimaced. "They're easy to come by in—umm, at home." I shouldn't be saying any of this to my commanding officer.

He chuckled. "I do know what you mean. A life in service can mean change in an instant."

I nodded enthusiastically, glad he understood. "What about you? Did you leave behind a special someone?" I tried to keep the tone of the question like a new acquaintance getting to know him, instead of a Protector and a commander wading deeper into treacherous waters.

He shook his head. "No, I've spent the last many years trying to rise through the ranks. My love for the service to our people hasn't left me with much space for anyone."

"What gave you such a passion for, umm, the Fey family?" I asked. "Don't get me wrong, they have been there for me my whole life. Even still, I don't think my appreciation for *Moriale* would keep me from finding love."

He looked at me for a long time before wiping his mouth with his napkin and setting it on his plate. I thought he wasn't going to answer me until he said, "I was in love once, when I was a much younger man. I was still with her when I entered the service. Shortly after, I realized that she was part of something those we serve wouldn't approve of. I begged her to stop, but she wouldn't. She chose her illicit activities over me. I was ultimately forced to be the one to bring her in. I was heartbroken, but it made my path forward clear. I needed to do everything I could to help the mission and prevent anyone else from falling in with the wrong people."

"Wow," I said. "I'm so sorry that happened to you."

He glanced out the window to the mountains beyond. "It was a long time ago. It's ancient history now." He smiled sadly and looked back at me.

"Ancient history?" I smirked. "You can't be that much older than me."

"It's funny how time feels sometimes." He reached out to briefly touch my hand resting on the table. Although the graze of his fingers on the back of my hand was quick, the tingle it left lasted a long while.

The bells outside rang twice and made us jump apart.

"I need to go work on those dresses."

"Feel free to stay for lunch anytime."

As I walked back to my room, I considered how before today, Lev felt like a nice distraction, someone that fit into the mold of Lina and George's expectations, but wouldn't become anything more. Yet, that lunch made it seem as though I wasn't the only one feeling an unlawful attraction on this mission.

I had to remind myself that Lev was my superior in the Protectors and my advisor in this ruse. Neither of those situations allowed us to be anything more than colleagues. It didn't matter if he was handsome—he was my commander and in charge of this mission.

I needed to keep my guard up around him. He seemed easygoing enough, but ten years in the Protectorate taught me to never get too friendly with your superiors. They would think less of you for being unprofessional or they let you think you could open up to them, only so you would reveal when other Protectors were doing things against the rules.

I had been burned by that a few years ago when I had been eating lunch with my superior at the time. She was so easy to talk to. I told her that I was tired that day. I had been up half the night helping George back over the wall around the Compound. He had stayed out past curfew and didn't want to be caught. Lina and I kept watch and assisted with a gusts of wind that landed him back safely in the Compound. I had mentioned this casually. She just laughed at my funny story and gave me no reaction that made me think she would report it. But she did. George, Lina, and I spent two months assigned to the underground sewage system, clearing blockages with our magic. It was a smell I would never forget.

I would need to keep my defenses up around him. Besides, there were plenty of other handsome men in this realm. Like Ransom.

Nope, that's an even worse answer, Ness.

The afternoon was not much fun. I took a much quicker bath than my sore muscles would have preferred and got out of the tub still stiff from the morning's training and filled with dread about the upcoming task. I was happy to see my sunburn healed when I glanced in the mirror and replaced by the beginnings of an olive tan.

As I went through the trunks, I tried on outfit after outfit that was wrong in some way, while Wynn's words about attitudes of wielders in the Empire ran through my head. Especially how we took the work of the mortal Protectors for granted. By the time I was on the last trunk, my morale had sunk low from both the clothes and the validity of Wynn's words. The pile of clothes that didn't fit was significantly larger than the pile that did. It appeared the original Aurora was a similar height, which was good. It would raise fewer questions with the seamstress in Port Mora.

I did find some fashion in the last trunk that I favored. I had brought plain black leggings with me, the only part of the Imperial uniform I was allowed to pack. I paired those with loose-fitting white tunics that had just enough detail to be fashionable while still being practical. These shirts were both to my taste and fit me. I added a corset with shoulder straps that covered my bust with shoulder straps, lacing in the front with utilitarian cordage. These were adequately adjustable for my body and allowed me to move freely, and had the benefit of supporting my chest without having to bind my breasts under my shirt. They could also be worn with the additional knife sheaths I kept finding throughout the trunks.

Aurora had really liked knives. She wore them on her belt, her thighs, in her boots, and I even found a sheath that could be worn on the inside of a forearm, to conceal a knife up her sleeve. Maybe I would have liked Aurora. She had been practical, wielding weapons that worked well with her slight frame, and her taste in fashion wasn't bad.

The reality, however, was that she probably would have scared the shit out of me.

CHAPTER SEVENTEEN

I told Ameal about the excessive number of knives in my trunks as we moved through the morning's stretches during the next training session.

"I noted that as well while searching your room," he said. "I still want you to train in all the other forms of defense here, but we will start working more with knives until you're proficient at those."

I opened my mouth to ask him what his preferred weapon was, but was cut off by Wynn and Jo approached us in the courtyard. "Mind if we join?" Jo asked. "I don't want to get soft in these two months."

"I only had a month of training before we came here. I need to pick up everything I can," Wynn said. Personally, I didn't feel either reason was good enough to choose to be awake at this hour, but to each their own.

We started to go through drills. Wynn must have had some natural inclination for this, because her movements were far more seamless than my own. Training went by much faster with Jo and Wynn there. Plus

I got more breaks, since Ameal was now checking three people's form with each movement and not only mine.

Lev and Jo didn't bring up the witches again in the lesson that morning, to my disappointment. I didn't have time to eat with Lev again, because I needed to meet Wynn to start making a meticulous list with exact measurements of all the alterations needed on every dress. I wouldn't have enough free time to go to Port Mora myself, so we needed to be very detailed with our fittings here.

On the morning of the third day, our training crew was getting warmed up when Lev joined us in the courtyard.

"I have been notified that we will be expected at the first event in two days. It will be an evening of drinks and music," he informed us. "Dress is semi-formal, and we will be expected in the great hall at six in the evening."

I breathed a sigh of relief. I could handle that. There would probably be far less talking required of me than the initial dinner, if we were supposed to be watching entertainers.

Lev stayed to join our training session, saying he would participate as frequently as he could. Ameal bristled at Lev's presence, as though training was the most important thing and if he wouldn't be there every day, he shouldn't bother to come at all.

The first week slipped into a routine of training, lessons, and dresses.

During one of the afternoons with Wynn in my dressing chamber, I floated the idea to Wynn about befriending the castle servants, while she made intricate notes of every way I was not Aurora. I ran my hand along one of the waist-high shelves that surrounded us on two sides, with enough room to hang shirts above them. The other two walls had rails to hang dresses from with high shelves above. Wielder lights illuminated the space in a soft glow.

"The servants are in contact with every delegation here. They probably hear things that we would want to know," I said as she measured the bare distance between my shoulder blades that the dress I was wearing didn't cover.

"This one needs a full five inches more fabric to button," she said as she turned to write it down on the piece of paper sitting on the shelf.

"Mother's hairy legs!" I exhaled loudly. "Was this woman a willow branch?"

"You think they're more hairy than average?" Wynn said with a smirk, double-checking a few measurements before signaling that I could take this one off.

"That is true about the servants," she said at last. "They do hear everything, but don't you think they're already reporting to Queen Elara? She seems smart, like she wouldn't overlook them as a potential resource."

I pulled the dress off over my head and handed it to her. Wynn folded it neatly with the paper and placed it in the stack going to Port Mora. I grabbed the next dress in line and wiggled into it.

"You're probably right. I don't want to force you to get friendly with anyone you don't have to. I know that would be painful for you, having to be nice to other people," I joked as Wynn pulled the lacing at the back. She tugged it far tighter than it should be.

"Too much!" I gasped, batting my hands behind my back at her.

"I can be friendly when I want to be." I could hear the smile in Wynn's voice as she loosened the dress.

I gulped down a breath. "You could have fooled me." I rubbed my ribs while she made notes on this dress.

She chuckled. "Fine, I'll try to talk with the other ladies' maids and valets at the next dinner. I won't promise anything. Everyone here is on their own mission."

I knew she was right, but I was still hopeful that we might find a way to gather information that didn't solely rely on my acting abilities.

On my sixth day in castle Nix, after training and strategy sessions, I went directly to my room to bathe and change for the evening entertainment. Wynn and I didn't have time to work through another set of dresses before the event, and my self-esteem was grateful for the reprieve.

I picked one of the dresses from the small selection that fit. This one was purple with gold embroidery around the hem, and the top was corseted, which was part of the reason it would work for me. Although as I tried futilely to press the swell of my breast down further into the dress, I thought that this amount of cleavage seemed slightly indecent.

Wynn came in to help me finish dressing and tamed my hair into a regal-looking arrangement. I hadn't fallen asleep on it while wet this time, and it looked decent in the half-up style. I checked the mirror in my bathing chamber and liked the look of myself.

Our daily training was adding a nice tan to my cheeks. Before coming here, I had been very fair from ten years of working mostly inside the Compound's buildings, but now the warm color that underscored my face and arms made me look healthier.

The tables in the hall had been arranged around a low, circular stage. To the sides, buffets of different types of wine dotted the room. Local taverns didn't carry this many varieties of wine, not even considering that I would never have been able to afford trying all of them. I wished I could sample every one tonight, but if I had that many goblets of wine, someone would need to carry me back to my room.

Queen Elara hadn't been kidding about inviting locals. There were at least three times as many people in here as there had been during the welcome dinner.

The minstrels played popular songs from Nixia and were quite good, even if I only recognized about half of them. I sat next to Wynn and Lev, waiting for an opportunity to present itself. Jo and Ameal roamed around and spoke to a few other personal guards from other parties.

While Lev went to get us wine, I looked around. My dress was far from the most scandalous in the room, which made me slightly less self-conscious about the fact that my breasts had never been so exposed in a public forum before.

Everyone was chatting in small groups, sipping their drinks. I tried to imagine which of these people might have searched my room that first night.

I felt eyes on the side of me and looked around to see Ransom engaged in conversation with one of his guards. I wasn't sure why I felt like someone had been looking at me, as he was clearly engrossed in what he was doing. My gaze lingered on him. He looked nice tonight, his hair half pulled back with the rest falling to just above the tops of his shoulders. Being accepted as an unofficial leader was probably very easy when you looked like that.

His tailored outfit showed off his broad, muscled form. He would have no problem carrying me to my bed if I had too much wine. My mind flashed with a quick visualization of that, and it made warmth bloom in my cheeks.

What is wrong with me? Stay focused.

Mira Galfrey sat down next to me in Lev's empty seat, drawing me back from my thoughts. Her glossy black hair swished in a curtain around her fine-boned features, which were set into a stern expression.

For such a slight woman, she commanded so much of the space around her.

"Aurora," she said, not looking away from the musicians in front of us.

"Mira." I looked ahead, following her lead.

"I heard they will play *All the Flowers of Spring* tonight." Her regional accent made the comment sound more mysterious than it really was.

"*All the Flowers of Spring*, you say?" I repeated, trying to keep this conversation going while having no idea what to say.

"Do you not like that song?" She finally turned her head to study me with her shrewd brown eyes.

"I'm not familiar with it," I said honestly.

"Really? I thought it was sung all over Moriale." She raised a brow. Shit, why hadn't we covered popular songs yet in my lessons? I remembered my ladylike posture and straightened. Her expression rearranged to one of appraisal. "Well, you should listen closely to it tonight. If it turns out to be to your liking, let me know."

Lev began walking back toward us with goblets of wine in his hands, weaving his way through the groups of people chatting.

"We can discuss it again after you've heard it and had time to consider its charms."

Mira disappeared into the crowd before I could get any more clarification.

I turned to Wynn. "That was weird, right?"

She nodded, tapping her foot in time to the melody that filled the room. "We're already at a meeting of rebels. Why not say what you mean?"

"Yeah, exactly."

Wynn shrugged. "I guess we better listen closely to that song."

Lev sat down next to me and handed me a goblet just as the song ended. "Apologies, ladies, there were many people I needed to exchange pleasantries with on the way," he said with a smile, as though acting the part of advisor was his life's greatest ambition. "I think I'm making a little headway on gaining the trust of the advisor from Kind."

He lifted his glass to *clink* against mine and his eyes lingered on me.

"And next, we shall play for you *All the Flowers of Spring*," the singer announced.

"Were you able to make a connection with Mira? I saw her over here," Lev said to me as the musicians flipped through their songbooks to the correct page.

"I'll tell you after this song. It's one they used to play in the tavern I frequented. I want to hear it again," I lied quickly. I wanted to figure this out for myself and show Lev I could be good at this mission.

"Which tavern in the City allowed people to play this song?" Lev asked.

"Shhh!" Wynn and I hushed him at the same time. Lev held up his hands in apology.

The song was a beautiful tune with many verses, between each of which the chorus was repeated.

Have you seen all the flowers of spring,
Together great beauty they will bring,
They were never meant to be tame,
In one garden, bound as the same,
Their seeds together must capture the wind,
Only combined can they all ascend.

When the song ended, I quickly drained my entire cup of wine while Lev was briefly distracted by the appearance of the advisor to Nixia.

"Lev, it seems you know where they're serving the best wine. Would you mind hunting me down another glass?" I asked when he turned back to me.

I added a smile at the end, twirling one of my curls around my finger. I don't know why I was being flirty with him—he was my advisor and would have gotten the wine for Aurora without that. The stress of the Gathering seemed to be making flirting my default.

He smiled back at me. "Sure. I'll be right back."

As soon as he was out of earshot, Wynn and I leaned in toward each other. "Right, so which issue do you want to address first?" she asked in a low voice.

"The song," I replied equally quietly. "What's the other issue?'

"That you're bad at flirting, but also that it strangely worked on Lev."

"Don't get me started." I rolled my eyes. "I did it to Ransom the other night too. Apparently it's where my brain goes when it's out of other ideas. I have no idea why I have no finesse with it, or how it has worked for me all these years."

"I think how it worked has a lot to do with how you fill out that dress," she snickered, eyes flicking down to my chest.

"Wynn, come on. We have five minutes before Lev comes back, and I want to figure this out. The song!" I hissed above the rustling and chatter around us.

"I've heard something similar before, but it's different from the way they sing it in the East. The version I know is about animals working together, not flowers in a garden, and the whole end part is about deceiving a hunter in Moriale, not covering the grave of the gardener who tried to tame them. I never thought too much about it before, but in this context, it feels pretty obvious that it's a call to overthrow the Emperor."

"Yeah, clearly the different types of flowers that *used to grow so freely in their native fields* are the people from all over the Empire being shoved into the gardener's rows of the Emperor's rules," I whispered as I replayed the song in my head.

"I think Mira wanted you to hear the part about how the flowers can't thrive in the single garden as they did under their own suns."

"So all this just further confirms what we already know. Everyone is here to organize a rebellion against the Empire. They all want to be the rulers of their own lands again. Isn't my presence at this Gathering proof enough that I would *like that song*?"

"Maybe she's asking if you're ready to act?" Wynn reasoned.

Mother's tits, Wynn was probably right. All the leaders were here because they felt the same way. What everyone would be trying to determine over the next few weeks was the others' plans of action. "Fuuuuuck," I breathed.

"What?"

"What am I supposed to say? How am I—" I cut off my incriminating words. I couldn't even voice any of these concerns in this castle, much less in the middle of an event full of people who believed I was Aurora Fey.

I had no idea how to respond to Mira's invitation to discuss rebellion and even less what the East's plan of action would be.

I had to talk to Mira, though. This was exactly the type of information the Empire wanted, the reason I was sent here. There would be information only available to Aurora Fey.

I already felt like I was an inch away from revealing I was an imposter at every turn. How evident would it become to everyone else once I started talking about this earnestly? I didn't think I would be put in this position so soon. I had no idea if the East was ready. What if they asked for proof of my intentions, and I couldn't give them any?

Then there was the Empire's side of this. Would the Empire be satisfied with the information I got at the Gathering, or would they continue to use me to meet with these rebellion leaders afterward? How far would this ruse have to go? Would this only end once I was found out? Killed?

I could feel my panic consuming me, and I wasn't able to stop the spiral of dread from carrying me down further and further into an abyss. My world narrowed in, replaying everything that happened in the last two weeks, for the last ten years, that led me to this moment in dizzying flashes.

"Hey!" Wynn said as she grabbed my arm. "Are you okay?" I was breathing hard and staring off in the distance. If I could have answered, I would have said no.

Lev returned. As soon as he noticed my face, he set down the cups of wine on the nearest bench and rushed to my side.

"Are you alright?" he asked, his brows pressed together. He rested a hand on my arm. With his other hand, he raised my chin up to meet his eyes.

"I—" I tried to explain the swirling dread that had inundated me, but couldn't think of a way to say it that would not raise suspicion if overheard. This frustration only added to the sea of emotions inside me, which started to overflow in the form of tears welling in my eyes.

Lev noticed this and said loudly, "Oh, Miss Fey, I think we've indulged enough for tonight. Let's get you off to bed."

He hooked his arm through mine and escorted me from the hall. There were many eyes on me as I crossed the room. I glanced toward Mira to see what she thought of her would-be ally, but she was in conversation with Chancellor Parisa of Gallia. Ransom was eyeing me from a few feet away with an unreadable expression.

I looked down. Better they thought I was a lush than a traitor.

CHAPTER EIGHTEEN

"Thank you," I said once we weren't in jeopardy of being overheard.

"I would have been a cruel man to have done nothing," he said without glancing at me.

We arrived at my room, and he escorted me inside. Once the door was shut, he finally faced me for the first time since leaving the hall. The walk had cleared my head a little, or at least organized the whirlpool of thoughts into a stream flowing in a single direction.

"I started to think of all I had to do for us to be successful, of all I don't know. It hit me in that moment, how big all this is. And it was too much," I explained.

He nodded. "You were thrown into this so quickly. I know you would have benefited from more training, but the fact was that we didn't have any more time to give you. It came down from the highest authority that we needed to do whatever it takes to get you here."

"I understand that. We barely made it for the start of the Gathering as it was. It's just hard," I said. I felt silly and small. I wanted to convey to him that I didn't think this was his fault. In fact, he was trying very hard to make sure I was armed with as much information as I could retain. Tears threatened my eyes again.

What the fuck was wrong with me? Ever since I'd left Capital City, my emotions were always just below the surface, ready to spill out at the slightest inconvenience. Naturally, anger at my tears only made them build more, blurring my vision.

"Hey. It's alright," Lev said, cupping my chin. The warmth of his hand seeped into my face, as his rough calluses from years of training brush against the softness of my cheek. "I know there's so much to learn, but you're doing really well. Having that aside with Galfrey was a great start. That's why we're here."

I looked up to meet his cerulean blue eyes. They were safe and steadying, an anchor against the waves of my rushing anxiety. I held on to his gaze until warmth started to creep through my body. It felt so comforting to be seen in this place. My cheeks flushed.

His eyes dipped to my mouth. I chewed my lower lip as my thoughts started to wander down a much different, irrational pathway. I glanced at his mouth, at how full and soft it looked. His thumb moved from my cheek to brush where I'd bitten.

My heart was pounding in my chest. He was my only safety in this castle, and I wanted to be as close to that as I could be. My body lessened the space between us. The heat of him and the scent of leather and soap were all around me.

A door slammed shut somewhere in the hallway beyond my door. Both of us jumped back, jarred from the trance we were in.

He was my superior. We were here for the Empire. Any heat in my body, anywhere in regard to him was not a good idea. In fact, it was against the law, and could not happen. He gave his head a small shake, tousling his soft blonde waves as he moved to the door.

He turned back just enough for me to see his clean-shaven jaw tense before saying, "Goodnight, my lady."

I stood there in silence, watching the door close after him.

It didn't take me long for me to wish that Lev had stayed. Not in the heated way I was thinking of minutes before, but because I wasn't able to take this dress off by myself. I needed help with the laces in the back that Wynn had securely tied me into.

I swallowed my pride and went to the rope by the door between my room and Wynn's. I hoped she had already returned from the hall. If not, I would have to wait by the door all night until I heard her come in. Or sleep in my dress, but that sounded terrible. I was a woman who enjoyed her sleep, and I had not been getting enough in the past few weeks as it was.

Shortly after pulling the cord, Wynn opened the door.

"Oh, thank the Mother. I need you to get this dress off me," I said.

"You know, you're not my usual type, but I suppose my options here are limited," she said drily, making a circling motion with her index finger.

"Ha ha," I said while I gave my back to her. She began to untie the lacing and loosen the dress. I held up the front of it as I turned back to her. "Thank you."

"Are you doing alright now?"

"I'm better," I said slowly. "I just got overwhelmed. There's so many fine lines that I need to walk perfectly to make this work, and I'm not ready for it."

"Well, you have to be. We're already here and everyone is expecting you to be the Fox of the East."

"Fox?"

Wynn nodded. "It's what the people of Moriale called their leader. It's supposed to represent being cunning, swift, and vicious or something like that." I raised my brows. "It's meant in a good way," she added.

"Shit. There's so much I don't know. That's the type of thing that will expose me for who I am," I said, shaking my head.

"Well, I'm here. I can help with the minutiae."

"I thought I was supposed to not get you killed and you were supposed to take care of the dresses?"

"You're growing on me. Like a wart."

I snorted a laugh that was certainly unladylike. I enjoyed feeling this companionship with Wynn. She was the kind of prickly person I found interesting. However, like with Lev, I had to remind myself to take a step back, since we were both here in service to the Empire. Though I couldn't know exactly where her priorities actually lay, I trusted her more than I should.

"You're growing on me too," I said.

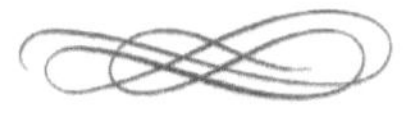

The following day, I had off from training. I requested a late breakfast be brought up to my room, but when the breakfast arrived, it was enough for four people. I knocked on the door to Wynn's room to see if she was interested in joining me.

"I'm always available when food is involved," Wynn said.

There were few unfamiliar dishes that Wynn was unafraid of. "What are those flat breads you're eating?"

"Have you really never had sweet cakes before?" She raised her brows as she tossed a golden brown disc on my plate.

"Essentially all of my meals have been provided by the Imperial Compound—I mean, Stronghold!"

"Relax. I don't think anyone is eavesdropping on your eating habits. You should put butter on it."

"Yeah, well. *Stronghold* has given me meals for the last ten years, and before that, my mom worked in the Compound and usually our food was brought home from the kitchens. Sweet cakes weren't something they had."

Wynn laughed as I tried it. "A whole new world is opening up to you. Here, try it with honey too."

After she left, I looked through the rest of Aurora's items. A few more knives along with their sheaths were nestled among her belongings. I particularly liked the one that crossed over my back, allowing me to keep large knives, or maybe short swords, within reach over my shoulders.

I pulled out the few books Aurora had packed and smiled widely at the exact novel I debated bringing and had thrown against a wall in the First.

Yes, I probably would have really enjoyed knowing Aurora. She was a little less intimidating, knowing we had the same taste in books.

I hated that she had died in some unknown part of the sea and would never be laid to rest in the embrace of Father Earth. No one deserved a death like that, and she was the Fox of the East. Someone I could only hope I might be a passing imitation of. I could never achieve the leadership she did.

She should have had a better end. And a longer life, no matter her views on the Empire.

The more I stared at the book, the closer tears came to the surface. I let them flow out of me unrestricted. It was the kind of snotty sobbing I could only do alone. They were the first tears since the Old Square that I didn't try to stifle, and the release was desperately needed. After a while, the tears petered out and the aching inadequacy lessened. I knew I was a mess, but I could do this. I had to so I could go back to my life. I had to.

I sorted the minimal jewelry in the trunks and stowed the items in the dressing chamber drawers, except my mother's necklace. I put it on for the first time, letting the comfort and memory of my previous life rest close to my heart.

I hung up all the clothes that fit, and I put away the undergarments and the leggings I had brought from my personal collection. I lined up the pair of boots from the First next to the shoes Aurora had packed, allowing myself to feel settled now that the trunks were empty.

I was tucking the trunks onto a shelf when I noticed the last one was the same size as all the others on the outside, but seemed smaller on the inside. I pressed my hand around the bottom, feeling for any sort of handle or latch that might reveal a compartment I missed. Maybe it was where she hid her expensive jewelry. But it was the same as the others. I flipped the trunk over and found nothing abnormal about it.

I unsheathed one of the knives. I cut out the lining from the entire trunk, ripping away the fabric to figure out this secret underneath. The bottom was just solid wood. No rattle inside hinted at any hidden treasure.

I couldn't find anything out of the ordinary about it. I tossed the knife back on a shelf, deciding the trunk just had a thicker bottom. The craftsman who made this probably mismeasured somewhere and hid his flaw with extra wood in the bottom. How many times had I seen a Protector cut corners because they were hungover during a shift? It was only an inch or so difference. I was being ridiculous.

CHAPTER NINETEEN

Feeling foolish for tearing apart a perfectly good trunk, I wanted to get away from my room. I decided to go stretch my legs, and went to visit Sugardrop in the stable. I brought along her namesake treats and fed her sugar cubes until she forced them out of my hand. I patted her nose and spoke to her for a bit, admittedly longer than I should have talked to a horse who couldn't talk back.

I went back to my room to spend the rest of the afternoon reading the book both Aurora and I thought worth bringing to Nixia, feeling closer to her with every page.

The next day I went back to my new routine. I trained in the morning, had lessons with Jo and Lev after breakfast and worked with Wynn on the dresses in the afternoon. Lev acted as though nothing had happened at all. Although, I did notice that he met my eyes less than normal when we worked together.

By the time the rebel dinner occurred in the second week, I was better prepared for the types of conversations I would have and entered the great hall considerably less nervous than I had been on the first night.

Wynn had informed me that all the ladies' maids and valets were seated together, all the guards together and all the advisors together. It amused me to know that she was suffering just as much as I was during these meals. She had to sit with all the ladies' maids and discuss fashions or gossip, especially now that she was going to try to befriend them. She would much rather be with the guards talking about how the sword designs differed from region to region than the latest hairstyles.

This evening, the seating arrangements were slightly altered. Tonight, Mira was seated next to Queen Elara. I was next to Mira with Ransom on my other side. It felt as though the queen wanted Mira and myself to finish our earlier conversation.

After her introduction to the group, the queen sat and directed her conversation to her other side to talk with the Chancellor of Gallia and Queen and King of Kind while the servants brought out the trays of food. As we were being served, I found out from eavesdropping that the first names of the royals from Kind were Atla and Row. I was sure the Emperor already knew that information, but it was a small win I could build on.

During our second course, I took a deep breath to steady myself. I had put it off long enough. This was why I was here. I shifted in my seat to face Mira.

"I never got a chance to speak to you again after the performances the other night. I was feeling unwell, and needed to retire early." I hoped she wouldn't pry at that.

Mira set down her silverware. "And?" She placed her elbows on the table, interlaced her fingers, and rested her chin on them, pinning me with her look.

"I did enjoy the song. And I have heard it many times in Moriale in different iterations. I wasn't familiar with the title as it is here. Or the ending." I repeated what Wynn told me the night of the performance.

She gave a pointed look as she took a drink from her glass. "Well, the ending, saying that this spring is the time to sow the seeds back in their homelands, was new to this particular performance, to my understanding."

"Ah, do you plan on planting a garden this spring?" I mirrored her as I reached out and took a drink from my goblet, hoping my throat would actually work enough to swallow.

"I do indeed, but it is hard to plant a garden alone. I was thinking I would have a much greater success if you and Solterra were planning on planting a garden this spring as well. We could compare our blooms, create a garden of greater beauty together."

I could do this. I could be Aurora, who wanted to speak up for her people, to take control back from the Empire. She was strong, she was ready.

"I have seeds waiting for me to sow back in Moriale. I would be pleased to plant them this spring."

"Wonderful," Ransom said from my other side. It made me jump and spill a little wine from my cup onto the table. I had been so focused on our conversation, I had forgotten that Mira and I were not the only two people present. In fact, at his words, I realized the royalty and the chancellor on the other side of the table were quiet, but when I looked up, they all were drinking or eating as though not listening.

Ransom laid a hand on my shoulder as he said in a low voice, "I was a little worried when I first saw you, Fox, that you weren't ready to be part of something bigger. I'm glad I was wrong. We only have six weeks left to perfect our plan."

"That's not much time to plan a garden as intricate as ours should be," Mira said, now leaning back in her chair. She raised her glass and took a drink. All the leaders at the end of the table followed suit in her toast.

Once no one was paying attention to me anymore, I realized the warmth of Ransom's hand was still seeping into my shoulder. I brushed it off and gave him a look. His expression as he pulled his arm back made it seem as if he had forgotten it too.

"I'm not sure how I feel about everyone calling me a fox."

"What else should I call a little creature who appears cute and touchable, but is truly vicious and powerful?" Ransom laughed. "And if provoked, I'm sure you're not afraid to bite." He ran a finger along one of my curls hanging down my back. "It works out nicely that you're from Moriale."

"If you think I'll bite, then why are you playing with me like I'm your tame pet?" I asked with narrowed eyes. He wasn't really bothering me that much, but he was extremely good at ruffling me. I needed to try to get the upper hand before I fell into his seductive trap.

He laughed again and raised his hands away from me, dipping his chin in apology.

"Forgiveness, Fox. I've found my success through collecting things of beauty or power when I come across them, and you are both," he said, leaning closer until only the two of us could hear. "Usually, they come to me willingly, but it's more fun that you're making me try."

I tried to hide my flush by bringing my wine glass to my lips. He was too good at this. I was already in his stupid trap.

I didn't notice him get even closer until his breath tickled my neck, sending goose bumps down my spine. He was so close, I could smell the woodsy, citrusy scent coming off his hair. His mouth was against my ear and his voice was barely a whisper. "Don't worry. I won't stop until I make you come."

I dropped my goblet on the table and half the wine sloshed out. The loud *clunk* it made against my plate drew the attention of most of the table.

"Sorry," I mumbled as I blotted up the spill with my napkin.

When I whipped my head to Ransom, cheeks burning, he had already straightened and was nodding along to the royals from Kind, but I caught the faint smirk on his lips. Everyone was acting as if nothing happened. Had no one witnessed him whisper that?

At least I was right—he used his suave front and good looks to get what he wanted in the Southern State. I couldn't let his flirtatious act fluster me again.

"Here I was thinking you found your success by being a brute," I said to him quietly.

He looked at me and raised a brow. "You shouldn't believe everything you hear."

"And you should know I'm not a thing to be collected. Or toyed with."

"I'm not so sure about that." The corner of his mouth kicked up as his gaze went to my lips. I knew it was an act, but damn, he was good at this. Heat was scorching through my body, and I was intensely aware of the way the fabric of my dress felt over my skin. I couldn't figure out how he slipped under my guard and made my heart pound so easily.

Did Agora have access to some sort of aphrodisiac he could add to his cologne?

"I suppose next dinner, I'll request to sit away from you if you can't control your urges," I said, trying to relax my thighs that were pressed tightly together.

Queen Elara arched her brows in interest. She turned back to Queen Atla and King Row, long blonde hair slipping over her shoulder, and said, "I do always forget, the hardest part of any gathering is trying to keep everyone out of each other's beds."

"Oh, you're no better," Queen Atla said. "Besides, it's hard to avoid such dalliances when there's a great concentration of extremely attractive people all together." She eyed Mira across from her, then Ransom on my other side, skipping over me. King Row's gaze followed the same path his wife's before smirking at her.

Aurora probably would have been attractive enough to catch Queen Atla's eye. Being skipped over loomed in my thoughts, that it was obvious I wasn't good enough to be one of them. The constant inadequacy I felt during this impersonation stung.

Ransom made several motions as though he was trying to discreetly catch my eye throughout the rest of the meal, but I couldn't handle any more of him tonight, and ignored them all. I kept my mouth shut and stared at my plate through dessert.

When the meal ended, I practically ran back to my suite. I was so flustered that I paced around my sitting room to burn off the agitation. I was mad Ransom thought he could toy with me and that I fell prey to his games so easily. I was mad that Queen Elara thought we were interested in a romantic relationship.

There was a knock at my door. I threw it open in a huff, expecting to see Wynn gloating about some part of my embarrassment she overheard. Instead, it was Lev.

He let himself inside, locking the door in his wake. "We should debrief on anything you overheard tonight. It looked like you were more involved in the conversation at that end of the table."

I felt guilty that I had just been thinking about the effect Ransom had on me. He was a prick and a rebel. Queen Elara was wrong about us flirting.

If anyone should warm my bed, it would be Lev. He was attractive, kind to me, he was on the same side as me, and he actually knew who I was. When Ransom flirted with me, it was to further his rebellion. Lev's interest was genuine. He was the type of stability I needed in my life.

Wait, fuck. Lev was off-limits too. Everyone was off-limits for the next two months. Sharing my bed with anyone while I was in Nixia was simply a terrible idea.

"Sure, yes." I sat down at my table. "I did get some information tonight."

Lev sat down next to me and pulled over some parchment and a quill. Excitement danced in his eyes. "What did you find out?"

"The Northern and Southern States are going to start to push back in the spring. They wanted to be sure the Eastern State would be ready then too."

"Ready for what? To march on the capital? To start organizing men? To start sending letters to each other? And by spring do you mean the equinox, or when the weather starts to warm?" His pen was still poised at the top of the page.

"I–I'm not sure. The conversation sidetracked after that." I went from feeling like I had a great triumph tonight to a complete failure in a matter of seconds. "I suppose that's not much detail at all. Sorry."

It was stupid to think I had good information to report tonight. It was literally one sentence on his paper, which he could have figured out himself from listening to the *All the Flowers of Spring*.

"Next time, try to get more specifics. Numbers, timelines, locations, anything you can. It was your first time doing this, though. It would have been suspicious if you had harassed them for details tonight," he said, easing some of the pressure I was feeling in my chest.

"I suppose that's true. I'm certainly not friendly with them yet."

"I'll send this tidbit off to the Empire tomorrow with Jo. It's better than what we came here with. We didn't know they planned to move in a few months." He stood and folded the paper neatly. "What was so captivating that a bunch of rebels stopped talking about rebellion?"

"What do you mean?"

"You said the conversation got sidetracked after this."

I stood from the table as well, blushing. "Queen Elara said something about rebellions being a pain in the ass because everyone tries to sleep with each other."

Lev laughed. "I suppose she would know. Fae have a reputation for being promiscuous."

"What? Really?"

"Yes, fae may live a long time, but children are rare for them. I suppose it's not for lack of trying, though. Apparently those with magic have quite the libido and aren't afraid to act on it. Maybe the two things are related—the more you share a bed with someone, the more chances you have of pregnancy." He shrugged nonchalantly, as though he wasn't currently speaking to a fae. I had magic, even if I wasn't allowed to use it here, and fell into the group he described.

"It's all just speculation on my part. Anyway, who was trying to find their way into whose bed? We could use that to our advantage in the future."

"Oh." It made me feel disloyal to tell him I spent my dinner engaged in suggestive banter with Ransom. "Queen Atla said a similar thing about everyone here being so attractive. Then she looked at Mira and Ransom like they were part of the menu." I left out the part where I had not been included on that menu.

I should *not* care about that. Maybe there was something to that libido speculation of his.

"Is that all? I saw Dimitris whispering to you. What did he say? Knowing his reputation, it was probably something crude."

"No. It was nothing to worry about." What Ransom said was suggestive, maybe even salacious. I wasn't sure why I wasn't telling Lev about Ransom's tactic with me. I shrugged and began coiling a loose curl around my finger.

"As for not being included in Queen Atla's bedroom plans, maybe you're not to Atla's taste. But did you really want to be invited to share someone's bed with so many others?"

"No," I said, releasing the curl and letting it bounce back. The word came out with such force, it surprised even myself.

"You're still very young in your long life. I think if you live for a few more centuries like the king and queen of Kind, your tastes would open up a bit." He laughed.

That was a thought I hadn't entertained yet. My life so far had always been focused on the immediate future—getting out of Nixia alive, finishing my service, getting out of the Protectorate.

"It would have been nice to at least be considered."

He looked at me, his eyes still bright, but I could sense that the cause of the brightness had shifted. He was assessing me, as though unsure if he should say what he was thinking. "It's important that you're considered by the right people." He stepped forward until he was inches from me. I had to look up to meet his eyes.

When Lev spoke, his voice was lower. "There are those, outside of these *leaders*, who wouldn't mind if you're the type of dish that needs to be savored alone." His hand reached up and gently tucked the curl behind my ear. He cupped my cheek. "Someone whose beliefs match your own, who makes sure that each flavor of you is tasted to its fullest."

Warmth from his hand coursed through me as the deep purr of his words resonated in my chest. My body was already on edge from the dinner conversations, and the heat quickly found its way between my thighs.

I closed the distance between us.

I wanted a reprieve. A reprieve from this heat in my body. A reprieve from the stress and chaos my life had become. A reprieve from concealing myself. I wanted him to see me. I wanted to taste him the way he talked about tasting me. I wanted safe harbor from the storm of my life.

He guided my face with his hand. His mouth claimed mine. I leaned into it, enjoying the press of him against me. The ache in my core was growing more insistent. My breasts felt heavy and my nipples, pebbled with desire, relished the friction of my dress crushing against his chest.

He grabbed my lower back with his free hand, sliding it down to the curve of my ass. His other hand slid around to the nape of my neck. I opened my mouth to him and he responded without hesitation, flooding me with the warm taste of him.

Fuck, I wanted this, wanted him, wanted to forget everything else outside of this kiss, the teasing during dinner, the inadequacy, the loneliness. I needed more, more friction, more of his stability and security. I rolled my hips into his, feeling his desire as I moved against him. He nipped at my lower lip. A soft moan escaped me.

He dropped his hands from me. He stepped back.

"You aren't—" he stammered as he rubbed his lips. "We can't. I'm sorry."

He grabbed the paper and left my room without so much as looking back at me. I stood in the sitting room for several minutes after he was gone, trying to hold on to the temporary bliss.

Despite my efforts to forget sex existed and pretend that nothing happened with Lev, I spent a fair portion of that night lying awake and remembering exactly how his lips felt against mine again. This tangled in a confusing way with what Ransom whispered in my ear at dinner.

I tried to focus on only Lev, how his bare skin would feel against me after the press of our clothed bodies had been so pleasurable. The warmth of his chiseled chest pressing against my breasts with no dress or tunic between them. How his hands would run down my sides with feather-light touches, the calluses on his hands skittering over the swell of my hips. I imagined his hands grabbing my ass harder, drawing me to him. Those strong fingers touching my sensitive nipples, then slipping down between my legs.

My own hand moved between my legs with what I imagined him to be doing to me. Him sliding against me, feeling the wetness at my entrance. Then, his fingers slick with my desire, he would draw back up to the apex of me, circling the nerves there. He would build the tension that I wanted to release so badly as he palmed my breast with the other hand. I moaned into my pillow.

I won't stop until I make you come echoed through my mind. He would plunge his tattooed fingers into me. The steady rhythm of his fingers moving in and out of me, harder, faster, coiling me tighter. I could practically feel the soft brush of his citrusy hair on my cheek. Drawing forth more moans, pulling me closer and closer. Thumb still teasing my clit perfectly, other hand rolling my nipple between his fingers until I spilled over the edge.

My release found me alone in my darkened bedroom.

CHAPTER TWENTY

The following morning, Wynn and Jo left for Port Mora. Jo was tasked with sending Lev's report to the Empire, while Wynn took all the dresses to the seamstress. They wouldn't be back for two days, at best. I wasn't looking forward to training with only Ameal and Lev. Worse still would be my history lesson in the afternoon, where it would just be me and the man who kissed me and ran. And who I then pleasured myself to.

It was going to be a long few days.

I really wished George and Lina were with me. They would have made fun of me about all this, sure. But they also would have been able to give me sound advice as well. I wouldn't have hesitated to tell them about the encounter with Lev, even if it was against the law. All three of us had a tendency to bend the rules. And if I had told them about my private exploits after he left my room, well, it wouldn't have been the first time we discussed self-gratification. Even if Wynn hadn't left for

Port Mora before I got up, our friendship was not deep enough to admit that I violated Imperial law with Lev.

Thankfully, when I arrived at training, Ameal was alone. We were nearing the end of our time together when he informed me that I wouldn't have afternoon lessons with Lev and that we would resume practice after a break for breakfast.

"Why?" I asked, while using a knife to fend off Ameal's attack.

"Because you can use all the training you can get." He easily disarmed me, proving his point.

"No—ahh!" I rolled to prevent a particularly sneaky stab from Ameal, who was now wielding my own knife against me. "I mean, why am I not having lessons today with my advisor?" I didn't even want to mention Lev's name, since there was a fair chance saying it out loud would cause me to blush. Ameal might have been quiet, but I got the impression he noticed everything, and I couldn't risk him picking up on that.

"I'm not sure. Lev didn't say. Just that he was otherwise occupied this week and until Jo returned, you wouldn't have lessons. I took the opportunity to fill your time." He pointed to the way my boots were planted in the grass. "Pay attention to where your legs are when you're in defensive stances." He lunged again.

"Please, no more hand-to-hand after breakfast," I panted as I tried not to trip over my own feet. He was right about needing to pay attention to where my legs were.

"You need to find your flow through these movements. Your body should feel like water slipping over rocks with your swings." He finally relented on his attack. I couldn't believe he could lecture me without losing his breath while also backing me into a corner. He studied me for a moment as I gasped for air, hands braced on my knees.

"But I'm pretty sure you'll be sick if we try to do more of this after you eat. Plus the day will be warm by then. I think I'll give you a little reprieve, we can do archery and go for a ride." He picked up his satchel and began to collect the various practice weapons we abandoned throughout the courtyard.

When I returned after eating, we practiced archery for an hour, which we were both pleased to see that I was decent at. I hit the target every time and even got more accurate shots than him.

I didn't bother to hide my excitement as we headed for the stables. I could always trust Sugardrop, no matter how uncommunicative she was. She was the one friend in this castle whose motives I actually knew—snacks.

Ameal took me on an unfamiliar trail further up the mountain, into the stand of trees I could see from my windows. We rode in silence along the mountainside, but I liked the quiet. The peace surrounding me was starting to absorb into my mind. This place had dramatic beauty, a ruggedness that I found myself loving.

The winding trail led us to a picturesque meadow higher up the mountain with a clear stream running through it. It was totally blocked from the view of the castle, giving it the feel of a private sanctuary surrounded by snow-capped peaks. Birds chattered in nearby trees over the soft rush of the stream. The bright green grasses of the meadow and the flowers littered about swayed gently in the sweet breeze playing on my skin.

I had the sense of entering the song *All the Flowers of Spring*, when the seeds had been sown back in their native lands. Purple, red, and tiny yellow flowers sprinkled the field with their beauty.

This looked like the portraits I'd seen in the Imperial Compound of landscapes I had always dreamed about visiting, but I'd been too trapped in the bleakness and grime of the City to realize such places could actually exist. Just weeks ago, those places were like some fantasy put on canvas, but now I knew these dreams were real. I could be part of them.

I looked at Ameal, mouth agape from the unparalleled beauty he'd brought me to. "Thank you."

"I thought you might like it," he said, with what I would have described as amusement if I didn't know Ameal. He dismounted from his white, dappled horse and began running his hands along the tops of the tall grass as he walked, like he needed to ground himself in this place. I joined him in the grass and crouched down to look at some of the flowers near where he was standing.

"I know you grew up in Capital City and hadn't really left before. I figured you might need to see this place," he said quietly. "I know we won't be overheard here, but it's hard to shake the habit." He turned toward me, looking at me with his bright brown eyes. "Sometimes we all need to remind ourselves that better places exist. It helps us be able to fight for them. You needed to be reminded that what you've always known isn't all that's out there. Better places can be reached. You can reach them."

He was right, I did need this. I felt at peace for the first time since coming to Nixia.

Then Ameal did something I never expected. He smiled.

CHAPTER TWENTY-ONE

Our few days alone together allowed Ameal to become more relaxed around me. His instruction became more detailed, going from "block your right" to "flow your arm up to block your right." Still not the most helpful, but I was becoming more fluid and the movements came more naturally.

Wynn informed me upon her return that she would have to return to Port Mora in two weeks to pick up some of the dresses. It would take a while to do all of them, so Jo and Wynn would need to go back occasionally to pick up what was done and send the coded messages to the mainland for the remainder of the trip.

It barely seemed worth it to have the dresses altered once I realized how much time I would spend without them. I would be in the same four gowns for half the Gathering. I wasn't sure why I cared. I'd lived most of my life only owning, at most, two dresses at the same time. I reassured myself by thinking Aurora probably wouldn't care if she only had four outfits.

The event that evening was a storyteller. He spun a wonderful tale about a monster that had taken over the land by slowly tricking the people of that kingdom into thinking he was benefiting them. He pitted the people against each other so they wouldn't try to throw him out, until a group banded together to oust him.

However, the storyteller got highly offended if anyone else spoke while he was on stage. This made it impossible to connect with any of the other leaders in any meaningful way. After the event, I tried to corner Mira for the details I failed to retrieve during the previous dinner, quickly walking past Queen Elara inviting Parisa and Queen Atla to tour the castle the next day.

"Mira," I touched her shoulder as she stood from her chair. "I wanted to further discuss your garden." She stopped, turning toward me. I drew back my hand and straightened my posture.

"What about it?" she asked slowly.

Shit, were we supposed to keep using code, or could I just ask her outright? "Are you planting your garden when the snow breaks? Or at the equinox?" She surveyed my face with narrowed eyes. "I just want to be sure mine *blooms* at the same time as yours."

My eyes darted toward where Lev was talking in a corner with a burly, ginger-haired man. Mira saw that glance. "Maybe you should figure out what your own garden is doing before concerning yourself too deeply with others. I will be sure the weak are weeded out before my plans are shared."

She turned on her heel and left the hall.

The following day off, Wynn appeared at our shared door with a tray of food.

"I suppose seventh day breakfasts are now our thing?" I stepped out of her way and cleared off my table.

"There are worse traditions."

"I want to hear all about Port Mora, but we'll have to eat fast this morning. Queen Elara invited the leaders on a tour of Castle Nix in an hour, and it feels like something I shouldn't miss. Like a bonus event this week."

"Do you think she would care if I joined?" Wynn piled her plate with an impressive amount of food.

"I think it's normal for fancy ladies to be accompanied by their lady's maid." I shrugged. "Who else will keep me from debasing myself with someone below my station?"

"If you think I could do that, you have overestimated me, my lady." She chuckled as she started on the fruit she'd plated. "Why didn't you have lessons with Lev while we were gone?"

I blushed involuntarily as my kiss with Lev flashed through my head. "We sort of had a tense moment after the dinner. I was under the impression I got great information, but when he came to record it, I didn't have anything that actually mattered. It left us in an awkward place. I'm not sure if he's avoiding me or now feeling as hopeless in this mission as I am."

She watched me as she chewed her toast, eyes narrowed. "Are you sure it was just awkward *information* that passed between the two of you?"

I could feel my throat heat with blush. "It couldn't be anything else. He's my commanding officer," I said evenly. "Lev is very serious about his duty, and I respect my station." She eyed me for a moment, sighed and returned her attention to selecting her next strawberry.

After breakfast, we hurried down to the entrance hall to meet up with the other leaders. Chancellor Parisa and one of her guards were milling around, talking to Queen Atla and Frange, her advisor.

Wynn and I stood off to the side, trying to look like we belonged. Mira and Ransom weren't here. I suddenly worried that state leaders weren't supposed to come to this.

"Here to find out all the secrets of Nixia, Fox?"

I looked over and saw Ransom for the first time in casual clothes. He was wearing a simple tunic and a dark, leather jacket with his hair pulled back into a knot, revealing that the lower part of the sides and back of his head was shaved close. It produced the image I had in my mind of Ransom Dimitris before I met him. His gray pants weren't tailored to him like the clothes he wore to dinners and events, but they did hug his thighs in a way that snared my eye. This man did not have to try hard to impress.

Mother, he was right with my dumb nickname. I was just a fox leaping into his trap.

I was saved from trying to come up with some quippy retort by him walking away to the other leaders to join their conversation. Queen Elara and Mansby, having appeared while I was distracted, were now with the other leaders.

"I see it now," Wynn said, the side of her mouth kicking up.

"See what?" I was still looking at Ransom as he strolled away, his pants just as flattering from behind as they had been from the front.

"Why your brain just happens to default to flirting every time you talk to him. If someone looked at me like that, I probably would too." She smiled coyly at me. "Should Lev be worried?"

"Wynn! No. To both. Wait, what does he look at me like?"

She laughed. "Come on, the tour is starting."

We got a historic background of most of the castle from Mansby, with tidbits thrown in by the queen about particularly noteworthy events that had taken place in those locations. Most of those incidents had to do with famous people and what they had done during parties.

"And over here, we have the marble statue of our third king's favorite horse," Mansby said. "It was carved by renowned sculptor Hinkle Fingly, a master of his craft."

"Yes," Queen Elara said, "and once during a spring equinox party, the singer, Fondslo Durrinberry, climbed on it. He fell and broke his cheekbone. He had to cancel six shows before it healed. He never really could hit high notes the same way again after that."

We made it out to the gardens, which I hadn't seen yet, despite spending every morning in a nearby courtyard. The flowers here were different than the ones I was used to in the Imperial Compound. I inspected small cobalt flowers that grew on tall stalks and had shoots coming off them like streaks of a firework as Mansby talked about a statue behind him.

"So that's Queen Elara's type?" Wynn muttered.

"Hmm? What do you mean?" I said, still bent over the blossoms and running my finger along the silken, blue petals.

"Aren't you listening? This was the statue they erected for Queen Elara's late husband after he died." She waved her hand at the bronze man presiding over the area.

I straightened and looked at it. "Oh, no, I'm not listening. I tuned out Mansby after the fourth room."

A deep chuckle came from Wynn's other side. Ransom was eavesdropping on us.

"I suppose he was quite good-looking," I said to Wynn as we continued to survey the statue.

"The fae always are," Ransom said. He caught my eye and gave a quick smile before turning back to the statue. I would have marked it as part of his strategic flirting, but Aurora wasn't fae. I didn't know what to make of that comment.

We continued through the garden until we came to a small, open area where the only feature was a large granite boulder surrounded by pathways.

"And this, of course, is Nuvimia," Mansby said as he waved a hand toward the rock. "Our unlocking stone."

"The pride of Nixia," Queen Elara said from nearby, as though she was introducing us to her child. I hadn't noticed her falling back to where we were in the group.

I had never really thought about whether there were more unlocking stones than Cavilth. My confusion must have read as angst, because she said, "I know Moriale's was destroyed when the Emperor took your lands. It must be heartbreaking to know your people have lost such a treasure."

"I suppose it's a good thing we can still use Cavilth." I couldn't take my eyes off the gray rock in front of me.

"Yes, I've always wondered about that," she said.

"What do you mean?" Wynn peered over me to look at the Queen, then quickly looked down and bobbed her head in deference. "Sorry, Your Majesty, I didn't mean to speak out of turn."

Queen Elara gave her a long, appraising look. "No trouble. I believe *every* guest in my castle should have their voice heard."

Wynn's shoulders relaxed as she looked back up. "Thank fuck." She slapped her hand over her mouth as I whirled toward her, eyes wide. Queen Elara laughed loudly and waved her hand as though to brush it off.

"A fae can only have their powers unlocked by the stone of their native land," she said. "At least that's true in Gallia, Kind, and Nixia. A magic wielder born in Gallia cannot use Nuvimia to release their powers. But it seems those born in Moriale, Decca, and Solterra can use Cavilth. I've always wondered how the Emperor pulled that off. It made his claims of uniting those kingdoms somehow into a reality, like even the Mother and Father approved of his villainy."

"I've wondered that as well," Ransom said, still standing near Wynn and me. "Especially since Solterra has produced no wielders in memory. Some think it's because the fae bloodlines aren't strong enough there. Or if you are a Child of the Mother, you say it's because Agora is too full of sin to allow for wielding."

"But you have wielders in your city, right?" I asked.

"Oh, yes." He smiled. "But none that were born there. I think when you live a few hundred years, the walls of Capital City start to get boring and the fun in Agora becomes irresistible." His last word became a purr that caused a slight shiver down my spine. A smile spread across my own cheeks.

Queen Elara shook her head. "The Emperor's policy is archaic. Only letting you touch the stone once."

"What do you do here?" Wynn asked loudly.

"Wynn!" I hissed. She could only press her luck so far.

"It's fine." Queen Elara eyed Wynn again, moving to my other side to be next to her, like proximity to royalty might make her behave more appropriately. "My people can touch Nuvimia as many times as they wish. Most people's magic is developed enough by the time they're seventeen to be unlocked, but some need more time and come back every solstice to try again. We've never had anyone older than twenty-seven be unlocked."

"*Twenty-seven!*" Wynn and I said at the same time.

"How much time do they have to spend in your guard to touch that rock ten times?" Ransom asked with a laugh.

"None," Queen Elara said. "I don't need to coerce my people into my service."

"What do Kind and Gallia do?" Wynn asked, her eyes intent on Queen Elara. "Your Highness."

Queen Elara smiled, clearly enjoying Wynn's fearlessly brash comments from a lady's maid to a queen. "They are similar to us, but I believe Kind does not let anyone over thirty try."

"So you're telling me," Wynn said, "there could be people in the Protectorate who touched Cavilth, had nothing happen, served their three years, and went on with their lives. But they could still have magic that could be unlocked?"

"Yes," Queen Elara replied.

"Have you ever had anyone who didn't get a chance to touch Nuvimia, for whatever reason—say they were abroad until they were over thirty—and had magic unlocked?" Ransom asked over me. He had taken up the space on my other side when Queen Elara moved closer to Wynn.

"That situation has never arisen, to my knowledge. Most people make the journey to Nuvimia a priority before they are that old. If they don't come by then, they usually aren't interested in being unlocked," Queen Elara said.

I watched Ransom as he looked at Nuvimia and ran a hand down his chest, smoothing his shirt. The expression on his face was a mix of emotions, clearest among them curiosity.

"Wynn, how old are you?" Queen Elara asked, pulling my attention back to them.

"Twenty-five," she said.

"Oh, you still have a chance when you get back," Queen Elara said delightedly. "If you want to venture to Capital City."

"Psh, unlikely. My family doesn't have any wielders in memory," she said.

I wanted to add that either way, the Emperor wouldn't let her touch it a second time, but then I remembered that she was Wynn, guard to Aurora Fey who had never touched Cavilth, not Wynn, Imperial Protector who had touched Cavilth a few weeks ago.

"How old are you, Ransom?" I asked.

"What? Thirty-two." His attention snapped back to me. "Why? How old are you?"

"Don't worry, she's of age," Wynn said with a devious smirk.

"Ha ha." I threw Wynn a dirty look. "Twenty-seven."

"How old are you, Your Majesty?" Wynn asked with a polite smile.

"A queen never tells," Queen Elara said with a wink as she walked back to the front of the group.

"Walk with me," Wynn hissed in my ear. I followed her over to Nuvimia, where I used my skirt to block the view of Wynn slipping her hand along the stone.

"Anything?" Ransom asked from right behind me. I jumped so hard, he put a hand on my shoulder to steady me.

"No," Wynn said in the quietest voice I'd ever heard her use. The disappointment etched in her face tugged at my chest.

"It's not a solstice. And you weren't born in Nixia," I whispered.

Ransom reached his other hand behind me and brushed the stone. "Just a rock," he muttered.

Wynn and Ransom left to follow the group. I let my fingertips brush the granite as I passed, and a faint gray glow briefly glimmered where I grazed the rock. I looked around to make sure no one else had seen what just happened, but everyone else was already on the other side of a hedge, hearing about how a famous diplomat had once gotten stuck in a topiary during a game of something called "horseless jousting."

CHAPTER TWENTY-TWO

Lev was still "occupied with other things" during the first few days of the following week. I had my history lessons in Jo and Ameal's room. I wasn't sure where Ameal was during my lessons, but I never saw him. He was probably out running to the top of a mountain for fun.

Jo had documents and books that he hadn't brought to Lev's room yet. They focused less on the history of Moriale and were more about the current state of the East. He had literature produced in the state, drafts of songs sung in taverns there, art made in their mountain towns.

"Why do you have all these in here?" I asked.

"They were on the boat," he replied. "I was excited to have them. They give us a much clearer picture of the sentiment in the East. Our strategy needs to be based around the direction the wind is blowing."

"Which way is that?"

"Well, that large pile over there references the East as *Moriale* or mentions the Empire in some negative way. This very small pile over here uses the Empire's perspective or speaks neutrally about it."

"So the wind is blowing to spread the seeds away from the gardener's clutches," I muttered to myself as I leaned over the table, poking through the piles.

"Indeed," Jo agreed quietly.

I whipped my head toward Jo. "This seems important to the role I'm playing. Why didn't you share this with me before?" I trusted Jo, but it felt neglectful not to give me such critical information. It would help me be better in this role, and therefore help all of us survive.

He frowned. "I was asked not to."

"Why? That feels like setting me up to fail." I crossed my arms as my brows furrowed.

"The thought was that you are new and untried as a spy to the Empire, so we couldn't be certain this information wouldn't slip from your lips to the wrong person. I disagreed from the beginning. You are risking all our lives. The least we could do is give you all the information." He shook his head. "I wondered this whole time if I should disobey orders and tell you. When I found out it would just be the two of us, I couldn't help but leave these laying around." He winked and smiled, but his lips became taut as he waited to see how I would respond to him defying a direct order.

"Can I meet with you in the afternoons when we start meeting with Lev again, if we don't get through all of them?"

His smile brightened again. "We can arrange that."

The following dinner, I was seated between Parisa and Mira. Between the two, it was a hard call who I would rather talk to. I needed to give Mira more time before she believed I was ready to confide in, so that left me with the leader of the kingdom to our west, well known in the Empire for their cruelty.

"As soon as the Gathering ends," Queen Elara was saying to her, "we'll start bringing in supplies from Port Mora for the winter. We have to be so cautious about being snowed in with the keep up this high."

"Yes," Parisa said, tucking her auburn hair back from her face. "Our council is held in the mountains as well. It's great protection, but a pain for logistics. I'm always happy when I see spring start to thaw."

This was my opening. I leaned forward, inserting myself into their conversation. "Yes, spring is my favorite too. And do you think you'll plant a garden this spring, Parisa?"

"What?" She faced me, utter confusion etched in her brows.

"Are you going to *sow* some *flowers* this spring?" I spoke slowly, angling my head to try to better convey the meaning.

"I suppose the gardeners will, they usually do." She was still looking at me now with her eyes narrowed in uncertainty.

Seriously? Was Gallia not using the same coded words as the Northern State?

"So nothing *extra special* is being planted this spring in Gallia?"

"What are you talking about?" A long moment passed as her confused gaze continued to rain down on me, then her mouth opened to make a small circle. She twisted her body forward and spoke loudly across the table. "Dimitris, Moriale is looking for a shipment of Keyf weed." She quickly pointed between myself and Ransom before turning back to Queen Elara.

Ransom smirked at me as I blushed deeply and shook my head. "No," I said quickly. "It was a misunderstanding. I—never mind."

"You know Agora has everything." He smiled wider, twirling a dinner knife around his fingers. "Just ask and you shall receive, Fox."

After yet another dinner where I didn't get any information of value, Lev decided it was time to resume our afternoon lessons. I guess he figured I needed help more than we needed to avoid each other. It had been a full week since we kissed. I had no idea what he had been up to in the meantime. I had rarely seen him during that week.

Another week was slipping by, my days now feeling very full. My combat training with Ameal, Jo, and Wynn was getting increasingly better. I was able to block more, stay standing longer, and even get in a few hits on all of them.

The lessons on the East with Lev and Jo were now considerably more uncomfortable. We discussed more of the history of the East after it was incorporated into the Empire. Every time I looked at Lev, his eyes were on me, but he would quickly avert his gaze when my attention turned to him. Any time Jo left the two of us alone, to get another book or use the washroom, there was a gaping maw of silence between us.

During one of those rare moments with just the two of us, I reached for a book, but wrinkled my nose as I extended my arm. It was still sore from training that morning, and I drew it back without finishing the movement.

Lev reached for the book. "Here, let me get that for you."

"Thanks," I said with a weak smile. "I don't think I'm built to use a big sword like Ameal or you."

"I don't think there's anything wrong with your build," he said, his blue eyes meeting my gold ones for the first time since we'd kissed. The pulsing tension between us was making my breath catch.

Jo came back from his room with the maps he needed, and our gaze broke apart.

These morning lessons were followed by secret afternoon sessions with only Jo that prepared me better for the Gathering than anything else had. He spoke to me about what he felt was happening in Moriale and towns where rebellious sentiments were strongest. He talked to me about how those sentiments correlated to the population centers in the East and how accessible the land was for moving large groups of people. I was learning military strategy along with the current state of Moriale, things that might keep us from getting found out by the others at the Gathering.

My biggest success was keeping everyone alive and not arousing any suspicion through another event. A group of acrobats performed in the hall, doing amazing feats of balance and strength. I mingled just enough to keep up the act that Aurora Fey was here to build ties, but stole away from conversations when they would start to press for details I didn't have.

I leaned against a pillar that Queen Atla and Chancellor Parisa were standing on the other side of and sipped my drink, pretending to watch the crowd. "Gallia doesn't want to risk engaging with the Empire until the other territories are involved." Parisa's voice carried to me. "Our army isn't big enough against the might of the Empire, and the people of Gallia are hesitant to lose more ground."

"Understandable," Queen Atla said. "We always put the needs of our people first. It's what any ruler worth their salt would do."

The acrobats finished their set, and further discussion between the two was blanketed by applause. I smiled as I accepted every breadcrumb I could find.

My seventh-morning breakfast with Wynn the following day was largely a silent affair, but at least we had reached the point in our relationship where the quiet was companionable, and not awkward.

I gazed out the large window, not seeing the mountain scenery, with a fork full of scrambled eggs frozen halfway to my open mouth as I thought about how I should approach Parisa again. Wynn let out a loud sigh. "Fine. What do you need my help with?"

"What do you mean?"

"I can hear you thinking all the way over here."

"I didn't—" I sighed, setting down my fork. There was really no point in denying that I needed help anymore. "Anything, really. Lev can only help me so much and he needs this mission to go well, but I'm failing it for him. I don't know what I'm doing. I'm trying everything I can think of. I'll take whatever you can give me."

She looked at me, brows lowered and set down her coffee cup. "Get two hairpins."

"Why?"

"Because you shouldn't feel like you're doing this alone. I'm going to do more to be there for you, I promise."

I went to my bathing chamber where I had discarded a few the night before, wondering what sort of hairstyle she was going to show me that could help the mission.

When I came back to the sitting room, Wynn was reentering from the hall door.

"What were you doing?"

"Locking the door between our rooms," she said.

"Why?"

"I'm going to show you how to pick a lock," she said and gave a mocking curtsy. "Like a lady." We sat down on the floor in front of our shared door. "Now, hand me those hairpins."

She showed me how to insert the pins into the lock and catch the mechanism inside, then had me copy her movements. She had me repeat the process, locking and unlocking the door until I could actually tell what I was doing. We moved on to my door to the hallway. Once she was satisfied that I had the skill, she excused herself for the afternoon.

I kept practicing after she left and perfected it on the door between my sitting room and bedroom. Finally feeling accomplished for the first time in Nixia, I spent the remainder of the afternoon on a ride with Sugardrop.

The following day, when I walked into my secret lesson with Jo, I found Wynn sitting there as well. What we were doing was insubordination at best, punishable by death at worst. She had been very clear to me that she would prefer not to die.

I stood there in silence. I wasn't going to be the first one to speak and put anyone in jeopardy. I didn't know what they had discussed while in Port Mora, and I had decided to try to use better judgment before opening my mouth, a resolution that probably wouldn't last very long.

"I can help, and I promised to be there for you," she said. "Not just as Aurora, as Ness too." I gaped at her. It was the first time anyone had said my real name since before we left the First. "And I didn't only mean party tricks like lock picking."

"We discussed this possibility while we were in Port Mora," Jo joined in. "But Wynn came to me last night and told me you feel like you need more help. We need to give you everything we can."

"Sorry about that," I mumbled.

"First lesson." Wynn slapped her hands on the tabletop. "Stop that."

I jumped. "Stop what?"

"Apologizing, for everything—for anything. Aurora would never have said sorry for doing her best." Wynn smirked. "Even if her best was terrible."

I smiled in spite of myself. "So you didn't live as far from Stronghold as you led me to believe?" I took my seat at the table across from them. "You knew her?"

She took a deep breath, "No, I didn't know her, but I know what the rulers of Moriale were like. Before I joined the Protectorate, I worked in Stronghold as a guard to the Fey family, but I left when her uncle was killed. I wasn't part of the resistance, I didn't lie about that. But it was hard to work in Stronghold and not share those sympathies. Aurora came to Polis after I left."

That one piece clicked so many explanations into place. Why after only one month of basic training, she was far better in our combat practice than I could ever hope to be. And why she was so much older than the other recruits. Why she'd been so easily convinced to come on this mission, if she had known the people who were supposed to be attending. Why she was willing to even be my friend, if I was the only other known person with golden eyes in the empire.

I should have seen this coming.

I got the sinking feeling I now associated with being bad at my job. I had simply believed what Wynn told me and let my mind fill in the gaps with innocent information.

Then I remembered that Lev said people would think the same for me posing as Aurora. Oddly, that made me feel less of a complete failure. Maybe things really weren't as bad as I had let myself think.

I attended the next dinner in a repeat dress, and ignored the sidelong glances from those that noticed. Some of the ladies' maids hissed at Wynn when they saw me enter, but the first of the altered dresses would be available soon.

I was seated between Queen Atla and the advisor from Solterra, the burly ginger man I had seen Lev speak to before. He was kind to me, but mostly kept his focus to this other side where the other advisors talked.

I faced Queen Atla, hoping to leverage her conversation I overheard the previous week. "Big changes are sure to come in the next year." She pivoted to listen to me. "If tumult comes to the soil of Moriale, I want to ensure my people suffer as little as possible." I had her full attention now. "I'm such a new leader, I'm having a hard time knowing the most impactful way to ensure my people's needs are met first. I'm of course willing to do whatever it takes."

"As a leader should." She dipped her chin in approval. She should, I'd basically just repeated what she said during the acrobat performance back to her.

"Hopefully, I can get some ideas of how to prepare Moriale. What does Kind plan to do?"

"Kind plans to hold the same line we did in previous times of upheaval, but this time we will make sure to be prepared for—"

"Fox!" Ransom interrupted from across the table. "If you're willing to do whatever it takes..." He continued to stare at me with a sultry look that made my cheeks heat. He dropped his voice to a low growl. "I promise to meet all *your* needs."

That fucking ass, just taking any opportunity to mess with me. I was about to get valuable details from Queen Atla. I needed to salvage this interaction with her. I ignored him and turned back to Queen Atla. "Sorry, Your Highness, you were saying?"

But Queen Atla was looking indignantly from Ransom's continued provocative gaze at me to my flushed face and not paying attention to anything I just said. She huffed loudly and pushed back her chair with a loud screech of wood on stone before leaving the hall. I glared at Ransom.

He smiled, popping a grape into his mouth. "I couldn't pass up an opportunity to fluster you both at the same time." He slipped back into the other conversations around him with a smile.

Despite my failed attempts to get any information from Queen Atla, I picked up snippets from the others that made me think I had a tiny chance of appeasing the Empire with the next letter Lev would send.

Gallia was tired of the Empire's outposts across the river that cut them off from the silver mine. If they made a push, it would be to knock down the bridge over the river, cutting the outposts off from the rest of the Empire. Gallia could reclaim the silver mine for their own. There were no whispers if that was going to happen in the spring or if they were going to wait until the states were already deep in battle. However, this was a certain location and plan for a first strike.

Yet, I had no dates and hardly any numbers. Every time I came back to my room without those details, I was a little sad I would be disappointing Lev when I told him.

He had not been to my room to debrief after a dinner since the night we kissed. I kept notes on my own. I would give them to him when he was ready for an update. Privately, I hoped with each stroke of my pen that the news would impress him.

I tried not to dwell on it. I knew the lack of contact with him was for the best. He was my commanding officer. We needed to keep our heads focused on the task at hand.

None of that stopped me from waiting for a knock on my door after each event. I would tell myself I wanted to stay up and read a few chapters of my book before bed. But every time, my book lost its luster after a few pages, and I trudged to my bed alone.

During a lesson midway through the fourth week, Lev requested I fetch my notes. He coded them and handed the sealed letters to Jo to take to Port Mora the following day. Jo left earlier than usual to prepare for his trip.

I broke the silent study of his history books. "Do you think I should start trying to seek out the other leaders between events? It would be more chances to get intelligence. I could ask one of them to view the paintings in the East Wing with me or something."

Lev shook his head. "Do you really think you're actually ready for that? It would be even harder than what you've been doing to try something in an unstructured environment." He briefly touched a hand to my forearm. "I wouldn't want you to place yourself in that kind of danger."

I went back to the book in front of me and zipped the pendant on my necklace back and forth as I read through a passage. My eyes stayed fixed on a single point on the page as I pulled the metal along the chain around my neck faster, creating a louder noise.

Lev reached over and covered my hand with his, stopping the movement. "Wound a little tight?"

"Why wouldn't I be? I'm failing at everything. I haven't gotten a single piece of valuable information yet."

He let go of my hand. "I know the General feels that way."

"What? He does?"

"The latest letter expressed that he would like to have more information by now, but between us, I think he's just exaggerating. He wouldn't really discharge all of us early when we return."

"What?" That made me sit up and let go of my pendant.

He shushed me. "Don't worry, he won't do that. You got us in here and allowed us to confirm that a rebellion is being planned. That's huge for the Emperor. It gives him a path forward to retaliate against the traitors within the bounds of the magical treaty."

"Is the Emperor going to kill them?" I asked, unable to hide the hesitance in my words. I certainly didn't want war. But the thought of Mira and Ransom's lives being extinguished didn't sit well with me.

"He can't until they conduct an act of violence against him first." He studied my face. "But knowing they are plotting against him would give him the ability to detain them until the matter can be discussed."

"I really need to know more about this treaty." I looked down at my hands. "Do you think Queen Elara has a copy I can read?"

He slipped his finger under my chin to pull my gaze back to his. His thumb brushed along my lower lip in the gentlest of touches, sending a flutter through my body. His eyes were locked on my mouth, as though he planned to meet my gaze, but got distracted by my lips and couldn't look away. His hand slipped down until he was tracing the column of my throat and along my chest. His fingers touched the pendant of my necklace and curled around it, the back of his hand resting on the tops of my breasts. The heat of his touch warmed me. I could feel the weight of his hand through my whole body. He pulled the necklace toward him, and me along with it.

His lips met mine as he leaned forward. The kiss was soft, barely there. It was a reminder of the stability the Empire provided and what we were fighting for. I wanted to fall into it and feel safe and steady.

He let go of the necklace and dropped his head. "Of course, I can't resist you." He let out a single breath of a laugh and shook his head. "I think if Jo needs to leave early again, we should end our lesson. We certainly can't meet while he's gone." He stood and opened the door for me. "I can't keep kissing you every time we're alone."

CHAPTER TWENTY-THREE

I received a note the following day that the event for the fourth week would take place in the Western Courtyard at midday and to dress for sport. I didn't know what that meant. I really hoped that Jo and Wynn were quick on their trip and would be back in time to give me more outfit choices and advice on what *dressing for sport* meant, but I wasn't lucky. They hadn't returned by the morning of the sixth day.

I tried asking Lev about proper court attire for sport, but when I knocked on his door, he didn't answer. I couldn't find him since the kiss in his room and suspected he was avoiding me. Again.

Ameal was no help with this topic and told me he was going to wear what he always wore. I was so desperate, I considered asking one of the other leaders for advice, but that would have been admitting to them how out of place I was here, and I didn't exactly want to call attention to that. I also didn't know where they spent their time between events.

I ended up dressing in the leggings, shirt, and corset combination that had become my default. I wore my boots, since I was more mobile in those than the beaded slippers that were my other choice. I braided my hair into a coronet around my head to keep it out of my way and let a few loose curls fall around my face. I even added a few knives to the ensemble for good measure, since I had no idea what *sport* would entail.

I felt adequately sporty when I looked in the mirror before leaving my room.

I had spent so much time preparing these last few weeks, I was ready to do my job at this event.

I entered the courtyard chatting with Ameal and full of confidence, not glancing around until I was in the thick of the crowd, where my confidence evaporated entirely. My stomach plummeted and the blood drained from my face. My interpretation of the dress code was far from correct.

All the other ladies wore dresses that were flowy with skirts that weren't as full as usual and perhaps offered them a small amount of movement more than normal. They were adorned in glamorous jewels and the most ornate, ostentatious hats I had ever seen.

No matter how much I thought I was ready, there was more I didn't know. I was never going to win.

Ameal gave me an encouraging look before he broke off to go stand with the other guards. A silence followed me as I crossed the yard to the table that held food and drinks. I poured myself a cup of the first thing I could find.

Lev was nearby, talking to the pinch-faced advisor from Kind, Frange, and the ginger advisor from the Southern State. All three advisors were staring at me. I raised my glass with a shaky hand in their direction before taking a drink.

Ransom's advisor smirked at the gesture. "Ransom was right. You would love the lawlessness of Solterra, Miss Fey."

Lev scowled at me. I was unsure if it was due to my out-of-place attire or apparent friendliness with the lawless Southern advisor. I opened my mouth to respond, but Lev turned his body, blocking me out of the conversation. Message received—Lev had the advisors covered.

Not knowing what else to do, I made my way to where the rest of the leaders stood. Ransom clapped my shoulder. "Ha, the Fox strikes again. You're certainly dressed for the type of games I'd love to play with you." His eyes danced as they met mine. I didn't mind his flirtation this time. His ability to make light of the situation made my mistake feel less dire. A smile threatened my lips.

It turned out the sport we were here for was some sort of yard game with confusing rules that involved rolling colored balls the size of grapefruits across the grass, but not too far, or too close to balls of the same color. Wooden buckets sat upturned across the lawn and we needed to try to hit them, but not if your color matched the color on top of the bucket, along with approximately one hundred other rules that included exceptions for when the bucket was knocked to its side and when someone had already thrown their ball in a path that crossed yours. And probably if a cloud was directly overhead, you needed to roll the ball from between your legs. I wasn't sure. I stopped listening and conceded to losing. I had too many other things on my mind to even begin to keep all these rules straight. Instead, I worked on drinking the alcoholic lemonade that was being served.

Chancellor Parisa approached me as I stood at the back of the group of leaders. "Did you get your shipment all arranged with Ransom?"

"I wasn't—" It didn't matter, and I cut myself off by taking a drink from my cup. She could keep on thinking I was trying to get Keyf weed for Polis.

"Aren't you glad the oppressive heat of summer is finally waning and we can enjoy events such as this outdoors?" She gestured to the lawn and the extremely wide brim of her hat flopped with the movement, making a stuffed squirrel adorned with ribbons on the top meet my eyes.

I hummed agreement into my drink, keeping to myself that *enjoyable* was not on the list of words I would use to describe this day.

"Don't you have all those mortals in Gallia that can follow you around and fan you when you get too hot?" I asked, my irritation with my failed attire getting the better of me.

She laughed. "Oh, the propaganda from the Empire. What are they funneling into Moriale through those schools these days? We bewitch our mortals to do our bidding?"

"No, enslave them," I said, each word clipped.

She snorted loudly.

"I don't think this is a laughing matter. Especially since my mother was a mortal." Shit, I had unintentionally been talking about my own mother. It hadn't occurred to me that Aurora's mother might not have been and that could be known to the other leaders.

"Sorry, no, enslavement is not a laughing matter. It's just the ridiculous rubbish that the Emperor comes up with couldn't be further from the truth." She straightened her face to look at me seriously, the taxidermied animal on top of her hat wobbling precariously. "My husband is a mortal, and I trusted him enough to let him govern in my absence. Well, he's on Gallia's council, so, assist in governing."

She was married to a mortal? That was unusual. Mortals and fae sometimes did marry. A wielder could use their healing to extend the life of a mortal beyond their typical years, but they would still have a few hundred years without their love. She must really care about him, to be willing to face such heartache.

"Then why do you have bloodlines pure enough to still have pointed ears and all those other fae traits?" I asked. "They rarely show up in the Empire, but it seems almost every person in your party does."

"Why do you think we have them?" she asked, a smile still playing on her lips.

"Geographic isolation?"

She let out a cawing laugh that startled me. "Geographic isolation. No, it couldn't possibly be that the Emperor makes it so hard to be unlocked that only a small portion of your fae get to pass on magic traits." She calmed herself again and looked at me with mirth still dancing in her eyes. "You are so funny. Moriale should have warned us about that in their announcement. *Geographic isolation.*"

"What word did Moriale send out about me exactly?" I asked. "I never got to see those letters before leaving. I'm curious what everyone knows about me."

"Oh, only that you were very new to your position. And that they determined you would be heir about a month before you were forced to take over, so you had almost no court training. Clearly." She waved her hand at my outfit. "But also that you were capable, smart, and passionate about Moriale's liberty." She finished with a smile. "What I've noticed about you is that you're a little spy."

"What?" I breathed, frozen in place, trying to stop myself from giving anything away.

"You listen at most of the dinners and events more than you talk. You don't show your hand. It's smart to see what everyone else's plans are before you reveal your own. An observer is a good decision maker."

My fingers stopped crushing the cup I was holding.

"Well, I'm trying to learn as much as I can in this short time and make the best decision possible for my people." I was rather proud of my diplomatic-sounding answer. "Clearly, I need to spend more time observing what people wear to various court functions." I smiled and waved my hand at my clothes, trying to make light of it and build on this seemingly promising interaction.

"I love your progressive outfit. It makes me think that perhaps our next event should be more combative." She waved her fist in a fake punch, wobbling the squirrel even more and its ribbon came undone.

"That I might enjoy." I glanced to where the advisors stood, the salt of Lev's snub still in my wounded pride.

"Good to know you are ready for a fight," she said with a sly smile as she sipped from her cup. She looked at me expectantly for a few beats. "We can talk later." She walked off to Queen Elara's side.

Shit! She hadn't been talking about events. This stupid coded language had tripped me up again. I missed an opportunity to know the specifics for what Gallia was planning. I had let my disgruntlement for this game, the stress of the mission, and frustration about Lev cloud my mind and not seen the opening to get more information from her. I finished my drink, letting the haze of the alcohol distract me from this failure.

The group of advisors was coming my way, and I wanted to get to the next bucket before Lev could somehow sniff out my failure. However, before I could slip away, he cornered me.

"What did Parisa want?" he whispered.

"You're spending your day with her advisor, shouldn't you already know?" My annoyance was slipping out of me easily now.

"We advisors can definitely be shocked by our leaders." He eyed my outfit. I got a slight twinge of satisfaction at the way his gaze lingered on parts of me.

"If only my advisor was capable of keeping himself composed. He might not have had to avoid me and could have actually advised me on proper attire," I hissed.

"Aurora." His whisper was full of warning.

"She asked me if I was up for a fight."

"And?" He glared at me.

I didn't want to tell him I failed again. "She said we could talk later."

"Remember why we're here. You need to do *whatever it takes* to get the information we need. We've already gotten *distracted* enough. Stay focused."

I didn't appreciate Lev being openly frustrated with me when I was trying so hard to give him what he wanted. With Parisa, I had gone from thinking I had been found out to feeling like a failure in a matter of seconds. The constant ups and downs of this mission were taking too much out of me.

I started to walk away, but he grabbed my arm, squeezing it—not so tight as to hurt, but enough to spin me back to him. "Do whatever it takes, Aurora. We all are."

I wretched my arm from his grasp and stormed off.

Whatever it takes.

I got to the bucket with the rest of the leaders and treated myself to another lemony libation. Lev eyed me from where the advisors stood.

I understood that Lev and I couldn't have a romantic relationship, but it felt like he was overcorrecting to my detriment. I would show him.

I only had so much at my disposal at the moment. I pulled down the collar of my shirt and adjusted my corset, putting my cleavage on a display that rivaled the purple dress from my first week.

My head was buzzing pleasantly with the satisfaction that I looked thoroughly indecent, and I walked up to where Ransom stood speaking to King Row. I stumbled more than once. Apparently, there were some divots in the lawn the castle needed to fix.

"I don't know why Mira is complaining about the heat. This is nothing. In Kind, it's so hot that we can't even grow the same foliage as here," King Row said with a bragging tone as he sipped his drink and surveyed the field around them.

"Yes, I've heard Kind is quite the paradise." Ransom looked bored as his eyes traveled anywhere except King Row. His gaze landed on me, or more specifically, on my newly adjusted neckline. I watched his throat work as he took a drink with his eyes still focused on me.

King Row huffed, shaking his head as he left Ransom and me standing alone.

Ransom dragged his eyes back to my face. "Sorry," he said a bit distractedly. "The royals from Kind won't stop bothering me. I'm trying to be more obvious at these functions that my interest lies elsewhere. They're starting to make it hard to accomplish what I came here for."

My eyes quickly flicked to where the advisors were standing, and then back to Ransom. "I could help you with that." I stuck my chest out a little more than what was comfortable.

"Yeah?"

I went to flick my hair over my shoulder, but only when I was met with empty air did I remember that I was wearing it braided on my head.

"What's your game, Fox?"

I stepped closer to him, my chest nearly brushing against him. "Even a fox wants to have some fun every now and then." My hand traced a line of embroidery on the chest of his dark blue tunic. I could feel the hard pectorals under his shirt, and the next part flowed from my mouth in a husky tone as I looked up at him from under my lashes. "Maybe I could help you show Kind where your interests lie."

He was just staring at me.

Maybe that wasn't obvious enough. "They could lie in my bed," I said in a loud whisper.

He huffed out a laugh and grabbed my hand from his shirt. He leaned forward, his face so close to mine that we were sharing breath. "I don't know what you want, Fox," he whispered. "But I'm willing to bet that your cunt isn't worth my mercenaries or my alliance with Decca." He was so close to me, his words blew the curls that hung around my face. "I can tell you with certainty that a drunk fox is not what I want." His caramel eyes, that usually sparkled with light when he spoke to me, now felt hard and dark. "Or someone pretending." He released my hand and straightened up.

I looked at him, stunned. I wasn't expecting to be so quickly and completely rejected. This was his game. I was playing his game back at him. I wasn't trying to fuck him out of his alliance with Gallia. I was trying to make Lev jealous and maybe get a tidbit of information that might prove I was good at anything.

I hated espionage. Everything meant something else, and I was terrible at this fucking mission. I was drunk, stuck in a never-ending game of rolling balls at fucking buckets. And Ransom had definitely stared at my breasts.

"I wasn't—I don't want—" Tears started to sting in the edges of my eyes for the first time since I had cried for Aurora three weeks ago. I made myself take a breath, refusing to let them fall here, in front of him, but everything was getting blurry.

A series of emotions passed over his face too quickly for me to read. He raised his voice when he said, "Not today, Fox."

He moved to the next bucket. I stood there for a while after he left me, listening to the dull *clunk* of balls hitting wood and the soft laughter of polite conversation that was a fog around me.

I was a failure in everything I'd done today.

When I finally moved, I didn't try to continue on with the game. I trudged off the grass and into the cool shade of the castle. I stopped just inside the stone doorway and leaned against a wall, taking deep breaths as I tugged my collar back up.

I needed to get my emotions under control before I went any further. I could feel my magic humming just beneath the surface, having not used it in too long. If a fae didn't wield regularly, the well of magic would fill up and spill out when emotions were high. I didn't need to add accidental wielding to my list of failures for this mission. I would have to slip away to expel some soon or it would start pouring out of me when my guard was down.

The echo of boots on the stone floor of the hallway washed over me until Ameal leaned against the wall next to me. I couldn't look at him, and continued to stare straight ahead.

"We don't win every battle. Some days it's wisest to stop and rest. Get ourselves back together before trying again." He mirrored my interest in the opposite wall.

"So everyone out there saw me miss my chance with Gallia and throw myself at Ransom like a maniac?"

"I doubt anyone else was paying as close attention to you as I was when Parisa approached." He paused. "But, yes, I think everyone saw the Ransom thing."

CHAPTER TWENTY-FOUR

My humiliation wasn't dimmed by the lemonade for very long. Typically considered slow by fae standards, my healing had no problem scrubbing the alcohol from my system in record time.

That evening, I was laying in my bed, allowing myself to wallow in my embarrassment when my door creaked open. Wynn walked in carrying a box from the seamstress in Port Mora.

I practically threw myself at her. "Please never leave me again."

She deposited the box on my bed. "I stopped by Jo's room on my way here and Ameal filled us in on today's event. So Ransom really is your type, huh?"

"Oh, stop. I lost control of the situation and didn't know how to fix it. I keep trying to tell you that I get impulsive and flirty when I don't know what to do."

"Clearly, if your solution was to try to jump in bed with Ransom."
She frowned thoughtfully. "You could do worse, though."

"There was no wise lady's maid there to keep me in line."

"Well, I can't say I'll always be by your side. We only brought back a third of the dresses. But you already know I'll help you when I can."

She sat on my bed next to me and told me about Port Mora. It was nice to feel the normalcy of a town going about its daily life through her words. I got to forget for an hour that I was threatening all of our lives with my incompetency.

Mansby and a few other servants brought in a trunk of dresses. Wynn and I watched them carry them into my dressing chamber and exit my suite from our post on my bed.

I locked the door behind them. "I guess they're aware now that I needed to let my dresses out."

"Oh, you can be pretty certain the entire castle will know by to-morrow morning. The people here are efficient with their gossip, but I couldn't carry all those up here myself."

I sighed. "I suppose I've already given them plenty to gossip about. What does this really matter?"

"I did spare you a little scandal, though, and brought *that* box up myself." She pointed to the now-forgotten box on my bed that I had assumed was a personal purchase for Wynn.

"What's in there?" Dread built inside of me at the idea of another ugly surprise today.

"Open it."

I hesitantly lifted the lid.

It was full of undergarments.

They weren't the utilitarian ones I had brought from the Em-pire. They were all lacy, silky, far more revealing, and many were even see-through. Brassieres made of lace with unnecessary bows attached to them and that looked as though support was merely an afterthought, not their purpose. I held up what I assumed was a scrap of fabric, but the lace had ribbons coming from it in a T shape.

"What in the Mother's name is this?"

"Underwear. For your butt," Wynn laughed as she oriented them the correct direction in my hands to the way they were meant to be worn.

"These look like they are for other parts of me and decidedly not for my butt."

"Apparently the dressmaker was appalled to think that you would wear her hard work with the *ugly, outdated men's shorts people from the mainland use.* She forced me to bring these back to you. I think she slightly altered some of the dresses to be more in line with fashion here. Hey, maybe with these, Ransom won't turn you down next time."

I threw the pair of underwear I was holding at her, which she casually caught midair and tossed back in the box in a single movement.

"I would have paid good money to watch that dressmaker explain what all these are to you," I laughed.

"Fortunately for your coin purse, that didn't need to happen."

"What do you mean?" I gasped. "Is this what they wear in the East?" She chuckled. "No."

"Then how do you know this is underwear for my butt?"

"I've seen them in action here."

"Oh, I didn't know you had someone special here." George or Lina never would have kept a new partner from me, even if it was the Emperor himself. I was again reminded that Wynn and I weren't truly friends, no matter how much I'd come to like her.

"It's not exactly something I can draw attention to."

She couldn't confide anything in me that might reflect poorly on her. We were just associates, shoved together on the same mission. Of course she wouldn't share those personal details of her life with me when it could get her in trouble with the Protectorate.

The loneliness I felt in the company of others here was beginning to take its toll. Lev pushing me away, failing at this mission at every turn, Wynn keeping me at arm's length. It all dug at the emptiness inside of me.

"Well, I should head off to bed," I said, trying to sever the uncomfortable moment.

Wynn nodded and left without a good night.

I wasn't sure if Wynn was going to show up for our seventh day breakfast the next morning, but I woke early and dressed in hopes she would. She arrived at my door with a tray as though nothing had passed the night before, so I didn't mention it either. We ate around banal conversation for most of the meal. When I finally set down my fork, my thoughts were everywhere except with the weather we had been discussing.

"Wynn, I don't know what to do anymore."

"With what? That underwear? I am not the one to show you how to put those on." She smirked impishly. "I bet Ransom has seen things like that in Agora and would be willing to help."

"Which is it? Am I fumbling over Lev or sleeping with Ransom?" I snapped.

I was trying to be serious. Our lives were on the line and she was sitting here joking. I didn't need her to point out how clueless I was about everything. I was well aware.

The tension of the mission had worn me so thin, I was fighting with one of the only people I could probably trust. I sunk my head into my hands. "I'm sorry, this mission..."

She patted the top of my head awkwardly. "There's no law saying you can only be attracted to one person at a time. Nothing wrong with having a few options at your disposal." She bit into an apple and a feline smile spread across her face. "Do you want to know who I would choose if I cared for men? Now, I think Ransom would—"

"Wynn," I said flatly, "I'm serious." My desperation was enough for her to change her demeanor.

She sighed. "Sorry. *Serious* isn't my strong suit."

There was no point in hiding the truth from her. "I spoke with Lev while you were away. He said Drakemore wasn't happy with how little we've collected so far and is threatening to dismiss us from the Protectorate when we return."

"Ancient Bastard." She looked out the window. "I just can't believe you were thrown into this with no training. I mean, if you're found out, it's all of our lives. Maybe that's finally sinking in for Lev, that his life is on the line too."

"Thanks for your vote of confidence." I rolled my eyes. "I didn't really need another reminder that I'm going to get four *more* people killed, plus myself."

"You—" She looked at me through squinted eyes. "Oh, yeah. That executioner. Well, he was no great loss anyway." She shrugged and started preparing another piece of toast.

I stared at her. She had so casually dismissed the tragedy that started this chain of events leading to us sitting here. I tried to respond to her several times, opening my mouth and shutting it again, but only succeeded in making myself look like a fish.

It was such a stark difference in outlook, and it made me wonder about Wynn's past again. Was there even more she hadn't revealed yet?

I knew we weren't supposed to talk about my life before, even in private, but I couldn't hold it back. Wynn and I were never really good at sticking to that particular rule anyway.

"The executioner is the only reason we're here. If I hadn't failed to protect him, I wouldn't have been sent to the First and I wouldn't have asked for you to come on this mission with me."

She blew air through her pursed lips. "You really believe that? The *only* reason you're here is because you look enough like what people know of Aurora. The Empire would have found a way to force you into this no matter what. I think it was just a happy coincidence for them that they could blame you for that death and use it as an excuse to get you here." She chewed another bite of toast. "Or I bet they staged the whole incident to make you not question a thing."

I looked down at my cup of coffee.

Fuck, she was right.

Lev had told me I was the only person in the Empire who could pull off this impersonation.

I would have ended up here no matter what happened that day in the Old Square. Was it convenient timing that I had failed so egregiously the day before that the Imperial Protectorate needed to move me to the First? Or did they need to move me without question?

I had been too guilt-ridden to really reflect on that day before now, the service duty change, the Committee hearing. Now it felt painfully obvious.

Duty with the executioner was almost never just a single Protector. Except that day. The day a Protector who had never done more than observe that duty was moved to it. General Drakemore knew the crowds had been getting worse, and yet I was still sent there alone.

It was not a far step to wonder if some coin had been pressed into a few hands in a poor neighborhood. How much convincing would it take to tell a young boy that he would get to eat tonight if he distracted a Protector who was aiding in taking his father from him?

Wynn looked at me as she took a bite of bacon. "Look who's finally starting to see what could be possible."

The morning after the free day, Lev was at training with the rest of us for the first time since we'd kissed. He even asked me to pass him a practice sword at one point. I caught him watching me several times that morning, probably as many times as he caught me admiring his muscled body flowing through the movements.

On the walk back inside the castle, Lev came up next to me. "Your form looked really good today, Aurora." His eyes lingered on me for a moment before he hurried off into the castle. Maybe one part of my plan with Ransom had worked.

When I entered the secret afternoon lesson in Jo's room, Ameal was sitting at the table with Wynn. I hesitantly moved to take a seat next to Wynn, followed closely by Jo after he locked the door behind me.

"I pulled out this stack of missives for us to go through today," Jo said, pushing a pile of papers to the center of the table.

I looked between the pile of papers, Jo, and Ameal, until finally Ameal spoke. "Some notes came our way from the guards from other parties...after your very public conversation with the crime lord." Ameal leaned back in his chair, crossing his arms and glanced at Jo. "It seems you ruffled a few feathers. It was requested that I attend these afternoon sessions to help ensure your safety in the upcoming weeks and aid with some proposed future strategies."

I guess now Ameal was part of our group of collaborators, possibly unwillingly, but it was very reassuring to know that Jo was willing to risk exposure over my security.

"What did those notes say?" I asked.

Ameal responded with a look that shut my mouth and set me to reading through the letters on the table. The others joined in, grabbing letters and pointing out anything that seemed important.

"What does *Committee Authority* mean?" I asked.

"Where do you see that?" Jo leaned over my shoulder to look at what I was reading.

"Right here." I pointed to the page. "It says, 'The Protectors are getting more aggressive with their Committee Authority each month.' I never had Committee Authority. Did you?" Jo shook his head and looked at Ameal, who frowned.

"It means," Wynn said, "Protectors who are stationed away from the Capital or Rangers patrolling areas without duty stations can make judgments on offenders."

"So they can..." I didn't even know what that might mean.

"They can see a crime, decide if it was heinous enough to merit punishment and carry out the punishment without consulting anyone else," Ameal finished for me. "It's supposed to be used in only the most extreme circumstances. For people who are a danger to others and can't wait for the monthly caravans to Capital City to be judged by the Committee, but that doesn't always happen." By the tone of Ameal's voice, maybe he was more willing to be here than I initially gave him credit for.

Committee Authority sounded like a power people could easily exploit. Given my recent conversation with Wynn, I was unsettled by the potential abuses. The information compressed my chest and made it hard to focus.

I sat there surrounded by those trying to help me achieve the Emperor's goals. People who knew about this darker side of the Protectorate, but were forced to serve a cause whether they agreed with it or not. I had known some of the Empire's policies were less than ideal, but I hadn't been aware that they were like this.

I couldn't personally come to terms with all it meant while I needed to complete this mission, but it was information I needed to know to play the role of Aurora. The inability to process it tightened the squeeze in my chest that was a stifling reminder of just one more way I wasn't fit to be here.

"Now," Wynn said, "let's get down to it. We need to make sure you don't fuck up the dinner in a few days like you did that lawn game. Fortunately, you did give us one advantage that day."

Right, we still had to survive the next few weeks. "I did?"

"Everyone in that room is going to underestimate you," she said.

CHAPTER TWENTY-FIVE

By the dinner that week, we had a plan, and I was prepared to face the other leaders. Wynn, Jo, Ameal, and I had been plotting like the best of them. I was as ready as I could be.

My first course of action was to wear one of the newly altered dresses. I didn't agree with the seamstress's claims that these were *slight alterations*. The sleeveless black dress with a scooped neck that I had been excited to wear, was now a plunging neckline, dipping to expose more of my breasts in a new way. I couldn't wear this without some sort of undergarment. Or maybe glue. It made me realize the box from the seamstress was more practical than I initially thought. The skirt was tight enough that anything I owned would show through the fabric, so I had to venture into the realm of underwear that didn't cover my butt cheeks.

Resigned to my fate, I pulled the box down from the high shelf in my dressing chamber and dumped it on the floor. I found the underwear for my butt and a brassiere that allowed the plunge of the neckline. Feeling very foolish and uncomfortable, I put the dress back on and was amazed by the effect. Perhaps I owed some credit to the fashionable folks of Nixia. I had never felt sexier in my life, and this was just a dress to wear to a random dinner, not even the masterpiece I'd be wearing for the final ball.

I pulled down the topmost trunk from my stack, the one I had removed the lining from, and shoved all the other undergarments into it. I would clearly need these more accessible in the future and didn't want to leave them somewhere a maid might happen upon them. Wynn helped me braid my hair half back and applied a small amount of cosmetics to my face.

I didn't usually spend too much time on my appearance, but maybe I should. I looked like a different woman. The embodiment of a capable leader. Confident and ready for battle. Wynn gave me a few final words of advice before we headed downstairs. "Everything is ready. Play your part right and we know we'll get what we need."

I entered the hall and was pleased to see more than a few heads turn my way. I really hoped it was because I looked glamorous and confident, not because I made a total ass of myself the last time I was with all these people. I found that I was seated next to the head of the table where Queen Elara sat, with Ransom on my other side. Perfect.

"Is this me?" I said to Ransom playfully as I approached my chair, leaning over unnecessarily far in his direction as I took my seat.

"Mother's tits, Fox," Ransom muttered as he looked at the view I was providing.

"Tits indeed!" Queen Elara said with a wide smile. "This is why I wanted you here next to me, Aurora. I knew you would be fantastic entertainment with Ransom tonight after the lawn games." Queen Elara grinned at me then Ransom. I beamed at her as I situated myself in my chair. I twisted my entire body to Ransom, propping my elbow on the back of my chair to block Queen Elara from our conversation, and pressing my chest forward.

His eyes struggled to stay on my face. That bolstered my spirits that this was going according to plan, and had the intriguing side effect of making me feel sensual and desirable, which was a nice change after being snubbed by Lev.

"So," I said, "regretting your decision?"

He let out an exasperated breath and turned his back to me to talk to Mira on his other side. I pressed my goblet to my lips and pretended to take a sip of my wine as I suppressed a grin. That was the second course of action tonight—not get drunk, and keep my head in the moment.

I shifted back to chat with the queens and king about the climate here versus in Moriale. Since my lessons with Jo, I didn't feel intimidated by conversation focused on a simple topic such as the weather in a place I'd never lived. They had prepared me well to describe what life was like in the East on the day-to-day. When the conversation moved to more historical aspects around the architecture there, I was grateful for my lessons with Lev too.

Eventually the food was served, and Ransom had to turn back. I made sure to keep my back straight and chin up as I ate. With him being so much taller than me, he would be able to see down my dress, practically to my navel if he looked over. I was pleased to catch his eyes wandering a few times out of my peripheral vision.

When dessert was being served, Ransom leaned over to me. "Fine, yes. You're doing a great job making me rethink every decision I've ever made in my life." I smiled at my plate. "In my defense, you were completely wrecked off that lemonade, and I would never take someone to bed in that condition."

"I'm a little surprised that would have stopped a crime lord like you. Isn't all your power derived from not having any morals?"

"I have morals." He frowned. "They may not be the same as the Empire's, but I have them. And they certainly include not taking advantage of women who are clearly in a bad way."

I looked at him blankly, my brows raised. I knew far too many men who were good by the standards of the Empire, Protectors even, and yet they had no qualms with bringing home the most intoxicated woman they could find at the Blushing Pony, some barely able to stand as they left the tavern. So, it was no act when the side of my mouth ticked up. "Hmm, I think I might change my opinion of you too."

A smirk spread across his handsome features, and my heart was beating harder than it had been a moment ago.

I needed to get on with this before my mind wandered too far. "I think I've had enough dessert. Ransom, do you know if all the leaders' rooms are the same?" I was no longer bothering to keep my voice low.

"I think it's worth investigating." He set his napkin on the table.

Silverware clattered against a dish next to me, and I looked over to see Queen Atla picking her fork up off her plate and staring at us, open-mouthed.

"I knew this would be worth it," Queen Elara said with a giddy smile, her sharp canines on full display.

Ransom and I slipped away from the hall through a doorway near our end of the table, my arm tucked through his. We walked in a comfortable silence, the warmth of him next to me soothing my nerves for what was about to come.

Once we were both in my sitting room, I closed and locked the door behind us so we wouldn't be interrupted.

"Sit," I commanded. As I crossed to the cabinet to get out two glasses and a bottle of brown liquor, he sunk into the sofa by the fireplace and watched me pour a measure into the glasses.

"It's been entertaining to watch you progress through this Gathering, Fox." He was very pleased with all this, leaning back into the plush fabric, and spreading his legs wide. "I will admit, the tack you're taking now is the most enjoyable for me."

I handed him a glass while finishing mine in a single swallow. Setting the cup down on the side table, I stood between his legs. It was time. I shouldn't have been so nervous.

I placed my hands on his thighs and leaned in toward him. "Are you ready to finally do this? I'm so tired of my needs not being met here."

He leaned forward, inches from my face. "Look at you, Fox, playing with your food before you eat it." He ran a finger along my jaw. A tingle followed the path of his touch and sparked a thrill that traveled to my spine.

He took another quick look at the neckline of my dress, as though he couldn't resist. "But maybe you're the one who should be eaten," he said with such pounding intensity that I squeezed my thighs together as my stomach flooded with heat. Shit, was he going to make me actually enjoy this? "I told you that first night you looked delicious. I have no doubt it's true." He was looking at me as though he would like nothing better than to lick me and find out. I swallowed hard and tried to ignore the way my core was molten and my legs had suddenly gone weak.

"You're really good at this," I admitted in a much huskier voice than a moment ago. I slid my hands up his thighs, trying to play his game too. Unfortunately, it also made me take notice of the powerful muscles that were only separated from my hands by the thin material of his pants. How would those thighs feel bare and moving against me? Fuck.

"You're not so bad yourself," he said, his voice low. He leaned in a little further, reaching a hand up to touch my waist in a gentle caress. My skin was already hot and overly sensitive. The added warmth of his hand was almost too much. A breathy sound slipped out of me.

His eyes flicked down to where my hands were on his legs. "Go on, have a seat."

I held his gaze for another moment before straightening and walked to the chair next to the couch. He burst into laughter and leaned back.

"Too bad no one was here to see our performance," he said, shaking his head and finishing his glass as he crossed an ankle over his knee. "Queen Atla would have truly been appalled. Even I believed you for a moment. You're really getting much better at playing the role."

"You were pretty convincing too." I leaned forward in my chair to pour us both more of the liquor. "It was a steep learning curve. Thank you for giving me another chance."

"Your guards are smart. They assured me your actions last week were atypical and you *are* worthy of an alliance." He tipped his glass toward me. "I wasn't sure that we could use the scene at the lawn games to our advantage, but they convinced me otherwise."

"Who says it wasn't my plan all along to get people to underestimate me?" I took another sip, trying to exude confidence like I'd been practicing with Wynn.

He laughed. "Oh, my little Fox. It's really too bad we met like we did. I might try to convince you to come back to Solterra with me. You have so much potential outside of all this."

"Oh, please. That would have never worked."

He had no idea how incapable I really was. It was only with the help of Wynn, Jo, and Ameal had I come this far. Afraid that doubt had clouded my face, I quickly fell back to the sultry character I had been playing to cover it. "You would have never been able to keep your hands off me. If I followed you to Solterra, it would only be a few months before you were willing to give up control of everything in Agora just to have me every moment of the day." I joked with the most unlikely scenario I could come up with.

He smiled and exhaled a huff of a laugh into his raised cup, eyes twinkling at me. His look made that idea seem a little less far-fetched than it felt a moment ago. A shiver ran up my spine.

"So, are you ready to commit?" he asked, getting the subject back on track.

"I am." I leaned forward, my elbows on my knees. "But I need to know specifics. I can't pledge that my men will be ready if I don't know when I need them or where they need to be."

He considered this. "It's a risk to give anyone those pieces." His eyes flicked low on me again. "Even if I really do want to know what untying that tiny black ribbon on your brassiere reveals."

"Ha ha," I said drily, sitting up again.

His lips curved into a mischievous smile. "You may have played your part too well. It's difficult to think of anything else."

"As far as I can tell, it's only decorative," I sighed, gesturing toward my chest. "Completely frivolous."

"I wouldn't say that particular area is frivolous."

"I suppose that's true. It seems to do a lot of work to keep your attention."

He laughed loudly, the gold tooth near the back of his mouth glinting in the firelight. "You only say that because you aren't able to see how much attention I pay to the other side of you."

I wasn't sure how much more of this pretend flirting I could do. My body was having a very hard time remembering this was an act. A constant, needy ache throbbed between my thighs, making my underwear stick to me.

"You have to give me something for me to give you something."

It took my mind a moment to realize he was talking about the rebellion. "Fine. Thirty thousand men at the ready."

"Thirty thousand?"

I nodded.

"Mira and I plan to converge on the Capital at the same time. We were hoping you would join us. Take out the serpent at the head," he said. "Thirty thousand extra men would certainly make the job a lot easier."

"What about Gallia? They're making moves at the same time too, right?"

"It's not my place to say. You need to talk to Gallia for that. Hopefully by now, you know they aren't the blood-sucking monster the Empire says." He chuckled.

"I'm finding out."

We exchanged looks that quickly became too heated. I directed my attention to the fire, letting the cozy crackle wash over me, while my body decided all the other lusty reactions I was having were not enough and they should be accompanied by my nipples being almost painfully hard. I swallowed the rest of my drink to give myself something to do besides thinking about how I was never this turned on with anyone.

Ransom looked my way with a hazy stare and a muscle jumped in his jaw. He stood up, clapping his legs with his hands. "We have a good foundation here, but I think that was enough fun for one night. I can't have people thinking I ravaged you too thoroughly."

I stood to walk him to the door. "Maybe I want them to think I don't share. Keep you from spilling my secrets in Queen Atla's bed."

"You do not have to worry about that. My preferences skew away from willowy monarchs."

"And what do they skew toward?" I laughed.

His eyes moved over my body so quickly, I wasn't even sure it happened.

"We'll talk again soon."

He stepped into the hallway and didn't bother to keep his voice down as he said, "I'll give you some time to recover, Fox. Let me know when you can walk straight and then we can do it some more."

"It's just a matter of when you'll be ready again," I said with a teasing tone.

I closed my door and started to head to my dressing chamber to get out of this dress, pulling hairpins out along the way. I reached the entrance to my bedchamber when a knock thumped on my door. I figured it was either Ransom coming back to say something he forgot or Wynn and Jo to check on how everything had gone.

I was wrong.

CHAPTER TWENTY-SIX

"What happened between you two?" Lev stepped in my room, snapping the door shut behind himself.

"Nothing," I replied immediately, wanting to soothe his evident displeasure, but the reply was almost too quick, seeming like a lie.

"Tell me everything he did." He locked my door before facing me.

"I don't think you get to ignore me for weeks, then start making demands of me." I was still channeling the confidence I'd built in myself that evening. Moments ago, I had been excited to tell him what I found out, thinking it might give us a fighting chance with the General. But, he didn't trust me. Didn't he see I wanted to do well for him?

"Listen." His tone changed to a plea as he began pacing the room. "I know I've been avoiding you. I honestly don't know what to do around you. We're on this mission together. We have an objective we need to complete, the safety of the Empire depends on it. There are so many lives that could be torn apart if this rebellion happens. What we're doing here is so important. I can't jeopardize that.

"I told myself it was fine to spend time with you, get to know you, in fact that it would help our mission. I told myself it was harmless to flirt with you. And then we kissed, and I knew we crossed a line. I'm in charge of you. Fraternizing with an underling could get us both thrown out. I needed to be the responsible one and distance myself. For both of our sakes."

He stopped in front of me, taking my hands in his.

"When I saw you earlier this week, at the lawn game, I wanted to help you. But you pushed me away. I was trying to give you the space you wanted." He gestured at me, my dress, "Then tonight, you, look at you. You made yourself irresistible. There was probably more than one reason Ransom wanted to get you in private." He dropped my hands to scrub his face.

"I was beside myself wondering what he was in here doing to you, what information he was seducing from you. I heard him leave and had to come over here immediately to check on you."

The emotions that rolled through me at his words made my head spin. He was objectively handsome, he felt like my only sense of security these weeks, and here he was, laying himself bare for me. I couldn't totally put aside the hurt I felt these past few weeks from his distance, but I understood his reasoning. My silence stretched on as I reflected.

"What did he do to you?" he repeated. "I–I need to know."

The desperation in his tone broke my steely resolve to keep him at arm's length. "Nothing. Just talked about his plans. I was getting information from him about the rebellion."

He breathed a shaky sigh of relief, cupping my face. "I was a fool to think you would be alright without me by your side. I need you to know you're mine. You always have been."

His words melted the last of the ice in my heart toward him. "But what about…?"

"I'll take whatever is to come. Just be mine."

He was willing to risk his career? For me? When it had been more important to him than dating at all these last few years?

I leaned into his hand and looked up at him. His thumb stroked my cheek as he took another step to me, closing almost all the distance between us. The warmth from his touch traveled through my body, heating me all over. The arousal from the too-realistic acting with Ransom earlier still lingered and blended with the feelings of Lev's caring words.

I wanted more of his skin on mine. I wanted to not feel lonely here. I wanted to know I was important to someone here and not because I looked like a dead dignitary. I wanted to be someone's.

I understood what Ransom meant earlier about not wanting someone in his bed to be pretending. All those touches and looks with Ransom were laced with the knowledge that it was all for show, all a plot to get to an end. He thought I was Aurora.

Lev was real. He was here because he wanted me. He knew who I really was and wanted that part of me. He wanted Ness.

I closed the remaining distance between us, pressing my body against his and tilting my head up. His lips crushed down on mine. The kisses before had been gentle and tentative. We knew we shouldn't, but couldn't resist.

This time it was unbound, fierce, assertive. He urged my mouth open. I obliged, letting his tongue possess me the way his lips had. His passionate need was unraveling me fast. It felt like it was the embodiment of his faith in me that I so badly needed to see. His callused hands cupped the soft skin of my cheeks. The heat in my core created a throb between my thighs again. My body was more than ready.

My hands slid around him, feeling reassurance in the strong muscles of his back through his tunic. His hand on my face slipped around and wove into my hair, his other hand grabbing my waist, pulling my hips hard against him where I could feel his pressing desire.

His lips moved from my mouth, trailing down my jaw, my throat. The hand in my hair pulled slightly, exposing more of my neck to him. His mouth traveled lower, kissing down to my collarbone to the tops of my breasts exposed by my dress. The press of his lips sparked heat everywhere they touched me, flooding my body with the desire for more.

I couldn't stand the clothing separating us any longer. I tore at his tunic with my hands, pressing it up over his head. He broke his touches just long enough to take the shirt off, then my hands were back on him, touching every hard inch of his torso I could. Crashing his lips against mine once more, the force of it bumped me into the table behind me.

He grabbed my hand and pulled me to the bedroom, and I kicked off my slippers on the way. When we got inside, there was a frenzy as his pants and shoes came off. He kissed me as though everything important to him depended on it. The desperate passion, the feeling of being wanted so badly stoked the heat in my blood.

His hands found the high slits on the sides of the dress. Reaching under it to travel up my leg, he found the band of my underwear and pulled it down. The cool flush of air on my most overheated parts pulled a small gasp from me. This night had been too highly charged. I couldn't hold myself together anymore.

He guided me by my hips to sit on the bed, and leaned me back. He took off his own underwear before leaning forward again, kissing me, letting his mouth move down my body, along the places the neckline of my dress exposed. His lips pressed soft dots of heat into my already blazing chest.

He bunched up my gown around my hips with slow movements of his hands, stroking my skin as though he needed to memorize the feel of me.

He slowly trailed his hand toward the part of me so desperate for touch. Slipping his fingers between my thighs, he circled around my clit with his first two fingers. Mother Creation, this was the friction I had been craving since I got to my room. I was already so slick and sensitive, needy noises kept slipping out of me.

I gave in to it and ground my hips without constraint against his hand. The teasing ache that had been building in me since dinner turned molten once more. He moved his hand lower still to feel more wetness at my entrance, and another low sound rumbled from his throat.

"I'm glad to know that you want this as much as I do." His strokes plunged inside of me. I threw my head back against the bed and let out a moan. He drew his fingers in and out slowly, coiling the tension in me tighter and tighter. I was on the cusp of release. The lingering arousal from this evening had made short work of it.

The frustration of this mission, the loneliness, the fear, it all tumbled out of my mind when my muscles tightened around his fingers. I hadn't finished riding the wave of calm when his hands drew back.

He shifted his position and the press of his tip was at my entrance. He thrust into me and paused with his forehead pressed to my collarbone for a second, savoring the joining before moving again. After that, it was a continuation of the frenzied kiss we'd shared. We needed to prove this was worth the repercussions if we got caught. As he moved in me, I focused on him, his enjoyment.

I wanted him to be happy with me. He would be happy if this mission went well. Ransom had given me what I needed tonight. My mind flickered to the memory of me leaning over the crime lord earlier, the fiery feeling of his firm thighs under my hands.

I refocused my attention on the feel of Lev inside me as his hands squeezed my hips, pulling me harder into him.

Trying in vain to regain the tension that my thoughts had let slip away, I tightened my muscles around him to heighten the sensation. His movements became wilder, faster, with forceful strokes that sought to claim more of me until he reached a climax.

Once he rolled off me, we lay next to each other for a long while, our panting breaths the only sound.

"This is certainly my most enjoyable assignment yet." He ran a finger over the swell of my hip. "When business and pleasure mix."

I laughed as I forced myself away from the refuge of the bed, my dress falling back over my legs as I stood to go to my bathing chamber to tidy myself up. I spun to look at him from the doorway, almost afraid he would disappear as soon as he was out of sight.

"Will you stay the night, or do you need to leave?" I asked tentatively.

"I should really get going. The longer I stay here, the greater our chances of getting caught become."

"That makes sense." I smiled weakly and went into the bathing chamber, trying not to acknowledge the waves of emotions flowing through me. When I returned to the bedroom wearing a robe, Lev was completely dressed and standing ready by the doorway.

"We need to get down the details of what Ransom told you tonight before I go."

"Oh, right. It won't be hard, I didn't get much from him." I walked out with him to my table.

He quickly jotted down what I told him from Ransom as I collected my discarded shoes from around the sitting room. With a quick peck on my lips, he left my room for his own.

It took me a long time to fall asleep that night, despite how tired I was. When I did, I had dreams of the crowd surging against me in the Old Square and getting knocked to my stomach, like so many nights before. Then the scene started playing out differently than it ever had before. When I looked up from the ground, Lev was offering me a hand to get up, but before he could grab me, he noticed Jenkins struggling and rushed to help him instead. I laid my head back on the gritty cobblestones, accepting my fate as the warmth of blood dripped out of my nose and across my cheek.

I wanted to close my eyes in the dream, but I couldn't. I was forced to watch from the ground as Jenkins was beaten and stopped breathing. Lev never made it to him. I didn't know where he went.

I couldn't look away from Jenkins lying motionless on the ground. Tears started to mix with the blood running down my face. Then, I was scooped up into strong arms, cradled against a firm body.

"Ness," the man holding me said, his deep voice was familiar and soothing. "Ness, you can't help him. You never could. You don't belong here."

My head turned away from the pain and guilt at the sight of Jenkins. The bright sun, high in the sky, forced the man holding me into silhouette. He began to walk out of the square, changing the angle of the sun to my eyes, but before I could see his face, I woke up.

CHAPTER TWENTY-SEVEN

I didn't get a chance to spend personal time with Lev for the rest of the week. He received some missive from the Empire that caused him to need to spend a great deal of time alone in his room.

Training started to run longer than normal. I began to eat a quick breakfast and go directly to my lessons with Lev and Jo. We spent more time than normal going through the complex history of particular towns and how they related to the Great War, but I didn't mind. It was evident that Lev was pleased to be in my company again, and every time Jo stepped away, he found a reason to touch me casually. A brush on my arm as he reached for a paper, a hand on my shoulder as he brought me tea, his knee bumping my leg under the table.

From there, I went straight to have a late lunch in Jo's room where we held unsanctioned lessons. Jo, Wynn, and Ameal had come to the conclusion that I should be the one providing all the information to Lev, so we also had daily reports where they relayed what they were picking up from their connections at the Gathering.

After we finished eating, we started working on what we wanted to achieve these final few weeks with the other groups and my new connection with Solterra. They all said they would work with their contacts as well. It felt nice to know that this mission wasn't totally on my shoulders anymore.

By the afternoons, I was exhausted, still covered in my own dried sweat, and could not wait to finally make it to my bath. One such afternoon, as I opened the hot water tap, I realized I hadn't felt that sense of melancholy at my small loss of superiority. In fact, I was pleased to think that I didn't need to expend any energy to make this bath. Then, I was delighted to think that every day after training, Wynn, Jo, Ameal, and Lev got to have relaxing hot baths. I smiled as I touched the hot water pouring into the tub. I liked the idea of getting to spend my energy elsewhere. More than that, I liked the idea of my friends enjoying this too.

The event that week was another group of musicians, but this time, they included instructors who taught all of us the steps to the dances. Queen Elara, wanting to continue her idea of fun, assigned Ransom as my partner, and placed us next to King Row and Queen Atla.

Ransom walked up to me, dressed as handsomely as ever. I really wished my enemy wasn't so attractive. "Fox, you look stunning this evening, as always." I glanced down at the relatively simple dark green dress with gold embroidery on the bodice, but nothing was particularly special about it. He must have been furthering the lovers ruse. I put on a grin as the music started to play around us, keeping my eyes on his face and making us look like a content couple.

Queen Atla approached us with a sneer on her face. "Look at her," she said loudly, her eyes raking over me with Ransom. "She looks more boring than pond water."

"Don't fret, darling," King Row said. "I've heard he's only with her to get access to Moriale's armory. Once their deal is signed, he'll tire of her and we'll get our fun." They walked away to their space on the dance floor laughing. My false smile faltered.

"Ignore them," Ransom said, adjusting his hand on my waist for the dance.

I realized Ransom and I did have to pretend to be a couple to continue our plan that kept me informed and the royals from Kind further away from him, but there were no rules about what kind of couple we were pretending to be.

We began to move through the steps of the song, then as we pulled apart and Queen Atla swished past us, I loudly proclaimed, "The servants had to throw those sheets away after what we did to them. Unsalvageable, they said."

Ransom's brows shot up in surprise, but he was also smiling. Queen Atla's audible huff made both of us shake with barely contained laughter.

"The people of Moriale are tired of giving our crops over to the Emperor," I muttered as a spin brought me in close to his ear. He gave a quick nod in acknowledgement.

Another set of steps brought us back near the royalty of Kind once more. Ransom's deep voice clearly said in their direction, "I didn't think I would like it, but you were right to insist. Next time, we'll use more oil." This time, King Row gave an indignant huff at the comment. Both of us barely kept it together long enough to swish away.

On the next movement that drew our faces near he said, "Solterra doesn't have much of a population, but we do have connections to mercenaries beyond the mist." The mist was lightest near the Southern State, so I took this as a credible bit of information. However, even if he sent word the moment we returned from the Gathering, the mercenaries couldn't arrive before next summer over that distance. I realized then he'd mentioned the mercenaries to me before, but I'd been too focused on other things to note it then.

"So you can't mobilize before summer?" I whispered when we were far from other ears again. He gave an almost imperceptible shake of his head.

We were next to Queen Atla and King Row once more. "I'm still sore," Ransom said, just a second before I started with, "I'll make sure the strap is tighter next time." The royals scoffed, dancing away from us and out of their designated space as Ransom and I shared in unbridled laughter.

The song ended and we found a pillar to stand against. A servant was walking by with drinks, and he snagged two cups from the tray as he passed. He handed me a cup of what turned out to be blackberry wine.

I watched him over the rim of my cup. "That was almost too easy."

"I hope I'm never so bored with whoever I marry that I end up like them."

We watched the king and queen bicker their way off the dance floor.

"Do crime lords want to get married?"

"I prefer 'Rogue Governor.' The Empire does recognize my leadership, after all." He surveyed me as he took another sip. "And I'm not entirely opposed to the idea."

"Ah, this Gathering has you seeing the benefits of a political marriage?"

"Oh, Mother, no."

A slower song was starting, and a servant came to collect our glasses and usher us back to the dance floor. Ransom took my hand and waist, holding me much closer for this dance. I wrapped my arm around his shoulders, leaning close and breathing in the pleasant smell of him.

"More like, I can now see the benefits of the right person," he said quietly, restarting the conversation that I had figured was over.

"How will you know it's the right person?"

"When it's the right person, I won't be able to let her go."

I looked up at him, meeting his eyes. "Oh, I thought it would be that they would use the appropriate amount of oil the first time."

He gave me an unreadable look as the corners of his mouth kicked up. Something about it made me laugh. I stifled the snicker by leaning my cheek against his chest until I got myself under control again.

When I lifted my head back up, he was looking at me with his sparkling brown eyes, and tucked one of my curls behind my ear. We continued to move in slow circles, the heat from him soaking into me and making me feel more at ease than I had in a long time.

The song finished. Couples all around us were clapping and heading off for refreshments. He released my hand, but left his arm around my waist as he guided me off to a corner of the room. The warmth of his arm remained on me while we stood by a wall for another round of drinks and more whispered information.

The cold of the castle pressed against me as soon as Ransom dropped his grip on me at the end of the night.

Wynn was already in my room, helping me out of my dress when Lev arrived to get my report. Not able to figure out an excuse for him to hang around, he left after I gave him the information on the mercenaries. He gave me a look that said we would try again later. I wasn't bothered by his departure. My thoughts were still lingering around what Ransom had said about knowing when someone was the right person.

The following day there was no training, and I was just sitting down in a chair by my fireplace to read when a knock came from my door. Assuming it was Lev returning in the morning to do what we could not the night before, I jumped up to answer it. However, it was a servant dropping off enough breakfast for a small army. Fuck, how I had forgotten about seventh-day breakfasts with Wynn?

When the last of the food was set on my table, Wynn walked in through our shared door. "Jo and Ameal should be here shortly."

"Why?" I asked.

"To find out how last night went, obviously." She sat down and spread a napkin across her lap.

"Ah, well, you know I already told Lev."

"I know. I think Jo and Ameal want to review *our* tactics, not information. How you felt you did, knowing what we've been teaching you. How this new partnership is going. You know, that type of stuff."

I leaned over to look at my door that was still ajar from the servants. Lev might still plan to come over, if his thoughts were in the same place as mine.

"Everyone is fully team Aurora Succeeding. We have a vested interest in that." She sat at the table and piled eggs and fruit onto her plate.

Jo and Ameal walked through my door a moment later, closing it behind themselves.

"Leave it unlocked. Lev might show too." I said it as much for Lev as I did to caution them.

Lev did step into my room moments later and looked around at the assembled group. I was glad I warned the others he might be here, as it gave Wynn, Jo, and Ameal time to adjust. Lev, however, was wholly shocked to find the entire rest of the delegation of the East eating at my table like we did this every day off.

Realizing there wouldn't be enough chairs, Wynn begrudgingly abandoned her eggs to grab one from her room through our shared door.

When she returned with the chair and silence blanketed our group, thick and heavy. I cleared my throat, searching for any way to break through the clicking of silverware. "Wynn, what's that fruit you're eating? I don't think I've seen it before."

"Really?" she asked in disbelief. "Places like Kind export it all the time. We used to have it occasionally at home."

"I guess I've lived a very sheltered life. No sweet cakes or imported fruit for me."

"It's called pineapple." She pushed several yellow wedges onto my plate. "Have some, it's delicious. And Ransom will appreciate it if you do." I had no idea what she meant by that, but Lev coughed into his coffee and Ameal snorted while chewing his eggs. Jo and I exchanged confused looks.

I decided to redirect the conversation rather than wade into whatever that was about. "We already know from the other night that Ransom and Mira are planning on working in tandem to storm the capital at the same time. They want the forces from the East to join them, and they figure they will be able to easily capture the Imperial Compound with their combined numbers."

"That's expected," Jo said. "That's why we're all here, right? To coordinate efforts. But we talked through this before, the South doesn't have the numbers."

Hopefully, Lev wouldn't pick up on the fact that we had discussed this without him. I pressed on before Lev had time to think about it. "Last night, I got confirmation that the South plans on using mercenaries. From beyond the mist."

"Did you find out what Kind's role is in all this, or Nixia for that matter?" Lev asked. I looked down at the food I was pushing around my plate with my fork. He already knew I didn't have any further information from Kind or Nixia.

"No, I haven't. I've been focused on the biggest threats so far." I looked around to Jo, Wynn, and Ameal. "Have any of you heard any whispers? Surely the other delegations are having their own group meals, sharing details of their days."

Jo shook his head. "The others have been tight-lipped around me as far as that's concerned."

"I've been building trust with the other guards." Ameal stabbed a slice of melon on his plate. "Especially from Solterra. They're easiest for me, since I was stationed in Agora before coming here. Maybe they'll get too comfortable and let something slip."

"You don't need to try too hard. *Aurora* already has Solterra taken care of," Wynn teased. "If you become their contact, she'll be sleeping with Ransom only for fun." Jo and Ameal chuckled.

They knew nothing was actually happening between Ransom and myself. They had been working with me for days and helping me formulate my plans. Ameal's connections to the Solterra guards was truly for my benefit, ensuring that Ransom and I were on the same page with our act.

Lev stiffened, though, his shoulders going tight like Wynn's words undid the truth I had already given him. I wanted to laugh along with the others, but I felt the need to make Lev feel more at ease. This thing between us was so new and fragile.

"We're not actually having sex," I said with an eye roll.

"We know," Wynn said. "It was just a bit of light groping." I couldn't resist that and burst into laughter with Jo and Ameal. Wynn gave a self-satisfied smile. Her words felt for the first time like I was talking to Lina and George again, the easy camaraderie and teasing feeling like the friendship I was forced to leave behind.

Lev forced a small chuckle as he tried to match the energy of the rest of us, but it was apparent he didn't think it was funny. I couldn't tell if he didn't like the jokes of me being with someone else, or if it was his need to stick to the etiquette of being our commander. It was so obvious that this was all in jest, it must be the latter.

"I know this is all fun and games, but if you get tired of this tactic with Ransom, just let us know. We can help you find a new plan," Jo said.

I knew he was trying to look out for me, making sure I wasn't pushing myself into situations I was no longer comfortable in. Oddly, this strategy with Ransom was one I was good at and didn't want to stop. Ransom and I had fallen into this easy alliance of sharing information over a flirtatious performance, and it was fun. Plus, I was finally contributing to our mission in a meaningful way. "No, I'm not tired of it," I said with certainty.

"Are you sure? You don't *have* to present yourself as promiscuous and vapid to everyone at the Gathering. We can find lots of other means to our end." Lev stared at me as though his eyes could force me to change my answer.

I stared back and didn't respond. I could understand him not loving the idea of the woman he was involved with pretending to be with someone else, but this was for the mission. Why was he trying to take this away from me?

"Oh, boo-hoo," Wynn said. "A woman finds an advantage that men don't have, and she's good at it! Then immediately men want to take it from her. Big surprise."

"That's not what I was getting at," Jo said quietly.

"I know," I said. "You are just looking out for me. Thank you, Jo."

The tension remained in the room, so I added, "What about you, Wynn? Do you have any *special* connections that are giving you information?"

She gave me a long look, silently communicating that the next time she laced up a dress for me, I wouldn't be able to breathe the entire night.

"Not really. I usually sit next to the lady's maid for Queen Elara. We chat a little, but she hasn't given me anything worth sharing. Mostly that Nixia needs to know where everyone stands before the queen will make any decisions, but I don't think that's news. Breaking the treaty is a big deal, and she won't make that decision lightly."

"I've spoken a bit to the other advisors," Lev volunteered. "I've made the most headway with Frange, the advisor from Kind. She hasn't said much of importance, only that the king and queen are not enthusiastic about another war. They may not have been in charge during the Great War, but the memories of the economic difficulties it brought still haunt their island."

"Economic? They don't worry about the deaths of their people?" I asked, brows pressing together. It was unfathomable to me that rulers would place the value of their trade over the people they served.

Lev shook his head. "No, they didn't send any soldiers into the fray last time. Their alliances and treaties only allowed them to supply goods to those fighting the Emperor's unification. Ships, swords, food, that sort of thing. Wars cost a lot of money, and the other kingdoms were grateful for that help."

"Hmm," Wynn hummed. "Well, maybe you should take a page from Aurora's book and fool around with old Frange, see if you can convince Kind to share a little more."

Ameal, Jo, and I looked between the two of them as silence stretched across the table. Lev let out a bemused grunt and shook his head.

There was no more talk of our interactions with the members of the other groups for the rest of the meal. After we were done eating, Jo and Ameal left with mumbled excuses that I didn't hear over my swirling thoughts.

Lev and Wynn were having an unspoken competition to not leave me alone with the other.

No one was a winner in this extremely uncomfortable endeavor, as we all sat in an ever-expanding silence, sipping our very cold coffees.

CHAPTER TWENTY-EIGHT

Finally, Lev relinquished my company to Wynn and left to go finish his latest report to the Empire.

As soon as the door snapped shut behind him, Wynn's posture relaxed. "I thought he would never leave and I would have to guard you all day." I raised my brows at her. "I didn't want him to take my snide remarks out on you once I left."

"Do you think he would do that?" I set my cup back on the table and looked at her.

"We all have eyes, Ness." My name, again, was a jolt through me. I was so unused to hearing it.

"What do you mean?"

"He's got some sort of sway over you I don't understand. It's like you think if you can please him, it will take back what happened at the Old

Square. He can pressure you into anything, even thinking it was your fault I was out of line at breakfast."

"I don't think that's true." Yet I couldn't stop my shoulders from slumping at her words.

"Really? You were jumping through hoops to reassure him just thirty minutes ago. After you didn't make headway the first few weeks, he ignored you, but that didn't deter you, you just tried harder for this mission. It was pretty obvious to the rest of us. Only after you got some good information, suddenly he's able to spend time with you again. I'm not sure why you're his punching bag, but I don't like it. Why do you think we decided you should give all the information to Lev? It's not to make it less confusing for him, it's so he would understand your value."

Damn, Wynn was really starting to feel like an actual friend, being protective of me. But she was also wrong. There was so much more to Lev's interactions with me than what she was seeing, and it pained me to not be able to correct her. Plus, what she was saying made me seem so...weak.

"If I didn't keep trying, it would have been bad for all of us. We all need this mission to go well," I said. "And he's under a lot of pressure. If we don't get enough information, the entire Empire could be in jeopardy, and that would cost Lev his position in the Protectorate, everything he's worked for his whole life." The reason I was always on the back foot when I talked to Lev was because the mission overlaid every interaction we had.

She scoffed. "I don't think you need to worry about what happens to him after this. He sure as shit won't care what happens to you in three weeks."

I wanted to tell her how wrong she was, but I realized I didn't know if she *was* wrong. This fledgling thing with Lev was undefined and uncertain. I was steadied by him, but could I say it was anything more than infatuation with a person who had power over me in a time when I was powerless? Was his draw anything more than that of an attractive man showing interest in me during a period I felt worthless and was full of self-doubt? That was exactly what George and Lina had spotted as my pattern, trying to anchor myself in a relationship when I was unmoored.

I flirted with Ransom and that didn't mean anything. I wasn't tripping over myself to impress the crime lord. He was an attractive man, and he certainly acknowledged my worth with every conversation we had. Even when he thought I was trying to drunkenly sleep with him, he believed I was cunning enough to use it to get information from him or sway his standing.

"Maybe, maybe not," I said. "But if this goes well, he could be a powerful voice with the Emperor after this. It would be nice to be in his good graces."

"After this? You don't think he's not already?" Wynn rapped her knuckles on the tabletop. "He has the ear of everyone important."

"How do you know that?"

"I peeked to see who his messages were addressed to. The Emperor himself is taking his correspondence."

"Wynn! You opened those letters?"

"My hand slipped. They were poorly sealed to begin with. But I couldn't read beyond the addressee because they were coded."

I shook my head. I could only deal with so many problems at a time. "Well, isn't it good that they are for the Emperor? That means the Emperor is taking the rebellion seriously," I countered quickly, trying to stop her spiral against Lev before this could get out of hand. "That means he can stop this rebellion before it even starts. Maybe he'll be able to sway the Emperor into changing his order, and we'll be able to do something to prevent this mess before anyone dies."

Wynn was quiet for a long while after that. She leaned back in her chair and looked at me carefully. "Do you still think of the revolution as a mess?"

Sure, I didn't love everything the Empire did. In fact, during my time as a Protector, I got to see some of the more unsavory things it did to maintain peace. But life in the Empire was stable. We were provided education, given the chance to elevate ourselves by unlocking our magic or serving in the Protectorate. When I had no idea how to survive on my own, joining the Protectorate had been Mother-sent. They gave me housing, food, money, and most of all, a place to belong.

Plus, deaths would come with an armed conflict in the Capital, which was full of unarmed families. I couldn't stand the idea of Polly and Jarvis losing everything if war destroyed the Blushing Pony. I wouldn't let the many innocent lives there be forfeited to someone else's game.

However, my thoughts nagged at me. The more I learned about current life in Moriale, the more I could understand the sentiments of the rebels. It was evident through Wynn's lived experiences and the documents Jo pulled from the boat that the Protectors stationed in Moriale felt it much easier to simply eliminate troublemakers, rather than jail them until the monthly transfers to the City for hearings.

When that evidence had started to pile up in our meetings, I had tucked it away from my emotions. My mind and heart were finite vessels, already too full of the mishmash of my life and said *nothing more right now*, closing the lid on those details to decide later if these downsides to the Empire were worth it for all it gave to us.

"Wynn, I get it. I really do. But I'm just trying to keep myself alive, keep all of us alive through this mission. If we're found out as imposters, we won't live long enough to choose a side in this rebellion. If we lose sight of the mission now, we don't stand a chance." My chair creaked as I shifted to look at her better. The sunlight from the window next to us illuminated the passion in her eyes.

Disbelief creased her face as she grabbed my hand resting on the table. "Now is the perfect time to think about this. If you wanted to, you could align with them here, prove you're on their side before the Empire gets a say. It could be the thing that *saves* your life. Moriale could have our culture and traditions back that were stripped from us. We could rule ourselves again and not be forced into the Empire's starve or serve policies."

"Yes, but that's a dream." I wanted her to see reason. "We don't know what will happen, even if there is a rebellion. I don't think anything the Empire has done is bad enough to condemn the lives of all the innocent families living in Capital City. To lose all these people to a cause that may not succeed, I'm not sure if it's worth it."

"Ness." She shook her head, releasing my hand and leaning away. "It's really time that you consider that your great education provided by the Empire might not have told you the truth about everything. Maybe they lied to you to keep you docile and against the rebels. Life could be better for everyone."

"What do you mean? They wouldn't lie about our history just to make us feel good about ourselves." Even as I spoke it, I knew it was possible she was right. I had never questioned it before. I was too busy just living my daily life. But here, I was forced to reconsider everything. Every interaction, every word said and unsaid.

"I went to an Imperial school as well. I also grew up in Polis. I lived the differences between those two experiences." Wynn ran a hand through her hair. "Have you considered at all why the Empire sent us here with the specific instructions not to interfere with the rebellion, only report on it? It seems to me that if the Empire truly cared about mortal lives, they would be having us do everything we can to stifle this fight before it starts, even if it meant losing us. I think they want this rebellion to start so the Empire can finally have the excuse they need to rid themselves of the loyal residents in the old kingdoms."

She stood and walked to her door. "Just think about it. And after you think about it, remember that everything you say to Lev goes straight to the Emperor's ear."

CHAPTER TWENTY-NINE

Wynn's words chased me through the routine of the sixth week. Training, planning, acting out our plans, making reports, and lessons, both sanctioned and unsanctioned, were all clouded by the ominous feelings crowding my chest.

At the dinner that week, I was seated next to Mira. This would have made me nervous a few weeks ago, but now a small exchange with her was an opportunity I wouldn't miss. "I've heard Ransom hasn't just been spilling himself into you lately, but also spilling some secrets," she said with a devious smirk on her lips.

I paused, unsure where this was going.

"It sounds like his plans for the future now heavily involve you." She dabbed her mouth with her napkin and looked at me, keeping her voice low. "I'm not sure what you've told him that is making him adamant that you are crucial to his plans, but you are part of this now whether I trust you or not." She eyed me up and down. "I can't decide if his plans are because you have something important no one else knows about yet, or if it's because you're the only warm place he's stuck his cock in a while."

I set down my silverware and gave her a bored look. This whole conversation would have embarrassed me beyond speech a few weeks ago, but it didn't even faze me now. I knew Mira didn't really care if I was or wasn't sleeping with Ransom, she cared about this rebellion. Everything here was a means to that end.

"I guess I could see if he's interested in a threesome, if you're so curious," I said.

"Ha, I know better than to get between a vixen and her mate. Foxes are known to be monogamous, after all."

It was good to know my relationship with Lev remained a secret, but an odd thrill went through me that this observant woman thought Ransom and I were truly together. It was a validation of our skills to know our act was that convincing.

"We're here with a purpose," I said. "I'm doing what I need to achieve my purpose. Naturally we're coordinating efforts. Never mind anything else that's going on. That's only for the Gathering."

She frowned at me. "So what do you know of Decca's plans from him?"

"That you plan on converging on the Capital at the same time as him." I faced her more fully.

"And I'm sure you know that he is relying on mercenaries that will not be in our realm until summer, at best," she asked without a question.

I nodded. "I also know my army would help turn the tides in your favor. How many men do you have?"

Mira smiled. "Tell me yours and I'll tell you mine."

"Thirty thousand that I can count on."

"Fifty thousand."

I didn't know the Northern State was that populous, or was she getting forces from elsewhere as well?

Before I could push the subject, she said, "When this gets hard, you will need a good reason why you are doing this, Aurora. I'm tired of the Empire controlling the lands my family cared for and leaving them in ruins. I wish Solterra was ready sooner, but I am willing to wait, if I get the payoff I want. I hope you are thinking hard about what you want and why you want it."

She stood, setting her napkin on top of her dessert, and left the table. Maybe I should have followed her to try to get more, but the conversation felt closed for now. Plus, I wasn't ready to walk away from this cake yet.

As I enjoyed bites of decadent chocolate, I looked across the table to see Ransom seated between Queen Atla and Queen Elara. He looked at ease in their discussion, but I noticed the little crease between his brows that I had come to recognize as him being done with whatever conversation he was in. It showed up a lot when Queen Atla was near. I smiled to myself. He caught my eye, as though hearing my thoughts, and smiled back.

Wynn and Jo left mid-week to send more letters and pick up the last of the dresses in Port Mora. Lev kept all the lessons as we normally held them. Just before midday, he looked over at me.

"You're wearing that necklace again," he said, pointing to the crystal I had my fingers wrapped around as I read the passage in front of me. "I don't recall it from Aurora's trunks, but the Moriale quartz seems the type of jewelry Aurora would wear."

"It was my mother's." I hadn't realized I was touching the pendant, but it brought me comfort.

"Hmm, I heard she passed away in your last year of school." I looked at him in confusion. "It was in your file from your previous commander," he answered my silent question.

"I didn't realize the notes about me were so thorough."

"It didn't include anything about your father." He leaned back in his chair.

"I wouldn't imagine that it would. I don't even know who he is. Every time I asked my mom, she would say, 'If he was worth knowing about, he would have stuck around.' Apparently he left Capital City shortly after my mother found out she was with child." I shrugged. It was ancient history in the scheme of my life, and I never bothered to spend much time thinking about it.

"You really have no clue who he might be?" he asked.

"None," I said. I pulled the pendant along my necklace chain, then I remembered it annoyed Lev, so I dropped the crystal.

"Too bad."

"My afternoon is free, if you'd like to spend a little time together," I said.

"I wish I could, but I have more reports to work on and we need to limit our interactions. The more time we spend together, the higher the chance we get caught. I would hate for the Protectorate to think we didn't gather enough information because we were too busy with each other."

"Right." I looked down at the book in front of me.

He leaned over and touched my hand. "You're still mine."

I gave him a weak smile before leaving.

I went straight to the stables to take Sugardrop on a ride, but ended up spending more time waiting for her to be readied than actually riding. It started to rain after only a few minutes. Sugardrop's indignant snorts and frequent stops under trees made me turn back.

When I returned to the stables, I wasn't the only person there returning their horse. Chancellor Parisa from Gallia was handing hers off to a stable hand as well.

"Too bad about the weather," I said to her with a smile, trying to use this time to my advantage.

"It certainly is." She smiled at me. "I haven't seen much of you these past few weeks, Aurora."

"Would you like to walk back together?"

"Please." Her smile widened enough to show off her sharp canines.

My mind raced through all the possible topics I could broach with Parisa and what Lev would want me to ask. Images of our lesson today flicked through my mind and how he'd brought up my necklace. The last time he had touched that necklace, he kissed me after I asked about the treaty.

"Forgive my ignorance," I said. "I've had so much to learn in such a short period of time, my advisor hasn't gotten to the finer details yet. What are the consequences of breaking the treaty?"

She frowned at me as we walked across the grass, the fine mist of rain rolling down our faces. "That was a big one for your advisor to leave out. I can't remember the wording exactly, but Elara has a copy in her library. It's something along the lines of 'Should anyone born of a land that signed the treaty make a move against the Empire, all those that act against the Empire will lose their magic.' It's a good motivation to stay where the Emperor put us."

"Yes, indeed. That's quite the decision," I said. "Then have Ransom and Mira already decided they would rather live in a land free from the Emperor than ever have long lives or the power to wield?"

She chuckled. "Have you? I suppose they are the only ones who could truly answer that question. Your lands will be hard to maintain without the protection of wielders who are loyal to you and them. That's why we're even having this Gathering, to prepare and for us each to decide if everyone is ready to take that leap. It's a big decision to make. The witches tried to stop the Emperor once, and it cost them their lives." We walked for a bit in silence. "The mist, that's the geographic isolation you should be thinking about."

"But we can travel beyond the mist," I said.

"Mortals sometimes can, yes. Fae tend to never return from that crossing."

"I didn't know that." I frowned. "I have wielder friends that want to travel to other lands."

"Bad news for them, and for yourself if you ever want to be unlocked. Territories rarely choose leaders that don't have fae blood," she said as we entered the castle.

"You think I have fae blood?"

"Ha," she laughed drily. "I know you do. It's obvious to those that know how to spot it. It's not all sharp teeth and pointy ears. The way you go completely still when you're startled. The attractive draw they all have, even before they get that flawless skin from fae healing."

I had never been grateful for my poor healing abilities until now. Even after I was unlocked, I was susceptible to sunburns and other things fae generally didn't have to worry about. That terrible sunburn during the welcome dinner had helped me fit in as Aurora.

"Mira and Ransom must be fae too, then."

She raised her brows at me. "That's exactly my point." She turned to go up a stairwell to her room, leaving me in the hallway.

I sighed, mulling over her words about the treaty and the mist. There was always something new to think about.

I was spending an exceptional amount of time outdoors in Nixia compared to my time in the Compound, and aside from my time on the boat, I hadn't experienced sunburn again. In fact, the sun of Nixia had only given me an olive tan that left my skin glowing.

In my room, I took a luxuriously long bath, trying to soak out the conflicting feelings I had settling in my chest. I rarely had free time at any point in my life. What did I possibly want to do with myself this evening?

I sat up so forcefully, water sloshed out of the tub and onto the floor.

I wanted to read through that fucking treaty.

CHAPTER THIRTY

I quickly toweled off and headed to my dressing chamber to throw on the first dress I touched and the nearest pair of slippers. I wound my hair into a quick bun and stuck a hairpin in it.

Once out of my room, I had to wander around the castle for a bit before I remembered from the tour that Mansby had mentioned the library being in the South Wing. We hadn't visited it then because nothing salacious had ever happened there with anyone famous.

I climbed several flights of stairs to find an impressive collection of books that made the bookshelf in my room look miniscule. It was comprised of several large rooms connected by stone archways, each filled with shelves lining the walls and the center of the room lined with tables and chairs. Wielder lights cast an amber glow over everything, since the high windows only provided the dim gloom of the now-raging storm outside. Several of the tables had people working at them.

I chose to start exploring in a deserted section. Each step through the stacks brought forth a stronger smell of parchment and old ink. I ran my hand along the shelf to the right as I read the labels, a light grit rubbing my fingers as I left trails in the dust. This was going to take forever.

"Can I help you find anything?"

The dark-haired librarian appeared from nowhere, making me jump as though I was doing something wrong, but when I turned to her, she presented me with a kind smile.

"Umm, yes," I said, "I'm rather new in my position and I need a refresher on the treaty from the Great War. Could I possibly read Queen Elara's copy?" I wasn't sure if this was uncouth, but hoped for the best.

"Certainly!" Before she whirled around, her eyes narrowed on the faint trails my fingers left in the dust. She waved her hands, causing a breeze to rush past us, leaving the shelves spotless in its wake. She started back the way she came, showing off her pointed ears as her long ponytail swished behind her. "It's just over here. And of course, it's only to be studied in the library."

She brought me to a far corner of the library, where several glass cases contained ancient-looking documents. "Normally, I would say you have to view the treaty through the glass, but as a head of state, I can take it out for you, if you'd like."

"Please."

She smiled again as she produced a ring of keys from an invisible pocket on her long, black dress and unlocked it. She gently lifted out the scroll and set it on the nearest table. "Just put it back when you're done, and the case will lock when you latch it."

Then she was gone just as mysteriously as she had appeared.

I read over the treaty with the title *Treaty for Peace Following the Great Imperial War - Kingdom of Nixia Copy*. The document was not as enlightening as I hoped. It stated almost exactly what Parisa had said to me when leaving the stable and nothing new besides the boring political

jargon outlining the exact boundaries of each territory and concluded with the threat of losing magic for breaking the agreement. I read
through several more times, until the sun had set outside, turning the
glow of the storm into a pale haze beyond the windows, and the only
light came from the wielder lights shining from the ceiling.

I deflated a little at this lack of revelation my gut insisted would
occur. I really thought reading this would bring me some clarity. I'd
expected some obvious answer to the warring ideas inside of me—was
the Empire good or bad, or rather how dark was its shade of gray? I
thought it would be some sort of compass to know which direction I
should allow myself to be pulled.

The disappointment seeped out of me in the form of Earth magic
and poured into the paper. Shit, my magic was just slipping out of me.
I hadn't really wielded since we got to Nixia, and the well inside of me
must be overflowing. I had reached the point where too much magic was
built up inside me, and now it was spilling out when my emotions were
high. I would have to find a way to release some of the buildup soon.
This mission was too stressful to have it so close to the surface.

I was about to stand to return the treaty to the case when I saw the
words on the parchment were glowing a little—all except the paragraph
at the bottom. I pushed a little more magic into the document, to reach
those words. The faint glow was slowly seeping down and almost there—

"Is this what you always wear to study, Fox?"

I jumped up and pulled my hand back from the document, the
magic fading instantly. I looked up to see Ransom strolling toward me. I
rushed to place the treaty back in the case and closed the lid on it just as
he made it to my side.

Still facing the case, I glanced down at my dress, smoothing the front
of it. I thought I had thrown on a simple red frock, but, upon inspection,

it was entirely too formal and scandalous for a library. I hadn't realized the thing was moderately transparent and my undergarments were clearly visible through the red lace.

"Well, I didn't want the seamstress' work to go to waste," I joked. "There aren't enough events left for me to wear them all."

I could tell he was looking at me differently. He opened his mouth, but didn't say anything.

Shit. Had he seen me use my magic?

I looked around. There was a door in the corner of the room. I grabbed his hand and pulled him through, disregarding the "restricted" sign hanging on it. The door closed over behind us, the only light coming from the murky twilight pouring in from the high, grimy windows. Once my eyes adjusted, I could tell we were in a disused room of the library, clearly intended for storage. The tables and chairs in the middle were all broken in some way. The mostly empty bookshelves here were even dustier and had no labels. The books sported broken bindings, ripped covers, or loose pages.

I pulled Ransom as far away from the door as we could get before speaking. "Say it."

"What? That we're clearly not supposed to be in here?"

"What were you going to say, Dimitris?"

"I was going to tell you how nice you look, but..."

"But what?" I asked fiercely.

He cleared his throat. *"Nice* didn't seem sufficient."

"I don't think you hunted me down in a library to say that." My eyes narrowed. Maybe he hadn't seen me using magic after all, but his expression told me there was still more he wasn't saying.

"Fine." He smiled and raised his closed fist out to me. "I wanted to return something to you. I—"

We both heard it—the sound of footsteps from the room next to us. We snapped our heads to the door that hadn't closed entirely behind us. Shit, the footsteps were definitely getting closer. I didn't want to try to explain to anyone why I had dragged Ransom into this room for seemingly no reason. I certainly couldn't say, "Oh, I thought he saw me using magic and I didn't want him to publicly accuse me of being a traitor." Besides, who would believe it when I was barely dressed and everyone already thought we were intimate?

I looked back at him. "I guess we're just lovers in the middle of a clandestine meeting." His eyes shot from the door to me, his brows raised.

"Kiss me," I ordered. He nodded enthusiastically, and his hands were on me like that's where they'd always wanted to be.

The warmth of his palm seeped through the thin fabric of my dress instantly as his hand splayed on my back, pulling me toward him. My chest was pressed against his, and I let myself believe the tingling heat in my core was just his body heat warming me and not immediate desire. My heart was racing in my chest, but that must be because we were about to be caught and not because his body against mine felt so right.

I tilted my face up and caught the hint of a smile before his mouth was on mine. Our lips met in a gentle brush that sparked a fire from where we were touching and traveled down. The smooth press of his soft lips felt designed just for this moment, just for how they would feel against mine.

Holy shit.

Kissing had always been fine in my opinion. Never great and really just something I did on the way to other, more satisfactory activities. Not this kiss, though. It could nourish my soul. I pressed my hips to him.

His fisted hand grabbed my hair and tilted my head up. I wrapped my arms around his neck as I parted my mouth and ran my tongue along his plush bottom lip. When he opened for me, I was consumed. The feel of his tongue claiming mine stoked the heat in my core to an inferno. The kiss became blazing and hard, like we needed to use this opportunity to let our fire rage or it would burn us alive.

He pushed me back until I was pressed against the nearest bookcase and unleashed himself on me. The force of our bodies shifted the bookshelf and made a few tomes tip over, but there was no room to care about that, no room for air when this was giving me so much life.

I arched my back harder, needing to touch more of him, but the fabric of my gown was in the way. I released his neck to hike up the skirt until I could hook my leg around his hip. The feel of his hard muscles under my leg felt so incredibly right. I ached for more of him.

His hand immediately moved from my hair to grab my thigh, holding it in place and keeping every part of my body flush to his. I rolled my hips against him as much as the position would allow, and this time a satisfied groan escaped my throat as the center of me found friction against the hardness in his pants. I was scared more of my magic was going to spill out from this, but I couldn't stop. It was humming in my breastbone, making every touch spark against me.

My fingers wove into his hair as his kisses began slipping from my mouth and along my jaw to my neck and collarbone. I felt like he was worshipping me. Offering a tribute to my sacred, tingling skin. The feel of his mouth on me was divine. I was burning for more in the wake of every kiss.

I tipped my head forward into his silky black waves, my nose filled with the cedar and citrus scent, wanting to devour as much of him as he was getting of me.

The door creaked open, the light from the library spilling over us.

"Excuse me! This area is off limits to guests." I stiffened in his arms, already having forgotten the reason we were doing this. I peeked around him to see the librarian standing about fifteen feet away from us with her hands on her hips. "You both need to leave now!"

Panting, he slowly released my leg, making sure I stayed steady as he did. We adjusted our disheveled clothes and walked out without making eye contact with her.

In the hall, I was trying very hard to remind the aching, molten feeling between my thighs that it had been an act. Hadn't it?

Once we were several flights of stairs away from the library and about to separate to our guest wings, I turned to Ransom. That had been something, hadn't it? Something wonderful and fulfilling. I wanted to say something that encompassed what just happened, what would come next, and everything I was feeling.

Stop. He's pretending. You should be pretending.

"Do you think that was dramatic enough for them to start including the library on the castle tours?"

He smiled at me and briefly touched my lower back before splitting off to head toward his room.

Back in my suite, I was not letting my thoughts wander over the fact that kissing Ransom was far better than any other kiss I'd ever had. Everything about it had been superior to all other experiences. Any time my mind strayed to him, a desperate need ached in me.

As I was getting ready for bed, I discovered a second hairpin I hadn't put in myself. It was silver and the end was formed into a snarling fox's head. There was no question in my mind that this was what Ransom had been trying to return to me.

Before I fell asleep, I realized that Ransom hadn't known I was trying to hide using magic. I didn't think a crime lord would mind being found in a restricted area, even if he was a guest in this castle.

He had agreed to kiss me very quickly for a person with nothing to hide.

That night I woke up with the memory of his lips on me and my core throbbing for more of what I'd felt when I was pressed against him. To my great frustration, bringing about my own release seemed to heighten this desire.

Only once I woke up the next morning did I remember Lev.

CHAPTER THIRTY-ONE

During the event that night I sat in the second row of chairs between Mira and Ransom for a production of a traveling play.

So far, it appeared the librarian wasn't a gossip, and I would keep that little performance of ours a secret as long as I could. I wanted to ask him about the hairpin, but with Mira nearby, it would have to wait. Instead, I tried to whisper more information out of them, to the scowls of the performers.

"If I start sending my troops the third week after the equinox, they'll arrive a month before yours," I said quietly.

"I can't send mine any sooner. The mountain passes will still be snowed in," Mira countered.

"We've been through this," Ransom said. "The mercenaries won't be there until summer solstice at best anyway."

An actor on stage cleared his throat loudly and when we looked up, he was glaring at us. After being shamed into silence, it was turning out to be a rather boring event until the intermission, when the advisor from Gallia approached Queen Elara. I hadn't paid any attention to the man before that night. The soft glow of the wielder lights illuminated his flawless beauty and shined on his sandy hair as he tapped her on the shoulder.

"Yes?" Queen Elara said, with a look that someone gets when they realize they just stepped in something and now they need to look at the underside of their shoe to find out what it was.

"Your Majesty," he said with a bow. The three of us leaders of the states really should have been using the intermission to talk, but we were all too engrossed in the scene unfolding in front of us.

"What the shit is this?" Mira whispered from my left.

"I had not yet had a chance to speak with you during this Gathering and thought I should take this opportunity to introduce myself," he said.

"If you really must," Queen Elara said.

"I am Rumo, and I am pleased to make your acquaintance," he said, undeterred by her complete lack of interest.

Ransom reached over and squeezed my knee through my dress, confirming I was watching this too. His eyes wide and fixed on the scene in front of us, I could feel his barely contained amusement vibrating through the touch. I put my hand on top of his and pinched it, silently battling him against the laughter that now threatened to spill out of both of us.

"Very well," Queen Elara said, making a brushing motion with her hand at him to dismiss him.

"Yes, well, if you need anything from Gallia or myself, simply let me know and I will be there in a heartbeat." He was either not getting the message or still thinking he had a chance to be the next king of Nixia.

"Thank you." Queen Elara pivoted back to the royals from Kind on her other side, and Rumo touched her shoulder and leaned in to her. If we weren't seated directly behind them, we would not have been able to hear what came next.

"That includes warming your bed," he said, with a small smirk as though this was everything she had been waiting for.

Queen Elara, unruffled, swiveled back to him. "I would rather resurrect the Great Spiked Dragons and ride one without a saddle than you." She flicked her wrist to her guards, who promptly escorted Rumo from the room. She stood, looking sharply around and shouted, "Parisa, get the fuck over here and answer for this."

The queen and Parisa exited the hall together in hurried steps, under the watchful gaze of every guest and servant of Castle Nix.

Mira, Ransom, and I exchanged looks and broke into laughter. As we regained ourselves, Mira glanced to my knee, where Ransom's hand was still placed and covered by my own. I withdrew my hand back to my lap. I hadn't even noticed it was still there.

His hand remained on my knee for most of the second act. It would be suspicious if I asked him to move it now that Mira was watching. I also didn't ask him to stop him when his thumb started making idle brushes back and forth along the side of my leg. We had an act to keep up, after all, never mind that it felt reassuring.

When the play ended, Ransom leaned over, still holding my knee, and with his other hand pointed to the necklace I wore. "May I?"

I nodded. He ran his index along the fine chain draped over my collarbone. His touch left a trail of tingling flesh in its wake, sending a pleasant hum through my body.

"What a fitting necklace for you," he said.

I smirked as I looked at him. "Is it?"

When his stroke reached the pendant, he wrapped his fingers around the quartz crystal and leaned so close that his lips brushed the shell of my ear. "It's beautiful." He lifted the stone and pulled it along the chain to one side. "It radiates power." He slid it along to the other side. Each clink of the pendant against the chain created a throaty *zip* that traveled down my spine. "And all I can think about is how it feels in my hand." He pulled it one last time, making the loudest sound yet. He leaned back and we exchanged smiles, my cheeks very warm all of a sudden.

Lev walked past us with a cough and a pointed glare. A quiver of shame rippled through my body. I stood, making Ransom's hands fall away from my necklace and my knee. I didn't really want to delve into the feeling or the sadness at the loss of his warmth. I told myself I was tired, that I hadn't been sleeping well since I left Capital City. This whole mission had all my feelings mixed up between the man I pretended to be with in public and the man I was actually with behind closed doors. Plus, that kiss had really confused things further.

Without remembering the walk there, I found myself back in my suite. I undressed and took down my hair with just as little attention to my actions. My thoughts were still in the audience of the play. The confused emotions swirled in me. I had pulled on my sleeping clothes when there was a knock on my door.

"There's always a fucking knock," I mumbled as I threw on my robe and padded over to the front entrance.

"Hi," Lev said, taking in my robe and the silk scarf covering my hair as he stepped in.

"I didn't get anything new tonight," I said, feeling the fatigue of this whole mission settle over me. I wanted to cut to the chase so I could go to sleep alone.

He nodded. "You seem to have this act down. You and Ransom were being overly affectionate tonight. It looked so convincing, I think I'm starting to believe it too."

I really didn't want to deal with this right now, I was so exhausted. I pinched the bridge of my nose and closed my eyes. "Lev, you should know that was for the mission."

He reached out and brushed my shoulder. "Then why have you been avoiding me?"

I released my nose and looked up at him. "What? I'm not. You said you were busy."

"It feels like you're avoiding me. Always asking me to spend time with you when I have reports I need to complete. And last day off, you invited everyone over so we couldn't be alone. Then I watch you get groped by Dimitris a few nights a week. It feels like your interest is getting pulled elsewhere." He stepped closer to me. "It's like you're forgetting that you're supposed to be mine. That I'm the only one you can trust here."

Mother, I didn't want to be talking about this right now. Why did I have to reassure this man on top of trying to sort out my own feelings? I reminded myself he was also on this mission and under a lot of stress, just like me. It was getting to both of us.

"Tomorrow is another off day," I said. "Why don't we plan on dinner together? An early dinner, so we have plenty of time for you to know exactly where my interests are."

He smiled and gave me a quick kiss that left no trails of heat or tingles in its wake.

I lay down and fell asleep quickly, only to be trapped in the same dream as a few weeks ago.

The press and suffocating panic of people around me in the Old Square. My fall. The pain and helplessness. Lev reached for me, but instead went to the aid of the executioner, never to be seen again. The warm drip of blood down my cheek. The faceless man picked me up with warm, comforting hands and the scent of cedar as my necklace moved on my chest. I pulled my eyes from the horrors around me, and I woke in a cold sweat.

CHAPTER THIRTY-TWO

Seventh day breakfast was now officially expanded to the unsanctioned crew, as they all showed up without invitation from me. Wynn and Jo had finally returned late the night before.

I got the impression it was a game of cards that kept Wynn and Jo in Port Mora so late, and not mission duties. Wynn was pretty pissed she'd missed the action when Ameal and I recounted what occurred with Rumo and Queen Elara during the play. I told her that was what she got for gambling, to which she threw a piece of toast at my face. The jam side hit me on the cheek, leaving a raspberry smear in its wake.

Jo let out a snort of laughter, "You two fight like my sisters do. I can't wait to have family breakfasts again. Don't get me wrong, though, this is a very nice substitute." I paused, scrubbing my face with my napkin as Jo's words nestled their way into my heart.

"Are you decided? You're going to go back to them after your service is up?" I asked.

"I am," he said. "Even if it's just for a while. I miss them. My niece and nephew are probably this tall now." He held his hand up to his chest. "I joined the Protectorate thinking I could make the Empire a better place for them. But now I think it's time to be a little closer to them."

"I'm very fortunate," Ameal said. "I was allowed to be stationed in Agora after my training."

"Is that where your family is?" Wynn asked.

Ameal nodded. "I don't even have to stay in the Protectors' barracks there. I get to go home to mom's cooking after a shift."

"That would be nice," Wynn said. "It's a shame I didn't get assigned duty in Polis."

"I hear they rarely assign people back to their hometowns if they are from the North or the East," Jo said. "Conflict of interest."

"Then why does Ameal get to have his mom's cooking every night?" I asked, wrapping my hands around my cup of coffee to let the heat soak through to my fingers.

"Agora rarely sends anyone to the Protectorate," Ameal said with a shrug. "People just don't want to go. I've never known a wielder to come from Solterra, so it doesn't seem worth the risk to most. Plus it's hard to keep Protectors assigned to the docks, so we get lots of exceptions. Being stationed in your hometown, not having to live in the barracks."

"Why's it so hard to keep Protectors there?" Wynn asked.

"They usually find out they can get paid better at one of Ransom's businesses and don't extend their contracts after their duty is up. Or they get bored, because duty is mainly collecting taxes on imports." He smirked. "Or the more devout are shocked by our ways of sin and flee."

"Sounds like a fun place," Wynn said as she selected her next piece of bacon.

"Maybe you could request a transfer when we get back," Jo said.

"Maybe," she said.

"Please wait until after the winter solstice to request it," I said. "That's when I'm done with my service, and I don't have it in me to make any more new friends."

She smiled and patted my back.

When the others left after breakfast, I bathed, making certain every part of me smelled and looked how it should. As I tried to select my dress, I was torn between a lovely gray-blue gown that was more in line with Imperial fashion or a shimmery green number with pink beaded accents cut in the Nixian style.

Making my way down the hall to his room that evening, I was feeling as nervous as I did on our first lesson after we kissed. Lev opened the door with a smile. He had the table cleared of its usual books and maps to be set with flowers and candles around covered dishes.

"I thought you might enjoy a romantic meal for a change," he said with a half smile.

"You didn't have to do this," I said. It felt like so much more than this random evening warranted.

"You deserve this," he said as he moved to wrap his arms around me. "You've been working so hard for the Empire. You should have a night of pleasing experiences." He lowered his mouth to my ear. "Dinner could wait."

I should want that, but I couldn't think of anything I desired less than to try to be intimate with a man I was having such conflicting feelings about. Lev was risking a lot for me, but I was starting to notice the pressure he put on me, which Wynn kept pointing out. And I was hiding the unsanctioned lessons from him. And the kiss with Ransom. And how kissing Ransom felt.

"Let's eat first. I'm famished," I lied. He nodded, clearly disappointed.

We sat down and started to eat around a tentative conversation that was too forced. I poked at the food on my plate while his story about some border skirmish that happened six hundred years ago washed over me.

This whole mission was so much for me to handle. Add in the events in the Old Square right before I left, and everything I needed to unravel on this mission, but hadn't had the time to. I should have been focusing on the mission and myself, not avoiding the unpleasant work of untangling my emotions. I'd known this for a while now, but his droning story induced a meditative state that finally allowed my mind to find clarity.

I set my fork down and looked at him. "Nothing good can come from this. Can it?"

He quickly cut off his explanation of ancient defensive positions and looked at me, slightly shocked at me interrupting him.

"We could get in trouble being together," I said. "We could get distracted from the reason we're here. And it's not as though we can continue this when we get back to the Empire."

His silence continued, and he gave a slight nod. It was apparent he simply had nothing to say to counter my argument.

"Thank you for dinner." I stood from the table.

We should never have been together, it was too complicated from every angle. We both knew that. It had been stupid to act on this in the first place.

I was a broken mess, and he was the string I had been using to try to tie myself together. I just needed to get through these last two weeks in Nixia. Then, I promised myself, I would let myself fall apart entirely if I wanted to.

With nothing else to say, I left his room and walked down the hall away from him. I had certainty in each step for the first time since I was sent to the Old Square as my hands brushed the tiny pink beads of my dress.

CHAPTER THIRTY-THREE

We had two weeks left until the autumnal equinox ball. Jo had come through for the mission by talking to Parisa's lady's maid to find that Gallia would only attack *after* the other states converged on the capital. They would target the silver mine on the Gallian side of the border river to reclaim what was once theirs. Only after that would they consider supporting the states' rebellion within the Empire.

I had been taught in school that the mine belonged to the Empire. There had been no lesson about the Emperor seizing it in the midst of the chaos of the Great War. Once I looked at a map, it was apparent the silver mine was very clearly on the Gallian side of the Partidus River. That review might have been prompted by Wynn throwing a map at me in response to my shocked expression at the news.

She was having to prod less and less to get me to rethink my knowledge of the Empire taught to me in primary school. I didn't let myself dwell on what that might mean for my future. My goal for the time being was to give the Emperor enough information for him to not kill us. And for us to not get caught by any of the other kingdoms, so *they* didn't kill us. Reconsidering my personal identity as a loyal citizen of the Empire would have to wait.

Ameal looked truly regretful to have to inform the unsanctioned crew that a Nixian guard had passed along that their commander would be willing to send us home with some extra armaments. But only if I was willing to have sex with the commander. He felt some extraordinary ability in the bedroom was the only reason Ransom would still be so dedicated to me. It was another grain of rice added to what had become a mountain of rumors about us.

We also found out that Kind planned to back the resistance efforts. They still had not committed to anything tangible, only that they would allow free trade and access to their goods to those involved in the uprising. They also hinted that once this all started, they would place an embargo on the Empire, but the Empire's goods were too important to them to start this right away. Their first priority was to keep their people safe and fed. I couldn't really argue with that, since it was essentially my perspective for my life right now.

The second day of that week was a beautiful one. The fall colors were starting to dapple the mountainsides. The sky was a clear blue with a warm sun that begged to be enjoyed. Jo caught me staring longingly out of his window during our afternoon session.

"Do you want to end here today?" he asked.

"How much more do we need to cover?"

He smiled. "It doesn't really matter what we cover if your head is elsewhere."

I nodded and glanced out the window again. "True, I guess I could use a walk. Organize my thoughts." When I looked back at him, his brown eyes were filled with sympathy.

"Do you want me to join you?" he asked.

The loneliness that had been gnawing at me since I left Capital City answered. "Yes, please."

Jo and I took a path out of the courtyard and along the mountainside that we could see from our windows. The crunch of dirt beneath our boots mingled with the songs of birds and the whistle of a soft breeze through the trees around us.

We were a good distance away from the castle when Jo finally spoke. "How are you doing?"

I tugged on my necklace and looked off into the trees. "Well, I mean, I'd obviously like to be getting more detailed information from the other leaders, but I'm not sure what else I need to pry for."

"That's not what I mean," he said.

We walked for a little longer before I responded. "Not well," I answered honestly.

"Do you want to tell me about it?" His request held all the gentleness of a protective older brother who found out a boy at primary school had broken his little sister's heart. I reminded myself Jo probably had plenty of experience with exactly those types of conversations.

"I just want my old life back. It wasn't glamorous or lavish, but I had friends I could trust. People's lives weren't in my hands. I didn't have to constantly wonder if I'm making the right choice." I sighed. "I wasn't so terrible at my job."

"This is a job that people usually prepare for over years and years, and you had no training," he said, as he held up a low-hanging branch for us to walk under.

"Well, yes. I'm trying. I'm doing it as best as I can. But that is never good enough. I'm always failing."

"You've made huge strides and gotten tons of information." He studied my face. "Is that what Lev is saying to you behind closed doors?" I didn't respond. "What *is* Lev saying to you? Ameal thinks he's just upset that he didn't get to be the one to come up with the plan you're using, but Wynn thinks he's outright abusing you somehow." He gave a weak smile to try to cut the harsh words.

"Really? You all have been talking about me?" I couldn't hide my frown. "What do you think?"

"We're worried about you." He looked over at me. "And I think you're a person who cares an awful lot about the people around you. But I think your caring has made you so desperate for this mission to go well that you aren't..."

The chatter of birds around us filled in the gap left by his unfinished thought. I didn't want to know yet another way I was lacking.

Jo touched my shoulder, forcing me to look at him. "You're going to have to decide for yourself who you want to be," he said. "It took me almost twelve years in the Protectorate to figure that out. I could keep extending my service and letting someone else tell me what to do, or I could end it. Take control of my own happiness. I could go be with my family again." He gave a small smile.

"I'm trying." I kicked a pebble on the path off into the grass. "I'm a little too preoccupied with keeping everyone alive right now to fix whatever's wrong with me." I shoved my hands in my pockets and started to walk again. Once I made it off this island and finished my service to the Imperial Protectorate, I could think through what I wanted to do with my future, who I wanted to be.

"No matter what you choose, we'll support you." He smiled at me again. "I'd like to think after we're back, our friendship won't end. Your service is up soon. You could come visit my family's farm in the Central State."

I smiled back at him and nudged him with my elbow. He hooked his arm through mine, and we returned to the castle in a better mood. Even if I didn't solve anything, talking about what was going on with me made me feel so much lighter. It was nice to have someone I could show a tiny part of myself to.

I was learning so much about the Empire, maybe I would focus on learning more of our history when I got back. I could have a better understanding of why things are the way they are. I could work out whether the rebellion was justified once supporting it wasn't a matter of my imminent death. It wouldn't be that much longer before I would be home.

Yet, my heart sank a little that I only had two weeks left to tease Queen Atla. Or watch Mira's shrewd observations. Or spend time with Ransom.

I only had to get through one more dinner, the event in the seventh week, and the final ball. Queen Elara had decided to cancel the dinner for the eighth week to ensure the ball was as magnificent as possible. I'd also heard it was because she wasn't interested in spending any more time around Rumo than she had to.

After the ball, everyone would be heading back to their respective states and kingdoms to return to normal life and start enacting their plans.

I could do this. One dinner, one event, a ball, then back to the First. My service to the Empire would be done a few weeks after that. Then maybe I would visit Jo. Small farming towns usually had work for passing wielders. It would be so fun to get to meet the family he was constantly talking about. Or I would head back to Capital City to Lina and George. I would make money doing whatever wielding was needed around the City until they were done with their contracts and I could figure everything out.

The last dinner should be an easy one. I was just supposed to keep my ears open in case any final tidbits fell into my lap.

I dressed in a velvet gown with long sleeves that belled out toward my hands. It was the type of fancy dress I never would have been able to afford in Capital City, and it was finally cool enough to allow me to wear it.

Naturally, the seamstress in Port Mora had seen fit to alter the back of this dress with a dangerously low cut, exposing me to nearly my ass. Wynn pulled one side of my hair back with a fancy comb and let the rest fall down my back. She was better at being a lady's maid than she gave herself credit for.

The night of the dinner, the seating arrangement was the same as the very first night. I listened to the chatter around me throughout dinner, but not hearing anything of value, I began speaking to Ransom. I was comfortable enough with him that I had no issue lacing the truth about my life before with being Aurora. I was telling him about an exploit with George and Lina and carefully replacing Capital City locations with places I knew of throughout Moriale.

"Yes, so then when we went to Port Erasmus, my friend had a sailor draw him a picture of exactly what he thought that would look like," I smiled at Ransom as he laughed. "Needless to say, I kept the drawing to this day." I leaned across the table to reach the water pitcher and refill my glass. "I actually have it upstairs in my room—" Ransom placed his hand *very* low on me as I stretched over. His touch was light, not groping, but still I snapped back, his hand sliding up my spine when I moved.

"What are you doing?" I hissed quietly. I didn't want to ruin the image we had created for everyone else, but it was a step further than our normal game for him to be fondling my ass in the middle of dinner.

"Sorry, you were exposing yourself to half the dining room," he whispered. "I thought you—and Frange—might appreciate a little more modesty."

I blushed deeply. "Thanks."

"Couldn't you feel the dress slip or the wind on you?" he chuckled quietly. The feel of his rough hand on my spine was reassuring. My long curls danced across the back of his hand as we talked.

"This fucking dress is nothing but a cool breeze down my backside. Pair it with the underwear they use here in Nixia, and I would never know if the whole thing came off."

His look shifted and a muscle ticked in his jaw as he pulled away. "Do you think you're going to miss your time here, Fox?"

"No."

He raised his brows. "I think I should be offended by how quickly you answered that."

"I just mean it will be nice to get back to normal life. Not have to worry about the secret second or even third meaning of every word and action. Of every single person around me," I said as I scraped up the last piece of berry tart on my plate. "Or how to wear the fashion of Nixia." I waved toward my back.

"Ah, yes, running a state. So much easier than constant parties," he teased. Then he leaned in very close to me. "But I guess you wouldn't know much about that."

My mouth went dry. I schooled my expression before looking at him. "Of course I still have a lot to learn. I'm very new to my role." I hoped I was covering the immense panic inside me.

He stared at me hard. "So you are. I'm still trying to figure you out, Fox, even after all these weeks."

"Oh?" I wasn't sure if I had taken a breath in the last few minutes.

"Yes, at first I thought you were one thing, but now you've become something else entirely in my eyes. Trying to separate your desires from the things you do just to please others keeps me up at night," he said, his eyes never leaving me. I looked at the strong line of his jaw rather than his eyes.

I didn't want to lie to him, for whatever reason, and it wasn't because he had slipped his uneaten slice of tart onto my empty plate. I breathed deeply and found words that were honest and I could manage without falling down this slippery slope. "My only desire is to live. At the end of the day, at the end of this, we all just want to live our lives. Can you blame me if I've been protective of myself to get to that end?"

He gave me a skeptical look and watched me a moment longer. "No, I can't, little Fox. You're right. That's what we all want at the end of this." His tone sounded gentler than it had a minute ago.

He leaned in close to my ear, so close his nose brushed my face, and I listened for whatever he was about to whisper. After a pause, he moved his head a fraction of an inch and pressed a gentle kiss on my cheek. He smirked as he stood from the table, his eyes flicking to the back of my dress before he left the hall.

I touched where his lips had been. When I moved my arm, I found a small piece of parchment had been slipped under my left sleeve while I had been focused on Ransom to my right.

I looked over and Frange had disappeared, gone to the washroom or to talk to someone else at the table. I hadn't noticed anyone else around us, but then again, I'd been pretty focused on what we had been talking about.

I took the scrap of paper and unfurled it under the table.

Join me in the hallway through the door you and Ransom left through two weeks ago.

I looked around to see who my mystery conspirator might be, but it was impossible to tell. With dinner mostly over, people moved freely about the room, almost no one still in their seats. It was most definitely ill-advised to follow instructions from a random note without knowing who I was meeting. On the bright side, I was wearing more knives than usual. The high slit of the dress allowed me to be able to wear one on my upper thigh and the long sleeves let me put one on my wrist.

This was one of my final chances to get any more information. I should take advantage of it. The recklessness was probably fueled by the adrenaline still coursing through me from my talk with Ransom.

I didn't have any pockets, and I couldn't leave the note here, even as tiny as it was. I slipped the note into my still-full wine glass under the pretense of running my finger around the edge. Waiting until I was sure the ink was ruined, I took a drink from the cup, allowing the paper to pass into my mouth. I wiped my mouth with my napkin, spitting the paper into it. I wadded up the destroyed paper until it was an unidentifiable mess through the napkin, and I placed it into my uneaten bits of food, under the guise of leaving my napkin on my plate. Even if anyone were to find that lump in the discarded food, they probably wouldn't know it was once a tiny piece of parchment. And they certainly wouldn't know what it said.

I smiled to myself, thinking I was finally getting better at espionage.

With that done, I walked out of the hall through the designated door, trying to make it seem as though I were only going to see to my needs.

The shadowy hallway was empty. I raised my hand to touch the hilt of my knife on my thigh as I moved along the flagstone tiles. I couldn't know who would go through the trouble to meet me in such secrecy.

Another dim hall branched off this one, the arched ceiling creating a darker shadow to hide in. That was where I would stand if this were me trying to speak to someone in secret. My furiously beating heart drowned out the soft sound of my slippers against the floor, as I unsheathed my knife in a fluid motion.

I heard from behind me, "Why are you slipping away?" Lev's voice.

I turned to glance at him for a second, then whipped my head back to the other hall. A tall figure ran away at the other end. I sprinted after it. I had been training hard for the last few weeks and could sprint faster than I've been able to before, but I was no match for the distance. The other person was already gone from the next hallway by the time I got to the corner. I put my knife away, knowing my target was lost.

Footsteps pounded from the way I came, Lev was almost to this hall.

"What in the Mother's name is happening?" he asked as he caught up to me. "You're dashing down dark hallways with knives drawn?"

The note felt to me like the type of thing the Emperor shouldn't know about yet.

"Someone else was out here. I was trying to see who it was, but they started to run." Though they didn't run until they heard Lev. "It might be useful to know who was sneaking around."

"Everyone is sneaking around." He held out his arm to escort me. "I was getting worried that you were having more secret rendezvous without telling me." A tight smile stretched across his face. "The possibility of you meeting up with any other man still bothers me."

I hadn't really thought much about Lev since the night I ended this thing between us. In fact, this interaction made me realize I had felt less burdened in the past few days.

"It's easy to miss you, you know. I saw you walking arm and arm with Jo yesterday."

I glanced at him to see if he was really that jealous, despite him agreeing that we would never work beyond the confines of this island. He hadn't fought for staying together very hard that night.

"It really doesn't help that the fashion of Nixia suits you to an irresistible degree," he said, his eyes darting toward my backside.

"Well, we're almost to the end," I replied, not sure what else could be said.

"Yes, we are."

CHAPTER THIRTY-FOUR

With only a few days left, we agreed to not have history lessons anymore. Instead, after training, all of us would meet in Lev's room to discuss the final details we might be able to wring out of anyone there. With the whole group as a buffer, it wasn't bad.

Privately, the unsanctioned crew also decided to stop meeting. Wynn, Ameal, Jo, and myself wouldn't need those private meetings at this point, and it would be too conspicuous with all of us leaving Lev's room and filing in next door.

Fresh from the bath, I picked a deep blue gown for the event that week while still wrapped only in a towel. The gown's neckline required a specific brassiere I remembered seeing when I first got the dress back. I went to the trunk and couldn't find the one I needed. In my frustration, I discarded my towel to have full use of both hands and dumped the entire box of garments on the floor, going through them one by one until I found the brassiere I was searching for.

I began folding them and neatly stacking them into the box. My finger caught on a bit of rough wood that was exposed since my decision to cut out the lining. The rough patch looked like a gouge in one of the corners, but as I leaned in, I dropped the stack of underwear I was holding. The spot in question was a thin arrow with the tip pointing into the corner, and the top of the arrow was a crude carving of a fox's head.

I dashed to my nightstand and grabbed the fox-headed hairpin Ransom had given me. I shoved the point of the pin in the indicated corner, where there was a slight gap at the meeting of the two sides and the bottom. The space was only slightly larger than—well, the point of a hairpin. I pressed down into the bottom and manipulated it in the ways Wynn showed me for picking locks.

There was a muffled *click*.

The hairpin had unlatched something, but the bottom of the trunk was exactly the same.

I didn't understand. I heard it.

I ran my hands over all the sides again, prying at every edge I could. I tried pressing the pin while pushing and pulling each panel, yet nothing. I pulled until a sheen of sweat broke across my forehead.

What the fuck.

Footsteps were coming from my sitting room. Shit, Wynn was here to help me get ready, and I was still completely naked. I closed the trunk with the hairpin still inside and shoved myself into the brassiere I set aside and first set of underwear I touched, which happened to be quite a bit more lacy and see-through than anything I normally wore.

I stood, my heart still hammering in my chest, as Wynn entered my dressing chamber. She took in the rapid rise and fall of my chest, my sweaty brow, provocative ensemble, and the underwear explosion around me with a slightly open mouth.

As she grabbed the dress to start helping me into it, she shook her head slightly. "I don't want to know what you were just doing."

The final event before the ball was subdued. Queen Elara had set up tables in the hall with various games of chance we could play. I was already playing a game of chance with my life and couldn't find it in myself to be engaged with gambling, especially when my mind kept slipping back to the trunk in my room. I wandered around the tables with my drink, speaking to no one.

I was leaning over Wynn's shoulder to look at her hand of cards, when a touch found the small of my back. I prayed to the Mother that it wouldn't be Lev's when I stood up.

"Not in the mood to play tonight, Fox?" Ransom's deep voice flowed over my shoulder. I exhaled in relief.

"You know I'm always in the mood to play with you." I straightened and Queen Atla glared at us from across the table.

"Walk with me." With a smile he offered his arm, and I took his bicep with both hands, abandoning my drink next to Wynn.

He steered me away from the group, to a quieter corner of the room. "I need to speak with you."

"I thought that's what we were doing right now?"

"No, we're walking."

"Ah, forgive my ignorance. This is, after all, my first rebel plot," I said with an air of great revelation. We both snickered.

He looked at me, mirth still glittering in his eyes. "Fuck." He smiled widely. "You—" He cut himself off with a small shake of his head, the wielder lights shimmering on his black waves.

"Isn't that the idea? This whole Gathering has been about you fucking me," I joked, trying to make light of his loss for words. "My magical cunt that's breaking alliances or making them, depending on who you ask." The weight of everything these past few weeks was welling up in me, and amusement quickly evaporated from my tone. The flood of frustration broke free and poured out of me in a cathartic dumping of the rumors I'd been hearing for weeks. Gossip that Wynn, Ameal, and Jo had been reporting back and I knew Ransom had heard too. I couldn't stop my mouth once the words of others started rushing out of me. "Or maybe I'm just a warm place to stick your cock, but also possibly the best lay you've ever had. Maybe I'm the woman that makes an honest man out of you. Perhaps I was a lady of the night before I was tapped to lead the Moriale rebellion, and all the tricks I know are the only way to ensure your assistance in the upcoming war. Or maybe fucking me gives you magic powers to win this rebellion. No one knows. Not even me."

He made a move like he was going to touch me, then thought differently, his hands brushing my arms. "I'm so sorry, Fox."

"Why? Why be sorry for me? I signed myself up for this. I agreed to this." My words were sharper than I really intended.

"I signed myself up to run Agora. It doesn't mean I go to sleep every night proud of what I had to do each day." He presented his elbow for me to take once again.

His words made me feel less alone. The void left by releasing those rumors felt less like humiliation and more like relief. I pressed my body in closer to his as we walked.

"I am going to miss you, Ransom." I didn't really intend to tip my head in and rest it against his arm, but it happened naturally. He squeezed my hand against his bicep and dipped his cheek to brush it to the top of my head with it. It felt like an oddly real moment for two people acting. A lot of them had lately.

Our circuit of the perimeter of the room led us back near the gaming tables. Lev's eyes shot to us. I was still holding on to Ransom's arm with both hands, and I had closed the distance between the two of us so we were walking with our sides pressed together. I knew how this looked to him. But it also completed the picture for everyone else that we were lovers. I found myself not caring about either opinion, and was glad to have Ransom's companionship.

When I got back to my room, I looked at the pile of clothes I'd left in my dressing chamber and the trunk I still couldn't figure out. It felt like one big window into the mess I was, and I decided to leave it until tomorrow.

The unsanctioned crew left my room after our weekly seventh day breakfast, and I no longer had an excuse to put it off. I went into my dressing chamber to pick up the mess I left the night before and to stow away all the clothing I wouldn't be wearing before leaving.

With most of the items packed away except enough outfits of leggings, shirts, and corsets and my dress for the final ball, I was proud of myself for being the type of person who would pack a week ahead of time. Not the disaster I came here as, who shoved everything in a sack and hoped it was good enough.

I tried to move the trunk of delicates back into the corner, but it was snagged on the rug somehow. After trying to move it unsuccessfully for several minutes, I kicked the trunk in frustration. The trunk toppled over, leaving its exterior bottom panel behind on the floor, with a book sitting on it.

So that was where the secret compartment was.

I wasn't expecting it to be accessed from the outside. Honestly, that made more sense. I couldn't imagine Aurora cutting the lining out and stitching it back in every time she wanted to access the book in front of me.

A book!

I scrambled over to it. It had no title on the front and was bound in brown leather with an embossed fox's head on the cover. I opened it and immediately realized that this was Aurora's diary. I flipped through a few pages.

Mother Creation, I wished I had this for the last seven weeks. It would have been a lot easier to imitate Aurora if I had access to her personal thoughts this whole time.

I started reading the diary there on the floor of my dressing chamber. It appeared that she'd started this journal right after her uncle died. She had been suspicious of the circumstances of his death, worried a plot was forming against Moriale. She suspected whoever took the seat of power would be in danger, and she wanted to keep a record of the events around her. She wasn't sure who could be behind this, if it was someone within her family, a competing family in Moriale, the Empire, or another kingdom trying to arrange things to their benefit. She had the trunk with the secret compartment made by one of the few craftsmen she trusted.

Sitting there on the floor, I read through a fair portion of the diary. I was hungry for her words. I wanted to soak them in, and hearing her voice through this diary was the only way I could try to give her the respect I knew she deserved. To listen to what was important to her and carry that information back with me into the world. The diary made her feel so real to me, a friend I had never gotten to meet.

Holding it, I was reminded the dressing chamber I was sitting in was supposed to be Aurora's. The tragedy of her death battered me once again. The image of her body sinking to the bottom of the ocean alone was painful. I wouldn't want that for anyone. She deserved to be buried, returned to Father Earth as we all should be. The tears rolled down my cheeks and dripped from my jaw to the rug beneath me on the floor.

I read a passage about how the Protectors stationed in Polis found an eight-year-old girl spending a coin from a purse that had recently been stolen from a visiting noble. She was buying a loaf of bread. The Protectors didn't question the girl. They didn't find out if she had stolen the purse or only found it.

They pulled her out of the bakery and killed her in the street.

Eight years old.

No Committee hearing.

No holding cell.

No chance.

This is what Committee Authority was being used for.

Aurora wrote letters to the Emperor to try to get him to answer for the actions of the Protectors. She got no response. Her men who went to Capital City on her behalf were dismissed on petition day because the nobles had taken up all the time allotted. They were given no special audience.

Their pleas went unheard.

There would never be any answering for that child's life taken.

The Empire had been feeding me countless lies in the schools they told me I was so lucky to attend. I had always believed they gave everyone a chance. I believed that everyone's parent could find work with the Empire if they were struggling, like mine had. I had always believed the Empire gave to its people and protected them, but in reality, it was taking everything. It was killing our children.

I slammed the book closed at the injustice of it. These lost lives. The girl. Countless other deaths like this plagued Moriale, mentioned in the letters in Jo's room. I'm sure this happened in Decca and Solterra too.

The magic that was typically a gentle hum in my chest was rumbling throughout my body. Fire ignited along my arm, licking at the pain that festered inside me. I let it burn.

Aurora had been young, kind, and pure. She only wanted the best for her people. She was brave and strong. She was willing to give up her life, her freedom for the freedom of others. An idea I was far too weak to ever consider.

That passage was one of many about how the Protectors stationed in Polis treated the people of Moriale. Aurora tried to stand up to them and was ignored. She wanted the power to protect her people against the Emperor, who cared so little for the people of her land.

I was spying for the Empire to take down a rebellion that I could no longer deny needed to happen. All because I wanted to make it out of here. I wanted to keep from causing a wave that might prevent me from having peace. What was that peace worth now that my eyes were open to all these people who lived without it?

I snuffed the fire that had erupted from me and stood to try to step away from the unfairness in those pages—but no matter where I went, the words followed me, along with my own shame in the role I had taken in helping the Empire for so long.

CHAPTER THIRTY-FIVE

I left my suite and dropped by the kitchens to acquire some snacks. The servants didn't even question my request, despite having served a small feast to my room just hours before. I made my way to Sugardrop and got her ready to ride by myself.

"Do you feel like running, girl?" I patted her neck and handed her an apple.

She snorted, but my understanding of horse wasn't good enough to know if that was a yes or no. I guess I would find out. Sugardrop made it clear her answer was a *no* by refusing to do anything faster than an amble. That was fine, I got to enjoy the fresh breeze and the beauty around me on the journey.

We rode the trail I'd taken that day with Ameal and went back to the serene meadow in the mountain pass. I tied her to a tree, wandered far enough away from her, and ensured we were alone. My well of magic was brimming and wielding was slipping out of me far too frequently to ignore that any longer.

I stood at the edge of the little brook that meandered through the grasses and looked at my reflection in the water. I needed to calm my magic before I used it to be able to bend the elements to my will properly. I watched it, observing it, slowing my own breath to be in time with the water's ripples over the stones at the bottom. I let myself be filled with its steady movement. The babble it made. The sun warmed my skin the same as the water would feel its rays on its surface. I let myself be consumed by the flow. Be engulfed by the sweet smell of wildflowers and grasses.

It washed away all the chaos and pain that surrounded me. I knew the Empire didn't always act in the best interest of its citizens, but the rebels would surely cost lives for what might become a line in our history books. Had I already done too much damage to the rebellion by reporting to Lev all these weeks? Would it be my fault if it failed? Could I help in any meaningful way and still keep the lives of our crew safe?

I allowed the pressure burning inside me to come to the surface and merge with the flow from the water. I raised my hands and with them, all the water lifted from the bed of the stream for twenty feet on either side of me, the pleasant hum of wielding tingling through my fingertips. I pulled up the column of water to eye-level and looked through it, twisting the water to see it from every angle. Fish still swam through the waters. I could see the little trout skating back and forth, unimpressed by their sudden change in altitude.

I raised the water higher. I wanted to see how far I could push myself. It went up and up until the sun refracted through the clear stream, cascading tiny prisms of rainbows down around me. I let several portions of it down to the ground, creating clear archways across the meadow. I stepped under one, surprised at how easy this was. I should store up my magic for weeks at a time more often if it allowed me to make such beautiful displays without tiring me. Maybe it would be one of my plans after I was out of the Protectorate.

I gently brought all the water back to its channel and let it skitter over the smooth rocks once more. The meadow looked like it had when I first arrived, fish back to their normal lives. I wondered if the fishes' experience was how this rebellion would feel to us. The world completely changed around me for a time at the hands of another, unsure what was going to happen next, if life would ever return to my familiar riverbed. Then, after a while, brought back to the life I'd always known as though it were nothing. No sign around me to even mark what had passed.

I played with the water some more, making rain showers in parts of meadow, waves in the creek, and little transparent walls around me until I felt empty.

I returned to Sugardrop to find that she had emptied my saddlebag by rubbing it against the tree during my absence. She was helping herself to all the apples when I walked up. I cleaned up our mess, shoving the half-eaten apples into the bag before heading out.

My head felt clearer now. My gut told me these were capable leaders and their cause was important. They would succeed despite me. I would have to spend my final week here doing as much as I could to aid their cause to try to make up for what I had done. I wasn't exactly sure what I could do, but I would start with not reporting anything else important to Lev. I might have to invent some findings to keep everyone else safe, but I could handle that.

Sugardrop took her time heading back to the stables, and I didn't bother to hurry her. The magic I had released today had balanced me and leveled my emotions, as opposed to the drain I usually felt after.

We were just coming around a bend in the trail when I was confronted with the crunch of grass. The scuffle of dirt under heavy feet. A deep huff.

Fuck.

Sugardrop couldn't stop her feet fast enough on this decline to keep us hidden from view. Standing ahead of us and blocking our path was a bear. It was so large. Staring directly at us. It stood on its hind legs.

I tried to remember what Lina said. I should try to look big, but I was already on the back of a horse—how much bigger could I get? Plus, from my point of view, the bear was winning the *who's bigger* game.

Its snout twitched as a breeze blew the scent of the half-eaten apples toward the bear.

Double fuck.

It was surprised and hungry, two of the things Lina said were bad.

Sugardrop was nervously prancing her feet, wanting to get away. I couldn't blame her, but I held her firm with the reins. I tried to slowly reach back and untie my bag from the saddle. I would just throw the food into the woods and hope the bear followed it.

Two much smaller bears appeared around the corner. Shit, worst-case scenario—a mother bear, protecting her cubs, who was also hungry and who I had surprised. I changed my mind, the food would not be a good enough distraction.

Mother blessed, I did not want this today, or really any day. The bears probably felt the same way.

I just wanted to get back down to the castle safely.

I blew out a slow breath and tried to assess my options. I did have knives on me, but I didn't want to hurt them. They were just out here living their lives. Plus, those cubs were really cute, their ears looked so soft and round.

I also didn't want them to hurt *me*. I hoped they couldn't smell fear, because I knew I reeked of it.

I had my magic, even as diminished as it was after the meadow.

Magic, the obvious answer.

I pulled on the breeze blowing across the trail, the very one that had been betraying my bag of apples to the bears, and strengthened it. I pushed the air along the animals and toward the woods, trying to direct them into the trees. The mom got back down on all fours as the gentle breeze increased into a gust and began to press on her, but she didn't move. I shoved harder with the wind, channeling more of myself into it and blowing fur on her side so aggressively, I could see where the hairs parted. The cubs were starting to act bothered by the wind, tripping and wiggling about, but didn't seem to want to go without their mom.

Come on. Just move.

I flowed the magic out of me harder, pushing out all that I had left in me. I cursed the fact that I wasted so much energy playing with that water.

The mom bowed her head against the wind, pointing her nose into it, and looked even more agitated, but I could tell she was starting to question this standoff.

I plunged deeper into my magic, pulling from everywhere I could, but there was none left to give.

The well was empty. The constant, gentle hum was a faint tickle.

I was up against a wall, but the wall was starting to give. I tugged against it inside me, drawing on my magic unrelentingly.

Then it gave way.

My well of magic was no longer contained. Like a sudden crack of lightning unleashing a thunderstorm, my magic broke free and torrents of power were unleashed, flooding my body. I could pull in magic from my whole being, from the warmth of the sun dancing on my skin right out to the tips of my fingers. The hum started again, louder and more powerful.

I was inundated by a sudden burst of energy and a gale erupted all around us. Sugardrop and I were untouched, the air near us perfectly calm. Yet all around us, branches swayed, needles from trees sprayed across the ground. The boughs of the trees groaned under the force of it.

The mother and her cubs scampered into the woods and up the hill to get away from the windstorm on the trail.

I squinted my eyes against the dirt and debris blowing in the air and squeezed Sugardrop's sides to urge her forward, past the point in the trail where the bears had gone. When we were a safe distance from the bears' path, I turned back to look.

It was a scene of decimation.

The dirt was exposed with no plants standing. Branches were bare and snapped. Nothing remained along that section of trail but dead, shattered land. I quickly looked ahead again, not wanting to see more.

I tried to shake the image from my mind for the rest of the ride. The trail was such a beautiful, peaceful place that I took solace in. I had tried to protect myself without harming the bears, only to ruin a piece of the haven I treasured.

That night, my dreams of the Old Square involved a young girl, about eight, hanging from the gallows. I forced the crowd away from her with magic I shouldn't have, but before I could go to her, Lev was standing in front of me, blocking my way. As he raised his hand, I woke up.

CHAPTER THIRTY-SIX

The midmorning meetings were cancelled for the final week. This gave me a little time before I had to report anything else to Lev. I couldn't help the Empire anymore, but I didn't know how far I could push our mission without endangering everyone.

I found I had little regard for what would happen to me if I disobeyed the Emperor's orders, but I wanted Jo to go back to his family's farm. Jo, who I had seen talking to Parisa's lady's maid during my walk the prior day.

I wanted Ameal to get to eat his mom's cooking. Ameal, who worked so hard to make sure I was protected and prepared during this mission.

I wanted Wynn to be able to return to Polis. Wynn, who was constantly trying to advocate for me.

I didn't worry about Lev. Wynn had been right. He would be fine after this.

Training was largely a silent affair each morning, as we all focused on the final few days. Thankfully, Lev was not attending.

I decided to take rides with Sugardrop daily after training, but avoided the mountain meadow after the bear. I was too afraid to see my damage to the land. It felt like some admission of guilt to return the once beautiful place I had ruined.

My evenings were spent reading through Aurora's diary. I could only take in a few pages at a time before being overcome by the pain of her life cut short and needing to step away from the small piece of her soul I now felt responsible for. Guilt consumed me that I couldn't figure out a suitable way to honor her after I'd been helping the Empire for so long.

On the third evening that week, I was sitting in my bed, reading an entry in the diary almost to the end of the pages she had filled in. Another entry with a list. This woman was organized and liked her lists.

Seventeenth day of the Seventh Month

Today we made our stop in Agora. It was nice to have my feet on land. It took a moment to get used to the fact that the ground was no longer undulating under me. Hudson told me that it was called 'sea legs' and soon my 'land legs' would return.

We accomplished all three of our objectives on this stop:

1. *Purchase supplies from Solterra along the docks. More spices were procured from the lands beyond the mist. Our kitchens will be so thankful. I am particularly excited for the vanilla beans. We have been without them for months now. The merchant also talked me into a spice I have never heard of, cardamom, which has a delightfully tangy scent and I think the cooks will enjoy.*

2. *Perpetuate the illusion to the Empire that this is a trade voyage and nothing more. The Protectors at the docks verified our paperwork and gave us no trouble. Hopefully the ears of the Emperor will be satisfied with our purchases and taxes paid.*

> 3. *Meet with Ransom Dimitris to feel out his stance before going
>   into the Gathering.*

The diary tumbled out of my hands, bouncing off my thighs and onto my bed cover.

What. The. Fuck.

She had met with Ransom.

He fucking knew I wasn't Aurora.

He knew I was an imposter. It wasn't a hard stretch to figure out that I was from the Imperial Protectors, if I wasn't Aurora. They were the only ones that had the means to pull this off.

Shit, shit, shit.

I got up and began to pace around the room, trying to think through this.

Was this why he said he wanted to talk? Fuck, was this why he didn't react when my face was clearly giving away my lies?

If Ransom had known I wasn't Aurora since day one, why hadn't he said anything? He had even mentioned that her boat stopped in Agora the first time I met him, and he'd said he didn't see me.

Maybe he thought the Aurora he met with was a proxy? Maybe he had her meet with an impersonator? No, that didn't feel right. There was no reason for either of them to do that.

Had he told anyone else?

Why was he playing along with me?

He must have known that I was reporting back to the Empire.

Was that why I had been able to glean such little information over these months?

Was everything he *did* tell me completely false? I assumed it was—he was smart and wouldn't have jeopardized the rebellion.

That presented a new problem. When I returned from this trip and nothing I reported back turned out to be true, my head would be on the line.

I needed to talk to someone about this. This was too big.

Wynn, I needed Wynn.

I clasped my hands behind my neck as I paced to the door I shared with Wynn. I knocked and waited. There was no answer. I pulled on the rope to the bell in her room. I knocked again, practically pounding down the door. I knew it was no good. She would have heard me the first time. But I let my frustration out on the door anyway. I beat my fist against the plane of wood separating our rooms until it was bending under my force. The door began knocking back in protest.

Wait, shit. That was my main door. Someone was knocking on it. I wasn't exactly being quiet.

I straightened myself up, took a breath, and opened my door to the hall, ready to pretend I hadn't just been making enough noise to rouse the entire castle from a deep slumber. Jo and Ameal barged into my room.

"We heard hammering. What's going on in here?" Jo said, looking around as though an aggressive carpenter could be lurking anywhere. "We thought someone was breaking into your room. We could hear it sitting in our room."

"I–I needed Wynn. She's not in," I said lamely. "That was me knocking for her."

"How badly did you need her?" Ameal asked with a half smile, a rare show of humor from him. Too bad I was too distraught to enjoy it. "Is it...lady issues?"

"No." I closed my door and locked it. "Ransom knows I'm not Aurora."

It spilled out of my mouth before I could think better of it. I hadn't contemplated what I was going to say next. I trusted them enough, but they would surely ask how I found out about this, and I didn't want to tell them that I had Aurora's secret diary. My hard-won discovery of the book made me feel protective of it, but also, I hadn't finished reading all her entries yet, and I wouldn't let anyone take it from me until I knew all its secrets.

Ameal was shocked into silence. He went very still, staring at me. Jo's mind went to a different, relevant question that was equally hard to answer. "How long do you think he's known?"

I lied my ass off. "I'm not sure. Probably since the last dinner. He said something to me that...I don't know. I'm panicked and I don't know what to do next. I don't know if Ransom knows that all of us are impostors or if he thinks I'm tricking everyone, you included." Of course he would realize the entire delegation from Moriale was a sham if he knew I wasn't the correct Aurora. In fact, he probably met some of the crew when they stopped, but I needed Jo and Ameal to focus on our immediate survival and not on where I'd gotten this information.

"Well, we can—we can...I don't know what we can do about this, but it isn't the end of it," Jo said, nervously rapping his knuckles against the back of one of the chairs around my breakfast table.

"Do you think we should get Lev?" I asked. I didn't want Lev to know any part of this, but I knew they would protest that suggestion and keep the momentum going away from the questions I didn't want to answer.

"No," Ameal practically cut me off. Jo and I looked at him. "From a security standpoint, no. We could have a leak in the group. The fewer people that know about this, the better. What if Wynn let this slip over pillow talk with someone from Solterra? She's been very tight-lipped about who she's seeing."

I frowned at him. I would reveal the diary if the alternative was letting Wynn be my scapegoat. "The entire delegation from Solterra is men. It's probably that one lady's maid that's always offering to teach her how to cross-stitch," I said, waving my hand around as though I could physically dispel any accusation against her as I glared at Ameal. "I think we should place more scrutiny on the man who came from Agora and is friends with the guards from Solterra."

I nearly forgot that I knew I didn't need to accuse anyone of being a traitor to us, I was too mad that he would doubt Wynn, who was right there with us undermining the Empire.

Ameal crossed his arms, towering over me. "Being from Agora doesn't make me the enemy."

Jo held his hands up between us. "I think we all need more information first before we accuse anyone. We've all been working very hard to pull this assignment off. We don't need to turn against each other now. How did Ransom find out? How long has he known? The answer to both of those questions will help us figure out where to start.

"And I agree, maybe leaving Lev out of this is the right move. Involving him essentially involves the Emperor, we all know that. The Emperor is known to take heads first and ask questions later when plans fail."

I blinked at him. Jo had been the start of our secret meetings, but was always careful to keep his words neutral. I figured he held the meetings to protect me and ensure the mission went well. Whether he intended to or not, he had just admitted that he was aware Wynn had been opening the secret letters. It was the most anti-Empire sentiment I had ever heard from him. Maybe he was doubting our mission here too. *Later, Ness.*

"Alright, then what do we do? Do we think Ransom will kill us?" I voiced my biggest concern.

Ameal responded to that one, much more level-headed. "He won't. Like you said, I was stationed in Agora before coming here. I'm familiar with Ransom's way of doing things. He's not known for making rash decisions. He is ruthless when he needs to be, but I think we would already be dead if he didn't have some sort of game he was still playing with you—with us. He has some bigger plan for this."

"I agree," Jo said. "I think our best course of action is to keep going as we have been until we find out more. If he doesn't know that you know, let him think he's playing you. Maybe you can find out why he hasn't acted on this information yet."

While I didn't love this plan, it was the best we had at the moment, and they didn't ask for any of the details I wasn't willing to provide yet.

Both Jo and Ameal offered to start sleeping on the sofa in my sitting room, in case I was afraid of an attempt on my life. I declined their offers, but did stow a handful of knives around my room and under my pillow, just in case.

I lay in bed awake most of the night, wondering why Ransom could possibly want me to keep up the facade of being Aurora. It clicked around one in the morning that I *was* beneficial to him.

Every time I spoke to him, I would freely share the details I got from the others at the Gathering. He always appeared to be on the same page as me with those pieces of information, but him knowing I wasn't Aurora all along was a testament to how good of an actor Ransom really was. He could easily have been gleaning new knowledge from me and confirming his own findings this whole time. He was probably keeping me alive to be an extra set of ears for him. That would fit with why no one else knew the truth and why he never let on that he knew.

He had given me the hairpin. Did he know about the secret compartment? About the diary? Was he trying to get me to figure out that he knew I wasn't her?

I decided that I wouldn't tell Wynn after all. Ameal did have a fair point that she was pretty secretive about whoever she was sleeping with. That made me think there was something more to it than sex, and whether that was love or treachery, I couldn't be sure.

I had another odd realization in the middle of the night that was strangely comforting. Ransom had kissed me knowing I wasn't Aurora. And it had been quite the kiss.

CHAPTER THIRTY-SEVEN

When I went to training the next morning, Ameal looked like he hadn't slept last night, but still pushed me as hard as ever. It was unfair that the man could go without rest and still run further and faster than me. Wynn and Jo had gone to take the final set of dispatches to Port Mora well before I was up that morning.

"Are you going to make me train all day since we have nothing else to do?" I asked through gasps of air after we finished a round of sparring.

"I have things to do," Ameal replied coolly, his breathing completely even. "And maybe you should use your remaining unsupervised days to do the things *you* want to." He eyed me for a moment. "We'll just work until lunch."

I was anxious to finish Aurora's diary. I had been so shocked by the revelation that she met with Ransom, I hadn't even finished the entry I was reading the previous night.

I wouldn't have time to take Sugardrop out for a ride, but I couldn't pass on a visit to my sweet horse with so few days left.

"You again," the stable hand grunted.

I pretended I didn't hear his rudeness. He started over to where Sugardrop's saddle was stored. "You don't need to bother with that today, I'm only stopping by to say hello."

"Thank the Mother," he said, his relief visible. "I'll be glad to see the backside of that terror in a few days."

"What? She's so sweet." I was in complete disbelief that his bad attitude would extend to my gentle friend.

"She's only sweet to you. No one else can stand her. She bites everyone else in here any time they get near her gate," he said with a side eyed glance her way.

I petted Sugardrop's nose. She may be spirited, but I knew he was wrong as I fed her the apple and sugar cubes from my bag. I was having a hard time imagining giving her up in a few days. She was going to go back to her original owner, and I would go back to being horseless.

I wondered how much it cost to buy a horse and have it shipped to the mainland. Probably double what Imperial Protectors made in their entire service. I decided I would have to have one more ride with her tomorrow, just the two of us. I kissed her nose and told her as much.

"Well, I'll take her out tomorrow. Then you'll only have to worry about getting her ready to leave, and she'll be out of your hair forever," I told the stable hand on my way out.

"Two more times too many," he mumbled.

Back in my room, I settled into a chair by my fireplace, committed to finishing Aurora's diary, and picked up where I left off the night before.

3.) Meet with Ransom Dimitris to feel out his stance going into the Gathering.

I am certain that none of the Protectors saw me leaving for the meeting, although I did recognize one of the Protectors from the dock milling about Ransom's palace. He said he pays them for extra security when they don't have duty, and as long as they stick to guarding the outside, the commander of Agora has no issue with this.

Alright, this was getting me somewhere. Some of the Imperial Protectors moonlight as guards for Ransom. Ameal was certainly not someone I could trust, despite how much I had grown to like him. If there was any chance that he'd already been working for Ransom before coming here, then he would already know that Ransom was aware of my identity. It added another layer of mystery as to why no one had exposed me yet. It also made me wonder why Ameal had been training me in combat and defense for the last seven weeks.

Maybe Ameal didn't work for him.

My initial perception of Ransom was that he was surprisingly handsome and professional. I would have thought someone with his reputation would have been a bit more lascivious, but he was a proper gentleman.

Ransom made no promises about the future and simply said that he would give me more information as I gained his trust at the Gathering. I can't blame his overcareful attitude, since I feel similarly. What we are doing will most likely result in our deaths unless we are able to execute this to perfection. Although, this is hardly a worry to me, since the Empire has been after my head since the day I was born.

I tried to probe into the rumors that Agora has a secret grimoire from the witches of old. Ransom was even less forthcoming about that topic.

He only told me he was sure golden eyes would be beneficial to this rebellion. He also stated that his spies have reported there is another golden-eyed woman within the Empire. In fact, she is in the employ of the Imperial Protectorate in Capital City.

What? Ransom knew about me? It didn't sound like he knew who I was, only that I existed. And that information was worth sharing with Aurora?

It perhaps explained why Ransom hadn't blown my cover yet—he had some need for whatever latent trait hid behind my eyes. Maybe they held some ancient fae power that would help them work around the treaty. Maybe when Cavilth glowed so brightly for me, it *was* connected to my eyes.

I would have thought any who held the same power as me found in the Empire's midst would have been killed immediately. After all, I've had to spend most of my life hidden away so that the Empire's spies would not see my telltale eyes and order my execution. I wonder if they have some plan for her. They must.

It would be nice to meet at least one other person akin to myself. After the Gathering, I will work to see if I can arrange a meeting, if it's possible. We could learn so much from each other.

I rubbed at the pang in my chest for this meeting that would never happen. I wished I could have met her too. It was strange to think she knew of me.

But the same power as her? Aurora never went to Cavilth, and even if she had, making that rock glow brightly had not changed my power in any way. I reread the passage several times before I truly absorbed all the information it contained.

The Empire might have some plan for me. Some plan involving a power that I shared with Aurora because of our golden eyes. This was giving me more questions than answers.

There was only one more entry in the diary, and it was a fairly short one.

Nineteenth day of the Seventh Month

We are being pursued by another ship. I do not believe that they are Ransom's men, even though they are not flying any Imperial insignia. If I had to guess, I think we were spotted by a naval patrol off the Twelfth. We are nearing the Strait of Gallia near Kind. There will be little room to evade them there, if it comes to that.

We are prepared to do what we need to for the benefit of our people.

I have hope that if I should not survive this, there is another out there who may return balance to our kingdoms if I cannot, and give us another chance at justice.

I already knew how her story ended. Imperial records picked it up from here. I was glad Aurora's final day was still filled with hope that others would continue the rebellion without her.

While I lay in bed that night, I considered all I learned that day. Aurora had some unique power. Was it because of the golden eyes? If she had gotten the chance to touch Cavilth, would she have been the most powerful wielder? Powerful enough to overthrow the Empire?

She had said we were akin. Did that mean that I was more powerful than most? But I already knew I wasn't.

Except since I'd been in Nixia, my power had felt closer to the surface. I figured that was just because I wasn't using it and it was building up inside of me. Maybe that wasn't true, though.

The longer I thought about it, the more I knew what I needed to do the following day.

I slipped into my usual dreams of the Old Square. Getting crushed by a crowd, knocked down, looking up to see Wynn, Ameal, and Jo hanging in front of me. Instead of Lev, a beautiful, willowy woman came to offer me a hand. Her golden eyes were framed by long, wavy brown hair. I told Aurora to run and save herself, that we could meet another day. She tried to tell me something I couldn't hear over the crowd, and before she could flee, the Emperor appeared and slit both our throats. I woke up gasping, my face wet with tears.

CHAPTER THIRTY-EIGHT

When pale early light finally filled my bedroom, I looked out my window on a beautiful autumn morning. I dressed and headed down to the kitchens for supplies. A twinge of guilt resonated in my chest for standing Ameal up for training that morning, but then again, he was probably working with Ransom. Maybe.

The cooks were no longer surprised by my random appearances in their midst.

"What do you need, Miss Fey?" a portly man with short dark hair asked.

"Apples and sugar cubes, if you have them," I said.

"Ah, I think at this point, you can just call that *the usual*." He laughed. "That horse of yours must be a really kind beast to deserve to be spoiled this much."

"I think she is, but the stable hands might disagree," I said as I leaned my hip on a counter, waiting for the apples. I took in the scent of fresh-baked bread and the simmering sauce in the pot over the fire.

The cook chuckled. "Well, we all have the one that soothes us, right?"

He handed me the bag with the treats for Sugardrop, and I had another thought. "Do you have anything for me with vanilla bean in it?" I asked.

"Yes, as a matter of fact, I do. One second." He returned from the pantry holding a cloth filled with pastries. "Vanilla bean, pecan, and cardamom swirls. I made them up last night. You asked at the perfect time."

"Cardamom too? I've been wanting to try that, but I figured it would be too rare to ask about." I accepted the bundle in disbelief.

"Looks like the Mother wanted you to have pastries today, Miss Fey," he said, wiping his hands on his apron.

I ate one of the delicious pastries as I walked to the stables, wishing Aurora would have gotten her chance to taste them.

When I arrived, I saddled Sugardrop myself, since it was too early for the stable hands to be around, and they would be pleased I took over this particular task. She was sweet to me as I tacked her up. They were liars about her temperament.

We rode to the trail toward the mountain meadow. As we climbed further and further up the path, my stomach began to tighten over what we would find ahead of us.

The place where I'd encountered the bears was impossible to miss. We rounded the corner to find dead trees, and I took in the damage. I hadn't looked closely the day it happened, I was too focused on getting back to safety and I didn't want to acknowledge what I'd done.

Once I dismounted and tied up Sugardrop, I began to walk around slowly. I touched the brown, wilted flowers that blanketed the ground on either side of the trail, surrounded by the discarded pine needles on the forest floor. I ran my fingers along the dry, brittle branches of trees covered in crispy brown needles that showered down from the boughs at my touch, adding to the litter.

The ruins of this once beautiful place settled over me. I bowed my head and tears began to drip from my eyes. I shouldn't have been able to do this. I was out of magic before I got to this point in trail.

This amount of destruction required a huge amount of power.

There was no denying that the special abilities Aurora possessed, I did too. The normal limits of wielding must not apply to people with golden eyes.

If Aurora ever had her magic unlocked, what would she have been capable of?

No wonder Ransom thought a golden-eyed woman could turn the tides for this rebellion.

It was also no wonder the Empire wanted to kill Aurora. When I looked around, I couldn't fault the Emperor for thinking this power was too destructive to be allowed. I was only one person, untrained with this extra ability, and I had decimated this area. Could I really blame the Emperor when I had done this?

No, and the Empire would never allow this power to live.

Why had my power been so average since I'd been unlocked until now? I tugged on my mother's necklace as I tried to figure out what was different. Being outside Capital City? Being with Lev? The food in Nixia? Everything here was slightly different than back home. The water tasted like rocks and even the contraceptive tonic was a different color.

I sat down on the ground blanketed with needles and pressed my back to the barren trunk of a tree. I rested my arms on my knees propped in front of me, looking around at the blight I had spread. No animals would ever be able to forage here.

I had made a mess of this place, just like I had with my life.

Certainty settles over me that I would be sentenced to death by the Empire because of this power sooner or later. Aurora had said it in her diary, but I didn't want to believe it.

I wished I had more time to correct what I'd done. I had been feeding the Empire information for weeks. I would never be able to truly rectify my actions against the rebellion now if even half of what I had passed to the Emperor had been true.

I rubbed the dried needles in my hands. I didn't mean to take from them. I didn't mean to end their existence to prolong my own. My intent was not to destroy or harm. In fact, my intent was to make sure every being present walked away safely. I wished Aurora was here once again, this time to teach me about our shared powers and what had caused this.

Brushing my hands along the ground next to me, I moved the brittle spikes away and saw the dirt for the first time. Tiny green shoots were sprouting.

I flipped to my hands and knees and began brushing away more debris. The sprouts were everywhere, despite winter being just around the corner. They promised the flowers that lay wilted now would return before long.

I hadn't decimated this area. Had I started it anew?

I looked closer at the trees covered in dead needles. The trees themselves weren't dead. Close to the trunk, I could see tiny spots of green poking up. New needles had begun to sprout. I moved around to the plants along the path, and they all showed signs of new growth beneath the brittle exteriors.

At the last patch of earth I checked, I leaned my head forward to the earth and began to cry again. This wasn't a barren waste of mountainside, it was a beacon of renewal and hope. It had been wiped clean to protect myself, Sugardrop, and the bears, but it wouldn't stay that way. Maybe my wielding didn't have to cause destruction; maybe it could cause new growth. Aurora had mentioned that I might be able to help return balance in her stead. This must be what she meant.

I let my tears soak into the soil, an offering to the Father for healing this land and the Mother for creating newness out of the ashes.

CHAPTER THIRTY-NINE

I didn't fully know what my extra wielding abilities meant.

My thoughts eddied around all these revelations as I packed the remainder of my items away for the journey home. Trying to process them in a meaningful way. Trying to figure out a way I would get to live to see my next birthday.

I heard Wynn return to her room around noon that day, but I would have struggled to keep my newly realized powers to myself if I had seen her. Wynn's dalliance with someone else at the Gathering made her a liability.

I was unsure how much knowledge Lev had. The Emperor knew that somehow gold eyes equated to extra magic. It didn't seem likely that Lev would have gotten so close to me if he had known I was going to die by the Empire's hand at some point. Still, if that was what the Emperor wanted, he could order Lev to kill me at any time. Even if Lev wouldn't go through with it, I had to keep him at a distance.

By the time night fell, I was tired of thinking and getting nowhere, so I got ready for bed far earlier than normal. I hoped that sleep would relieve me from the dread that was steadily tightening in my chest.

I was washing my face and wondering if I should request a tea from the kitchens to help me sleep when a knock came from my suite door. It wasn't exactly late, but it was well beyond the hours of a normal visit, even from Wynn.

I stalked to the door. I didn't bother trying to figure out who wanted to see me at this hour. Imminent death made such things too trivial to consider.

"Fox," Ransom said by way of greeting and stepped into my room, quickly snapping the door shut behind him. He was dressed as if he had been walking outside in the cold autumn night, even though he only needed to traverse a few halls in the warm castle to get from his room to mine.

Shit, I had completely forgotten he'd said he needed to talk to me. When he mentioned it during the last event, it had seemed harmless, but after the discoveries in the diary, this could not be good.

I took on my Aurora stance from my first few weeks here, straightening my spine, throwing my shoulders back, tilting my chin up, and pressing my chest proudly forward. I looked Ransom in the eyes. If he was going to turn me in or kill me, I would meet that fate with dignity. I did wish I wasn't wearing only a Nixian nightgown, but I couldn't do much about that.

He took in the thin silk and trails of lace that barely covered me. A smile spread across his lips, and his eyes glimmering with the mischievous look I was so used to seeing when we put on our performances together. It was a devastatingly handsome expression on him. I didn't like how that made me flush, especially now that I knew how talented that mouth was. I wasn't a fan of the idea that I was going to die with these as my last thoughts.

"I did come here for business, Fox. But not the kind of business you're dressed for." He couldn't seem to keep the smirk off his face as his eyes skated over my form again.

"Then stop looking," I gritted out. "Besides, if I want to die in this or nothing at all, then that's how I'll go." I tried to remember where the closest knife I hid was in the sitting room.

His eyes met mine, the mischief gone from them. "We can't talk in here. Go put on more clothes—and shoes, and a coat. We're going for a walk."

I considered objecting, or going to my room to grab the biggest knife I had and trying to kill him first.

"I'm sorry for this nighttime meeting. I tried to talk with you after the last dinner, but Lev interrupted. It's now or never," he said.

I decided that I had too many questions I wanted answered, no plans for the future that assured my safety, and I had magic. I could go with Ransom and see if he could offer me any help with any of this. If his intent was to kill me away from everyone in the castle, I could always wield magic or stab him. Or use this golden eye magic too, now.

I pulled on lined leggings and shoved my feet into boots. Rather than change my top, I pulled on the heaviest jacket I had over my thin nightgown and went back to Ransom.

He poked his head out of my door and checked the hallway, then silently signaled to me to follow him. He led me out of the castle and along the shadows of a brisk courtyard blanketed in night. The frost on the grass crunched beneath our feet as we exited the keep walls through an isolated archway that was suspiciously left unlocked. I followed him into the dark wilderness beyond.

He led me up the mountain along a path I was unfamiliar with, my legs having to work hard to keep up with his longer stride. Eventually, we got to the top of a sheer rocky face on the mountainside. The gray rock was covered in boulders and pebbles until it dropped away, providing what was likely a dramatic view of the hills below in the daytime. At night, it was a darkened abyss. He sat on a boulder and waited for me to catch my breath from the quick pace on the steep incline.

"Is this as far away as we need to get to talk?" I asked.

He patted a second boulder right next to his for me to come sit on. I stared at him for a moment. Although it appeared he wasn't going to kill me, I couldn't guarantee I no longer wanted to stab him for leading on a silent march through the dark, freezing woods.

The tiredness in my legs won out and I sat next to him. "What?"

He smiled and pointed up over the line of the trees to the sky. I was sick of mind games, but had already come this far, so I sighed as I turned my head to the direction he was pointing.

I looked over the outlines of the surrounding mountains and my jaw dropped. A dazzling display of aurora borealis was lighting up the night beyond the castle. Bars of greens and blues rolled through the sky, streaming wisps of brilliant smoke along the horizon. I watched the colors shine like a beacon set by the mountains, their slow ripples pulsing over us, a wavering dance among the stars. I was so drawn into the calm bands of light, I was unsure how long I sat there. I only knew that I would never tire of this sight. The colors had slowly shifted, shimmering hues of pink and violet now undulating overhead as well.

"Ness." His voice was distant to where my mind was, but it pulled me back to him instantly. Hearing my name from him didn't send a jolt through me, like it had the times Wynn said it. My name said with his voice was a gentle caress to my soul, a balm after having heard it so few times in these stressful, lonely weeks. It was natural coming from him. The way his voice shaped those letters was the way it was always supposed to be said.

I finally pulled my eyes from the lights and looked at him. I hadn't realized my neck had started to ache while I looked up and rubbed at the stiffness.

"I thought you would appreciate it, even if it wasn't your name-sake," Ransom said, leaning back on his hands propped on the rock, a smile threatening his lips.

"Thank you." My voice was surprisingly rough.

I didn't want to change the softness of this moment, but I was running out of time. I cleared my throat before I went on. "I'm sure you know about the diary I recently found in the secret compartment of Aurora's trunk."

"Diary? What trunk?" He looked at me blankly. "How would I possibly know that?"

"You gave me the key to the compartment!"

"I don't think I did."

"That hairpin."

He laughed. "That? Ameal found it hidden in the boat and gave it to me to see if it meant anything. I couldn't find anything special about it, so I figured you should have it. I'm glad to hear it came in handy."

I looked down at my lap. "So Ameal is working for you?" I figure this was the case, but I was still sad to know he wasn't truly someone I could trust.

"He has for a long time now."

"Then I'm sure Ameal told you, I found the diary entry a few days ago that talked about her visit to Agora."

"He didn't know about the diary, just that you knew. We stayed up all night after that, trying to piece together how you found out." We watched the lights in the sky for a bit. "It's always seemed wrong to call you by her name, like it dishonored her. Plus *Fox* suited you, even if you're not from Moriale," he said, too lightly for how I felt.

I hunched to look down at my hands, picking at imaginary dirt under my nails. His words took something out of me I didn't know I wanted. "You don't need to tell me I'm a piss-poor Aurora. I can feel it in everything I do. I know I'm a constant letdown to her memory. I read her journal and she was so dedicated to her people. She wanted to give them freedom. Fight for them. The only thing I've ever wanted is to save my own neck." Tears pricked my eyes. These fucking tears. I had cried more in my time in Nixia than I ever remembered crying before.

"I think you want to save a whole crew of people's necks," he said, flipping my words on me. "Even if Ameal wasn't keeping me informed, I could see it in everything you did. You care a lot about getting your party out of here alive. Isn't that type of caring how revolutions get started?"

"I don't know. These last two months have made it very clear I don't know anything. Everything here shows me that all I've been taught and led to believe up to this point is a lie. I don't even know how to begin to sort it all out." I placed my feet in front of me on the rock and rested my chin on my knees, hugging my legs.

The cold was starting to get to me. I wished I had put on a shirt over my nightgown now.

I remembered I didn't have to pretend to be Aurora and moved my hands, stirring the air. I pulled sticks from the ground by the tree line over to make a pile in front of us. When they were arranged to my satisfaction, I switched my wielding to let a flame lick from the palm of my hand to the sticks until it kindled a small campfire in front of us.

I tucked my hands between my legs and body to wait for the warmth of the now-crackling flames to wash over me.

Ransom smiled at me. "Starting a fire without ever getting up," he said, shaking his head. "Impressive."

I looked at him blankly. This was wielding anyone could do. *Impressive* was not the word for it.

"If it's any consolation," he said, "you've been far more fun to work with these last few weeks than Aurora would have been. I don't think she would have gone along with a plan that allowed anyone to remotely think we were in item, much less openly try to get in my bed in front of the entire Gathering. Her standards were much higher." Amusement trickled through his words.

I scowled at him, dropping my legs down. "The day of the lawn game was already the most embarrassing thing I've ever done without it ever being mentioned again."

"Don't give me that, you let Lev in your bed. That's a pretty low standard." His tone was laced with disgust and something else.

My jaw dropped. "How did you— What do you— I didn't sleep with Lev."

"Don't bother lying. I know your tells, and Ameal has been keeping me informed of everything since day one, Nessamia Riseworth."

"Don't ever call me Nessamia again. And Ameal doesn't know about Lev and me."

He sighed. "Ameal does know, but only because Lev already kissed and told." I stared at him in disbelief that Lev would share that with Ameal. "I've been intercepting Lev's letters to the Emperor since the beginning. Ameal has been making copies of them before Jo sends them off."

"Wait, Lev wrote that we slept together in the letters? Why would he tell the Emperor that? It would just get both of us kicked out of the Protectorate," I said while trying to keep the emotions from my voice. Ransom didn't need to know how badly that hurt me. I balled my fists in my lap until my knuckles blanched and my fingernails dug tiny crescents into my palms. I couldn't believe he would report something so private. I felt so exposed and betrayed.

Ransom's brows pressed together, and he chewed his lower lip.

"Ness," he started too gently. "I really don't want to tell you this, but you deserve the truth." I braced myself for what he was about to say. If Ransom was showing remorse...

"Lev won't get kicked out of service of the Empire for sleeping with you," he said quietly. He reached into his coat and pulled out a bundle of folded paper.

"These are copies of the letters we have been intercepting from Lev. The writing below each line is the decoded message. We only broke the code last week. We don't have any of the Emperor's responses, but Lev's letters spell it all out. I'm so sorry."

CHAPTER FORTY

I slid off the rock to read the letters by the light of the fire. I didn't remember taking the pages from him or unfolding them.

There were so many of them. So many words to take in. My eyes flew across the letters, reading sentences here and there, my vision getting blurrier with each piece of paper, but quickly building the picture Ransom alluded to all the same.

Thank you for permission to do what is needed. She is still off-bal-ance from the quick turn of events and what we manufactured at the Old Square. She will be easily manipulated by authority figures. Seducing her into submission will take little effort.

-LD

✝✝✝

On the evening of the sixth, I kissed her and left her room, claiming that it was a forbidden attraction. She is weak and has been ensnared by this trap of leaving her desires unfulfilled. This should keep her eager to please me for some time.

-LD

✝✝✝

I am frequently separating her from Partson and Beckworth by sending them to Port Mora. She should have little opportunity to piece anything together with the help of others. I have continued to lead her on to great effect.

She is still too overwhelmed by the task given to her to see any of the ways we are using her. I am not worried about her ever figuring it out. She has never been bright enough to piece together our influence in her life over these many years.

-LD

✝✝✝

On the twenty-seventh of this month, Dimitris came too close to her, so I bedded her. Even though it was not strictly necessary for the mission, it should be effective in ensuring that Dimitris will not sway her easily manipulated loyalties. I didn't even bother to fully undress her, yet she believes this to be real enough to ask me to spend the night in her room. I, of course, would not. She is almost too easy to control.

-LD

✝✝✝

On the seventh day of the Ninth month, I invited her to my room for dinner, continuing the impression that I wish to be involved with her. She moved the conversation to the impossibility of our situation, and I had to say nothing to let her feel as though the termination of our "relationship" lies fully on her shoulders. This should keep her beholden to me with hope, long enough to complete this mission without worry of her straying into Dimitris's charms again. She may be desperate to please those around her, but I do not think she is so promiscuous as to take up with him now.

-LD

I wished these were fakes. Some ploy by Ransom to win me over. But these letters held details only Lev and I would know. I hadn't shared some of these things with Ameal, Wynn, or Jo. The date. There was the fucking date when I had sex with Lev. The fact that I never took my dress off that last night...

They went on and on. Everything was laid bare for anyone to see. How easy I was to manipulate to his plan. How he kept me from interacting with the other leaders except when he wanted me to.

I was wrong—drunkenly flirting with Ransom in front of everyone that day was certainly not the most embarrassing thing I'd ever done.

Falling into trap after trap set by Lev and the Emperor was.

I flipped through to the last page. It would probably be the one Jo and Wynn had just sent.

Instructions are clear. She has become very withdrawn from me since our last private evening. I am unsure how she is spending her time, but I fear she is too close to those that could give her the truth. I will terminate her as a liability before we leave. There is little more we can use her for in the next two months anyway. Hastening her execution will finish eliminating the gold-eyed threat.

   -LD

My hands were shaking, my entire body felt numb. My brain was filled with a strange buzzing. I couldn't think. I couldn't make my limbs move. Was I even breathing? But then, I let myself slump until I was on the ground. I burst into laughter. I lay over on my side laughing, facing the fire, tears falling freely until they turned into sobs.

I knew I looked deranged. Pine needles were matting into my hair. They were poking me through my leggings. None of it mattered. I was going to die tomorrow. I'd assumed the Emperor would kill me, but without a timeline attached to it, it hadn't felt real. Now, I wouldn't even be able to protect Wynn or Jo. It was over. I was the only other golden-eyed woman in the Empire, and I could do nothing. I would never know what could have been.

Ransom slid off his rock too and sat next to me. His thigh pressed against the top of my head as he collected the letters from the ground around me. His presence next to me was enough of a comfort that my sobs faded, replaced by rapid thoughts and his warmth.

I was a fucking joke. My whole life. Cavilth glowed brighter for me than anyone in memory and yet, my power was completely average until a few weeks ago. I had these gold eyes, the one thing that made me special, and they were a death sentence. I had always been a pawn in someone else's game, a thing to be used and set aside. A means to someone else's end. I was special somehow, and I would never understand what exactly that meant.

I must have said some of this out loud, but I didn't remember my mouth moving.

"You're not a joke. You are powerful, even if you've never been allowed to use it," Ransom said evenly. It didn't feel like he was trying to pacify me, but that was what he really thought. He stroked a strand of hair away from my face.

My emotions washed over me too quickly. It was like standing too deep in rough waters, waves pummeling you, and each time you tried to stand up, a new one knocked you over. I wasn't going to be knocked over again. The firm presence of his thigh against my head was the only part of my life that felt nice anymore.

I sat up. "Fuck me." I began to unbutton my coat.

"What?" he said, looking at me and not moving. That was stupid, he should be taking off his pants.

"Fuck me. I've got less than a day left to live, and I don't want to die knowing Lev was the last person I slept with. It wasn't great. Besides, you're way more attractive. I'll die happier knowing he wasn't able to keep me from being promiscuous or whatever the fuck he said." I tossed my coat to the side as I toed off my boots.

He stood up at the same time I did. Good, he was going to start getting undressed. I didn't want to be naked in this cold longer than strictly needed. I bent over to slide off my pants and underwear. I felt a breeze all the way down my front. Right, this nightgown. I was probably on full display to Ransom.

"Ness," he sighed deeply and rubbed his eyes.

"After that kiss, it's pretty clear we both would enjoy this," I said as I got my pants over my socks. I looked up, and I was at the perfect height to see a promising outline growing on him. I stood and grabbed the hem of my nightgown to start lifting it up.

He grabbed my wrist, stopping me. "No."

"No?!" I practically screeched at him. "Listen, no one is that good of an actor." I waved my free hand in the direction of his pants. "Let's just fuck and then you can let Lev kill me or you can kill me or whatever you need, your choice."

I tried to take off my dress again, this time with one hand trapped, but couldn't.

"Ness, it's not—stop," he said firmly. "I told you I don't sleep with women who are clearly in a bad way. You are *very* clearly in a bad way. And I don't want you dead, either."

I looked at him until the part of me thinking this was a good idea got smaller and smaller. When it totally disappeared, tears started again, silently pouring down my face. I don't think they ever really stopped since I started reading the letters. I was a mess. Trying to get him to have sex with me while crying and covered in pine needles on a freezing mountainside.

"You're right. You're right. You're right. Sorry," I rambled. "No, I–I don't want to pressure you into something. That's the last thing I want. I'm sorry. This isn't who I am normally. I just, I'm sorry."

I looked down at where he was still holding my wrist. The feel of his callused palm was stilling me, keeping me from getting lost.

When I looked back up, he was watching me carefully. He tugged on my wrist ever so slightly, but the invitation was clear. I took a step forward and allowed myself to be pressed into a hug that I didn't want to admit I needed so badly. He let me rest my cheek on his chest and be enveloped in his warmth until my tears stopped.

"It is a lot." His deep voice rumbled through his chest and into me. "It was a lot for me when we decoded those, and they aren't about me. It was sickening, the way he talked about you, and undeserved. Anyone would be thrown off after reading these."

I took a long breath and let him go.

The cold started to creep over me. I realized my skin was prickled and my nipples peaked against the silk of the nightgown as a small shiver ran up me.

He picked up my pants off the ground and dusted the needles from them before handing them to me. His attention went back to the lights in the sky. I was grateful, since there was no way I could put them back on without flashing some part of me to him in the short dress, and modesty had returned to me along with my common sense.

When they were on, he knelt in front of me and put my boots back on my feet, dusting the dirt off my socks first and handing me my coat before we both sat back down.

For a long time, the only sound was the crackle of the fire in front of us. I wielded more air to add sticks to it, allowing it to hiss and sputter and drown out the roar of shame in my ears.

"I'm sorry again," I said. "You've really met me at possibly the worst point in my life. This isn't who I normally am. That doesn't excuse it, but I wanted you to know that."

"Ness, I'm not judging you. I want to help you." He cocked his head. "I think we can help each other, really."

Ice slid into my stomach. There it was. The real reason he was being kind to me. He didn't actually want to help me through all these emotions. He wanted me ready to fight against the Emperor, so he could ask for whatever gold-eyed help he needed and I would have to agree.

"What do you want from me and when do I die?"

He looked over at me for a moment before sighing. "I want to get you safely off this island. I want to bring you back to Agora and hide you there from the Empire." I waited for it. "If that's not enough motivation,

I'll give you the second-best room in the palace. I'll pay you well, not like the Imperial Protectorate."

"The catch, Dimitris."

"You're not dumb, Ness. The Empire knows that golden eyes mean some sort of special ability. We need you to fight with us in the rebellion."

"And when do I die in this plan?"

"Hopefully not for a very long time." He frowned. "But I don't know anything about this supposed power. When the witches cast their final spell, they had to use their life forces to do it. I'm not saying that will be what's needed of you. I'm saying I don't know."

Fuck. I truly was out of good options. My best chance was to escape the Emperor with a crime lord, to go try to do something completely unknown, with a fair chance that it would cost me my own life.

That was my *best* chance.

Because my other options were certain death with Lev or trying to figure out some way to save myself in the next twelve hours. Even if I got off this island, I would spend the rest of my life running from rebel leaders who would now want me dead, and hiding from the Emperor.

"How long is this supposed to take? Do I have to spend the rest of my life with you?"

"That's entirely up to you." The firelight played off his handsome features as he looked at me. "However long it takes you figure out this power and turn the tides against the Empire. We'll be coordinating with Mira and Parisa to do it at the most advantageous time. Hopefully in line with when the mercenaries arrive this summer."

I sighed. "So everyone here knows I'm an imposter?"

He tilted his head in thought. "Queen Elara is very astute, but I'm not sure about her. But the royals from Kind don't to my knowledge. It was actually Mother-sent that Queen Atla ended up being so jealous of you. I was afraid she was going to spill real information to you about the rebellion at first." He gave a small chuckle. "When Mira found out you're an Imperial spy, she was not pleased. Really wanted to kill you right away. I've got her mostly under control with this plan."

"Shit, so I have no chance of having a life ever again, even if I can do this." I rubbed my forehead.

"Not true. If you agree to this plan, you will be formally pardoned by Solterra, Gallia, and even Decca," he replied. "We're assuming Kind, Nixia, and Moriale will follow suit once they know what has happened here and how you plan on making it up to the rebellion. They'll see this as penance for spying for the Emperor, even if we made sure we never gave you anything worthwhile to report back to him."

I sank my forehead into my hands, bracing my elbows on my knees. I stared at the fire in front of me, letting the licking flames lull me into a trance. I focused on the rolling glow of the coals as the last of my heightened emotions drained away from me.

"This is just going from being forced into one country's plan by Lev into being forced into six countries' plans by the Gathering," I said. "And the ultimate outlook for my life isn't that significantly better."

He shrugged. "I'm trying to give you a choice where I can. Unfortunately, the choices are to join the rebellion or be killed by Lev tomorrow."

"It isn't much of a choice. I can either not go with you and get murdered by any number of people. Or I can go with you and hopefully not die too soon in the future."

"I'm really sorry this is the position we're all in, Ness," he said. "But seeing as I'm your only chance at getting out of here alive, we've already arranged for you to come with me. In fact, Ameal should have already gathered your trunks and sent them to the docks while we've been out here."

"Ameal broke into my room and packed my things?"

"He's only taking what's already packed, and it wouldn't be the first time he went into your room when you weren't there. He went through your room on the first night to make sure you didn't have any extra secrets we needed to know about." He flicked a pine needle off his pants leg. "But mostly, it was an excuse to convince you to train with him."

"Ameal is the one who broke into my room on the first night? If he was the reason I was in danger in the first place, why did he bother to train me?"

"Well, there wasn't much breaking involved, you left your door unlocked." He shrugged. "At first, he didn't care much if you trained. I ordered that. I needed you to survive. The combat standards the Protectors have for their wielders are terrible."

"At first? But he helped me so much. He's my friend." I felt silly to admit that anyone here felt like a friend. "Or I thought he was."

Ransom nodded with a bemused smirk. "He started to like you. I don't know what you did to win him over, but as our plans progressed, he became a pretty fierce defender of yours." He laughed. "He hated our plan to pretend we were together, but he knew you were safe with me, so he never said anything."

"Why did he hate it then?" I asked, genuinely curious.

"He was afraid you would end up falling in love with me or something," he laughed again, looking off to the sky where the aurora borealis was fading to almost nothing. "That was before he knew you were with Lev."

I waved at the stack of letters on the boulder. "I was never truly *with* Lev. But either way, why did it matter to him? I know you were just using me too, but still, can't I do what I want?"

"It's not that. My reputation in Agora is not one of commitment. He didn't want you to get hurt." The flickering glow played off the flush of his cheeks as his fingers drummed against his thigh in restlessness. "I was never planning on hurting you, but you grew on me too. I came to really enjoy our time together, Fox. You're an interesting person, much funnier than I expected. And smarter." He looked forward, to the trees and the view of the mountains beyond them. "And Ameal kept me updated. Even when you felt like you couldn't do it, you never gave up on what you were supposed to be doing. It would have put his life at risk, and Jo and Wynn. You pushed through for people you barely knew. Then when you started to doubt the Empire, you couldn't give up on those around you. Even if you didn't have magic at all, you would be one of the strongest people here." He closed his eyes and shook his head slightly.

I wanted to do the same. His words had made my mind feel light and warm. It was so at odds with my situation. The cavity of darkness I'd carried in my chest was being patched together—not quite full and whole yet, but getting there.

"You're just trying to flatter me so I agree to go with you."

"If I were trying to flatter you, I would be telling you how very hard it was to say no to your recent proposition. But I think you caught a glance of that for yourself." He looked me in the eyes. "I want to give you a choice tonight. I know it's a mockery of a choice, far from true freedom. But it's all I can offer you right now. "

I exhaled loudly. "Well, you did also offer to give me the best bedroom in the palace and pay me more than I could ever spend in my long life."

"Second-best bedroom and reasonable pay. If you want the best bedroom, you'll have to share."

"What about Wynn and Jo?"

"There's plenty of room on the ship for them too," he said with a nod. "Ameal is already trying to plant the idea for Jo to come with us. It's been difficult, though. Apparently, Jo has been a bit cold with Ameal ever since a certain fox shouted that they shouldn't be trusting Protectors from Agora."

"Well, I was right."

He tipped his head in concession.

We both knew I didn't have any room to negotiate. His ship was the only way I could make it off the island. And I appreciated the last illusion of control over my life he was giving me.

"I have two friends in Capital City, still in the Protectorate. Anyone there would know they mean a lot to me. If I run from Lev, from the Emperor, their lives will probably be in danger too."

"Fortunately for them, I know quite a few professionals in Agora that are good at making people disappear."

CHAPTER FORTY-ONE

The aurora borealis had long since disappeared from the sky and I had no idea what time it was, but could tell it was late. Ransom and I walked back to the castle after putting out my fire. My body was spent and ready for bed by the time we made it to my suite.

When I opened the door to my room, Ransom stepped inside with me. I gave him a curious look. "I'm not sure if you're angling for a good night kiss or what here, but I'm just going to bed."

"So am I." He took off his coat and hung it on the back of a chair at the table. My entire body heated. He could not mean what I thought he was implying. I was still a woman in a bad way. I probably would be for a long time after those letters.

"I, umm, don't want you to fuck me anymore, if that's what this is about," I said sheepishly. It was surreal that those words were coming out of my mouth after I hadn't been able to stop thinking about his kiss for weeks now.

His lips kicked up to the side and he looked at me so intently, the heat in my body settled in my core. He leaned forward and tilted my chin up with his hooked forefinger, running his thumb over my bottom lip in a barely there touch. I sucked in a sharp breath.

"Are you sure about that, my little Fox?" he said, his voice deep and husky. His face leaned in closer to mine. The smell of cedar and campfire was coming off him along with the fresh, citrusy scent.

I wasn't sure.

"I'm sure," I said firmly.

"Good." His eyes were focused on me so intently while a smile played on his lips. "I'm staying here to guard you, and I have no doubt a night with you would consume my full attention." He ran his thumb along my lip one more time. "I'll wait until I can take my time with you."

A shuddering breath came out of me when the warmth of his hand left my face. It was good to know we were back to our act for the Gathering.

He sat down on the sofa and began taking his boots off. "Are you serious about staying?" I asked.

"There's a risk that Lev noticed you or your trunks leaving tonight. Don't you think he might try to end things a little early if he suspects you're up to something? You need someone to stay here and make sure that doesn't happen." His voice had an odd tone, like he was still trying to come back from what he said a moment ago. For the first time, I wondered if he wasn't acting as much as I previously believed.

"Why can't Ameal stay here?" I asked.

"Well, he did offer and you turned him down a few nights ago, so it would be very strange to Jo if you requested Ameal suddenly come over in the middle of the night," he said matter-of-factly.

He began to unlace his pants, and I almost yelled at him that we had just established that we were not having sex. I was hanging on to that resolution by a thread. Then I saw he had sleep pants on under his normal ones. I guess he had been planning this all long.

"Do you have a blanket I can use?" he asked as he arranged the throw pillows on the couch.

"Yes. Let me get it from the dressing room."

I couldn't believe this was happening. I didn't exactly trust Ransom yet, but he wasn't wrong. Tomorrow, I would be trying to sneak away on his ship, and if Lev found out about it, my odds of survival were much better sticking near Ransom. I hoped.

I did have a gut feeling he wouldn't hurt me, and that he was being honest about his intentions for tonight and his plan. I believed he did want me to survive. But then again, maybe I was still so thrown off from recent events I was simply being seduced by another powerful man in my life.

"I'll go in first, and make sure no one's lurking in the dark," he said, getting to his feet.

I followed behind him and tried not to focus too much on the way the sleep pants were hugging his ass. The memory of his hands on me in that dark room in the library kept popping into my head as I took off my coat, boots, and leggings while he checked my rooms. Great. My underwear was still on the mountainside.

"All good," he said.

I went into the dressing chamber to grab a blanket on a high shelf while he made use of the bathing chamber. I was still reaching up, straining with all my height to try to grab the thick woolen blanket tucked up there, when he came into the dressing room. Perfect, just in time to see my very short dress lifted up.

He didn't say anything about it, passing me to reach up and easily grab the blanket. Maybe he hadn't noticed. Hopefully his attention had been elsewhere.

He smirked devilishly and thrust a wad of fabric into my hand as he walked past me.

It seemed I had been wrong. My underwear had been in Ransom's pocket.

I thought I wouldn't sleep at all since I had a crime lord on my couch and an Imperial officer waiting to kill me, but my body was too exhausted to care. I fell into a dreamless sleep before I could even finish pulling the pine needles out of my hair.

The next morning, I threw on my robe and twisted my mess of curls up into a quick bun, securing it with the fox hairpin, which had become my favorite.

Ransom woke and wasted no time in getting dressed. I tried to catch a glimpse of him before he put his shirt on, but he was too fast for me and already dressed by the time I got into the room.

That didn't seem fair. If he got to see my butt last night, I should at least get to see his muscles or how far his tattoos extended under his shirt. I sat next to him on the sofa, waiting for teasing or awkwardness, but there was none of that.

"I think you'll like Agora," he said. "I may be partial, but the food there is far superior to Capital City. The vendors near the docks use spices that are so fresh and exotic. You won't have tasted anything like it before. Ameal told me there were a few dishes you'd never had before Nixia. You'll get to try so many new things there."

"Do you think someone as uncultured as me will fit in?"

"Agora is full of people from all walks of life, and I think someone who has been kept as confined as you will thrive there."

I laughed and wondered if I should request breakfast for both of us when the clock chimed nine, and he went to stand by the door.

"Keep as many knives on yourself as you can all day, Ness. I would love to get you out of here before the ball, before Lev can catch on, but we need the day to prepare everything."

I nodded, joining him by the door. He raised a hand and tucked an errant curl behind my ear. I wanted to thank him for making sure I would get out. For trying to keep me safe. But I also knew he needed me for his plan, and the words died in my throat. I tugged on the curl now dangling behind my ear, pulling it straight, then letting it bounce back into a spiral. His eyes were fixed on the movement as he chewed his cheek.

"If you knew I was a spy, why did you kiss me in the library?"

Ransom opened his mouth, but closed it again when my door opened. Ameal poked his head in. "You're all clear all the way back to your room."

Ransom slipped out with a quick glance back at me. "Lock your door."

I soaked in the bath and picked the remaining pine needles out of my hair as I contemplated my life.

Lev's betrayal stung as deeply in the light of day as it had when I read the letters. Maybe more so now that I'd had time to think about how long and how profoundly he had been deceiving me.

I needed to get to Jo as soon as I entered the ball and convince him to come with me.

There was also Wynn, who I wouldn't leave behind, but her al-legiance might be with her mystery girlfriend. If it was a lady's maid, it would likely be fine. But if it were Mira, would she have spread her sentiments about killing me to Wynn?

Everything was unknown. If I couldn't do powerful enough magic, my head would still be on the line, just sometime in the future. I wasn't naive enough to miss that. What if the magic I needed to use took my life? What shit choices.

I began to understand Aurora's rationale for taking her own life. It was some semblance of agency to pick your own death over one someone else gave you. Maybe if Lev captured me tonight, I might follow her lead.

I put on the undergarments that had been left out, the ones designed for my dress I had been saving for this evening. I wrinkled my nose at the knowledge that Ameal had been in here collecting my trunk and had seen them laying out. I looked at the tiny bows and unnecessary ribbons and grimaced. This was probably the feeling a person would have if their brother saw their undergarments.

When I'd first set these aside to wear tonight, right after Wynn brought them from Port Mora, I thought that Lev might be seeing them after the ball. He could get to peel the beautiful dress from me and be greeted by the sultry fashion underneath. Now that idea made me nauseous.

Wynn came in to help with my hair about an hour before the ball. She was already dressed in a simple, floor-length gown, hair looking like it always did, falling straight to her chin.

She lined my eyes with kohl. I looked powerful and self-assured, with rouge on my cheeks and lips, the way I always imagined Aurora. While she applied the colors to my face, my hair dried in its usual curls. We decided against fighting that battle. I sat in front of the mirror as she stood behind me, gently twisting back my hair into a low bun. The style allowed some curls to be free and frame my face. She grabbed the fox-headed pin to fix it in place.

"Did you use that one on purpose?" I watched her in the mirror.

"No, it was just the one on the top of the dish," she said, eyes still on my hair. "But it's appropriate for tonight."

Wynn was quieter than normal as she worked. I wondered if she felt the charge in the air as well. The feeling that whatever happened tonight would change our lives, and possibly our realm forever.

"Finished," she proclaimed. I looked up at myself in the mirror and was pleased with the effect. I looked ready for this ball, regal in a way that I had never known was possible before. I wished I would be able to truly celebrate tonight instead of just trying to survive.

I slipped off my robe and pulled on the heavily beaded dress. The fabric underneath was a midnight blue, but with gleaming blue, green, and opalescent beads and gems encrusting the dress. It truly looked like a display of the northern lights incarnate, an aurora borealis for Aurora's last evening.

I had been so excited when this dress came back from the seamstress. It was my favorite by far. I'd imagined twirling to the music at the end of a successful mission in it. Now I would be lucky if I lived long enough to change out of it.

True to Nixia fashion, the neckline gave a generous view of my chest. The fabric hugged every curve of my body. I wondered if this was how the seamstress had been able to add the extra inches I needed to all these dresses, by removing all the fabric that would cover my chest.

Ness from a few months ago would have hated this and the attention it was sure to draw. It would have been a dress she didn't deserve. Now I couldn't care less about the attention. Everyone here already knew everything about me. I'd been under their eyes constantly, and this wouldn't change that.

The Ness tonight only hated that this dress was probably part of some creative plan by Aurora that I could never have conceived. She probably would have been able to use this dress to her political advantage in some brilliant plot.

I just wore it to be a pretty little pawn in someone else's game. It could be the Emperor's game, where Lev would defeat me. It could be Ransom's game, where I couldn't be sure of the ending. But it was all another move made by someone else.

I was powerless.

"Your trunks are already gone?" she asked, looking around the dressing chamber.

"Yes." I turned to walk out.

She grabbed my arm to spin me back to her. She put her hands on my shoulders to keep me locked on her. "Ness, I really am your friend, you know." There was so much sincerity in her eyes. Life was too short to not believe her. *My* life was too short.

I sagged in her arms. "My trunks are on Ransom's ship."

Her hands stopped digging into my shoulders. "Thank the Mother. I was really worried there for a while when you were sleeping with Lev." She dropped her hold on me.

"What? How did you know that?"

"The apothecary has been delivering your contraceptive tonic to your lady's maid all these weeks. I've just been leaving it on your table after I got it." She shrugged. "Who else could it be for? Ransom isn't foolish enough to actually sleep with dignitaries he needs to use for alliances."

"Why didn't you say anything before now?"

"I tried to warn you that I didn't like how he treated you, but you didn't want to hear it. You barely trusted me. And I was already being pretty blatant about my stance on the Empire. If I had told you I knew all your secrets, you would have run from me." She scrunched her nose. "Plus, how embarrassing for you."

I sighed. "Yeah, I see that now."

"But I'm really glad you're going with Ransom. I really didn't want to have to fight on opposite sides of the battlefield from you."

I had figured Wynn was truly against the Empire for so long that this confirmation was no surprise to me, but how she fit into the rebellion was still uncertain.

A bell chimed outside in the courtyard, letting us know it was time to go down to our fate.

CHAPTER FORTY-TWO

I walked into the great hall of Castle Nix, and it was barely recognizable as the room I had spent so many previous nights in. The long table in the middle was gone, and instead smaller, tall tables surrounded the perimeter draped in velvety cloth. Lengths of fabric dotted with wielder lights arced from the ceiling, making it feel more intimate. The low stage that was used for the entertainment events weeks ago now held a group of musicians. Banquet tables to the side were laden with food and drinks, their rich scent wafting through the room.

Most of the attendees were already there, but I didn't see Jo. Or Ameal. Or Ransom. Wynn had wanted to stop by her room before coming down, so I was on my own.

I made my way to the table of drinks and stared at the goblets of wine, debating whether I would like to face my destiny tonight drunk or sober. I chose a route somewhere in between and decided to have one glass of mulled wine.

As I sipped from my goblet, I surveyed the room. All the ladies were in their beautiful ball gowns, hair intricately piled and braided on their heads with jewels glittering from every part of them. I had forgotten to add any jewelry besides my mother's necklace, which I hadn't taken off in weeks now. I didn't really mind. It was the only ornament I was attached to, along with the fox hairpin I was wearing.

The men all looked dapper in their finely tailored outfits, with hair combed into tidy styles. A few couples danced near the musicians, but the party was still rather tame.

Damn, the mulled wine was really good. I wished I hadn't just decided to keep my wits about me.

The nervous tension was too much in my system. I couldn't stand still and wait. The doors to the courtyard were open on the opposite wall, and I decided to head into the cool night air. If the remaining beats of my heart were numbered, I'd like to feel them under the night sky.

The crisp breeze prickled goose bumps along my bare arms. I strolled further along the cobbled walkway to a fire burning in a chiminea a few feet away. My insides mellowed with the last drink of my mulled wine. Warming myself by the flames and staring at the starry sky, my body became less rigid.

The night was clear. I could see the milkiness spilled around the middle of the sky that was never visible in Capital City. An almost-full moon glowed down on the courtyard, illuminating everything. I allowed myself to breathe deeply and enjoy this moment of tranquility before I would be cast into the unknown.

Then Lev appeared at my side, ruining everything.

The wine hardened in my stomach. I reminded myself that I just needed to placate him for a bit longer. He didn't know I was planning on leaving without him yet. I would keep this smile plastered on my face for a few more hours, until I could get away. I could pretend that I was going to board the boat with him and return home tomorrow morning. That I didn't know he was going to kill me.

He slid his hand around my waist, startling me. Even when we were whatever we were, he didn't display any affection publicly. "Aurora, you look unbelievable. I hope you saved a few dances for me."

I was appalled that this man who intended to end my life in a matter of hours wanted to put his hands on me. Wanted to dance with me. I remembered his last letter, his concerns that he didn't know what I was up to, what I was learning. This was his ploy, to try one last time to find out what I knew and who I was working with before he ended me.

This fucking piece of shit. I tried to pull away from him, but he drew me closer to him.

He dipped his nose toward my throat, seeking to graze my skin. I leaned my head back, dodging his attempt.

"What are you doing, Lev? We're over." I finally managed to free myself from his grasp.

"Wouldn't you like one last night together? One more chance to satisfy each other before we have to return?" he asked, the perfect portrait of a hopeful lover.

"No, I most certainly would not." The lid wouldn't stay on my anger much longer. I had every intention of walking away from him.

His hand shot out and gripped my upper arm like a vise, pulling me around to face him again. He squeezed harder, a bruising force holding me in place. "What is going on with you? You've been so eager to please me until recently." His words dripped with crudeness, making me feel dirty for the truth behind them. "Did Dimitris finally get his prick in you?"

I was done.

I was done being his puppet. I was done with him thinking he could manipulate me. Done with everyone thinking who I was fucking would control my life and my thoughts.

"Nothing is the matter with me. In fact, I'm probably the best I've been since getting to Nixia."

He scowled at me, dragging me by my arm up against his chest. I could barely believe I ever wanted to be this close to such a disgusting man.

"Who have you been talking to? What did you find out?"

"Everything," I snarled, summoning my fire to my arm and burning his hand off me. I had never tried that before. Only after it slipped from my arms that day in my dressing chamber did I consider that magic didn't have to only come from my hands.

He jerked back, his palm shiny and red. Several emotions passed over his face before he schooled his expression.

"Tell me." When I didn't immediately comply, he struck me across my cheek with his uninjured hand. My head whipped to the side, and I tasted blood from my throbbing lower lip.

A knife pressed at my chin before I could look up again. I tried to think quickly about what I could feed him without revealing too much, what would allow me to walk away from him and this courtyard. I slowly looked at him, following his pull of the blade.

"I know you sent Wynn and Jo to Port Mora all the time to keep them away from me. I know there's information the Empire isn't telling me that might have changed how I carried out this mission." I laced in enough of the truth to be plausible. "I figure you wanted to protect me from whatever they know."

His posture slackened once my words reaffirmed his subpar expectations of me, ignoring the fight I put up seconds ago, as though that too was part of the erratic behavior he expected from me. "I had to lie about that for everyone's good. You were too weak to handle the truth. You barely kept it together as it was. You could never have managed this mission if you had known how important it was to the Emperor. You were always just a set of golden eyes."

Underestimating me was his mistake. I looked up at him through my lashes, playacting the docile creature he saw me as. "How important is it? I never did get to find out."

He smiled at me, pleased he could so easily bring me back under his authority. He reached out and brushed a curl from my face, lowering the knife. It took all my willpower to not recoil from the touch.

"I suppose we're at the end now, and you've been such an amenable little thing that I can tell you. This mission was important enough to send someone very high up in the Empire. My rank is greater than I've led you to believe."

That revelation was not worth this act. I didn't give a single shit if he was a captain or a commander. I stepped back slightly and dropped my demure posture.

Seeing my response, he added, "You know me better as General Drakemore."

"What?" I breathed.

"Surprising, I know. I did my best to keep it under wraps," he said, self-satisfaction oozing from every word.

"Why don't you look the same?" The question tumbled from me. I had seen General Drakemore the day before I met Lev. I had been seeing him throughout the Compound for the last ten years.

"It's amazing what a shave and growing your hair can do for a person's looks," he said with a smirk. "I've been telling you since the beginning. Keep as close to the truth as you can and people will believe what you tell them. Did you even know my first name was Levien in the ten years I watched you in the Compound?"

My stomach churned. I had never spent enough time in the company of General Drakemore to think about what he might look like under his beard. Now that I knew the truth, I could see it.

I was too hungry for the truth to pretend to be passive anymore. "What—Why would you need to be here?"

"Poor little Ness, always five steps behind," he chuckled. Apparently he was ready to drop his act too. "Fortunately, the Emperor and I were the only ones able to survive that terrible plague that killed off everyone alive during the age of witches and shortened the life span of all the other fae. We remember. The magic that the witches used isn't gone forever, it only needs to be released by a High Witch."

"High Witch?" I asked quietly.

He gave a humorless laugh. "It's such a wonderful twist of fate that you don't even know what you are. Two High Witches born at the same time. Proclaimed by these mutinous shits to be the heralds of a new era, the sign to start a coup. You needed to be watched carefully.

"When I found out about your existence, I thought you might just be the downfall of our Empire too. A reborn spirit of a witch of old, here to pick up where they ended hundreds of years ago. I ensured you would make your way into the Protectorate so I could keep you from falling into rebel hands until I figured out exactly how you would play into all this.

"Fae power combined with your High Witch golden eyes. You could have been a powerful weapon with both wielding and witch's magic at your disposal. I needed to make sure I was the one who wielded you." The flickering light of the fire in the chimenea cast dancing shadows on his face, giving him the ominous look to match his words.

I had witches' magic? The destructive power that we were taught to fear? No. There had been new growth on the mountain trail.

His humorless grin turned my stomach. "Imagine how pleased I was when you were so easily quelled. You didn't believe in yourself from the start. It was too easy to always pair you with the strongest wielders we had so you would feel less than from the beginning. You so easily believed it when the tonic started to take effect. I stationed you in the Compound, training the new wielders, so I could watch you. I knew I could end you at any moment, but you were still tied to the Empire and you were harmless. Why not keep you around in case you came in handy?" He was enjoying his moment in the sun, all of his plotting finally acknowledged. I was trying to decide what my next move needed to be to get away from him. Maybe I could use his self-absorbed monologue to sneak away.

"Then you did come in handy—not as I had expected, but here we are. You served your purpose and now I can rid the world of you. Once the others we came here with are gone too, everyone will forget about you, and it will be like you never existed."

The General grabbed for my arm again. I didn't know what he had planned for me, but I wanted no part of it. I stepped out of his reach and swung my wine goblet as hard as I could, hitting him in the face. He reached to touch the spot I struck, hissing, "You bitch!"

I spun and came face to face with Ransom, smiling with his hands in his pockets. "Tsk, tsk, Lev, that's no way to speak to a lady." He shifted his attention to me. "See, you didn't even need me to— Why is your face red?" His hands were out of his pockets, reaching for me.

Drakemore moved trying to block me from Ransom. "She doesn't need saving, Dimitris. It's just a little spat," the General said as he straightened his hair. I was glad to see a bruise blooming on his cheekbone already.

"Some spat," Ransom said with a frown. "Join me, Fox?" He offered me his arm. I took it quickly and began walking, not enjoying the idea that my back was to Drakemore, and expecting another strike at any second.

Thankfully, the General didn't follow us.

We paused just before the doorway, and I looked back to the chiminea. Drakemore was nowhere in sight. I leaned back against the cool stone wall for a breath, getting to truly look at Ransom for the first time tonight. He looked damn good. His tailored shirt and pants highlighted the muscles underneath, his hair combed to an usual tameness, pulled back from his face in a knot at the back of his head.

I knew I looked a mess at this point. My hair had come loose in the bun and was falling all around my face from my struggle with the General. Ransom already knew I could wield, so I didn't try to hide it when I focused my Earth magic on my face until the stinging in my cheek and pain in my lip disappeared.

Ransom's hands came up to either side of my head. I ducked away from his touch and raised my arm to protect my face, my brain still ready for a fight.

"Whoa, sorry. I should have warned you. I was trying to get your hair in order, so you didn't walk in there looking like you fought off a bear." He smiled as he looked over my appearance. His smile melted into a frown when he noticed Drakemore's handprint bruised into my upper arm.

"Ness," he said tenderly, eyes on my arm.

"It's fine. Fae, remember? It'll be gone soon," I said dismissively. I wanted to forget the interaction with General Drakemore happened at all.

He nodded. "Can I?" he asked, as he reached toward my hair again, this time far more slowly.

"Please," I consented, leaning in to him.

He was surprisingly gentle as he tucked the silken curls back into the bun. I wanted to melt into his kindness. When he finished, he looked me over. "There. A vision once again."

"Thanks, Ran."

He paused, his eyes trained on my face.

"What? Do you hate 'Ran' as much as I hate 'Nessamia?'" I teased. "I won't call you that again, if that's the case. Or I might start calling you that a lot more if you annoy me."

"No, it doesn't bother me at all. You can call me Ran." He cleared his throat. "We need to get to the boat as soon as possible. He's going to be hunting you now. Are Wynn and Jo ready? I can go grab my men."

"No, I need to get them." I didn't want to tell him that I had still been dragging my feet. I knew I was being foolish by not acting faster.

"Hurry and round them up, Fox. I'm going to go get everything set in motion." He looked at me again and leaned forward. I had the briefest notion that he was going to kiss me again and a thrill ran through me at that idea, but he turned it into a brush of his hand along my arm, and then he walked away. Where he'd touched me left a path of tingling warmth for a long while after he was gone.

CHAPTER FORTY-THREE

My time was running out. Ransom was right. Lev, or rather Drakemore, might not have followed us in that moment, but there was no way he was done with me. At least, not while I still breathed.

I needed to save the unsanctioned crew.

The hall was crowded now and filled with noisy chatter over the songs of the musicians. More people had begun to dance near the stage, making it harder to find anyone in the moving swarms of bodies.

I spotted Jo off to the side of the dance floor, standing near a large group of ladies' maids who were waiting to be asked to dance by the guards. As I reached Jo, Drakemore returned from the courtyard through a door across the room. I grabbed Jo's arm and pulled him behind the group of ladies whose very full dresses blocked us from the General's line of sight if we ducked down slightly, but also made me unable to track Drakemore's movements.

"Jo, we're going to have to leave on Ransom's ship if we want to have a chance at living," I whispered to him hurriedly from our crouch. His eyes went round.

He set down his drink on the floor. "Alright, let's grab Wynn and Lev—"

"No!" I cut him off. "Lev is actually General Drakemore, and he's the one that wants to kill us." My hissing whisper caught some looks from a few of the ladies' maids.

Jo chuckled at me. "Good one. You almost had me." He made to stand up, but I yanked him back down.

I should have left out the part about the General's secret identity. It forced me to explain too much in the time we had. "No, I'm serious. He altered his appearance, but it's him, and we were never supposed to return from this mission."

Something on my face or the desperation in my voice must have been enough for Jo.

"What do we need to do?"

"We need to find Wynn and Ameal, or Ransom," I said. "Ameal is working with Ransom, so he can help us get off this island. But I'll be honest, I don't know what will happen once we go with him." It was the briefest possible explanation I could give.

"I knew Ameal was up to something. Why didn't I listen to myself?" He shook his head.

"Yeah," I said. "But at least we know Ameal was working with the person trying to save us from the person we thought we could trust. So maybe your deeper instincts were right to keep it to yourself."

"That hardly makes me feel better."

"You can deal with that later. We still need to find him or Ransom to actually make it out of here. And we need to get Wynn."

"Right, let's stick together."

My heart was beating faster than a hummingbird's wings. I stood and spun in a slow circle, trying to see Ameal or Ransom while attempting to stay out of view of Drakemore. Of course neither of those mountainous fuckers were in sight when I needed them.

I hooked my arm through Jo's and began to walk to an exit. I passed Mira chatting with Chancellor Parisa. They both eyed me as I walked by them. I had no idea what they were talking about. All I could hear was my own blood pounding in my ears. I wondered how much power Ransom really had to stay Mira's hand if she truly wished me dead. By the look on her face, he was barely keeping her in check. I quickened my pace.

Jo and I rushed out into the entrance hall. A frantic look around didn't reveal anyone we were searching for. Jo glanced over his shoulder.

"Shit, Lev is following us," he murmured into my ear.

I spotted a door that I was fairly certain led to a storage closet or pantry. Either way, it would work fine for a quick hiding spot. I yanked open the door to the dark space, revealing it to be a little of both. Shelves filled with bushels of apples and empty pitchers were next to brooms leaning in a corner. We both scrambled inside, and I closed the door behind us as quickly and quietly as I could.

We waited and listened to Drakemore's heavy gait storm across the entryway. Hopefully, he thought we went straight outside and was following that path.

"Where did Ransom say to meet him?" Jo's voice came out of the darkness next to me.

"He didn't. He said to find him or Ameal, which presently, is not helpful at all."

"Alright, I suppose the most likely place for you to bump into Ameal would be the hall. We're going to have to go back in there. It seems that Lev is searching the grounds for you, so we might have a little time until he comes back—"

Jo's words were cut short by the bright lights flooding into our dark sanctuary when the door was yanked open. Standing with one hand on the handle and the other with fingers interlaced with Wynn was Queen Elara, blonde hair tumbling gracefully down her shoulders. Her laugh dropped off the moment she saw us standing in the closet.

"What are you doing here?" Wynn snipped.

"I would ask the same of you two, but I think that answer is pretty obvious," I said, unable to keep the wryness totally out of my voice.

"What's that tone for?" Wynn asked sharply.

"It's for your stupid secrets. It's for purposely making me think you're fooling around with someone who wants me dead."

"No one said *I* don't want you dead," Queen Elara chimed in with a mockingly helpful tone.

Wynn shot her a look. "Yeah, well, I couldn't exactly tell you I was actively trying to sabotage the Empire's plans this whole time with foreign royalty."

"Wynn," Jo exhaled, like a disappointed father.

"Fuck, Wynn. I— Never mind. What's important right now is Lev going to kill us." I wasn't going to mention that Lev is Drakemore yet. I didn't think Wynn would let that detail go as easily as Jo had.

"Mother's hairy legs. I knew that he was a bastard from the start," Wynn said.

"Shit, he wants to kill Wynn too?" Queen Elara asked, worrying her lower lip.

"Yes," I said firmly.

"I am bound by the treaty to not help," Elara said. "I can no longer harbor you. You'll have taken an active role against the Empire."

"I've been doing that since before I joined the Protectors," Wynn said as she rolled her eyes.

"Yes, but once the Gathering ends tonight, you can no longer be my guest and under that protection. You need to get out of Nixia tonight," she said.

"That's fine, because we need to find Ameal or Ransom to get on their ship," I said.

"Ameal? I think I missed some details here," Wynn said.

"Later," I said. "There's a lot to tell you."

Queen Elara looked into Wynn's eyes. "This has been so nice and so needed," she whispered to Wynn, her hand on her cheek, their foreheads pressed together. "You helped me remember to enjoy life again."

"I enjoyed it too," Wynn said softly, as she raised Elara's hand in her own to place a kiss on the back of it. "You reminded me it doesn't have to be all or nothing."

They exchanged a tender kiss. I wished I hadn't been intruding on this intimate moment between the two of them, but there wasn't much I could do about it in this tiny closet. I looked over to Jo, who was staring intently at a broom.

"Ready?" Wynn's voice drew my attention back up. Queen Elara was gone.

The three of us entered the great hall and surveyed the room to find our fortune had finally shifted. We spotted Ameal against a wall almost immediately and didn't see the General at all.

We crossed quickly to where he was leaning his shoulders against the stone wall, arms crossed, one leg propped back so that his foot rested on the wall. His usual all-black attire was much nicer for tonight.

"We're ready to go with Ransom," I told him without preamble.

He nodded, pushed off the wall with his foot, and began weaving through the hall smoothly, like he had been planning for this moment all night and had already plotted his path amid the crowd. He nodded discreetly to the two guards from Solterra in the hall as we passed them. Apparently, it was a signal they had been waiting for, and they fell in line with our parade to the door seamlessly.

When we got to the stables, we met with Ransom along the rear side of the building, standing in a shadow. Sugardrop and a few other horses were already saddled and tied to a post a few feet away. Ransom told Jo and Wynn he hadn't prepared their horses yet. The guards and Ameal went inside the stable to help them saddle their mounts, leaving the two of us standing alone.

"Did Sugardrop give you any trouble? She's got a bit of a reputation for being a pain," I said.

"No, she was easy," Ransom said. "You don't have much time to change. Here." He tossed a bag to me. "I don't have any for your lady's maid, though. We couldn't get her trunks."

I opened the bag to find lined leggings, boots, a loose tunic, and my leather jacket. As I pulled each item out, I hung it over the low wall next to me.

"Thank the Mother I won't have to try to ride in this dress," I murmured.

"Or you could thank me," Ransom teased.

I shot him a narrow-eyed look before waving to my dress. "Help me get out of this thing."

"I thought you'd never ask," he said in a low voice that made heat curl in my stomach, despite the circumstances.

He stepped up to me and gathered the skirt in his hands at my hips with deft movements that did nothing to help the blood coursing through my body. This wasn't the right time or place, and honestly, with my recent experiences with men, it was probably better I swear them off altogether for a while.

He helped me pull the bunched material over my head and shoved it in a bag. I had forgotten what I was wearing underneath that dress—the provocative, lace-trimmed brassiere and assless underwear with little bows. When I looked up from my glance at my undergarments, Ransom was staring at me with dazed eyes, his mouth slightly open.

"I'll remember this is what you like when we get to Agora, Ran," I said, turning his low, sultry tone on him as I leaned a fraction closer.

"Trust me, I won't forget, Ness." His voice was rougher than it had been. The corner of my mouth ticked up as our eyes locked. My gaze fell to his lips. I stepped toward him, and his large hand enveloped my hip.

"Ness." The word breathed across my lips. When had we gotten so close together? I tilted my chin up, pressing my chest to his.

A loud *thunk* inside the stable jolted us from our moment. His hands were in his pockets before we even finished stepping away from each other.

I laughed off the heat devouring my body as I grabbed my clothes off the low wall and pulled them on. We didn't have time for this.

CHAPTER FORTY-FOUR

I added several more knives and a small sword to my person from the bag Ransom had provided, and I climbed on to Sugardrop as the others brought their horses over to us.

"It should be much faster to go down the mountain than the half day it takes to get up here," Ransom said. "But still, we need to move as swiftly as possible."

We began to make our way to the trail. We didn't see any sign of the General as we went. I should have used my time alone with Ransom to tell him that Lev was Drakemore and explain it, instead of getting distracted by his stupid, lush lips.

I moved back along the line to Wynn to see how she was faring with riding in her dress. I had to look her over several times to try to understand what I was seeing when I noticed her riding normally. Her dress appeared to be split in two?

"What is happening here?" I asked her.

"What do you mean? We're escaping with our lives." She gestured to the path ahead.

"No, your dress," I said. "How are you able to ride in it?"

"Oh, it's a split skirt. The seamstress in Port Mora had it in her window. It looks like a dress, but it's not. I knew it would come in handy." She shoved one hand into a hidden pocket in the skirt, or pant leg, and she grinned. "I billed it to Lev's account."

"How long do you think it will take to get back to Port Mora?" I asked. This sense of dread wouldn't ease until Nixia was a dot behind me. Probably even then, I would still be filled with worry until we were tucked away in Agora.

"It takes far less time to go down a mountain than it does to go up it. Jo and I usually took about two hours to get down. At this pace, probably closer to an hour," she said.

"You're kidding. Wynn, you and Jo always took two or three days to send the letters. If it didn't take that much time, what were you doing?" I asked.

"Usually drinking beer in town. Fishing. Playing cards. Just not being at the castle, really." She shrugged. "It was harder than you probably think to keep all my secrets from you."

That was a strangely nice thought, to know that Wynn chose to avoid me because her only other option was to befriend me.

We couldn't speak much once we were on the slope of the mountain. The trail was too narrow to ride two abreast. The horses were pushing as fast as they could, but it was dark out. We needed to focus. Despite the brightness of the moon, the shadows of the trees frequently left the path in a cover of darkness.

I allowed myself to feel the cold air of autumn and darkness of the night sky sink into me. The glow of the moon kissed the backs of my hands and my face every time we stepped out of the shade of the trees. It was filling that well of extra magic that was hidden inside me. I guess now I knew it was witch's magic. I stepped back from conscious thought and let myself be in the moment. I calmed my frayed nerves and centered my erratic mind. My heartbeat was finally returning to normal. My body swayed with the movements of Sugardrop. My ears filled with the breeze rustling through the pine boughs.

My mind wandered to this power. How I shared it with Aurora. I mourned her death and how much she would have helped the world, no matter what form her power took. And selfishly, how she would never be here to help me.

At least now I could go to Agora in her place and help this rebellion.

My only goal when I was last on this mountain trail had been to leave Nixia alive and see my friends again. I was going to do that. Ransom said he would help me get my friends. My excitement at the prospect of living to see George and Lina's faces again, no matter how far in the future, made me grin like a fool to the night air.

When this was all over, just maybe I would get to see the world I spent my life dreaming of. The Deccan alpine towns Mira spoke of, I would get to visit them. I would get to see how Gallia was governed for myself. Queen Atla and King Row would be able to show off the isle they were so protective over.

By the time we reached the bottom of the mountain and hurried along to the docks, we couldn't waste another second. We handed off our horses to a longshoreman along with a small bag of gold.

I gave Sugardrop a kiss on her blaze. "Love you. You're a good girl, don't let anyone tell you otherwise. If I could take you with me, I would." She nuzzled into my hand, and I took that as a reciprocal sentiment.

We started down the boardwalk to where Ransom's boat was docked. My heart clenched at how close we were to safety. I couldn't believe I got them all here. I was going to get my friends out.

The waves themselves were following our progress along the slippery boards. Water lapped higher and higher with each stride we took, eventually hitting the boards under our feet. The spray kicked up, soaking the hems of our pants. Waves continued to build, washing over the boards. The next swell soaked us up to our knees. I was pushed back slightly from the force of the water.

The wave after that rose so high it created a wall of water ten feet tall, blocking our path and dousing us in the cold, salty deluge when it fell. The following wave roiled up in front of us into a wall blockading our escape and did not recede.

Standing behind us, just off the boardwalk on the dirt road, was General Drakemore, his arms raised in front of him, holding the water to block our path with his magic. He was still dressed as he was at the ball, but with the addition of a large sword strapped to his back.

The sight of the General blinded me with rage. I began to run toward him.

He was a dead man. I was going to rip that fucker apart limb by limb. Distantly, my name was shouted behind me.

I reached within me and drew forth a gale of wind to slam it into him as I ran. He dropped his focus on the wall of water, letting it crash back into the harbor in order to redirect my wind at the last moment, sending my air straight up.

With the water no longer blocking the way, most of the crew from Solterra grabbed the bags from the dock and scrambled to finish getting the boat ready. Ransom, Jo, Ameal, Wynn, and the one remaining guard were close behind me, running toward the General.

The anger inside me burned with such ferocity that fire magic came out of me without realizing it. I stopped on the docks, letting the flames lick from my hands, turning my raging inferno into fiery ropes whipping ahead of me. I had never manipulated magic in this way before. They darted forward, reaching for Drakemore like striking snakes, his own air pushing the flame back toward me.

It was a battle of fire and wind lashing against each other, a maelstrom of wills and power. The heat from the flame thrashed around us in a torrent.

He thrust his hand up, and I was shocked by a sharp sting across my shoulder blades. I whipped around to see a dozen columns of water rising out of the bay. They lashed about, striking anyone they could. I was battered across my chest by another column of water, knocking me back so hard that it was like being struck by one of the iron chains used to anchor the boats. My head slammed into the slick wooden planks. Stars burst behind my eyelids.

Jo grabbed my arm and steadied me as I rose. We both began to run toward Drakemore once more. I pulled on the columns of water the General was controlling and jerked them his way, releasing my control of them right before they reached him. As he was distracted, I paused and slid one of my knives out of a sheath at my thigh and threw it with a quick flick of my wrist. The cold metal left my fingers just as quickly as it had come into them.

The knife flew across the distance separating us from Drakemore, who was busy redirecting the water rushing toward him, sticking into his thigh as he was forcing the last of the wave away. He yelled in outrage and pain.

I couldn't help but feel satisfied at that.

He pulled the knife from his leg to allow his fae magic to heal the wound. In the time it took for him to react, the rest of my group converged on him, weapons drawn.

The quarters were too tight for the General to use magic effectively against so many opponents. He drew his sword from his back. Ransom, Wynn, Ameal, and the guard were blurs of movement and glinting steel. The blades flashing and ringing against each other idled my already buzzing head. I hadn't moved since throwing the knife. I gave myself a little shake, forcing Earth magic through my body.

I couldn't use magic offensively either with the others close to Drakemore, so I pulled another knife from my hip as I began to run toward the fray.

I hadn't taken a single step before Lev's sword went through the Solterran guard's body. The metal sank into his side, dark red pouring out after it. The sight halted me once again and drew the attention of all the others in the fight. I didn't know him, didn't even know his name, but the loss jarred me.

He had people who cared about him back in Agora, I was sure. People who were expecting him back from this trip. A mother's cooking to eat, a family to tease, a home to protect. My breath caught in my chest. I gripped the knife so tightly, the handle pressed divots into my palm.

But then, I saw it.

My chance.

Drakemore had to swing a wide circle to pull his sword from the body of the guard, and he needed to use his full body to do so. The others couldn't step around him, and it exposed his chest to me.

I firmed my stance and steadied my breathing as I corrected my hold on the knife and used the full force of my body to throw it as hard as I could at his chest.

The moonlight gleamed off the blade as it flipped over and over through the night. I forced my thoughts to the air it was cutting through, wielding the wind to take it to him faster, harder, as fast as a bolt from a crossbow. Yet, I watched it in slow motion.

He saw death coming for him, his eyes widened. I was going to enjoy watching the light leave them. My eyes trained on the place my knife would strike his chest.

Then all I could see was Jo's back.

Jo was in front of him.

Jo was in front of the knife tumbling through the darkness. Jo had launched himself at Drakemore with his sword, seeing the same opportunity I did to end the General.

The knife struck with a muffled *thump*.

I watched Jo stumble forward with the handle protruding out of his shoulder blade. It was a hard hit, but not fatal.

I could get to him.

I could heal him.

I could pull him from the fight and make sure he saw his family again.

I would get to him and he would be fine.

He would hug his niece and nephew soon.

He would see his family. He would show me the farm. He would. He would.

The point of Drakemore's weapon erupted through Jo's back, covered in dripping scarlet death.

No.

It was as though time, which had slowed so I could watch my knife travel, needed to speed up to balance the scales. I hardly had any memory of my feet pounding across the remaining dock to the fight. Nor did I remember drawing the short sword on my back. Drakemore had already pulled his sword out of Jo by the time I reached him.

The dust was still settling from Jo's body when the first strike of my sword rang against Drakemore's. It was immediately evident that he was much stronger than me. I couldn't win this way.

My fear manifested in a ball of flames encircling my hand. I flung it at him, striking him on the neck and cheek.

He roared, grabbing his blistering throat.

"You fucking whore!" His scream rent through the night.

I was vaguely aware of Wynn and Ameal using the moment to pull Jo's body to the side. I didn't need Wynn's sob or Ameal's rough shouts of "Jo!" behind me to confirm what my heart already knew.

I struck at Drakemore again and again. I might not be stronger, but I was faster. And angrier.

"The ship!" Ransom's yell was accompanied by a tug on my arm.

His ship was ready to go, the small crew had unmoored it and was bringing it closer. It would soon be at the end of the nearest dock. It was a short run, but the ship was also in motion. We needed to meet it at the right time to jump on board.

I flicked my attention back behind me. My slight reprieve allowed Drakemore to build his own ball of flames.

"Run!" I screamed.

The General threw the ball of flames—not at us, as I expected, but at the ship. It struck the deck in a sizzle of smoke and steam. The walls of water that pummeled over the harbor earlier had soaked everything, and the drenched wood didn't ignite.

I knew we couldn't be so lucky twice. I pulled a hard wall of air into place between Drakemore and our escape. His fire lashed at it. I was too unfocused with trying to run, time the coming jump, and maintain the wall. His fire broke through the air and hit me in my lower back. The flames seared me as they scorched through my jacket, the smell of the burning leather and the acrid tanning chemicals singeing my nose.

I fell on my face and rolled to my back to smother the flames. My freshly healed lip from Drakemore's slap earlier had broken open again with the fall and blood ran down the side of my face. I raised to my elbows to see the General rushing toward me in one direction and Wynn, Ameal, and Ransom sprinting to the ship in the other.

I jumped to my feet with energy I didn't think I still had and forced a wall of water up in front of Drakemore, cutting him off from us with his own trick. I looked at my friends. They were almost to the ship.

"Come on," yelled Ransom back to me. "Now, Ness!"

I could feel the General's powers battering into my wall of water. He pushed harder and harder. I couldn't run and keep them safe. My shield of water was forced back under his barrage, retreating closer and closer to me. A hot wetness dripped down my cheek and I couldn't tell if it was blood or tears.

I was supposed to die on this island. I didn't deserve to leave this island without Jo. The hope of escape was only so I could potentially stay alive a little longer. I might as well die protecting the rest of them. I could keep Drakemore off as long as possible, then give myself over to him. I was the one he wanted anyway. It would give them enough time to get away. With them, the rebellion could come to fruition. They could carry out their plans and help their people. They would have to find another way without me.

"Get on the ship, I can hold him off!" I shouted back.

"Don't be too sure about that." Drakemore's voice was audible over the rush of water in my wall.

He was close. The wall was thinning. My energy was dwindling. I could feel the warmth of his flames through the water, searing my face and hands.

The water began to bubble and steam. The heat from the mist scalded the palms of my outstretched hands.

I dropped the water wall completely, running to the end of the dock. Wynn and Ameal jumped toward the ship. Instead of protecting my back from the General, I used the wind to guide their leaps, making sure they landed on deck. I didn't see Ransom on the dock. He must be already on board, I couldn't imagine it any other way.

I knew that choice to help Wynn and Ameal was my last and allowing them safety had ensured my death. Drakemore was on me at that moment, encasing me in a globe of wind, cutting off my surprised scream as soon as it started. The air moved so fast and mixed with the spray of the ocean, I couldn't see or hear anything outside of the roar of my cage.

It swirled tighter to me, pinning my arms to my sides. I started to feel lightheaded, the air was being pulled right out of my lungs. I couldn't breathe.

This was a painful way to die.

I closed my eyes and focused on the hum of my magic. It always brought me comfort. The moonlight had bathed my skin on our trek down the mountain, and it had been so soothing. I let that memory take over my mind.

I was surprised to find that the feeling of moonlight was still enchanting my skin. I drew the feeling from my exterior and pulled it into my magic. I wanted all those sensations that calmed me together in my final moment.

My lungs were burning. The need for a breath was so great. It was getting fuzzier to think.

The two powers touched, the humming of moonlight and magic melding together. They glowed inside me. They strengthened each other, expanding within me, filling every part of me with humming light. When there was nowhere left for the light to grow, it erupted out of me, shattering the prison of wind.

Groaning cracks of exploding wood battered me. Splashing, screams. I couldn't understand the words. I couldn't see or feel.

I had given everything in me. There was nothing left.

The blackness was overcoming me as I slowly slipped into the unknowing.

It turned out death was dark. Death was a sensation of falling.

It was a cold, rushing drag against my whole being.

Death was nothingness.

CHAPTER FORTY-FIVE

After the dark, there came a glowing brightness. The way sunlight felt behind closed eyelids. I didn't have any eyelids to open. Just the dim glow that was more prominent at times and dimmer at others.

Next there were sounds.

The waves of the sea. Splashing and dripping.

Birds screeching.

Creaking.

Gentle mumbles that made no words, spoke no languages, but had the cadence and lilt of human speech.

There were smells too.

A salty brine in the air.

A pleasant cedar scent like the mountains in Nixia mixed with a freshness of citrus. They brought me a strange sense of serenity.

Then I could feel softness around me, a gentle sway rocking me.

My body wrapped in plush warmth.

The After must exist amongst the waves.

Then pain came. Overwhelming pain that consumed my knowing until darkness pressed in once again.

CHAPTER FORTY-SIX

Before I could open my eyes, I knew I wasn't dead. There was no way I would ache this much if I didn't have a body. I tried to take stock of what was touching me. I was in a bed in a tiny wooden room. No, I was swaying, and I could hear the sounds of the sea. I was on a boat.

There had been a boat. It was very important. But I hadn't reached that boat.

Every part of me hurt. My legs felt as though I had run for miles, my arms were more sore than after a day of double training with Ameal. My lower back and palms ached worse than all of it.

I cracked open a bleary eye to see my hands were bandaged as I raised them in front of my face. A thick salve seeped out from the wrappings. My torso was wrapped as well.

The narrow bed was for one person and tight against a desk. It had white sheets on it that were lightly scented with the cedar and citrus smell my brain registered. I nuzzled my nose into the pillow to pull in the scents like they could heal me too.

I was wearing an overly large tunic that was soft and comfortable against my skin and clean leggings from one of my trunks. I wasn't sure who'd cleaned me up, but they removed the unnecessarily sexy undergarments I had been wearing the night of the ball. Thank the Mother, I was done with those for a while.

I looked over to the desk again. A form was dozing in the chair, head tipped back against the wall behind her, reddish black hair unkempt.

"Wynn," I croaked.

She jolted forward. "Ness! Thank fuck, I was so worried you weren't going to wake up."

I tried to respond, but all that came out was a scratchy grunt.

"Oh, shit, let me get you some water." She grabbed a pitcher and cup from a tray on the desk and began to fill it. She reached out to hand me the cup, but I couldn't sit up enough to take it.

"Let me help," she said, setting down the cup and coming over to prop me up to a seated position. She then handed me the cup, which I drank in a single swallow. She refilled the cup and handed it to me again.

"What happened?" I asked before draining my second cup.

"What's the last thing you remember?" she asked as she reached out to fill the cup once again.

"I died," I said between sips. "Or something like that."

"I'm guessing you mean when you basically turned into the sun." A smile lifted the corners of her mouth. She sat back in the desk chair, satisfied that I wouldn't need another refill for at least a few seconds.

"Yes, please explain from there." I continued to sip the best-tasting water ever created.

She chuckled. "Well, we don't know what happened, but you started to glow in that ball of air Lev trapped you in."

"Drakemore," I corrected.

"What?"

"Lev is actually General Drakemore. I'll explain later. Go on." I reached out to refill my cup again.

"Right, well then it got much brighter and your light exploded out. I've never seen anything like it. No one on the ship has. It was like a different kind of magic.

"It knocked Lev, Drakemore, whoever out. You blew up half the dock and fell in the water. Ameal and I were already on the boat, and we couldn't go after you. I'm not sure exactly what happened, but the next thing I knew, Ransom was swimming up to the boat with you. We pulled your ass on board. Lev, Drakemore, was up by then and saw your lifeless carcass being pulled onto the boat."

"So is he following us?"

She shook her head. "There's been no sign of him. We think he thought you were dead, well, because we all did." She toyed with the hem of her shirt and watched me drink my water.

My brain slogged backwards through the memories of that night. "How did Ransom catch the boat? I was barely able to make sure you and Ameal got on."

"I'm not sure how he was able to swim that fast, but I think the boat caught a bad current because the water stopped us, like it was waiting until we pulled you two up. I'm really not sure, maybe all the wind Le—Drakemore used to trap you caught the boat." She shrugged.

I let her story sink into me for a moment. "Nereids," I mumbled.

"What?"

I shook my head. I really only had one question at this point, though I was sure more would come later. "Wynn, can you help me to the head?"

CHAPTER FORTY-SEVEN

I found out that I had been asleep for two days. After I returned to the tiny cabin with Wynn, she brought me two days' worth of food, which I ate all of. While I did, Wynn checked my burns under the bandages. My fae healing must have been working again, because they were much better and she removed the gauze altogether. Once I had my fill of food, water, and sleep, I began to remember more of what happened that night before my explosion on the docks.

"Jo," I whispered, before my heart broke into thousands of pieces.

Wynn dipped her head, looking at the bandage bundled in her hands.

"I think I need to get some more sleep. I'll come to you when I'm ready to be up. No need to check on me."

She nodded and left me to wallow in the sorrow.

When the door thumped shut behind Wynn, I looked out the small window and stared into the infinite, glittering sea. I had certainly been responsible for Jenkins' death and that weighed heavily on me, but this was something else entirely, since it was my hand that had thrown the knife.

Jo, who was always on my side. He was the best of us that had gone to Nixia, and now he was the only one not getting to return. The gentle waves became blurry as hot tears rolled slowly down my cheeks.

I spent the next few days in the cabin sleeping, eating, or crying, in between long stretches of nothingness. Trying to feel nothing, think about nothing, but I failed at that too, just like I'd failed to get Jo safely back to his farm in the Central State. At one point, there was a knock on the door followed by Ameal's voice asking if I wanted to talk. I ignored him and hoped he would think I was asleep.

I didn't know how long our voyage was supposed to be and was too afraid to go and ask anyone. I couldn't face Ameal or Wynn. It was my fault our friend was gone. I hardly left the cabin and when I did, it was usually in the dead of night, so as not to run into anyone else. Trays of food and pitchers of water were left at my door daily, so at least one person on this boat didn't hate me for what I'd done.

Late in the evening on that sixth day, I was sitting up in my bed and looking out the tiny, circular window over the desk. I watched the innumerable waves pass the ship in shimmering blues and tried to lose myself in it.

My door creaked open.

"Best view on the ship." Ransom walked in carrying my tray and pitcher. "That's why I chose this one for my cabin, even though there's a bigger one next door."

"This is your room?" I pivoted to look at him.

"It normally is. This trip, I've hardly been in here," he said as he set the tray and pitcher on the desk.

"Hardly? When were you in here?"

"Wynn and Ameal needed some breaks." He shrugged. It was one thing that Wynn sat with me before I woke up or even Ameal, but it was different to know Ransom has been keeping vigil over me as well. "And it took both Wynn and myself to get you settled the first night. You needed a lot of cleaning up."

A thought passed through my mind, probably an unimportant one, but my cheeks heated. "You saw me naked?"

"I've seen women naked before, believe it or not." His voice was devoid of the usual teasing and flirting he would have laced the comment with a few days ago.

He changed the subject, which I was grateful for. "You look much better. We weren't sure you would survive that."

"So I heard." My fingers played with the ends of the braid I had corralled my hair into. "I wish I hadn't."

"Well, I'm glad you did." Ransom pulled out the desk chair and sat on it, directly in front of me. He was so large and the room so small that he was already in my space before his knees were bumping against mine. Now, his presence overwhelmed me as he took up my entire line of sight, especially with him leaning in toward me.

"I don't think Jo's family would feel the same way if they knew I threw the knife that killed him." I tore my eyes from my hair to look at him. I wanted him to see the honesty in them, that I wasn't fooling myself.

"Lev is the only reason Jo is dead," he said firmly.

I turned my head away from him, looking out of the window again. "You're wrong." I kept my eyes on the waves lapping at the ship outside.

"Even if Drakemore's sword took Jo's life, he never could have done it without my knife."

Ransom shook his head and sat up straight in the chair, giving me back some space.

"Do you think that if Jo knew he would die, it would have changed anything he did that night? Do you think he wouldn't have fought by your side until his last breath no matter what?"

I had no words for him. The emptiness in my chest took my ability to talk into its void.

"I heard we were fighting General Drakemore?" Ransom asked after a moment.

"Yes," I said, turning back to him. "He altered his appearance. I can't believe I never recognized him in all those weeks. Just another way I failed everyone."

"How well did you know him before?"

"Not well at all," I said slowly. "He called me a High Witch earlier in the courtyard. Is that the power you need?"

"We'll be able to figure out the truth of all that in Agora, but at least we have someplace for you to start." He leaned back in his chair, crossing his arms. "That's not the reason I came to see you. Tomorrow evening we'll arrive in Agora, and you need to get yourself ready. There are things you'll need to know."

"Like what? You're actually married and we can't pretend to be paramours anymore?" I said with an eye roll. Nothing would really surprise me at this point. Although the thought did nettle inside me, and I found myself apprehensive of his response all the same.

"Like the fact that you are an Imperial spy coming to Agora. I can't exactly reveal that to anyone there. People talk. It would be all over town before nightfall that I was harboring the enemy. Someone might mention you to the commander on the docks and the Empire could figure out you're not dead pretty quickly."

"Can't you tell them the truth? That I'm there to support the rebellion," I said. "If the Empire is already the enemy, that should be an easy one."

"See, that's where it gets tricky. The people of Agora hate the Emperor, but they don't exactly know anything about the rebellion yet, so we can't say that either. Most people are generally against ideas that would upset the life they know, as wars tend to do."

"Fine. What am I supposed to say?"

"Nothing," he said. "Lay low. Stay in the palace as much as you can."

With how I felt right now, getting to stay away from other people all the time was Mother-sent. "I can do that."

He sighed deeply. "I don't want to do this to you, because I know what you've just been through." He shook his head and leaned forward, running his hands along the stubble on his face.

"What now?"

"So, you know your question?"

I didn't. I was asking a lot of questions. "Which one?"

"About me being married and us pretending to be together?"

Yes, I remembered that question. I'd also noticed how he ignored it. I waited, my stomach in knots. I was about to have yet another blow to my emotions.

"Well." He breathed out. "The second-best room in the palace is actually connected to mine. It's supposed to be the queen's room."

"It's fine if your wife wants to keep her room," I said, surprised at how hollow my voice sounded. "I didn't come with you only for the second-best room in the palace."

He smiled weakly. "No, you can have the room. It's been empty for decades. But remember how I said people talk? Especially the people that work in the palace. If you take that room, they're all going to think it means we intend to get married. The staff, my family, everyone will think that."

"I can use a different room."

He huffed a laugh. "I think it's actually the best cover for you being there. Wynn can say she wanted to join my guard, no one will question it. Ameal has always worked for me. But you will be scrutinized. I think letting everyone know I found my great love at the Gathering, which was thought to be a trade conference, is going to protect you the best. There will be far fewer questions around your presence if everyone just thinks we're together. You don't have to change much of your backstory. You grew up in Capital City, even that you used to be a Protector and can wield won't be a big deal. You can say you were at the Gathering from the Moriale delegation and decided you couldn't leave Nixia without me. All of that is essentially true."

He was right, I didn't love the idea. I didn't want to lie about who I was anymore. I was looking forward to some time not being entangled with men, pretend or real. Yet, what he was saying also made sense. Ransom ran Agora. I would be protected by being associated with him so closely.

I nodded.

"I will warn you, my family is going to be...enthusiastic about me bringing you home. Be ready for that," he said.

"Why?"

He rubbed the back of his neck. "There has been a lot of scrutiny over getting me to settle down and secure the family line. This will end that." He grimaced.

I didn't know what to say to that.

"Also, Ness," he said. He tightened his grip on his knees. "I've been playing nice for weeks. I needed to be on my best behavior to win alliances at the Gathering. But that is not who I need to be to run Agora."

"What does that mean exactly? You're going to start being horrible to me?" I shrank back from him. If he was going to treat me the way Drakemore had at the ball, I would probably take my chances jumping off this ship right now.

"No. And in the palace, I can mostly be myself." His whole demeanor shifted. "But the things you might hear about me, might see. They may be unpleasant." His eyes lost their bright quality as he leaned forward. I shifted uncomfortably on my—no, his bed. The way his tone lowered worried me. He was more intense all of a sudden.

"I own many businesses," he said. "Shops, taverns, lounges, inns, gambling dens, brothels."

"So?" I snorted. I'd thought it was going to be much worse. "Half the nobles in Capital City have money in places like that. It's not anything shocking to me."

"I do this while overseeing the well-being of the people who live there. I keep the Imperial Protectors at the docks in check and out of our lives."

"Again, this doesn't sound that different from what's in Capital City."

"Yes, but in Agora, the leash is off. People come there for what they can't get in the rest of the Empire. The shops sell illegal goods. The lounges serve illicit drugs and feature dancers of a much more exotic nature than the Capital would ever allow." He kept those darkened eyes on me. I shifted again. Those things would certainly not have been allowed under the Emperor's nose.

He leaned in further, his forearms braced against his thighs.

"I keep people in line with what's acceptable and what isn't. Sometimes, for a person who is overindulging in the delicacies of Agora, that line is easily blurred." His expression was even more shadowed than it was a moment ago. My breath caught in my throat. "I do whatever it takes to keep order. I don't like to get my hands dirty if I don't have to, but I would never ask my men to do anything I wouldn't."

His tone left no room for uncertainty that he would do anything for Agora. That was why I was here, wasn't it? Some desperate hope to better the lives of the people of his city, a hope that we both knew might cost me my life in the end.

He was not joking about the man in Nixia being an act. Everything about him was different now. His posture radiated menace and power. The planes of his face were harsher and his eyes that usually sparkled brightly, looked dark and heartless.

"I have been known to kill people, torture them, let their lives' work burn to ash." He leaned so far forward that our faces were less than a foot apart. I swallowed drily. My heart was racing.

"Tomorrow, you are coming into port with a different man."

I had no idea what I was about to get into.

And no way out.

ACKNOWLEDGEMENTS

First, thank you! Thank you to everyone who has read my words and made it to the end. To everyone who cheered me on and helped get the word out about this book. To everyone who liked posts, signed up for my ARC, and shared it with the world. I'm so happy I got to share this with you.

I will say, I started writing this book during a time when I felt very alone and overwhelmed (bad) while my husband worked out of town for months, but I have been overwhelmed (good) by the love and support I received for this novel.

Top billing on the long list of people that deserve all the love are Jesslyn and Amy. Everyone needs a Jesslyn and an Amy in their lives. Their relentless support, responding to my millions of texts, listening to my ideas, reading this book nearly as many times as I did, getting coffee/brunch with me when I needed to talk through things, and just overall awesomeness has me spiraling through the cosmos. This book would not be what it is today without you ladies, and I couldn't be happier about it. I would never leave out the support and cheering coming from Megan and Malena either. You are the JAMMM that fills my jar. My unsanctioned crew.

A massive thank you to all my beta and sensitivity readers, both hired and volunteer— Katie and Stephanie, even if life got in the way. Jessica, Cathy, Lauren, Bria, Luna, Leo, and Alexia. Your enthusiasm, love, support, and guidance were so huge for me and helped me go from a girl with a word doc to a girl with a novel. Every time I heard that you told someone how amazing my book was, my heart grew three sizes.

A second shout out to Katie for my author photos and keeping my secret as long as you could.

There's also a shout out due to Kris for enduring being the loose framework for a loveable character and all the ridicule that comes with it. I'll throw in Tom for potentially selling my book on etsy, but mostly just sending me memes. Casey for ordering my birria tacos for me. And Hasan for coming out of hiding to know how many too's to put in a sentence.

Also a thank you to anyone I may have missed that gave me love and cheered me on through this.

I need to thank Vivien Reis for my beautiful cover art. You made it better than I could have hoped!

My dear editor, Ana Hansen, you are supportive, a cheerleader, and an amazing editor. Don't worry, you have so much job security because I learned nothing. I will still use comma splices and incorrect homophones with reckless abandon, and I will capitalize at Complete Random. Knowing that someone I didn't know thought my jokes were funny kept me going. Thank you for answering my infinite questions as I learned the process. You are the best.

Finally, I have to thank my family. My son, who told me I should "put a bear in it" and so I did. My daughter, who is whimsy incarnate and always willing to dress up as a fairy with a sword. I hope neither of you ever read this book. Last but not least, my husband, who was eternally supportive of this pursuit. He took on bedtimes, grocery runs, and so much else single-handed so that I could grab a few minutes to write, revise, edit, market, you name it. He's my adventure buddy and my HEA. Let's keep making good stories with our lives together forever.

ABOUT THE AUTHOR

Marley Ferguson resides in the Midwest with her husband, two kids, and dog. When not writing, she likes to have her own adventures hiking in the outdoors or traveling to new places.

Follow Marley on Instagram for the latest news @marleywritesbooks

Books by Marley Ferguson:
Rebellion in the Mist – Book 1
Magic in the Wilds – Book 2